MORIARTY

Sherlock Holmes' Nemesis lives again…

Forced to flee England and live in America in the 1890s, Professor James Moriarty returns to London in 1900 to find that his huge criminal empire, his 'family', has been infiltrated, raided and plundered by the coming crime boss, Idle Jack Idell. He also has evidence that one of his closest lieutenants, a member of his self-styled Praetorian Guard, is betraying him. Trying to reform his old family, tempting 'straying sheep' back into his fold, he engineers a plan to assassinate Idle Jack, but when things go horribly wrong, Moriarty is faced with an even bigger problem.

MORIARTY

MORIARTY

by

John Gardner

Magna Large Print Books
Long Preston, North Yorkshire,
BD23 4ND, England.

British Library Cataloguing in Publication Data.

Gardner, John
        Moriarty.

        A catalogue record of this book is
        available from the British Library

        ISBN   978-0-7505-3183-2

First published in Great Britain in 2008 by Quercus

Copyright © 2008 by The John Gardner Estate

Cover illustration © Vintage Collection by arrangement with
Arcangel Images

Published in Large Print 2009 by arrangement with
Quercus Publishing PLC

Magna Large Print is an imprint of Library Magna Books Ltd.

Printed and bound in Great Britain by
T.J. (International) Ltd., Cornwall, PL28 8RW

For Trish
Then, now, and forever

Sometime when you have a year or two to spare I commend to you the study of Professor Moriarty.

– Sir Arthur Conan Doyle
Sherlock Holmes in *The Valley of Fear*

Ex-Professor Moriarty is the Napoleon of Crime ... organizer of half that is evil and nearly all that is undetected.

– Sir Arthur Conan Doyle
Sherlock Holmes in *The Final Problem*

Contents

Author's Introduction
to the Moriarty Books

There is need for some explanation regarding this volume and how it came into being. Therefore certain facts should be made clear at the outset.

In the summer of 1969 I was engaged in research concerning the current problems and operational methods of both the Metropolitan Police and the sprawling criminal underworld of London and its environs. During this period I was introduced to a man known to both the police and his associates as Albert George Spear.

Spear was at that time in his late fifties, a large, well-built man with a sharp sense of humor and lively intelligence. He was also an authority on criminal London – not only of his time but also of the previous century.

Spear was not without problems, being well known to the police, with a record of many arrests and two convictions – the latter carrying with it a sentence of fifteen years for armed bank robbery. In spite of this he was a thoroughly likable man, whose favorite pastime was reading any book that came to hand. On our first meeting he told me that he had read all my Boysie Oakes books, which he found amusing and entertaining rubbish – a criticism not far removed from my own view.

One night toward the end of August, I received a telephone call from Spear saying that he urgently wished to see me. At the time I was living in London, and within the hour Spear was sitting opposite me in my Kensington house. He brought with him a heavy briefcase, which contained three thick leather-bound books. It is as well to say here that the bindings and paper of these books have since been subjected to the usual tests and indisputably date back to the second half of the nineteenth century. The writing contained in them, however, cannot with absolute certainty be dated, the results of chromatographic analysis and further tests being inconclusive.

Spear's story concerning the books was intriguing, the volumes having come into his possession via his grandfather, Albert William Spear (1858–1919), and in turn his father, William Albert Spear (1895–1940).

My informant told me that he had not really examined the books until recently. All three generations of Spears seem to have been involved in criminal activities of one kind or another, and Spear remembers his grandfather talking of a Professor Moriarty. He also claims that his father spoke much about the Professor, who was apparently a legendary figure in the lore of the Spear family.

It was on his deathbed that William Spear first spoke to Albert about the books, which were kept locked in a strongbox at the family home in Stepney. They were, he claimed, the private and secret journals of Moriarty, though at the time of his father's death the younger Spear was more concerned with the activities of one Adolf Hitler than with the family legend.

Although Spear was an avid reader, he had not read or studied the works of Sir Arthur Conan Doyle until the late 1960s – a strange omission, but one that did not worry me since I was also a latecomer to Dr. Watson's chronicles concerning the great detective. However, when Spear began to read the saga, he quickly came across the few references concerning Holmes's archenemy, Professor James Moriarty, and was immediately struck by the descriptions in the Holmes books that had bearings on some of the things his father had told him.

One night he became so intrigued by both the similarities and paradoxical inconsistencies that he began to examine the books he had brought for me to see.

The pages were in good condition, and all three books were crammed with careful, rather sloping, copperplate handwriting. One could make out certain dates and street plans, but the remaining script was at first sight unintelligible. Spear was convinced that his father had told him the truth and that what he possessed were the real Professor Moriarty's private journals, written in cipher.

I cannot deny that my first sight of those books gave me an immense thrill, though I remained on guard, expecting the sharp Spear to put in a plea for hard cash. But money was not mentioned. It would please him, he told me, if someone could decipher the journals and perhaps use them to good advantage. His interest was purely academic.

In the days that followed, I came across a number of immediate inconsistencies, not the least of which was the fact that the journals continued for many years after the spring of 1891 – the year in which, according to Watson, Holmes disappeared at the Reichenbach Falls, presumed dead after a fight with Moriarty, only to reappear in 1894 with the story that it was Moriarty who had perished. If these journals were those of the same Moriarty, then obviously someone was either glossing fact with fiction or there was some strange case of mistaken identity.

My own knowledge of ciphers being small, I eventually took the books to my good friends and publishers Robin Denniston (who has had much experience with codes and ciphers) and Christopher Falkus. After many long hours of arduous trial and error, coupled with applied science, the cipher was broken. The result is that at the time of this writing, some one and a half books have been decoded.

Quite early in this operation we realized that the documents could not be published as they stood. Even in these permissive times there is little doubt that Moriarty's inherent evil – which lurks on every page – could cause concern. Also, the memories of too many revered and famous personalities would be subjected to wanton rumor and scandal.

We decided, therefore, that it would be best for me to publish Professor Moriarty's story in the form of a novel, or novels. This is why some of the locations and events have been slightly altered – though in some cases, such as Moriarty's involvement in the Ripper murders and the so-called de Goncourt scandal, there is no point in concealing the facts.

A further reason for this form of treatment is that Spear disappeared shortly after handing the journals to me. As I have already stated, we cannot positively date the writings, so it is just possible, though I do not believe this, that Albert Spear, with a mischievous sense of humor, has taken some pains to perpetrate the second-largest literary hoax of the century. Or maybe his grandfather, who is much mentioned in the journals, was a man of imagination? Perhaps the publication of these volumes may bring us some of the answers.

I must, however, add one final acknowledgment, which is, I believe, of interest. I am deeply indebted to Miss Bernice Crow, of Cairndow, Argyllshire, great-granddaughter of the late Superintendent Angus McCready Crow, for the use of her great-grandfather's journals, note-books, correspondence, and jottings – papers that have been invaluable in writing these volumes.

Before the Tale Begins

In the summer of 1969, so the story goes, three bulky leather-bound volumes changed hands in the sitting room of a small, pretty little house in Kensington. I was not to know that these books, crammed with tiny ciphered writing, maps, and diagrams, were to take me – almost physically at times – back to the dark, brutal, and secret places of the Victorian and Edwardian underworld in London.

It is now common knowledge that these books are the coded journals of James Moriarty, the diabolically cunning, highly intelligent criminal mastermind of the late nineteenth century known as Professor Moriarty.

The known felon who handed the books to me, on that hot and heavy evening all those years ago, went by the name of Albert George Spear, and his claim was that these books had been kept by his family since they were given for safekeeping to his grandfather, who was Moriarty's most trusted lieutenant.

I have already told the story, in the foreword to *The Return of Moriarty*, of how the cipher to the journals was finally broken and how those who advised my professional life quickly realized that it would be impossible to offer these extraordinary documents to the public in their original, unvarnished form. For one thing, they present grave legal problems; for another, there are incidents contained in them of such an evil character that, even in this permissive age, they could be accounted a corrupting influence.

There is also the small possibility that the journals might just be a hoax, perpetrated by Spear himself, or even by his grandfather, who figures so largely in them. I personally do not believe this. However, I think it quite possible that Moriarty, the great criminal organizer, has, in writing the *Journals*, sought to present himself in the best possible light and, with his consummate cunning, may not have told the entire truth. In some places *Moriarty's Journals* clash strongly with other evidence – most notably the published records of Dr. John H. Watson, friend and chronicler of the great Mr. Sherlock Holmes. In others it clashes with the evidence I have been able to amass from the private papers of the late Detective Superintendent Angus McCready Crow, the Metropolitan Police officer assigned to the Moriarty case toward the end of the nineteenth century and during the early years of the twentieth century.

Taking these matters into account, my closest advisors most wisely felt it was more appropriate for me to write a series of novels based on the *Moriarty Journals*, occasionally altering names, dates, and places wherever this seemed advisable. This has been done, leaving me with only two items that require further examination.

First, after the publication of *The Return of*

Moriarty and its sequel, *The Revenge of Moriarty*, it became apparent that some reviewers were not as familiar with the work of Dr. John Watson as they claimed. There were those who appeared not to have heard of the fact that Moriarty had come from a family composed of three brothers, each of whom bore the name James. Now, I will admit that some Sherlockian scholars do seem to make heavy weather of this fact. Heaven knows why, because the situation is crystal clear when you examine Dr. Watson's sources. It is further clarified by the Moriarty journals in my possession.

Take Dr. Watson's written word. References are made to Professor Moriarty, Mr. Moriarty, the Professor, and Professor James Moriarty in five of the cases written up by Dr. Watson. They are *The Valley of Fear, His Last Bow, The Missing Three-Quarter, The Final Problem,* and *The Empty House.* Further, a Colonel James Moriarty is referred to in *The Final Problem;* and a third brother, reported to be a stationmaster in the West Country, is spoken of in *The Valley of Fear.*

Sherlockians, to my mind, often seem to have difficulty with the possibility of the three brothers Moriarty each bearing the same Christian name, James. *The Moriarty Journals* certainly solve that problem. As far as I can make out, James is a family name, and in the *Journals* Moriarty makes it plain that the three brothers regarded this as an idiosyncrasy, and spoke of each other as James, Jamie, and Jim. In the *Journals*, Moriarty claims that he is, in fact, the youngest brother, a criminal from an early age, who, incensed with jealousy because of his eldest brother's academic success, finally becomes a master of disguise and sees to it that his brother is disgraced and removed from the Chair of Mathematics in the small university where he is becoming ever more famous. Moriarty then tells us that he murdered his brother and, wonderfully disguised, took his place, so becoming a figure of awe to his underworld minions. This seems to me to have a certain validity, though for once Mr. Sherlock Holmes appears to have been taken in by the subterfuge.

Second, after the publication of *The Return of Moriarty* some voices were raised in strident – in a few cases, hysterical – concern that I had re-created Moriarty as a kind of nineteenth-century *Godfather* figure, leader of a vast army, a man with an almost unthinkable knowledge of crime and the coarse language and manners of the Victorian underworld. Indeed, many seemed genuinely upset that the question of sex and licentiousness had barged into the formerly placid world of Baker Street – placid, that is, except for the drug abuse and certain unspoken vices. To those who were, and possibly are, upset, I can only apologize.

To some, this view of Moriarty seems to be unpleasant and vulgar, as though the Sherlockian world was being violated while it sat quietly doing crossword puzzles. I have news for them: The Victorian and Edwardian underworld *was* exceptionally vulgar and unpleasant, and the text of the Sherlock Holmes cases leaves us in no doubt concerning Moriarty's place within the

Victorian underworld. In *The Final Problem*, Holmes speaks of Professor Moriarty as '...[the] deep organizing power which forever stands in the way of the law.' He mentions Moriarty's involvement in 'cases of the most varying sorts – forgery cases, robberies, murders....' Moreover, he describes him as 'the Napoleon of Crime ... the organizer of half that is evil and nearly all that is undetected in this great city [London] ... a genius, a philosopher, an abstract thinker. He has a brain of the first order. He sits motionless, like a spider in the centre of its web, but that web has a thousand radiations, and he knows well every quiver of each of them ... his agents are numerous and splendidly organized...' and so on in the same manner. Is there not something familiar about this description? Something resembling a *Godfather*-like criminal family? Indeed, in the nineteenth and early twentieth centuries, to be a member of such a family was to be a villain.

To me, Moriarty's place in the criminal scheme of things is obvious, plain, and straightforward and should be accepted at its face value.

All the reader needs to know at the start of this book is that in May 1897, pursued by Sherlock Holmes and Inspector Angus McCready Crow, Professor Moriarty was forced to flee London. At the start of this work he has returned, quietly and without fuss; and we hear little of either Holmes or Crow during this episode.

I need say no more, except to declare my heartfelt thanks to the following for their great personal help in preparing this, the third book in a planned quartet: Otto Penzler, who provided the impetus for this third volume; my luscious agent, Lisa Moylett, who does magic things; Patricia Mountford, who gave me a wonderful idea, now embedded in the plot; Philip Mountford, for specialist assistance; and Jeff and Vicki Busby, for even more specialist help. Last but far from least, my daughter Alexis and my lovely son-in-law, John, plus my smashing son Simon all caused this book to be written by a generous and surprising present. They know what they did. Thank you.

1

Back to the Smoke

LONDON: JANUARY 15, 1900

Daniel Carbonardo could not distinguish the house until he was almost upon it. Daniel killed – that was his job in life: death. He killed for chink; murdered for geld; a few sovereigns and the person named was dead, while Carbonardo disappeared like smoke on a zephyr. Yet his favourite interest, next to murder, was obtaining intelligence – putting people to the question.

It was said that Daniel had learned the trade of torture from within his family, who traced their ancestors back to the Tower of London: people who were begetters of truth, one of whom had come over in the retinue of Catherine of Aragon, daughter of Ferdinand and Isabella of Spain, first wife of Henry VIII.

Catherine of Aragon ended up in a convent; many in her retinue, including the Carbonardos, ended up broke, staying in England to work for the royal household, where some became great exponents in the extraction of truth from unwilling tongues. That particular work, gaining intelligence by torture, threat, pain, or promise, was on Daniel's mind tonight; and he knew it all, from the rack and the boot to Skeffington's daughter, and

27

even more esoteric methods of prising the truth from people disinclined to talk.

'She knows,' the Professor had said. 'She'll give you the name. There are three of them and Spear.'

Daniel felt he had heard words similar to those many times before. 'From your Praetorian Guard?' he asked, incredulous. 'You can't mean your Praetorian Guard, Professor!' and Moriarty nodded, slowly. 'The very same,' he muttered. 'We have a traitor, Daniel. Right at the top, among my most trusted. A traitor who has burrowed, like a little animal into my organization.'

'But who would...?' Daniel began.

'To whom would some turncoat sell his soul? Who?' Moriarty chuckled.

'Sherlock Holmes?' Carbonardo asked again and the Professor laughed louder, a high, animal bark.

'Holmes? Holmes? I think not. Holmes bothers me little these days. We had our moment of conflict and I think came to a mutual understanding. I doubt if I shall ever hear again from Mr. Holmes.'

'Then who?'

'There *is* one.' He rested the nail of his right thumb just below his eye, then ran it down to his jaw, tracing a line down his cheek. 'Angus Crow. Crow is a skilful policeman who has sworn to trap me. Indeed, it is his one aim in life. I am his one big case.' He paused, his head moving forward like the head of an old turtle, then swaying from side to side. 'And of course there are others. One in particular who has used my recent absence to plunder my former organization, my family.'

28

Carbonardo shook his head in puzzlement, finding it hard to believe that one of the Professor's closest lieutenants could be a turncoat.

The four men who comprised Moriarty's so-called Praetorian Guard were Ember, Spear, Lee Chow, and Terremant, who had been inducted into the Praetorians following the disappearance of the fine big lad Pip Paget.

Ember was a small, foxy, unpleasant little man, who acted as a contact, running between Moriarty and the lurkers, demanders, and punishers, the street men, the patterers, the magsmen, the dodgers, whizzers, dips, nightwalkers, dollymops, gonifs, and those who specialized: the petermen, confidence sharks, fences, assassins, and jewellers.

The two main members of the Guard were the Professor's true lieutenants, the distinctive Albert Spear and Terremant – Spear with his broken nose and the telltale forked-lightning scar down his right cheek, and the big tough known only as Terremant. This pair were leading street gangers, mobsters, men who made decisions and had the final say-so, most feared out in the highways, byways, and alleys of London.

Last, and possibly least, of the Praetorians was the evil Chinee, Lee Chow, who dealt with the Eastern foreigners and lowlifes, running opium dens and dispensing cruel justice. He was feared by all because he would do Moriarty's bidding, no matter what, and never turn a hair of his pigtail. It was known that one of his best tricks was to cut the cheeks from a man or woman, leaving the victims appallingly disfigured and unable to use their mouths as normal persons.

The Professor locked eyes with Carbonardo, who felt a nudge, partly of awe, partly fear, as he looked deeply into the dark, knowing, glittering eyeballs that had seen much evil and knew even more. Like many, Daniel tried to avoid looking straight into Moriarty's eyes, for they held a mesmeristic power that it was said could remove a man's own will and command him to do unmentionable things.

His gaze dropped, and he saw that Moriarty was smiling. A slight, cynical raising of the corners of his lips, an evil smirk that in no way crept up the face to bring warmth to the eyes.

'You think members of my closest circle, my business intimates, are exempt from duplicity?' he asked, the terrible eyes never leaving Carbonardo's face.

'Well, Professor... Well, I...'

'You have heard of Pip Paget, who at one time was counted almost as a son to me, a prime member of the Praetorians? Surely you've heard of him?'

'Who hasn't, sir? Who indeed?'

'Pip Paget saved my life, Daniel. Shot a murderous skunk dead and saved my life, yet he'd already betrayed me.' He thumped his chest with a clenched right fist. 'Me!' He thumped again. 'Me, who was a father to him, who had been present at his wedding, stood for him, provided his marital feast, blessed his union with another member of my organization ... my family...' His voice rose as if in anger, tumbling the words one upon another. 'Seen and blessed his marriage to that little jigster Fanny Jones. Me!'

Carbonardo nodded. He knew the story of how Paget had sold out details of the Professor's most secret hiding place to Inspector Angus Mc-Cready Crow of the Metropolitan Police Force, and passed on intelligence that almost led to Moriarty's downfall.

'You do well to nod, Daniel. It is meet and right for those who earn their stipend through me to know of my justice.'

Moriarty paid what he called a retaining fee to Daniel Carbonardo: bunce to ensure that he had first call on the man's services. It was a generous jingle of cash, enough to enable Carbonardo to maintain his pleasant villa in the thriving and rising area of Hoxton, the house just off North New Road, five minutes' walk from the parish church of St. John the Baptist: a modest home with the name Hawthornes, though there were no bushes or greenery adjacent to the terraced property – two reception rooms and a small study; three bedrooms; a privy indoors, a luxury; a little bathing room; and a basement kitchen with area steps.

It was down those steps, seventy-two hours previously, that the little old, bent hansom cab driver had come asking for Mr. Carbonardo, refusing speech with anyone but Mr. Daniel Carbonardo, enunciating the name with care, rolling the *R*s in almost an Italian or Spanish manner.

On being taken upstairs to the study and being introduced to the master by Tabitha, his one servant, the caller assumed a subservient manner, hands clasped low, head bent, waiting for the master of the house to speak. Daniel was brusque

31

with the man; indeed, he had immediate reservations about him: Old, bent, and with an unhealthy, greyish pallor, the fellow should never, he considered, be allowed to drive a cab.

'What is it, then?' he asked. 'I am a busy man and cannot spare you more than a couple of minutes.'

'You'll spare me more when you hear the purport of my business.' The man had the gravel throat of one who liked spirits and tobacco more than was good for him. He spoke low, quietly, in a way that set Daniel thinking of another whose speech was always low, the voice dropped to make certain you listened carefully.

Now, Carbonardo looked hard at the man's face, peering into his eyes, lifting his chin slightly as though searching for some clue. 'I know you,' he said at last. 'Harkness, isn't it?'

'The same, sir. Indeed. I've had the pleasure of driving you many times.'

Daniel Carbonardo took a pace back. 'You used to work for the Professor. I remember you well: Moriarty's private cabbie, right?'

'Oh, indeed right, sir. Yes. Moriarty's personal cab driver. But what d'you mean, *used* to work for the Professor?'

'Surely you cannot work for him anymore, for he's left the country. He's not been heard of for some years.'

'Back, sir. He's back.' The little man paused as though for dramatic effect. 'Returned to London, sir.' He continued. 'Back here in the Smoke. Back and waiting to have words with you. Waiting even as we speak.'

'Where?' Now Daniel's voice was hoarse, his throat dry, the news of Moriarty's homecoming making him wary, vigilant. Maybe even a mite frightened.

'Never mind the where or the why, Mr. Carbonardo. I am to take you to him instantly. Indeed, every minute we tarry will edge the Professor closer to irritation, something neither of us require, sir.'

Daniel shook his head in a small flurry of discontent. 'No! No!' he muttered, stepping briskly to the door. 'If you have orders, then take me now.' In the hall he shrugged into his dark green ulster, nodded to Harkness, then followed the cabbie down the front steps and into the waiting hansom.

It took near five and forty minutes for the cab to travel west, to one of those anonymous squares that had, over the past half century, started to appear close by the borough of Westminster. But at last they came to a halt, and Harkness called down to tell Daniel they had arrived.

'You're to go straight in and up to the second floor,' he called through the partition that separated cabbie from passenger below.

Alighting, Carbonardo found they had stopped in front of a fine, large, terraced house with broad steps leading to a solid oak front door. From behind the windows came the bright glare of electric light, and the area in which he found himself smelled of money: It was the kind of London square where men of substance lived and kept their families, tended by wealth, surrounded by luxury. These were the manner of houses fast taking the place of the crushed, cramped buildings that had previously made up a vast part of Westminster: the sprawling dense huddle of structures, leaning in on one another, tipping over and locking together to make up the rookery known as the Devil's Acre, a region that had teemed with men and women with whom Daniel Carbonardo himself would have had second thoughts about associating.

'You're to go straight up, sir. He has rooms on the second floor. Go straight up, there's no cause for concern. He's expecting you.'

The front door was unlatched, and inside, in the spacious hall, Daniel was puzzled to find no fitments or furniture – just bare boards, and stark stripped walls with outlines where pictures had once hung or furniture stood.

The heels and soles of his boots thumped against the wooden flooring, sending echoes loud through the house, and, as he made his way up the stairs, he was conscious of the gas mantles un-lit behind their glass bowls. What electric lighting had been introduced was obviously recent, and did not exist throughout the entire house.

As he reached the second-floor landing, Carbonardo heard a sound from below. The front door through which he had just entered creaked again, while a second footfall sounded, crossing and starting to mount the stairs behind him, a shadow passing over the scrubbed bare boards. Swiftly, Daniel took two steps into the passage that led, forking from the landing, off to the right. He turned and, flattening his back against the wall, barely breathing as he listened, watchful, to the footsteps coming closer.

Finally, as the interloper reached the top of the stairs, Daniel hardly dared breathe, lest the shallow rise of his chest call attention to him, silent in the shadows. He waited, conscious even of his heartbeat, thinking the sound might be so loud that it would give away his position. To his left he glimpsed a tall cloaked figure pausing on the landing, then crossing and opening the one door facing the staircase. He heard the footfalls, then the turning of the brass knob, the unlatching of the lock, and the sound of the door moving over what was probably a thick carpet as it swung inward. Before the door closed again he heard a single laugh, a throaty chime of what could have been either amusement or triumph.

Counting silently to himself to quell the alarm and jangling of his nerves, Daniel Carbonardo followed the figure who had moved so stealthily across the landing and into the facing room. Taking a deep breath, he turned the doorknob, pushed with his shoulder, and stepped into the room.

Moriarty smiled at him, one hand raised as he seemed to peel off part of his face. It took Daniel a moment to realize that what he removed was in fact a piece of stiffened molded linen that altered the shape of his cheek, as if he were removing half of Harkness's face to reveal his own beneath it. 'I told you that you'd give me more time, young Daniel, once you'd heard the purport of my business,' he said in the familiar voice, half whisper, half threat, and wholly commanding, one of the many facets of the Professor's physical

35

makeup – the eyes, the authoritative manner, and that distinctive voice, once heard never forgotten.

'Come, Daniel, let us sit, perhaps take a glass of good brandy wine. Come, make yourself comfortable.'

'You all the time, Professor! I could have sworn it was your man Harkness.' He looked around, for the first time taking in the room, feeling the deep pile Wilton under his feet, the coal fire roaring in the well-blackened grate, the old polished furnishings, the scent of beeswax in the air, the desk with inlaid red, gold-trimmed skivers, a pair of padded chairs, an ornate corner cupboard with a selection of leather-bound books on its shelves, good pictures on the walls, the heavy velvet curtains in a crushed gold shade complementing the creamy carpet.

'There.' Moriarty peeled the treated linen from his other cheek, then from around his nose until he was revealed as the man Daniel Carbonardo knew as Professor James Moriarty. 'I always enjoy taking on the role of another.' He straightened, a smile twinkling on his lips and in his eyes. 'But you know that, Daniel. You know how addicted I am to disguise, and how I delight in stepping into the shoes of other men ... and their bodies, of course.' He rubbed his hands together briskly. 'This weather, it can't make up its mind. Topsy-turvy.' The smile again. 'You know my man Terremant of course.' A gesture to the shadows at the farthest end of the room, out of which the big bully of a man stepped, appearing as if by magic.

'Terremant was at one time in charge of my people known as the punishers,' he said with a sly chuckle, as though the name amused him. 'When I had to say good-bye to Pip Paget I required a replacement, and good Terremant seemed to fit the bill, as they say.' There followed the conversation already recounted.

Then–

'I have work for you, Daniel. Important work. You must entice intelligence from an unwilling tongue for me.' Turning to the big man still half in the shadows, he said, 'Stop your ears to this, Tom Terremant. Stop your ears and freeze your brain.'

'Aye, Professor,' the giant of a man grunted.

'No,' Moriarty snapped. 'Go. Wait on the landing. I can trust no one.'

The big Terremant shrugged in good humour, then lurched from the room.

'And stand away from the door, Tom. Go down and see to my horse, Archie.'

Terremant grunted and closed the door behind him.

'My horse, Archie,' Moriarty laughed. 'Short for Archimedes. He's a good horse, but he belongs to my man Harkness. I bequeathed the horse to him when I last went away, what? Some six, seven years ago?' The Professor laid a finger against his nose, then tiptoed to the door, pulling it open suddenly to reveal the landing was empty.

From below came the sound of Terremant's tread as he crossed the hall to open the front door.

Moriarty came back into the room. 'Good. Now listen to me carefully, Daniel. Tomorrow you must go to a certain private hotel and make arrangements. Then, on the following night I require you to find out who has been upending

37

me, making a fool of me. You've doubtless heard of Sal Hodges, Daniel.'

'Why of course, Professor, yes.'

'Mmmm. Of course, and you still doubtless think of her as my bed warmer.'

'Well, sir. It's said that...'

'That Sal Hodges and Professor James Moriarty dance the horizontal jig, and that she's mother to my child.'

'Well, sir ...'

'"Well, sir. Yes, sir." Don't be shy, sir. Of course that's what's said, and to some extent it is true. Maybe is still true.'

Daniel Carbonardo nodded and said a silent affirmative.

'The night after next, Daniel. The night after next you must find out who the traitor is. She'll know, Daniel. Sal Hodges'll know, mark me.'

So now, two nights later, shrouded in fog, Daniel Carbonardo crossed the street and went lightly up the steps of the Glenmoragh Private Hotel. Standing in front of the door he took shallow breaths that formed little clouds from his lips, willing himself not to cough. From somewhere over the roofs came the striking of a clock: three in the morning. Silent, cold, menacing; the world muffled by the thick, bitter mist.

The weather had been strange: changeable. This morning it was cold and damp. Now, freezing fog hung dense across the square; you couldn't, as they said, see a hand's turn in front of you.

He had stolen the spare key when visiting on the previous afternoon under the pretext of seeing if Mrs. James had arrived, knowing full well that she had not. Slipping the key into the lock he turned it noiselessly, praying that the boot boy had done his bidding – that he had slid the bolts back and taken off the chains. He pressed against the heavy wood and the door swung open so that he could step inside and close it behind him, leaning his shoulders and long back against it, waiting for his eyes to adjust as he stood in the blackness, aware of the pleasant warmth even here in the hall, the carpet soft, yielding under the rubber soles of his heavy boots.

Sam, the boot boy, had told him number eight. Mrs. James would be in number eight, on the first floor, along the passage, then first door on the right. 'She'll only be there the one night,' he had said. 'Then she'll be off to see her boy at Rugby School, poor little bleeder.'

Fancy that, he had thought, the Professor's son at Rugby with the nobs. There were others who'd take care of the boy if need be; after all, he was son and heir to a huge organization and vast wealth. Daniel's job now was to frighten the woman into revealing the truth. Mrs. James, whose real name had been Sal Hodges. He remembered her well from the old days: the Professor's woman, his bit of regular hot tail.

After five minutes he could see through the darkness as good as in daylight, so he walked to the foot of the staircase, slipping his right hand inside his dark ulster and pulling out the knife, holding it well away from his body, point down, right hand firm around the carved horn handle, thumb against the crossguard, the nine-inch blade tapering to a needle point and a blood drain down the flat of both sides. 'Have care,' Mysson had told him. 'I've ground that blade sharp as a surgeon's scalpel. Just how you like it.'

Women were easy: Threaten to cut them on the face, then give them a small cut and they'd fold like a newfangled card table. Men were another matter: Go for their most precious organ, that was the rule. Go for it with a razor, give it a tiny cut, or with the hot tweezers, and they would inevitably squeak and squeal. Nay, scream and yell.

He was about to move up the stairs when he heard the hansom, the horse's hooves clopping in a steady rhythm, then faltering as it pulled up outside. Gawd in heaven, what could he do now? But the hansom moved on, the cabbie searching for a number: not this one, not fifty-six, the Glenmoragh Private Hotel, the hotel that did not advertise. 'We are recommended by our regulars,' Mr. Moat, Ernie Moat, the manager, bragged.

Hansoms may soon thin out, he thought, mounting the stairs slowly. The horseless carriage was said to be the coming thing, though he couldn't quite believe that: They were noisy, smelly things, difficult to control and not at all reliable.

When he reached the door he found that it had not been locked, not that it would have hampered him had it been secured: Daniel was as good with locks and lock picks as he was with weapons.

As he stepped into the room, the sweet scent of the woman enveloped him, the air infused by whatever she wore to hide her natural odours. For a moment he stood by the bed, his head dizzy as he looked down on her face, hearing her steady breathing and knowing it could suddenly end if he willed it. That was the usual job and that's what he really was: a doomsman, a reaper's henchman, a coffin nailer, and, more to the point, a priser, one who made people talk: a ventriloquist as some said, or a confessor to the more religious.

His left arm shot out, a big hand across the woman's nose and mouth so that she woke with terrible suddenness, looking into the dark. The other hand came down, the knife ripping her nightdress, exposing her breasts, then moving up. The point resting against her cheek, then balanced straight above her right eye.

'I'm going to ask you one question,' Carbonardo hissed. 'And when I take my hand from your mouth you'll not scream, or make noise. You'll answer my question; otherwise you'll say good-bye to your right eye. I'll have it out in a trice, and I don't joke about things like that. You understand me?'

He could see her staring eyes, wide open and fearful as she tried to nod assent. Carbonardo muttered that he was about to remove his hand when, without warning, vicelike fingers locked around his wrists; the knife was jerked from his right hand while the other was torn from the woman's face as someone turned up a gaslight and he saw that the woman was not Sal Hodges, and that men were swiftly around him, pinioning his arms to his sides and quietly telling him not to struggle – men Daniel recognized as trained hands, people who could move as one and would obey orders with military precision.

Daniel Carbonardo's world was suddenly

turned sideways, and he cursed, angrily spitting out the oath.

A match flared and a lantern was raised.

'Hello, Daniel,' said Idle Jack, grinning like a wolf in the thin light. 'We have need to talk.'

Carbonardo was seized from behind and quietly led, protesting, from the room.

2

Return of the Guard

LONDON: JANUARY 15, 1900

After Daniel Carbonardo left Moriarty alone in his rooms on the second floor of the elegant house on the fringes of Westminster, the Professor went out onto the bare landing and softly called for Terremant to come back up to him. 'Tom,' he called. Then again, 'Tom.'

He stood for a moment looking down at the empty hall and the stripped wood of the staircase with the brass fitments still in place for the stair rods, the borders smooth with varnish. For a moment he thought about Daniel Carbonardo out there now, getting things ready to put Sal to the question and solve his biggest problem. Then Terremant returned through the front door below, glancing up and nodding to his master as he climbed the stairs, nimble for one of such height, weight, and muscle.

Moriarty was pleased with his arrangements, for he had purchased the entire house through a third party – a solicitor whom he had used many times in the past. He was also pleased with his instructions to Carbonardo, for he knew he could rely on Daniel's judgement; he would get the information required. After that it would be a matter of dealing with the guilty party, silencing forever the man who was betraying him and those who trusted him.

There were three of them and Spear.

Through the same man, the solicitor, who was named Perry Gwyther, senior partner in the firm of Gwyther, Walmsley and Mercer, solicitors of unimpeachable good name, he arranged to have some of his own furnishings brought out of storage and taken to the house, where he personally oversaw the work of the good and honest man charged with making the rooms comfortable and to the Professor's liking: by name George Huckett of Hackney, Builder & Decorator, as he styled his business. In due course Moriarty would have the whole house restored, decorated, and furnished to his satisfaction, but for now the rooms in which he lived were enough and in good order. He had this living and working room, a bedroom, and a small room where simple food could be prepared. Next to the bedroom, George Huckett arranged for his plumber, by name 'Leaky' Lewis, to fit up a bathing room with a hand washbasin and a deep, raised bath on stylish claw feet – the water heated by a coke-burning stove under a great tank in the house's old basement kitchen and pulled upstairs by one of the newfangled electric pumps.

The house was only partially wired for the electric light, and in due course, when the entire house had been done, he thought he would perhaps have the revolutionary new telephonic apparatus connected. Moriarty was a man who rarely dismissed new inventions as passing fads. He was farsighted and could see how things like electricity and the more recent form of telephone communication, even wireless, could well assist him in his endeavours. The solicitor, Gwyther, maintained that within a couple of decades everyone would possess wireless receiving sets through which they would listen to the world's great symphony orchestras and outstanding actors. This would, Gwyther contended, hail the advent of a new understanding of great music, drama, and literature, for the most common of men would have access to the arts, in their own homes. Moriarty did not know how he felt about this, for he imagined that a universal entrée to the arts might well lead to them being devalued, and he liked things to retain their value.

Turning back into the room, Moriarty lit a wax taper from the fire, adjusted the wicks, and lighted his two oil lamps, simple brass pieces, each with a tall classic column on which stood the oil reservoir and lamp, each capped by a tall glass funnel rising from inside a decorated opaque glass globe. The light from the two lamps, one on his desk – a davenport with a piano front – the other on a drum table at the rear, spilled out as though filling the room with warm sunlight, giving the illusion of an added depth to the cream, gold-flecked heavy wallpaper and a fresh gleam to the polished furniture. Somehow, James Moriarty preferred the soft lamplight to the harsher glare from the electric light.

Now, the Professor advanced to the fireplace, above which hung the most striking item in the entire suite of chambers: the painting of Georgiana, Duchess of Devonshire, possibly Thomas Gainsborough's greatest portrait, painted in the 1780s and missing since May 25, 1876, when, on a warm, misty midnight, the Professor, with the help of Albert Spear and Philip Paget, gained access to the upper art gallery of Thomas Agnew & Sons, at 39a Old Bond Street in the heart of the West End of London, where he had cut and removed the priceless painting from its frame.

On that night, almost a quarter of a century ago, the famous painting hung alone in Agnew's first-floor gallery in Old Bond Street, a crimson silk rope keeping the more inquisitive viewers at a distance. This was where Moriarty first saw the painting of Georgiana, Duchess of Devonshire, visiting 39a Old Bond Street on the very morning of its theft, joining the line of people moving steadily through the main gallery and up the stairs to where Gainsborough's masterpiece was the sole item on display in the long upper room.

He was drawn to look at the painting not through any desire to observe a work of art, but to view something that had already sold for ten thousand pounds sterling, the highest price so far ever paid for a painting. And at that time it was reliably rumoured that Agnew was about to sell the work to Junius Spencer Morgan as a gift for his son J. Pierpont Morgan – now, almost a

45

quarter of a century later, the prime controller of American Finance, the wealthiest and most powerful man in the United States of America.

Indeed on that very afternoon in the present – January 15, 1900 – James Moriarty had heard another whisper: that the original painting was about to be returned to the Agnew family, having been discovered in New York. Indeed he knew this to be 'true' because he had arranged for an exceptional forgery to be smuggled into New York in the first place, and found in the second, plus identified in a roundabout way the original thief as being a confidence trickster called Adam Worth. Once Worth was publicly accused and the forgery had changed hands, becoming the accepted true and original painting, the Professor could relax.

The forger, one Charlie 'The Draughtsman' Dainton of Camberwell, had a head start on other copyists, for Moriarty allowed him to paint his brilliant replica while looking at the original; then, when everything was done and tidy, he took Charlie out on a celebratory picnic near the old university city of Oxford – ham, pickles, tomatoes, a large veal-and-ham pie with hard-boiled eggs, a flask of fruit salad, and an excellent bottle of Puligny-Montrachet that they cooled in the river, hanging the bottle in the water by a strong cord.

They sat on a secluded, willow-screened patch of grass, close to a riverside public house called The Rose Revived, and when The Draughtsman was sated with food and mellow with the wine, Moriarty leaned over and thanked him for his expertise and friendship, clasping, for a second, both of the forger's hands in his. Then, as the

46

forger smiled happily, the Professor slit his throat, holding down his hands until he bled out and his lungs collapsed. After that he weighed down the body with chains and old pig iron – which he had conveniently brought with him in a large trunk strapped to the rear step of his gig – then tipped the body into the river, washing the blood from his hands as he did so.

The body of Charlie Dainton was never recovered; it was as though he had never been.

This was on a Sunday evening during July of the previous year, so, having disposed of the only other person who could have given the game away, James Moriarty repaired to choral evensong in the chapel of Christ Church College, where the choir sang an anthem suitably based on the words of the Prophet Isaiah, 'And a Man Shall Be as Rivers of Water in a Dry Place,' a piece composed by Moriarty himself and sent, under an assumed name, to the choirmaster with a hint that he might be in the congregation on that day. After evensong, Moriarty walked around the corner to the Mitre Hotel, where he dined on roast beef followed by summer pudding, washed down with a pleasant burgundy.

Moriarty rarely thought of The Draughtsman again, except for those occasions when he regretted the fact that the man was not there when he could have been of assistance in pulling off some criminal endeavour.

And here, now, in the present, above his mantel in this suite of rooms close to Westminster, hung the true original, in all its glory: Georgiana, Duchess of Devonshire, formerly Georgiana

Spencer, half turned to her left with her right shoulder square to the spectator, a blue silk sash setting off her white dress, curls roiling from under a black feathered hat, her pert face closed as if holding a secret known only to herself, lips edging toward a smile and her eyes half mocking, half inviting, in what errand boys called a come-hither look.

Moriarty could not comprehend love. Lust he understood, but love – well, that was another matter. What he should really have considered was obsession, but he found it difficult to recognize that particular weakness in himself.

The magic of this piece of Tom Gainsborough's art never failed to have a profound effect on Professor Moriarty. He often thought that had his brain been equipped with taste buds, it would have been as though his mind had bitten into the most refreshing, deliciously ripe fruit, flooding his brain with juices that brought together all the great, exotic tastes – more than could ever be experienced in a lifetime.

From the moment he first saw the painting, Moriarty knew he must possess it, for having the picture would be like owning the duchess herself: She would be the rationale for his life, his inspiration, the shaft of light that made his criminal labyrinth crystal clear in his mind, a kind of profound love lighting the darkness of his being. What was more, he considered, he would not have to idly converse with the duchess, nor remember her likes and dislikes, purchase feminine fripperies to keep her happy, or make love to her. Moriarty enjoyed the delights of a woman as much as the next man, in some ways even more than the next man, but he found the whole thing became complicated once love marched through the door. Moriarty's memory was prodigious, but he knew that a man had to be possessed of second sight to keep up with the changeable tides of a woman. Albeit he would sometimes admit that the unpredictable beliefs and decisions of certain ladies could be part of a particular woman's charm, but often at a cost to a man's temper, or even his sanity.

That warm night all those years ago saw him going late into the streets with Spear and Paget, pausing outside Agnew's premises in Old Bond Street, signalling Paget into a doorway to act as their crow – their lookout – handing him his top hat and silver-knobbed cane, then lifting his right foot for Albert Spear to stirrup him up to the window, where he removed a small crowbar from a secret pocket in his coat and worked it into the interior lock, the sneck, of the casement, sliding up the lower part of the window, now released, and stepping inside.

He had never forgotten his own sense of amusement: What, he asked himself, would his colleagues think of him vaulting up the wall and springing through the window? Absurd, their imagining the Professor as they knew him, performing these burglar's acrobatics. Just as he had never forgotten the orgasmic thrill of taking out his little, pearl-handled folding fruit knife and using it to cut the canvas from its frame, then rolling it into a tubular shape to fasten it inside his coat before returning to the casement, briefly aware of a night watchman's heavy snore from

49

outside the door, and climbing from the open window and dropping into the street below, retrieving his silver-tipped cane and top hat from Paget, and leading the men back along the pavement and away from Old Bond Street with a feeling of near drunkenness.

From that night on, he kept the painting with him, wherever he went.

A talisman.

There was a cough behind him. Terremant stood in the doorway.

'Professor, you called me Tom, sir. My name's Jim. James.'

Moriarty dragged his eyes from the painting, reluctance in his face.

'Your given names are James Thomas. Is that not so?'

'Yes, but I'm known as James. Jim to be exact. When the lads want amusement they call me Little Jim – like Little John in the Robin Hood story.'

'Well, I have too many Jameses in my family, Tom. So to me, you'll always be Tom when I bother with your first name. Now, come and sit down. You'll take a drink?' He gestured toward a chair, his neck protruding and his head moving from side to side, the nervous tic inherited – like his older brother's – from father or mother, or even farther back in his lineage; it was an odd reptilian movement of the head, side to side, slowly to and fro. What we do presume from medical opinion is that the tic exhibited itself in moments of pressure or stress, and in view of the instructions Moriarty was about to give to his henchman, some stress would certainly be present. 'Your colleagues in what I like to call my Praetorian Guard return to London this very night, Tom.'

Terremant gave a small gasp. 'So soon?'

'Yes, they've come by rail and sea, ending tonight in Southampton, aboard the SS *Canada* of the Dominion Line. At this moment they will be bound for London and, I am assured by the Dominion Line's representative in Haymarket, they will be arriving in London at approximately half past the hour of eight tonight. You are to meet them in the saloon bar of The Sheet Anchor public house off the West India Dock Road, in Poplar, about half past nine.' He took up the bottle and poured a generous glass of brandy for Terremant, the amber liquid seeming to glow as if giving off a pulse of light. 'There, that will keep the cold at bay. Now, I have particular instructions which I've written for Albert Spear.' He strode with purpose to his desk and picked up four or five pages of a heavy white rag paper filled with the Professor's neat copperplate handwriting, which he scanned closely before folding it neatly, running his fingers and thumb over the creases to make the folds sharp, then sealing the pages in an envelope of matching paper.

'Drink,' he called to Terremant, and the big man took another sip of the brandy as Moriarty lit a small candle on his desk and went through the business of heating and dropping scarlet sealing wax onto the flap of the envelope, then completing the matter by pressing his signet ring into the wax, leaving a clean impression of his personal seal – a flowery letter *M* topped by a coronet and a dagger

51

running through the *V* of the *M*.

'There,' he said, walking over to Terremant, offering him the envelope addressed to Albert Spear with the words *By Hand* written in the top right-hand corner. 'You are to put this into Albert's hand and none other. He must read and act on the contents, which he will doubtless share with you. But he must act on the contents immediately. Understand? Immediately!' The word cracking like a whip.

Terremant finished off the brandy, took the envelope, and tucked it away in the inside pocket of his jacket. 'I'll do it all, Professor. Never fear. The Sheet Anchor off the West India Dock Road. I used to know it well. Half nine.'

'It's been under my protection for some years now, The Sheet Anchor. Poplar, you'll recall, is hard by Limehouse, where we once had our headquarters.' Moriarty smiled his grim grimace and nodded a curt dismissal. 'Mind you're not watched or followed, Tom Terremant. But go now and go well... Oh, and Tom?'

'Yes, Professor,' he said, just on the wrong side of surly.

'Don't let your tongue start wagging. Keep a curb on it. Not a word about what I've been doing. Not yet. Understand? What I've been up to here, and before, in Vienna. It's my business and it's for the sake of our family. You must be aware of that. See?'

'Of course, sir.'

'Well mind it.'

'Shall I bring the lads back here, guv'nor?'

'Not tonight. I've got them rooms at Captain

Ratford's place off Leicester Square. They already know that and I've got a pair of lurkers watching for their arrival.' He ran his thumb down his right cheek, nail against the flesh, tracing a line from just under the eye to the jawline. In fact the Professor had no such thing as a pair of lurkers watching. He had returned to London two weeks previously after an absence of several years to discover what he had long suspected: that his family of villains could no longer be completely trusted, just as he could not depend entirely on the close members of his so-called Praetorian Guard, and could depend only partly on his former mistress, Sal Hodges, mother of his son, Arthur James Moriarty.

Terremant went downstairs to the little cubbyhole that he had set up as living quarters among what probably had once been the senior servants' quarters near the spacious kitchens: sitting rooms for the cook or butler, he presumed, for the house had obviously been built for a significant family.

He had made the room as cozy as possible, with a comfortable bed, a small chest of drawers, a table, and an easy chair that the previous occupants had left behind. Once inside the room he closed and locked the door, for he had no wish for Moriarty to come in unexpectedly.

He took out the Professor's letter and dropped it on the table, then lit a small candle and warmed the thin blade of a pocketknife he had bought when in Switzerland with the Professor. Once the blade was warm he wiped off any stains or soot and slid it into the envelope flap, directly below where Moriarty had sealed the packet with wax. His experienced fingers moved the blade along the flap, under the wax, then up to the top of the envelope.

Terremant was an expert at opening the coverings to letters, envelopes, and more exotic foldings. He had started his working life as a footman to a large family here in London. There were several young people, both boys and girls, in the family and he soon discovered that the master – a highly placed man in the Foreign Service – insisted that his butler spy on his sons and daughters. In turn, the butler instructed the footmen in the opening of notes and billets-doux from would-be lovers, which they did the year round for a small percentage of what the butler was given by either the master or, as often occurred, the young ladies and gentlemen who paid so that the servants would look the other way.

Sitting at the table, Terremant smoothed out the letter and, with his finger travelling from word to word and line to line and his lips moving as he slowly read what Moriarty had written, the big man digested the entire message that he was to take to Albert Spear. The job took several minutes, for Terremant was not the fastest reader in England, having learned to read and write at a comparatively late age under the tutelage of Albert Spear himself. But the deception was finally done, and when he had finished and tucked the letter back into its envelope Terremant nodded to himself, as though the whole thing made perfect sense to him, as indeed it did.

He put on his greatcoat – the dark one with the

caped shoulders and the long skirts – and took from his pocket the Smith & Wesson revolver that the Professor had given him when they were in America, checking that it was loaded, cocked, and with the safety catch on, then returned it to his pocket. Then, putting on his somewhat battered hat, and picking up the thick, heavy stick with a knobbed head that he liked to carry when going abroad, James Thomas Terremant let himself out the door at the foot of the area steps that he climbed to the pavement and set out on foot, in the growing darkness, to start his lengthy journey to meet his three colleagues in Poplar.

He had almost disappeared into the murk of night as another dark shape detached itself from the blackness across the road and moved after Terremant with a sense of purpose and a silence borne of much practice and thick rubber soles on well-made boots.

3

Questions and Conversations

LONDON: JANUARY 15-16, 1900

There were no two ways about it: Daniel Carbonardo was terrified, thought he was *in extremis*, thought he was going to die, and wanted a priest because if he died without benefit of one he would go straight to eternal damnation, or at best to limbo, where the unbaptized babies go. As a devout Roman Catholic this is what Daniel Carbonardo believed, and it terrified him enough to loosen his sphincter muscle.

The two men who took him out and back down the front steps of the Glenmoragh Private Hotel were none too gentle: louts, tough as a jockey's backside, pugified and with no finesse to them, which was why he was frightened now. When you put a man to the question you did not usually want him to die, but there were sometimes accidents, and these brutes had not even the sense they were born with. With these two lumps of muscle – rampsmen, in popular jargon – an accident was waiting to occur. Daniel knew that he could sing his heart out and still end up very dead.

Outside, two hansoms were waiting, the cabbies alert, horses snorting, and he knew others from the hotel – two or three men, he thought – were going to the second while the pair of punishers bundled him inside the first cab, sitting themselves one on either side of him, holding his arms in steely grips. As he was entering the cab he caught a glimpse of someone outside, standing in the road, ready to grab him if he tried to leap from the far door. That at least was professional, the kind of thing the Professor's mob would do without pausing to think, like soldiers at a drill.

The cab began to move, fast from the off, and the bully boys started softening him straight away, slinging a sacking hood over his head and clouting him to the face, making his brain whirl and his ears screech. They didn't stop punching and slapping him for the length of the journey –

he guessed about a mile, maybe a mile and a half. Rock-hard fists came at him, hitting his jaw, cheeks, mouth, and eyes, leaving him in a little mask of pain, with one eye closed, a lip split, and one tooth less, spat out inside the hood.

'Come on, out with you,' one grunted when they came to a final standstill, the cab rocking on its springs, the horse still frisky after its gallop.

'Out, you cunning bastard,' the other growled, close to his face. 'Come on, you little Spanish bugger.'

He heard the door open, felt the chill night air, and was pulled so roughly that he went sprawling onto the pavement, banging his face hard, tearing his trousers, and skinning his knees.

They dragged him to his feet again, got his arms twisted behind his back, and frog-marched him up stone steps and into a house. He was aware that there was light and he could feel the warmth. Behind the musty smell of the sacking he thought he caught a whiff of women: powder and sweat and ripe, overused cunny. A knocking shop, he thought, and as if his captors could read his mind, he got a heavy blow to the face, a fist catching him just above the nose. Beyond the pain, and from somewhere above him, he heard a woman laugh: nervous, shrill, humourless.

Up more stairs, banging his shins, across a landing and stumbling, climbing again, a sharp turning of the stair and bare boards under his feet. They twisted his arms farther up his back, sending needles of pain through his shoulder blades, and one of them kicked him hard behind his right knee, almost bringing him down.

Then they tore off the sacking hood and started in on ripping off his ulster, tearing at his jacket and shirt until he stood bare-chested, breathing hard, his eyes swivelling about to see what he might see, which was nothing. He knew he was in a near-empty attic room, two dormer windows to his right and people moving among the shadows at the far end, which was very dark, illuminated by only two weak little candles standing on boxes on the farther side of a long, narrow bath, filled almost to the brim with water that sloshed around and looked as cold as the North Sea in a blizzard.

He felt both men place hands on his arms – one hand high above the elbow just below the shoulder, the other clamped around his wrist – then a hint of breath on the back of his neck and a further pair of hands closed around his head from behind, tipping him forward, his head going under the water.

Holding him down.

Struggle as he might, there was no way for him to break loose. His lungs were soon bursting, and the blood pounded in his head so that he thought it would explode. His whole world was shrunken now to a need for breath and the thundering of his heart in his ears.

Just as suddenly as he had been ducked into the water, so they pulled him out. No warning, just the harsh tug and he was above water, ears singing and chest heaving, mouth open as he sucked in air.

'Good,' said a voice. 'Now you know how bad it can get. Professor Moriarty came to your house in Hoxton, a couple of days back. You thought he was the cabbie, Harkness, who always drove for him in the old days, but it was the Professor himself and you were taken back to the house he's using near Westminster. Right or wrong?'

'Right,' Daniel heaved, still desperate for breath, the pain in his chest and the need for air overriding everything.

'What did he want, Daniel? You tell me or you'll drown, lad. I mean it. You're nothing to me.'

And down he went once more: hard under the water so that he was thrashing about, trying to turn his head from side to side, lungs on fire in need to be quenched by air.

Daniel was near certain that his interlocutor in the shadows was Idle Jack, whom he had glimpsed in the hotel bedroom when they had taken him.

Idle Jack was a coming man in the criminal fraternity, intelligent and with plenty of contacts, building his own family and not to be taken lightly: a barrister and a baronet whose nickname was easy to fathom for he was Sir Jack Idell, which he pronounced with stress on the first syllable – *Eye*-dell. So of course everyone called him Idle Jack.

The baronetcy had been inherited from his father, Roderick 'Roister' Idell, who had been a career soldier, distinguishing himself at the battle of Inkerman – the third great battle of the Crimean War. Shortly after Balaclava, and the famed charge of the Light Brigade, on the night of November 4, 1854, Major Roderick 'Roister' Idell of the 68th Durham Light Infantry led a reconnaissance party below the heights at Inkerman, where the British and French armies were established, and reported their strength and disposition to his commanding officer, Sir George Cathcart. Later in the battle, Idell saved the life of the son of a courtier to the queen, which was the true reason for the baronetcy – that and the Idell millions that came from the flourishing slave trade. The Idell millions, if we are talking facts, were mainly mythical, or eaten away in the upkeep of the house and estate in Hertfordshire and the town house in smart Bedford Square, which had cost Sir Roderick a fortune to start with, and by the time of his death, in 1892, was so run-down and threadbare that Jack's inheritance – title, houses, land, debts, and all – was more of a burden than a boon; indeed, some said that Idle Jack had little option but to go into a life of crime, which the wits said he'd already done being a barrister at law.

A collage of vivid thoughts concerning Idle Jack swamped Daniel's brain as they pulled him out of the water again, retching, reaching for air. Gasping, trying to see into that dark patch at the end of the room, where he knew there were people.

The commanding voice again. 'What did he want of you, Daniel, the Professor? Did he give you orders? If so, what were they?'

'Yes.' He could hardly get the word out, lunging for more air to feed his starved lungs. 'Yes. Yes, he gave me instructions.'

'Tell me, and maybe I won't let them duck you again.'

He told it all: how he was to go to the hotel, bribe the boot boy, discover how long Mrs. James would be there and in which room she was to be lodged.

'Mrs. James?' It was definitely Idle Jack. In the back of his head Daniel had the picture of him, there next to the bed, grinning his wolfish grin.

Hello, Daniel, we have need to talk.

'That's what she called herself.'

'Who?'

'You know who.'

There was a pause, maybe the space of two beats, then the hands were on him again and he was submerged once more, fighting for his life; and this was the worst yet, making him urinate in his trousers, brought to a fever of fear. He seemed to be out of air for longer than he could remember, taking a great gulp of water in, choking, and finally suffering the red mist, then the darkness as he hit unconsciousness.

'That'll teach you to play the old soldier with me, young Daniel,' Idle Jack said, his voice hard as a grindstone.

Carbonardo vomited water back into the bath, his lungs wheezing with the dregs still remaining.

'Who was this Mrs. James, Daniel? Tell me everything now, and tell me true.'

'Sal Hodges: the woman in charge of Moriarty's girls, the whores and the dollymops, the perfect ladies and nightwalkers, those in his knocking houses.'

'He had many such houses?'

'Some ten in the West End and several smaller shops elsewhere, places of sixpenny sinfulness. In the suburbs mainly.'

'Really? He should count again, I think. The Professor has been away too long and when the cat's away, the mice... Well, you know how it

61

goes, Daniel.'

Nearby, somebody chuckled.

In his mind, Daniel Carbonardo could see the man, Idle Jack, whose father had been called 'Farmer Idell' because of his ruddy complexion, the loping walk as though he tended a plough, and his slack-jawed face. Indeed, *Punch*, the 3d-a-week comic magazine, had once published a cartoon of him as 'Farmer Idell catching flies as he speaks to his farm labourers.' The drawing showed Roderick Idell – old 'Roister' himself, mouth drooping as he harangued a group of politicians over whom he held much sway. The son, Jack, was very like his father, and he exploited the somewhat foolish expression of his face by pretending to be 'sixpence to a shilling,' as the wags called it. He was, of course, sharp as a needle and dangerous as an angry adder.

'If you should see Moriarty again – which I would not advise – I'd tell him to take a good look at some of his pleasure houses. They don't all pay their profits to him anymore. Now, what did he want with Mrs. James, Danny?'

'He was after intelligence. He thinks someone near to him has committed treachery, supplying an enemy with hard facts about him and his plans.'

'So, what has this to do with Sal Hodges? He and Sal were as close as wax.'

'I don't know. He had suspicions. Said Sal would know who the traitor is.'

She'll know, Daniel. Sal Hodges'll know, mark me.

'And you were to squeeze the juice from the plum, eh?'

'Them were my orders, yes.'

62

There was the sound of shuffling from among the people at the end of the room, as though they were acknowledging some kind of truth.

'Good. You're a sensible man. Far more sensible than I expected from one who takes orders from the Professor.'

Daniel was about to try and speak, but he prudently changed his mind.

Idle Jack continued, quietly, 'Will you take some advice from me, Daniel? Will you?'

He nodded, and Idle Jack roared, 'Will you, Daniel?'

'Yes,' he croaked.

'Take yourself out of London, then. Take yourself into the country and hide yourself away. Get a job in some country school, maybe, as fencing master or in teaching calisthenics in a school for young women. Just disappear. You follow me?'

'I follow you, sir. Yes.'

'I warn you, Carbonardo, if you don't get lost and away from Moriarty and his mob, I'll hunt you down like the hound of heaven and next time I'll let my lads hold you under forever. And don't go near the Professor. The Professor's had his day. Finished!'

And at that moment there was a freak change in the weather. Though it was almost freezing outside, an enormous double lightning flash lit the sky, sending a few seconds of clear light in through the dormer windows.

In the flood of light, Carbonardo clearly saw Idle Jack Idell standing a little in front of a knot of people, and to his right Daniel thought he could see Sal Hodges, hemmed in by two burly rampsmen. Sal, he would have sworn, looked sore afraid.

There followed a massive thunderclap that sent a further shiver of fear through Carbonardo, and the floor seemed to move under him.

In Poplar, down near the West India Docks, in The Sheet Anchor public house they heard the clap of thunder but did not see the lightning flash, for the pub fronted onto a narrow alley off West India Dock Road that blocked out the light and made the landlord, Ebb Kimber, keep gaslights on in his house almost round the clock, for his receipts from the bar were never good enough to cover the expense of putting the electric in.

The thunder came just as they arrived, walking into the saloon bar: Albert Spear, Lee Chow, and foxy little Ember, all three of them smart, dressed in well-cut suits with greatcoats – men about town.

'Was that thunder?' Ember asked.

'Yea. Queer weather.' Spear sucked his teeth. 'Strange. Fog and ice when we got in, now there's a bloody thunderstorm.'

'The weather's changing. Said so in *Reynolds' News*.'

'Well, they'd know, wouldn't they, *Reynolds' News?*' Spear gave Ember what was known as an old-fashioned look and repeated '*Reynolds' News*' with a curl to his lip.

'Once I saw pouring rain one side of street and hot sunlight on other side.'

'Where was that, then, Lee Chow?'

'Was in Nanjing.'

'Blimey,' Ember smirked, 'I thought the nearest

you been to China was Wapping.'

'Ah, in my young days I spent many year in China.'

They came fully into the room, acknowledging an elderly man, sitting on his own by the fire reading the *Evening Standard*, and the two younger men at the bar with a woman who looked flighty with a smudge too much rouge on her cheeks, a ratty feather boa round her neck, and a cackling laugh that could wake the dead if the wind was in the right direction.

Divesting themselves of their greatcoats, the three men pulled chairs up against the wall behind a pair of round, marble-topped tables and Spear went over, rapped on the bar, and ordered three pints of porter.

No money changed hands, and the landlord greeted him warmly, calling him Mr. Spear, very correct, treating him with respect. Then the door opened and a tall man peeped in, as if checking on who had come into the saloon bar. On seeing Spear his wary eyes lit up.

'Mr. Spear,' he said. 'How nice to see you. Unexpected, like.'

'Will Brooking,' Spear acknowledged. 'Still lurking round here, then. Good lad.'

'Doing the job you give me, Bert. What? Six, seven years ago?' and the newcomer thrust out a hand like the head of a battle-axe. He had a craggy face, watchful eyes, and carried himself like an army man.

'See him before,' Lee Chow announced, taking a long swallow of his drink.

Spear rarely smiled, but he did now. 'One of

mine. Prizefighter he was – a boy of the Holy Ground. Used to go round the country fairs, with the travelling people. Keeping an eye out here, in the pub. Good to see him still doing his job.'

'Bet he hasn't been paid in a while.' Ember had an annoying, somewhat whining voice that went with his ratty, foxy face.

Ranged along the wall, they all had a good view of the door, ready to scrutinize any customer who entered, and they began talking about how good it was to be back in London. 'You could put me down in the Smoke and I'd know where I was in minutes,' Spear told them.

'Yea, by the smell of soot and smoke,' Ember said.

'Same for me in Nanjing,' Lee Chow added. 'It smell highly of pork. Ve-iy pungent, pork on the butcher stall in market.'

'Raw meat can niff when it wants to,' Spear agreed.

The man reading his paper asked if they were off a ship, and Spear gave him the fish eye. 'In a way. Who's asking?'

'Oh, I'm nobody. Just heard your Chink friend talking about China, so, naturally I wondered.'

'We've been out of the country for a while, but we're back now,' Ember said with stunningly obvious finality.

'I remember this pub from when I was a nipper,' Spear told them. 'I used to do the shivering dodge round here with my sister, Violet.'

'What is shivering dodge, Bert?' asked Lee Chow.

'Worked best in cold weather.' Spear smiled as if looking back through the tunnel of his memory. 'We'd come out in rags. Hardly anything covering us. Nothing on our feet. The trick is to stand there and look pathetic. And shiver of course. Mind you have to do it near a pub and where there are plenty of people about. You stand there, looking miserable and shivering like a leaf in the breeze. Always worked.'

Ember gave a dry little laugh. 'They still do it, kids do it in winter. I seen 'em. Fair brings tears to the eyes if it's done right.'

Lee Chow laughed. 'Shivering dodge,' he said.

'Eventually, if you stand there–'

'Shivering–'

'Yea, shivering, well, some person, usually a woman, she'll say, "Ho, Lord love us. Look here, Charles" – he was doing a posh voice now, exaggerated and quite funny, moving his hands, fluttering them around like a woman might. '"Ho, my goodness me! Ho dear, ho dear! This child. Ho my. Child, does your mother know you're out in this cold weather?" ... "Ain't got no muvver, miss." ... "Your father then?" ... "Ain't got no favver. Only me and me little sister in the whole world." ... "Ho my poor child." And if you're lucky she'd get her husband, or her gent, to take you to the pub and give you some bread and cheese and a pint of porter to warm you, maybe there'd be a bowl of hot soup 'n' all – nip of brandy, if you were working well. Sometimes you'd even come away with some money. Sixpence. Shilling maybe. You see, the blokes didn't want to look cheap in front of their women. They may have suspected you

67

were on the dodge, but the last thing they'd do is show meanness.'

'Yea, I done the shivering dodge an' all,' Ember nodded.

'And I'd wager that you were very good at it, Ember.'

'Once, a man give me a whole silver crown to show off to his girl, but he come back, clipped me round the ear, and took it from me. I even called a copper, said he was robbing me, but the copper knew the dodge and clipped me ear again.'

Lee Chow was delighted with all this, his sallow little face screwed into a wreath of pleasure.

'Hey, Spear.' Ember leaned forward. 'You ever do the dead man's lurk?'

'Oh, that was good if you had the gift of tongues. If you were a good talker. But let me tell you about a woman I knew: We called her Haggie Aggie. She was an old whore. Past it by then. So she was on the shivering dodge well into her sixties, near seventy. Used to station herself close to a good pub, and she'd rub ash into her face, make her pale and pasty like, mess her hair up with grease. And she'd do more'n shiver. She'd moan, an' do the fainting stagger an' all. A real performer. Beautiful to watch. Someone would always take pity and they'd get her to the pub an' give her a good glass of brandy. She'd move around, mind you, Haggie Aggie. She'd crawl round the pubs up the garden, up Covent Garden, where there're plenty of young men after a bit of how's-your-father. And they'd take her from pub to pub. She'd start eight or nine in the morning and she'd be pissed as a loon by midday. Really in need of a quack by noon. Half seas over she'd be. Too drunk to see a hole in a ladder. Pixillated. Oh, but my word, she didn't half smell an' all. Ponged something terrible. Don't think she can ever've washed. Smelled like a badger's touch hole.'

'Covered in fartleberries, eh?' Lee Chow gave a great guffaw, as if this was the funniest thing he'd ever said.

'Very witty,' mumbled Ember.

'Fart-e-bellies,' mused Lee Chow with an almost childish giggle. But he was a man who imagined a rousing breaking of wind to be the height of sophistication.

Lee Chow now asked Spear what this dead man's lurk was –'Ber', wha' dead man 'urk?' The Chink's short tongue sometimes made it difficult for him to pronounce his *L*s and *T*s. But he was inconsistent and some said he did it on purpose, to sound exotic, but sometimes he would forget.

Bert Spear started to explain that you had to be very careful: pick a recently deceased person and go round checking up on him. 'Then you'd go down the coffin maker, down the undertaker, and ask to visit the corpse, and you'd find out when the family were coming in and place yourself ready to bump into them, like. When they come out from the chapel of rest, after viewing the stiff.

'See, Lee Chow, they'd be overcome with grief, so more likely to believe any old bunny you spun them: how their dad had been a wonderful person and always paid you for odd jobs. "Only last week I did this, that, or the other and didn't see him to get the two guineas he would have given me. No... No, lady... No, I don't want any money now. It was

69

a privilege to help him out... Well, ma'am, if you insist.'" He laughed heartily at the memory; then the door of the saloon bar opened, and all three heads turned as though they were all on the same string. If you were looking carefully enough you'd have noticed Ember's hand duck inside his jacket, and Lee Chow's right arm reach around to his back where he kept his little scalpel-sharp filleting knife safe in a scabbard.

It was Terremant, shaking himself like a big dog, coming in out of the rain. 'Bloody hell,' he said grinning at his old friends. 'It's raining like a cow pissing on a flat rock out there. I'm drenched.'

The man by the fire made way so that Terremant could dry his coat by the flames, and Ember rushed off to get him a drink– 'Drop of brandy, please, Ember. Dry out me innards.'

They all huddled together now, heads low and muttering softly.

'Fart-e-bellies,' Lee Chow murmured, then went off into a peal of high laughter.

'Keep quiet and shut up, you evil fucking Chinee,' Ember snapped.

'I got a letter for you, Bert. From hisself,' Terremant said, sliding the envelope over the tabletop.

Spear turned it over, glancing at the seal and flap. 'You've read it, of course?' he asked.

'Could never break meself of the habit,' Terremant answered, raising his eyebrows.

'You'll come to a sticky end, reading other people's letters.' Spear broke the seal and ran his thumb up the flap, then pulled out the four pages.

'You've got to find another really big warehouse, like the one we had in Limehouse,' Terremant said. 'You're to buy it through that lawyer he's always using. Funny-named geezer.'

'Gwyther,' said Spear as though there was nothing strange about Perry Gwyther's interesting name.

'That's the one. You buy a huge warehouse.'

'Where?'

'Here in Poplar, or back in Limehouse, Shadwell, wherever you find one. But it has to be near the river. Like before.'

'Then what?'

'You get hold of an architecture and get him to design a place just like we used to have.'

'You mean an architect.'

'If you say so, Bert. You know me and words. You get him, take him out for a steak supper. Tell him what you want, let him make the plans, then report to the Professor. I know where he's staying for the time being, because I'm staying with him, seeing as how I'm looking after him.'

'And what've you been doing, Jim? You and the Professor?'

'I can't say.'

'Course you can, Jim.'

'I can?'

'We're all on the same team, old friend. You can share with us.'

'Yes,' he said, still a shade uncertain, remembering Moriarty's admonishment. 'Oh, I suppose so.' He paused as though still mulling it over. 'Well, we spent some time in Vienna. He was looking for someone.'

'Was he now. And did he find who he was looking for?'

71

'I think he did. German gent.'

'Not that bugger Wilhelm Schleifstein?' Ember snapped.

'No, not him. This one's a fellow called von something. I think it's von Hartzendov, or Hertzendorf, or something. I seen him somewhere before, but can't place him. The Professor had dinner with him a few times. He seemed very happy, but he's not happy now.'

'What's he unhappy about now, then?'

'Like a bear with a sore head. It's all there in the letter, Bert. He wants all of us to have a word with our people: all of them, the lurkers, punishers, whizzers, dippers, the madams, the girls, the blaggers, rampsmen, tricksters, and the gonifs. Since the Professor went away, family people have been leaving, defecting. Some forty percent of our people have gone. It's all in that letter.'

'Wha' is this?' Lee Chow asked. 'Wha' is defecting?'

'Defecting, Chow. Defecting means to change sides, go over to the enemy; it means to desert, to turn traitor.'

Lee Chow shook his head vigorously. 'Not my people. No' my men or women. No. Never my people.'

'I'm afraid they have, my old yellow friend. About a quarter of your folk have left the Professor's employ.' Terremant nodded, most serious.

'And he wishes us to speak to each individual?' asked Spear.

Terremant leaned over and tapped the pages of the letter on the table with his forefinger. 'It's in there, Bert. Each of us have to see our people and

72

count them off. Within reason, that is.'

'I'm glad it's within—'

And this was the moment when the door of the saloon bar crashed open and they heard the rain lashing down outside.

Later, Ember said he had never seen anything like it, except when he saw Maskelyn and Cooke's conjuring show at the Egyptian Hall. The large pistol appeared in Albert Spear's hand like magic. He was sitting there looking at the pages of the letter one minute; the next he had a revolver in his hand pointing straight at the door and the bedraggled boy who came tottering through it near to tears.

The lad was soaked to the skin and breathing heavily. 'Mr. Spear, sir. I got a hansom for the last few yards. I went on the bus, but I run the last five miles. I'm from the Professor...'

'Shush, lad,' Spear commanded. 'Don't take on.'

'You're young Walker, aren't you?' Ember almost spat at the boy, leaning over and taking a handful of the boy's sopping jacket, dragging him across the table. 'You're Paul Walker's little brother, always pestering me, wanting to be a lurker. What you doing out this time of night?'

Terremant touched Ember's arm. 'Hear him out, can't you? Since he's been back, the Professor's brought in some of the keen street kids. Them what can run and are brave. Calls them his shadows. The lad's jonnick.'

'What's the message, boy?'

'You're to go to Hoxton. Quick as greased lightning, he said.' He gave the address and added that they had to take Daniel Carbonardo. 'You

73

got to take him alive and breathing, bring him to the Professor. And you'll be fighting time: Get to him before he has it away on his toes.'

'Where?'

'I know where,' Terremant told them as they reached for their coats and Spear instructed the rampsman, Will Brooking, who had come through from the other bar, to look after the boy, get his clothes dry, then make certain he got back to the Professor, put him in a hansom.

As they hurried out to the waiting hansom, Ember asked Spear if he knew who Daniel Carbonardo was.

'I know him alright.'

'You know his trade?'

'I do, God help us.'

Spear was not a religious man, but Ember noticed that he crossed himself as he climbed into the hansom. 'Amen,' he said as they moved off, the cabbie urging his horse forward.

4

The Professor Reminisces

LONDON: JANUARY 16-17, 1900

Spear sent their cabbie in search of a second hansom when they arrived in Hoxton, stopping near the church of St. John the Baptist and walking through to Carbonardo's nice little villa.

There were three ways in or out of Hawthornes: the front door; the area steps behind the railings to the kitchen door; and through the gate in the garden wall at the rear of the property and across the lawn, past flower beds and a giant oak tree, to the back door, which led into a small utility and cold room behind the kitchen. To the right of the back door there was a wash house where, on Monday mornings, Tabitha could be found stoking the little fire below the 'copper' and stirring the week's wash with wooden pincers and the like in the soapy, scummy, steaming water, the walls rivering with condensation, the air heavy with the scent of the green washing soap.

As was his right, Spear took charge, sending Ember and Lee Chow around to the back. 'Into the garden,' he ordered. 'Walk right up to the house and show yourselves. He's in there, upstairs at the moment unless he's got a wife. Show yourselves but don't precipitate anything.' If nothing else, Spear used caution with men like Carbonardo, or anyone else with a deadly reputation.

'No wifee,' Lee Chow said confidently. 'Daniel live alone except when he get woman in.'

'What did he say?' Spear asked Ember, cocking his head to one side and frowning.

'He says Carbonardo has no wife; and that he lives alone, apart from when he has a pusher in.'

Lee Chow had known about the rear of the house and gave the impression of having worked with Carbonardo; he knew Hoxton and the area and Carbonardo's standing as a man to whom life was cheap.

The rain had stopped, leaving a cold, glistening

slick on the roads and pavements, the gutters running, and a clean smell in the air, the storm having passed violently on, moving north.

As they travelled in from Poplar, Albert Spear had showered Terremant with questions:

'What's all this about the Prof using boys? Shadows, you called them?'

'He's been seriously incommoded.' Terremant shifted on the bench seat, embarrassed by his words, uncertain for a moment whether he had used them correctly.

'Seriously incommoded?' Spear's voice went up an octave. Terremant wasn't good with words, and these two were unlikely intruders into his vocabulary.

'It's what he said. "I have been seriously incommoded, Terremant. Somebody's skimmed the cream off of my milk." Meaning a lot of the lads were leaving. He holds us responsible.'

'We weren't here. He told us to stay out. To back off.'

'Well, those we left in charge have been found wanting, and he's not a happy man. I've rarely seen him so unhappy. Mild as a hornet, he is.'

'Beware his sting then.'

'Aye, indeed. The gaffer can be a cantankerous bugger when he's a mind.'

'So he's got a load of boys to do men's work?'

'A lot of young lads want jobs. He's done it before. Ember's had young 'uns working for him in the past.' He made a grunting sound from the back of his throat, trying to clear it. 'If you want to know, Bert, I pointed him in that direction. There're not enough of our lads working, so he

76

put the boys on the lurk. He's got young lads watching everywhere. Even watching the place where he's living. I think one followed me down to Poplar tonight, and if he did, he's a good boy 'cos he ain't showed hisself.'

'But they're untrained. Inexperienced.'

'What's that matter? These boys're eager.'

Now, outside Carbonardo's house, Spear said, 'Just let him see us, eh, Jim? Not threatening. Stand on the steps here.'

'Yes, that's the way I'd do it, Bert,' Terremant said, and they saw Daniel Carbonardo come to a ground-floor bow window, probably his front room.

The assassin twitched the net curtain and peeped out.

Daniel Carbonardo saw them from behind the curtain covering the bay window of his front parlour. He recognized Spear and Terremant standing still and silent in the pool of light from the electric lamp standard in the street, outside his house.

He felt no true fear, and was happy that to a large extent his feelings were ones of safety. Of course the Professor would want to see him; of course he'd send his top men, even if he suspected them of treason. Then he wondered, for an instant, had they really come from Moriarty, or were they part of a darker game? For one fleeting moment he considered going out through the garden; he even moved to the door, then turned back. Spear and Terremant would have people at the back. They'd come to take him, and these blokes weren't for taking chances when they were intent on stopping someone. He went to his desk, took out the keys attached to a chain running from under his waistcoat, unlocked the top middle drawer, and activated the deep secret compartment in the desk's right-hand pillar. He took his long knife and his Italian pistol, with which he had armed himself on his return to Hoxton, and placed them carefully side by side in the secret compartment. He then slid the drawers closed and locked everything again, noting that his hand was shaking like a cornered weasel and reckoning that was a direct result of the water torture, which, in retrospect, still terrified him.

Going from the parlour into his small hall, he looked for a second at the valise he'd already packed to assist in his escape. Another ten minutes and he would have been gone. But perhaps it was better this way. He opened the front door, pulled it back wide, and stepped forward, holding his hands away from his body.

'I'm not going to resist you,' he called softly, and Terremant said, 'I'll look after him, Bert. You go out the back and bring in Ember and the Chink.' So Bert Spear stepped past him with a nod and a 'Good man,' while Terremant flexed his arms as a kind of warning.

He needn't have bothered: Terremant was six foot three in his stocking feet with a burly body to match, while Carbonardo was only five foot four and slightly built; of swarthy complexion, he had dark tousled hair and dark eyes showing some blue in them. 'Real little heartbreaker,' Sal Hodges had said the first time she set eyes on him, and Sal knew about broken hearts.

Spear found the back door on the latch, and upon opening it he bumped straight into Ember and Lee Chow.

Spear told them, 'He's buckled, ready to whistle for the Prof.'

'Good thing an' all,' Ember said.

'Watch him care-for-ee,' Lee Chow cautioned. 'Daniel is cunning fellow. Danger-ess man.'

They followed Spear through to the hall, where Terremant had come inside and closed the door. Daniel stood at the foot of the stairs with both hands on the wooden ball that topped the newel post.

'I've run me hands over him,' Terremant said. 'Clean as a button-stick.'

'He's a good boy, Daniel.' Spear put a hand on the assassin's shoulder. 'Not going to cause us any bother, are you, son?'

'Just want to talk to the Professor. Want to find out who peached on me. Then I can go and take care of whoever it was. I'm sometimes stupid. I was told to make myself scarce and I was going to, but I wasn't thinking right. Should've gone to the Prof straight off.'

'Who told you to go for a walk, then?'

'Would you believe it? Idle bloody Jack.'

'You'd better secure your house then, Daniel,' Spear suggested.

'Jack Idell come a shade heavy with you then, Danny?' Terremant probed.

'Yes, but I'll talk about it to the Professor.'

'Good.' Terremant nodded, no feeling in his voice.

'None of our business.' Spear shook his head.

'Oh, I think you'll find it is,' Daniel Carbonardo said with the ghost of a smile.

Professor James Moriarty sat back in his favourite chair, facing the fire and looking up at the Duchess of Devonshire, who always calmed his mind when things became difficult and his thoughts were frayed. He often wondered how a painting had the power to calm him, but there was no denying it. The Duchess did have that effect.

The whole business with Carbonardo naturally worried him. One of his young shadows had followed the assassin to the Glenmoragh Private Hotel with instructions to report back once Carbonardo had taken his leave.

The lad had, of course, returned with the startling news that his mark had been hustled out and into a hansom – an unexpected turn of events.

Moriarty had chosen these boys, some fifteen lads aged between thirteen and sixteen years, mainly for their fitness. They had to have stamina, he told them, and Terremant had brought him unusually good specimens – unusual because most street boys of that age were poor cases, what with the hard life and unappetizing and sometimes meagre victuals. Terremant's lads were in the main fit, strong, and intelligent.

The particular boy on the Carbonardo watch, a fourteen-year-old called William Walker, was a runner, able to keep up with the cab in which Carbonardo was spirited away, or at least keep it in sight so eventually he was there, watching the doors of the notorious house to which the assassin was taken. He also had the presence of mind to stay hidden nearby, even during the cloudburst that came an hour or so later. So he was quite near to the door when the bedraggled and shaken Carbonardo was brought out of the house, and he clearly heard one of the brutish rampsmen tell a cabbie to take him back to Hoxton. 'To his own gaff. He'll show you the way,' the tough had added.

Billy Walker quite clearly heard the cabbie reply, 'All Sir Garnet, Sidney,' and he noted that the rampsman was a burly oaf with a shaved head and a nasty scar running from the corner of his mouth, 'as if someone had tried to enlarge his norf and sarf.'

Billy Walker then showed intelligence by coming straight back to the Professor, who had quickly summoned another of the boys – Walter Taplin – and sent him, posthaste, to Poplar to seek out the Praetorians.

Many men in Moriarty's position would have worried, counting the minutes – all dragging like hours – before his old lieutenants reappeared with or without the hapless Carbonardo. But James Moriarty had trained himself to sterner stuff. He was not a man to chew his fingernails or worry himself into all manner of stews. There was nothing he could do about the situation, so he sat back, enjoyed looking at the Duchess, and thought how comparatively lucky he was. Sufficient unto the day is the evil thereof, as the Good Book says.

As he sat, warmed by the fire and the balloon glass of good brandy at his elbow, he thought long about times gone by, musing on his childhood back in Lower Gardiner Street in Dublin, some thirty-five or -six years previously; and before that, dimly, as if through a mist, he remembered the farm, out in County Wicklow, where he had been born. Then he thought of his mother, God rest her, Lucy Moriarty, the kind and saintly woman who was one of the best cooks ever to come out of the Emerald Isle. How did she find the time to do everything? For she also taught the piano and, oddly, he was the only son who had any talent in that direction. As he thought of his dearly loved mother, Moriarty absently ran his right thumbnail down his cheek, from just below the eye to his jawline.

Lucy Moriarty did not tie herself to one particular family, but hired herself out to households and organizations, having a set tariff for banquets, meals of celebration, or special occasions – *any number of guests, from three to three hundred upwards*, as her advertisement proclaimed. She had, it was known, been called to cook for royalty and for great men of the land, and many of her dishes could never be beaten by other equally talented cooks. It was said that her steak-and-kidney pie was the food of angels (the pastry being the lightest and most meltingly succulent that even truly knowledgeable palates would ever taste); that her lobster cocktail was ambrosia; and that a man would have to walk the length and breadth of Europe to enjoy the equal of her beef Wellington and horseradish.

Lucy Moriarty's one failing in life was her marriage. Her husband, Sean Michael Moriarty, the schoolmaster, was a man of irrational temper and a drunkard to boot. Sean Moriarty gave his wife three fine sons and precious little else. He treated his sons as though they were whipping boys to his conscience, and when he had finished leathering them he would, often as not, take his belt to his wife.

Until she could stand it no longer.

Moriarty could still clearly remember the night when his mother gathered up all three children and stole out of the house, leaving the cruel and unruly Moriarty asleep in his chair, deep in an alcoholic stupor. Which was how he spent most Saturday nights.

Lucy Moriarty had managed to squirrel away a substantial nest egg from her cooking jobs, and on that fateful night she had money enough to pay the fares for herself and the three boys on the ferry from Dublin to Liverpool, where her sister Nelly lived in comparative peace with her kind and hardworking docker husband.

Sean Moriarty never came in search of his family, and Lucy paid her parish priest for Masses of thanksgiving (never, of course, telling the priest the details or reason for her giving thanks lest Father O'Flynn counsel her to return to Sean and make good their marriage). She also said countless novenas to the Blessed Virgin, praying that Sean Moriarty would continue to be absent from hearth and home.

The strange thing about the Moriarty family, growing up in Liverpool, was that the three boys were all blessed, or more likely cursed, with the same Christian name – an eccentricity that could be laid at the door of their bibulous father.

The eldest was James Edward, the middle boy

was James Ewan, and the youngest had been baptized James Edmund Moriarty. Among themselves they differentiated by using mainly diminutives – James, Jamie, and Jim. All three, however, seemed to have inherited some talents from their clever, but flawed, father. The eldest, James, was a natural scholar, specializing early in mathematics. The middle son, Jamie, had organizational skills, plus a natural aptitude for the mathematics of war; he excelled in such things as the game of chess, and had a deep knowledge of history of famous battles, his favourite books being the works of great military thinkers such as von Clausewitz's *On War;* the great Chinese classic, Sun Tzu's *The Art of War*, and the similarly named *Art of War* by Machiavelli; while the ninth-century work *The Tau of War* by Wang Chen was his favourite bedside book (not unexpectedly, these books were also favourites of the youngest Moriarty). Inevitably, James was marked early in life for an academic career, while Jamie seemed destined for a military life.

So what of James Edmund, Jim to his brothers? Jim was the most secretive of the trio, guarded, with a cold touch of his father's legendary brutality. The one difference was that he kept that coldness and innate cruelty in check. He was also blessed with organizational skills that showed at an early age, when he drew around him boys whom he could lead into skulduggery – real skulduggery, not simply high-spirited youthful japes. By the age of fifteen, Jim Moriarty had led his cronies in a robbery that made the headlines in Liverpool, the theft of over three hundred bottles of fine wine and brandy from a secure warehouse in the docks area. A few months later, the same gang broke into a city jeweller's strong room and lifted thousands of pounds' worth of necklaces, rings, and other items. These are among the first things mentioned in the *Moriarty Journals*, which he began writing at the age of fifteen.

Back in Dublin, Sean Moriarty died suddenly of an unexpected ailment – a street robbery – when Jim was only sixteen years of age. Interestingly, he does not confess to this wanton crime (in the *Journals*), but he does admit to being away from home for five days coinciding with his father's death. Sean Moriarty was found beaten with iron bars and robbed of what little money he had on him. The crime brought a comment from a Dublin coroner, who remarked, 'A man can hardly walk the length of his own shadow these days without being set upon by hooligans or rampers: getting as bad here as it is reported in England. Which is saying something.'

James, the eldest, flourished academically, eventually studying at Trinity College, Cambridge, and quickly making his way in the world of academe, while Jamie joined the army and was eventually commissioned. For a time, Jim disappeared and was rumoured to be working for the railways as a stationmaster in the West of England.

The one thing that is, to quote Albert Spear, 'plain as Salisbury' is the growing pathological jealousy that grew in the youngest Moriarty's heart against his eldest brother. That, combined with the increasing suspicions of the authorities, led him to take the terrible steps that began to form the great plan for his future as a superlative criminal mastermind.

The immortality of the eldest brother, James, was assured early with his treatise on the binomial theorem, coupled with the Chair of Mathematics at one of Britain's smaller universities, and it was only when the youngest brother first visited James in that quiet intellectual backwater that he realized what fame his brother had already achieved. Moriarty would never forget that day: the tall and stooping boy he remembered now transformed into a man to whom deference was shown on all sides. The letters from famous men, congratulations and flattery; the already half-completed work on *The Dynamics of an Asteroid* lying on the smugly neat desk facing the leaded window looking out onto the quiet courtyard.

He thought now, as he waited in his makeshift rooms on the edge of Westminster, that it was during that visit so many years ago that he knew the full flush of envy as he saw James's real potential. His brother would undoubtedly become a great and respected man – and this at a time when he, Jim Moriarty, was harried on all sides, desperately trying to build himself into a man to be feared and respected within the criminal hierarchy of, first, London, and then the whole of Europe.

At the time of that first visit to the up-and-coming professor, young Moriarty had suffered a number of setbacks and more than anything, he needed some way of showing the underworld that he was truly a man of strength, a force with which to be reckoned, a leader with unique skills.

It was only after Professor James Moriarty was acclaimed for his work *The Dynamics of an Asteroid* that the professor's youngest brother saw clearly the way in which he could both further himself and scour the torment of envy from his brain. After all, he, more than any other person, knew his elder brother's weaknesses.

By the later 1870s, the tall, gaunt, and stooped professor, old before his time, was becoming a public figure. His mind, it was claimed, bordered on genius, his star seeming to be set ready for a rapid rise into the academic stratosphere. The newspapers wrote of him and there were predictions of a new appointment: the Chair of Mathematics would shortly be vacant at Cambridge, and it was common knowledge that the professor had already turned down two similar posts on the Continent.

The time was ripe for the youngest Moriarty to act, and, as with all things, he laid his plans as meticulously as the professor in his world used science.

Among his acquaintances, the young Moriarty had fostered the friendship of an elderly actor of the blood-and-thunder school, Hector Hasledean, a thespian whose one-man performances, in which he presented a striking range of Shakespearean characters from the hunchback Richard III to the old and embittered King Lear, were still much in demand.

Hasledean was by this time in his late sixties, and drew freely upon a lifetime of theatrical experience. A flamboyant figure in both private and public life, the actor, though much given to the bottle, had a huge well of talent, still retaining the ability to move audiences with his range of emotions but also dazzling through his ability to change his appearance. Audiences marvelled at this talent, and young Moriarty set out to learn from him the tricks of that particular trade.

Always certain of his victims' weaknesses, young Moriarty became an invaluable friend to the ageing actor, plying him with gifts of good wines and expensive spirits. He quickly won the actor's confidence, and one night before Hasledean lapsed into total fuddlement, Moriarty made his first approach.

He explained that he would like to play a trick on his famous brother and now sought the actor's help in teaching him the art of disguise – in particular, how he could appear before his famous brother as a replica of the great man. The idea appealed to the actor, who totally entered into the spirit of things, working with the younger man and teaching him the rudiments of disguise: choosing the right kind of bald-pate wig with the assistance of the greatest expert of the day, supervising the making of special boots with 'lifts' to give the added height, and designing a harness to help the young man maintain the required stoop. He also bade his pupil study the best books on makeup and disguise: Lacy's *Art of Acting*, *A Practical Guide to the Art of Making-Up* by Haresfoot and Rouge, and the more recent *The Toilet and Cosmetic Arts* by A.J. Cooley.

In a matter of some four weeks, the youngest Moriarty was able to transform himself into an almost unbelievable likeness of his revered brother. But this was only half the task, for Hasledean was now able to teach him the deeper secrets of becoming another character: the hours of preparation, the steeping himself in the known facts and thoughts of the professor, immersing himself in his brother's way of life: his past, present, and the goals and desires of his future.

It became the younger Moriarty's habit to prepare to become his brother by standing before a looking glass, seeing himself in the buff and thinking himself into his brother's body, drinking in his very character. This was a carefully studied process, for James Moriarty was already years ahead of his time, having evolved a system akin to that which Konstantin Sergeyevich Stanislavsky was, many years later, to offer the theatre in his masterwork, *An Actor Prepares*.

Moriarty would stand looking at his nakedness, and it looking back at him, as he emptied his mind, filtering in the character and presence of his elder brother until, even without the aids he had yet to apply, there was a subtle alteration, as though he became another person in front of his very eyes. Or were they indeed *his* very eyes?

As Moriarty looked back at himself in the glass at this moment in the ritual, he always experienced a sense of deep fear for a few seconds as the transformation was taking place in his head. This was the time when he would wonder which of them he was – the killer or the victim? It was just like that finally, at his own beginning and his brother's end; and having learned so much about disguise, Moriarty was soon able to transform himself into many other, and different, personas.

Once he had mentally prepared to become a likeness of his brother, the actual physical work became an almost automatic rite, beginning with the use of a long, tight corset to pull in his flesh so that he could take on the thin, near wraithlike proportions of the other Moriarty. This was followed by what appeared to be a more restricting device, the harness – a slim leather belt that passed around his waist and was buckled tightly. A series of crossover straps came over his shoulders and threaded through flat loops sewn into the front of the corset; from thence they passed down to buckles on the front of the belt. When these buckles were drawn tight, the effect was to pull his shoulders forward so that he could only move with a permanent stoop. Moriarty would next don his stockings and shirt before climbing into the dark striped trousers and lacing the boots with the built-in 'lifts' to give him added height.

All that was left now was to use the wig and the normal colours and brushes of an actor to produce the final transformation. He usually did this sitting at a dressing table: First, he tucked his thick mane of hair under a tight-fitting skullcap and began to work on his face with quick, firm, deft, and confident brushstrokes so that he gradually assumed the gaunt, hollow-cheeked look so easily identified with Dr. Watson's famous description of the archcriminal. Even with only the skullcap covering his hair the effect was remarkable, the pallor striking and the eyes sunken unnaturally into their sockets.

Then came the final and crowning part of the

disguise: a domed head covering of some pliable and thin material mounted on a solid cast. Externally the colour and texture was that of a normal scalp, and, when fitted in place over the skullcap, the effect was extraordinarily realistic, even at close quarters, giving the natural impression of the high bald forehead sweeping back and leaving only a sprinkling of hair behind the ears and at the nape of the neck. He would then make the few final adjustments and, once satisfied, he would finish dressing. Then, standing in front of a cheval looking glass, he would peer at himself from all possible angles.

Moriarty looked back from the glass at Moriarty.

The Professor always thought kindly of old Hector Hasledean, who, sadly, died in his dressing room at the Alhambra Theatre of an apparent seizure only four weeks to the day after Moriarty had mastered the art of becoming his brother.

After wholly mastering this ability of physical change, Moriarty's next step was to destroy his brother's career, his future, and his life.

Looking up at the Duchess above the warm fire, Moriarty began to let his mind drop back to those days when, still relatively young, he set about ruining James Moriarty's life, and then taking it. A smile flickered across his face, but as he slid back the years, he was suddenly rudely interrupted by noise from below in the bare hall.

His Praetorian Guard was returning with Daniel Carbonardo. He would have to leave his reminiscences and face the more urgent present matters.

5

Plot on the Boil

LONDON: JANUARY 16-17, 1900

The two boys, Billy Walker and Wally Taplin, had been left to their own devices down in the kitchens. The Professor had told them to rest, keep warm, and come up to his rooms when he rang the bell. The bells were on curved springs along a board, each with its printed label: one said *Drawing Room*, another *Dining Room*, and a third was tagged *Study*. There was no designation for the Professor's rooms, but he told them that did not matter. 'Nobody's going to ring any of the other bells. Just come when you hear the clattering. There'll probably be some chink in it for you.' And he smiled, almost benignly, like a kindly old uncle. He was in his Professor's gear: painfully stooped, shiny bald head, the lot. The whole meshuggener, as his Jewish friends might say. The whole crazy business. In spite of the smile, both boys felt chilled, as though a freezing wind had passed over them.

They were dozing by the fire that heated the tall water tank as though this was the only warm place in the world, but they woke, looking at each other in alarm, as soon as they heard the footsteps from up in the hall. Billy Walker was on his feet and up the stairs leading to the green baize door in the hall before Walter could even open his mouth.

'It's all right,' Billy said, grinning with relief on his return. 'They've come back. I heard Mr. Terremant doing the devil's paternoster going up the stairs; he's a right grumbler.'

Some ten minutes later, the bell clanged and clattered from the board in the passage outside the kitchen.

'We'd better both go,' Walter said, not wanting to face the Professor on his own. So they climbed the stairs and knocked at the door on the first landing.

'My good boys,' the Professor greeted them, and they knew enough to pay attention to him only. 'You are to run an errand,' he said, fishing in his purse for coins. 'You're to go along to the pub on the corner. You know it?'

'Duke of York?' asked Billy Walker.

'That's the one. You are to go to the Jug & Bottle and get two jugfuls of porter. You'll have to leave money on the jugs, but you're to ask for Mrs. Belcher, the landlord's wife. Say it's for Mr. P. and bring back some bread, cheese, and one of her special jars of pickles – two loaves of bread and a big lump of cheese. Tell her it's for eight hungry men. Got it?' He handed over the coins and nodded them out. 'I do this out of the goodness of my heart. I've plenty of gin and brandy here, but I know you prefer to quaff porter, lads.

'Good boys, those two.' He smiled his thin, humourless smile and cast his gaze around his lieutenants. 'They've done fine work for us tonight.'

'I've used both of them before,' Ember said, and the Professor nodded again.

'They told me. Said you was a hard taskmaster. "Mr. Ember's a very hard taskmaster," they said.'

'Bloody hell,' William grunted as the boys made their way downstairs. 'They look hard bastards when they're all gathered together.'

'Hard nuts, the lot.'

'Harder than pulling a soldier off your sister.' Billy gave a dirty little laugh.

'Speak for yourself. Didn't like the look of that Chink,' Wally whispered as they reached the door.

'No, that's Lee Chow, cuts people's cheeks out. Mr. Ember tol' me.'

'I can believe that.'

'I'd believe anything of those hard bastards.'

When they returned forty minutes later, loaded with bread, cheese, pickles, and the warmth of Mrs. Belcher's smile, they found the atmosphere in the Professor's rooms changed: cold and edgy now, where before it had been warm and friendly. Terremant stood up, cut them each a slice of bread, gave them some cheese, and told them to run along. Moriarty did not even speak to them, or acknowledge their presence.

'Didn't get any pickles,' Wally grumbled as they went back to the kitchen.

'Never mind. The Professor's a real gnostic, Wally. The genuine article.' By which he was paying a compliment to the Professor, meaning that he was full of guile, knowledgeable but good-hearted, a downy cove. (Jack Dawkins, the Artful Dodger in Charles Dickens's *Oliver Twist*, is a downy cove.)

The reason for the frigid atmosphere upstairs had been Moriarty's temper. He had given them all a right gobber hammering, mainly about the number of men and women who appeared to have left his employ and gone to try their luck with Idle Jack.

'I want you to start first thing tomorrow,' he told them, voice flat, showing no feeling. 'Get out there and see all our men and ladies and examine their brains. Then come back to me and tell me who's true and who's false. Who goes and who stays.

'Spear,' he rapped, still out of sorts. 'You already have my orders. Go and purchase a warehouse for me, then get a good architect and have him draw up plans to your specification. Do what has to be done. I want things to be as they were before. Just as I wish you to remember what Jack Idell is. They say that a child's way to the gallows is a pack of cards. I say 'tis Idle Jack. That perverted villain is the Jack of spades and the Jack of clubs, both.'

Spear gave a solemn grunt of agreement, signifying that he would do as asked, his mouth full of cheese and pickles.

'And as for you, Daniel Carbonardo, I suspect you'd like to even the score with Idle Jack Idell.'

'I suspect we *all* would.' Daniel didn't crack his face, all too cognizant of Moriarty's fury with Idle Jack's attempt to displace him, setting himself up in direct opposition to the Professor.

'Well, go out and do him, then. As publicly as possible.'

'That's all very well, guv'nor, but there're two problems.'

'They are?'

95

'Who peached on me; and where can I get Idle Jack when he's a sitting duck? He seldom goes abroad alone. Idle Jack's not idle about his protection.'

'The first's a matter of deduction, Daniel. I told you what to do. So, it stands to reason that the one who betrayed you must be someone you told. I certainly told nobody of where you were to go, or what you were to do. Not even these good fellows here. So... Well...?'

'I told no person.'

'I think you did, Daniel. Not the details. Not what educated men would call the minutiae, but you signalled your intentions to at least two people. Sam, the boot boy at the Glenmoragh Private Hotel. You asked him about a certain Mrs. James, you asked him to slip the locks on the door; you also spoke to Mr. Ernie Moat, the manager. People come and people go, Daniel. You doubtless tipped young Samuel the monish for his pains. And you know, Danny Boy, money doesn't just talk, it sings, and more ways than one. Veritable arias the monish sings. And if I was to put money on who sold you to Idle Jack, I'd put it on your boot boy.'

Carbonardo frowned, shook his head, and breathed out noisily.

'Then he should be taught a lesson.'

'Quite correct.' Moriarty was jaunty now. 'Terremant, my friend, help Daniel out, would you? Lay hands on this Sam and give him the thrashing of his life. Then offer him a job with us. Get him out of that hotel.' Turning to Daniel, he now addressed the other problem. 'You say Idle

96

Jack takes care of himself when he goes out?'

'The two rampers that took me, yes. They guard him practically everywhere. I'll need to get him alone if I'm to take him once and for all. I'd not like to fail with those two bullies around.'

'Ah!' Moriarty raised a finger, and his face took on the look of a man who had just solved some weighty problem. 'I think we may have the answer. Lee Chow, you little warped Chinese, go down to the kitchen and bring the boy back – the one who lurked so long outside the lady's boardinghouse where they took Daniel. The boy, Walker.'

Lee Chow stood, bowed, and shuffled out. He always did the bow because he knew the round-eyes with whom he worked thought it quaint and oriental. He returned a few moments later with Billy Walker, who looked white-faced and trembly, wondering what he was in for, full of fear.

'My boy,' Moriarty said, almost stroking the lad with his voice. 'My good boy. When they brought this gentleman out of the house tonight, where you lurked well, got soaking wet, and observed everything?' He indicated Daniel Carbonardo, who, it must be said, looked a fright with his bruised face, split lip, and the dried blood around his mouth where the tooth had come out.

'Yes, sir?' The boy's voice was shaking in a high register.

'The man who treated Mr. Carbonardo here so roughly. Tell me, what did he look like?'

'Hard, sir. Hard like the Rock of Gibraltar. I wouldn't like to be on the bad side of him. He's muscled all over, with a shaved head. Bullet-headed.'

97

'Clever boy.' Moriarty smiled and nodded with pleasure, leaning toward the lad. 'Now, he conversed with a cabbie after seeing Mr. Carbonardo into the cab?'

'Indeed he did, sir. I heard him.'

'And what did he say?'

'Told him to take the gentleman back to Hoxton, sir. To his own gaffe, he said.'

'And did the cabbie acknowledge him? Call him by a name?'

'Yes, sir. He called him "Sidney," sir.'

Bert Spear made a noise of disgust and then said, 'Sidney Streeter. He worked for me, Sid did. All-round ramper. A tough cove.'

'That cockatrice! I recall him,' Moriarty spat out, running his right thumb down his cheek, nail against the skin. 'Spear, before you look for the warehouse, go with friend Terremant and have a word with Streeter. If he's any sense left he'll come back and work for me.'

'Do we want him, sir?'

'Mmmm ... on a temporary basis.' He tipped his hand from side to side, fingers open, flat, palm down. 'He's guarding Idle Jack, Spear. We want him to pass on Jack's movements, put Daniel here in a position so he can pass *him* on, if you follow me.'

Spear nodded and drew a finger across his throat.

'Precisely.' Moriarty licked his lips. 'There's another thing, Bert Spear. I want you to find Sal Hodges. Don't hurt her, don't threaten. She may well have been taken unawares like Daniel. Just bring her to me and I'll do the business with her,

98

find out what's what.'

'I seek Sidney ou'.' Lee Chow's face went still; no grins now as he looked up toward the Professor. 'I a'ange Sidney.' Chilling, making a pledge. He would be responsible for bringing the traitorous Streeter back, a penitent, to Professor Moriarty.

'Very well, Lee Chow.' Moriarty raised his eyebrows at Spear. 'Better if Ember goes with our Chinese brother, eh?'

And Spear gave a confirmatory nod as Moriarty dismissed the boy, then raised his voice, making each word seem to spark from his lips, throwing back his head and barking out the most momentous announcement of the night.

'I want all of this dealt with, and quickly. You will start first thing in the morning, for it is now already near the devil's suppertime. Those of our men and women who have wandered in the direction of Idle Jack must be brought back into our fold. If they will not come, or if any of them appear to you not to be worthy of returning – by which I mean people who could still pose a threat to our family – then you must deal with them as you see fit. In these cases I suggest that if they pay the highest penalty, then you must make certain that they pay it as publicly as is convenient. I want no hole-in-the-corner mutilations, or bodies turning up in dark cellars three years hence, or under the ground and unaccounted for.

'Idle Jack must be demolished. I don't much care how you do it, but he should be swept away – him and whatever family he has already constructed around himself.

'Now, I'll tell you that I have a plot on the boil, and when that plot comes to fruition it will put all of us well out of the reach of the clutches of any Sherlock Holmes, Inspector Lestrade, or Angus McCready Crow, or any other rozzer or bluecoat who fancies himself my match. When I have completed this ploy, none of us will have to concern ourselves about wearing the broad arrows ever again. We will not have to fear Jack Ketch or any of his houses of correction. We shall be free to make our rich livings as we please without threat or hindrance. We will have a Royal Warrant, lads.'

There was spontaneous applause from the Praetorian Guard, followed by an excited murmuring among them.

'Go, then, and be about my work.' The Professor dismissed them; then, as if by an afterthought, he called back Lee Chow.

'Lee Chow, my friend. A small job for you before the night is over...'

And as he told Lee Chow what he required, the sly Chinese man's eyes widened. He was not a religious man, but he felt a dreadful fear, low in his bowels, then exploding through him so that he shook and almost lost control of his limbs. He would have to do what Moriarty asked, but it terrified him in a way he had never experienced before.

For his part, Moriarty had chosen well; he knew his Chinese underling could be garrulous and would be the first to carry a report of what he experienced to his colleagues, and so word would go out like ripples from a large stone cast into a still pool.

Lee Chow left the house, carrying a small

jemmy and some pick-locks – his charms, he called them – in his commodious pockets, and made his way to the nearest Roman Catholic church, where he broke in and committed an appallingly sacrilegious act.

In the Lady Chapel, where the Blessed Sacrament – the consecrated Host, which is to Christians the Body of our Lord Jesus Christ – is kept in a tabernacle on the altar, he broke into the tabernacle and stole the pyx, in which the Blessed Sacrament is kept so that it can easily be removed and transported to the sick, or those on the point of death, so that they may partake of the sacrament and undergo the last rites.

Lee Chow then went to St. George's Hospital, Hyde Park Corner, and there asked to see Nursing Sister Gwendolyn Smith, who was an old and valued accomplice of the Professor. The nurse nodded understanding and bade Lee Chow wait, finally returning with a small bottle, wrapped in linen.

'You can tell him,' she said, 'that this is the best. The child was born only two hours ago and I took it from the umbilical cord.' The bottle was made of thick dark blue glass and was warm to the touch.

To complete his master's instructions, last of all Lee Chow went to Moriarty's prime bordello, the one known as Sal Hodges's House in St. James's, where he demanded that their prettiest harlot, 'Bold' Bridget Briggs, come with him; so, together, they returned to the Professor.

Lee Chow handed him the two objects, wanting leave to fly away as quickly as was feasible.

101

He wished he could grow wings or be transported like people in the stories his mother used to tell him long ago. But Moriarty sternly bade him stay. 'Come, Lee Chow, you must witness this act. Get that tall glim' – indicating a candle – 'and follow me. You as well, Bridget. Come.'

They went together down the main staircase, and then farther, to the cellars, where the Professor unlocked an old door leading into a long, narrow chamber at the far end of which stood a table with five crosses etched into its surface: one at each corner and one in the middle. The stone walls had been whitewashed recently, though there was a trace of a dank smell when you went near them. This place was raw, bone-consumingly cold; it ate into you, like a rodent. Lee Chow began to quake; he did not like what was going on and what Moriarty was about to do. Some other sense told him that evil was close to him, swirling about Moriarty, and he was sore afraid. Strange, this, for Lee Chow was a strong, tough cove, yet somehow Moriarty's actions disturbed him, and he not even a Christian.

He was told to light the candles on the table, and when he did so he saw that they were black candles in brass holders. Between the candles, at the rear of the table, there was a crucifix turned upside down and slotted into a recess built into the table.

When he turned around, Lee Chow saw Moriarty preparing himself with robes: a cassock over which he got into a long white alb and an amice, which he pulled on over his head. Then a black stole and a maniple, the stole around his neck, threaded through a girdle, and the maniple on his left wrist. These, Lee Chow knew, were vestments worn by priests celebrating the Holy Mass, the greatest of the Christian acts of worship. As a priest vested himself he would kiss the stole and maniple, but Moriarty spat on them, and last he put on a gorgeous black chasuble, decorated in gold with a depiction of a goat within the symbol of the pentacle.

The Professor now ordered the harlot to divest herself of clothes. 'I shall have use for you soon enough, Bridget,' he said sharply. 'Just stay close to me, girl.' His voice cracking like a whip so that she wailed; she was a good girl, really, a Roman Catholic who went to Mass most mornings and prayed for custom that day.

The Professor smiled to himself. He knew that within days the superstitious men and women who worked for him would learn that he had danced with the devil, and thus they would fear him even more than before. And they would hold him in greater awe – all of them, the lurkers and punishers, the dips and whizzers, shofulmen, rampsmen, collectors and cash carriers, fences, cracksmen, macers, whores, and abbesses. All of Moriarty's family would know.

Thus apparelled in his vestments, Professor Moriarty called the whore to him: 'Bridget, come to me now. Now, just as you are.' And the poor girl was sobbing like a child, shaking in all her limbs, her fingers faltering with buttons and tapes as she stripped naked, quivering as though her last moments had come. Which they may well have done. Who knew? The child was distraught, blubbering, the sobs wracking her, like a seven-year-old caught out, breathless in her contrition and consuming tears. Pitiful.

Now, Moriarty approached the table that was his altar, followed with blundering steps by Bridget, who was so panicky that she could not walk straight. He carried with him a silver chalice and paten, stolen long ago from some country church. He spat on the altar and started to say the Black Mass.

And that is such an evil thing, dear reader, that I cannot even bear to describe it.

6

Decimated

LONDON: JANUARY 17, 1900

Albert Spear sought out, and found, his former bodyguard, a strong-arm by the name of Harold Judge. The Professor always laughed at the name. 'Is the judge with you today?' he would ask in jocular fashion; or, 'Has the judge got his black cap with him today?' – a reference to the piece of black cloth a judge draped over his head as he pronounced the death sentence, followed by a benediction, 'And may the Lord have mercy on your soul.' After which the chaplain would sonorously intone, 'Amen.'

Spear and Judge walked together across Hyde

104

Park to its northeastern corner, where the big marble arch had been moved, the one John Nash had constructed, based on the Arch of Constantine in Rome. Originally the arch had been made to front Buckingham Palace, but on erecting it they discovered the centre of the structure could not accommodate the passage of royal coaches. This caused a small embarrassment and the removal of the arch to the west end of Oxford Street (the northeast corner of Hyde Park), hard by London's great shops and department stores, glittering temptations to empty your purse.

Judge was eagle-eyed, watching every person they passed and paying attention to everyone who flowed around them, ready with a pistol in his pocket, a truncheon hidden by his long jacket, and a knife scabbarded on his belt – a walking arsenal. When you were as close to Moriarty as Albert Spear was you had enemies: the envious, people who harboured bad intentions against Moriarty himself and the many whom Spear had seriously incommoded over the years – those who would profit, financially or in conscience, by his demise.

Even on this chilly day, there were plenty of people about: Army officers, smart in their crimson or blue coats, rode on Rotten Row, together with ladies in stylish habits; in the park itself nannies were pushing perambulators and lovers passing the time, dallying under the trees, or strolling beside the placid Serpentine while boys of all ages sailed their model yachts. The rime of last night's hard frost still spiked the grass, and from far away came the sound of a military band, giving selections from Gilbert and Sullivan. In

105

this tranquil, unperturbed atmosphere thoughts of evil and criminal design seemed far away, but they were forever close to the minds of men like Spear and Judge. Times had changed, and the random violent crime of the early half of the last century had now settled into a different pattern, the evil warp and weft of criminal acts, organized and urged forward like an army on wartime manoeuvres. To be effective, the criminal class needed a leader, and in Professor James Moriarty it had found its field marshal.

Arriving at Marble Arch, Spear and his companion crossed the wide, busy road, dodging hansom cabs, omnibuses decked with placards, and the commercially viable conveyances advertising vans, while the pavements were crushed with people out to gaze at the winsome, beckoning windows, gorge themselves in chophouses or seven ale bars, or simply breathe the congested air, thick with the scent of horse dung and humanity – which was certainly preferable to the stench of human waste, which had, until the middle of the last century, pervaded the atmosphere of the metropolis, rising from the thickly polluted river Thames, the reservoir for London's daily tons of bodily solid litter, cesspool to rich and poor alike.

So they stepped around a hurdy-gurdy man, turning the handle of his machine to jingle-jangle 'Ta-Ra-Ra-Boom-De-Ay!,' Lottie Collins's hit music-hall song; and with Moriarty's henchman, Spear, muttering alternative words to himself, the pair disappeared into the burrow of streets and lanes north of Oxford Street, streets with names like Seymour Street and Old Quebec

Street, leading to Bryanstone Square and Montague Place. Here were good houses, mostly not as grand or large as the kind of mansion Moriarty had appropriated in Westminster, but houses valued by professional men, or the bachelor still waiting for Miss Right to come along.

Deep within this enclave, in one of the many old mews of the area, Moriarty owned a good-sized house of pleasure. Now, having viewed the house from the outside, Spear and his man, Judge, entered it and talked to several of the workers within. They were there some ten and thirty minutes, and later, Spear reported to the Professor, 'It's your biggest house, your largest money box for the girls. I can hardly believe what's happened.'

Moriarty nodded and gave an impatient gesture with his right hand, a kind of tired wave.

Spear told him, 'I asked for Dirty Ellen, who's always been abbess there, and they said she'd gone, didn't live there anymore. I waited a while and saw young Emma Norfolk–'

'Dark girl, pretty, button for a nose...' Moriarty gave a wink of a smile, warm, there one minute gone the next, a remembrance of things past perhaps, Spear thought.

'That's the one. I walked with her a short way and she told me they was rushed one night, a year or so ago. Rushed, crowded out, and the next day all the old protectors had gone. Most of the girls stayed, frightened to leave, as they was threatened; but all our toughs were gone, replaced: the men who did the protection, the fighters and the cash carriers. Overnight they disappeared like snow in sunshine. Idle Jack Idell's men there now,

107

aplenty, thick as glue.'

'And what of you personally, Bert Spear? What of your people?'

'I hardly dare tell you, Professor. When we left England I had over two hundred men and women loyal and true to us, doing everything you could think of. Now, I'd be lucky to pull in half of them. And I had three good Aarons under me, all on 'em Hackums: Hard Harry Wickens, Jawcrack Makepiece, and Glittering George Gittins...' An Aaron, one supposes, is a captain, Hackums being bravo bullies.

'I remember him, George Gittins. Big fellow with a lot of hair.'

'You used to call him a golden lad; his face has a healthy look from the sun, like a farmer's boy.' Glittering George Gittins was so called on account of his hair: It was golden and had such a sheen to it that one wag said, 'Take a glim near him and he'll reflect it and light up the street.'

'Yes, well Shakespeare says that golden lads and girls all must, like chimney sweepers, come to dust. But I'll wager the ladies think him a right belvedere.'

'He hasn't come to dust yet, sir. I seen him. They put frighteners on him, but George'd need a host of frightening. We've been decimated, though, Professor, decimated.'

'We have that, Bert.' The Professor paused and looked down at his fingers. 'So you're short-handed?'

'*We* are shorthanded, sir. My men are your men, Professor.'

Moriarty nodded absently, his mind elsewhere.

108

'You said the house was rushed, Bert. What's your meaning there? How rushed?'

'Some of the girls go out on the streets, as you know. Go out to tempt blokes, usually trying to attract men that are half seas over, three sheets to the wind, you know, to save themselves the trouble of chauvering them; letting the muscle take care of 'em in the house: strip 'em then shove 'em out, minus their cash and even minus their trousers in some cases.'

'Yes, so?'

'Well, one of the girls said they should've noticed that night. The lads they brought back were only putting on drunk, pretending. Idle Jack had likely lads on the streets where the girls go hunting – lads who looked like they needed their greens, some appearing swell. Lurking and lusting. They were younger an' all, while the walk-in trade were big set-up boys. It seems the house was full by midnight. Unusual. Then the trade started fights, took our lads to pieces. Cut 'em up. Ejected our hard boys. Took over.'

'And *your* people who've left?'

'Gone to Idle Jack like the rest. He's copped the lot. Working for him like they used to work for you, Professor.'

'And the same with Terremant's folk?'

'Exactly. That good house he ran near St. Paul's, that's gone to Jack, who's getting a lot of tribute which, by rights, should be yours, Professor: a might of hard cash from robberies, street work, the girls, garrotting, cash to keep things nice, blaggings, and the saucy books. Some hundred and a half men and women gone from

Jim Terremant's teams.'

'And what of Sal's house?'

'It appears untouched, but you'd have to ask Sal to be sure.'

Sal Hodges, who took care of all the Professor's whores, ran a good house herself, with the pick of the girls, just off St. James's. However, the general belief was that she paid less to the Professor than the other houses because of her relationship with him.

'You've seen her?' Moriarty asked, looking up sharply.

'No, I haven't laid eyes on her since we were all together in New York. I presumed that she'd gone to Rugby to see Master Arthur.'

'Never presume, Spear.' The Professor looked troubled for a moment. 'I think maybe it's time to fight back, good Spear. Take them at their own game. Gently to start with. Have one of your hard lads with you – same for Terremant – and make a little conversation with some of these backsliders.' Then, raising his voice, 'What's the cause, Spear? How's he tempting them?'

'Promises. He's promising the earth. Less of a cut for him; food and drink he's providing, he says. In the early days he claimed you wasn't coming back. Just straight talk that you was out, and he was in. Pop goes the weasel.'

'Lost sheep,' Moriarty mused, looking grave-faced, most serious; sad even. 'If you're unsure of anyone, then don't bring him back. Let them think everything in the garden's lovely, then throw a little surprise party. Allow the sun to disappear; clouds, maybe thunder and lightning.' He gave an evil grin and drew his right fingers over his throat. 'Understand?'

'We're not to take risks. That's sense. And perhaps I should make an example of one or two.'

Moriarty nodded, happy. He had always liked Spear, and prayed to heaven that he was not the traitor in their midst. 'Go, then, and come back to me in a pair of days. Don't tarry. Make haste.'

As Spear reached the door, Moriarty called him back. 'One more thing. The boot boy at the Glenmoragh? The boy, Sam?'

'Took care of that first thing, yes.' Spear told how he'd been up be-times and gone to a school supplies business just off St. Giles's High Street and purchased a cane of the kind they used in all schools for corporal punishment, for flogging. He was waiting with Terremant at the back of the hotel when Sam came off duty at half past eight. They had a cab ready and took the lad to a quiet house that Terremant knew of and had arranged to be vacant. 'Didn't want to bring him here, Professor, lest he didn't take his medicine proper. As it was, he was a mite difficult in the cab, so Jim Terremant had to cuff him round the head.'

In the basement of the house, Terremant held the boy by his wrists over a stuffed chair, while Spear flogged him. Twenty-four stinging strokes that had Sam gasping after three and howling after half a dozen.

'I swished him good and proper, told him to hand in his notice at the Glenmoragh, then come to me at my lodgings for a new job. Little bleeder could hardly walk when we left him. He won't

111

peach again, and he'll wear the stripes for several weeks.'

When it was over and Sam was taking great gulps of air, trying to control himself, his world diminished to the scalding area of his backside, Spear told him, 'You're never to go near Idle Jack nor his people again, otherwise it's your neck that'll be stretched, not just your arse stinging. Think on it, lad. And come to see me tonight. If you prove yourself true there'll be work and riches and responsibility for you.'

'Howled liked a wolf, wept like a willow,' he told the Professor.

'It'll be the making of him,' Moriarty said flatly, convinced.

'No more'n lads get at boarding school.' Spear, in the back of his mind, wondered how young Moriarty – Arthur James as he was known, son of Moriarty and Sal Hodges – was doing at Rugby School, and he saw what he could only describe as a kind of pause in the Professor's face, the mouth starting to open to form a word; then he altered his mind, eyes alight, darting somewhere else. Then a total change. 'Yes.' The Professor gave a series of small nods – *like a monkey on a stick*, Spear thought – *Indeed, yes. Make a man of him.* In his head Bert Spear shuddered, hearing again the terrible swippy-swish of the cane and the flat thwackering as it came down, cutting across the boy's buttocks. He did not envy boys who went to public schools and were beaten for the slightest irregularity. Spear's father had leathered him, but with his belt, usually across his back and shoulders, and he'd learned the art of turning away to avoid the worst. From what he'd heard of public schools, the beatings were laced with ritual and filled with pain – dreaded, like an execution.

'Out you go, Spear. Use your men wisely and bring my lost sheep into my pen, and if they won't come, put them to the slaughterhouse.' He gave a wheezing chuckle, as if he relished the idea of an abattoir, his head oscillating in that strange, slow reptilian manner of his.

Spear nodded, exchanged no more words, turned on his heel, and left to keep an appointment with Jim Terremant and his own golden lad, Glittering George Gittins, who wanted to prove his loyalty to the Professor.

As he went, Spear sang, under his breath, one of his favourite music-hall songs:

'And the tears fill her eyes,
While she fondly sighs,
He's getting a big boy now–
Ta-ra-ra-ra – all together now–
I'm getting a big boy now...
And I fancy it's time I knew how.
I'm getting a big boy now.'

While Spear and Terremant were off planning how to deal with the stray lambs, so Ember and the evil Chinee, Lee Chow, were heading toward another memorable moment: on the prowl for the man who had been described as hard as the Rock of Gibraltar by the boy Billy Walker, who added that he was muscled all over and had a shaved head – a bullethead. Sidney Streeter, once one of Moriarty's brutal boys, now seemingly

113

joined hip and thigh to Idle Jack and ready to do his bidding, his bodyguard – a sharer of secrets.

Lee Chow's reputation may give Sidney Streeter pause, Ember considered as the two murderous mobsmen made their way unerringly toward The Mermaid tavern in Hackney Wick, where Ember recalled Streeter drinking on most days around the noon hour.

They went by a double-decker omnibus, drawn by two docile nags, almost all the way, the vehicle advertising Nestlé's Milk, Pears Soap, and Virginia Cigarettes. Close to the Hackney Wick bus stop there was a stand for cabs, four of them there with the horses nibbling carrots and the cabbies dozing, whips in hand.

Moriarty kept a large number of people 'on the books,' as he put it: doctors, surgeons, undertakers, publicans, politicians, a pair of policemen, nurses, even lawyers, and, of course, cabbies. Ember looked up, getting off the omnibus, and saw Josiah Osterley, hansom cab license number 7676, his piebald horses named Valentine and Vivian, a growler-shover because he had a larger cab, four-wheeled, suitable to go on a growler around the pubs and fancy houses. Ember signalled him on, pausing to give him instructions. 'Not now,' he told him. 'But when we're inside. You stop outside and linger in case we need you.'

Osterley was a taciturn man; he didn't speak much. He nodded, indicating he would do anything they wanted; Ember had only to say the word.

They had to walk only half a mile now, reaching the tavern at a quarter after noon. And there was

114

Streeter standing in the Saloon Bar, drinks in and with two men known to Ember and Lee Chow – Jonah Whalen and Sheet Simpson, both formerly in Bert Spear's brigade, therefore Moriarty men.

The Saloon Bar was spacious, done out in a lot of mahogany panelling, with plenty of gilding and much glass, the glass ground and decorated with curlicues and flourishes. There was a girl, nicely dressed in a starched full apron, seeing to a hot box where she was cooking sausages and potatoes for serving all day long; and next door in the Public Bar they had a piano and were singing old music-hall songs quite raucously, even though it was not yet half past noon.

They sang:

'I'm a doo-ced toff of a fellow,
My makeup I reckon's immense,
I'm the Marquis of Camberwell Green–
I'm the downiest dude ever seen,
I'm a Gusher–
I'm a Rusher–
I'm the Marquis of Camberwell Green.'

'Sidney,' Ember called loudly to Streeter, leaning against the counter, and the little bullet-headed man turned around, automatically assuming the boxer stance, ready for anything. Ember took in the whole man and his clothing: the narrow trousers, none of these newfangled turn-ups, the cloth a worsted in a hound's-tooth check. A matching jacket, shorter these days, three buttons, all fastened, and his shirt open at the neck – no tie, no neckerchief, nothing for a fighter to catch hold of – while the trousers were cut simple and there was one vent in the jacket that meant easy access to whatever he had hidden behind his hip, one side or the other. A fighter's rig. A heavy topcoat thrown over a nearby chair and a hard bowler resting on top.

Sidney Gresham Streeter gave them a sideways look – sly, expecting trouble, looking for it – while his cronies had their eyes slipping side to side, not knowing where to look, concerned knowing Lee Chow's reputation.

'Hands on the bar,' the whippet Ember snapped in his high little voice, seeing Streeter's arm starting to stray toward his back, just behind his right hip, and Lee Chow came up beside him, one strong hand clasping the right wrist, a wicked knife in his left hand, a humourless smile decorating the Asian's face, slant-eyes glittering.

The landlord appeared behind the bar, like the Demon King in a Christmas pantomime. 'Here, here,' he growled. 'None o' that. We don't want no trouble here.'

'No t'ouble,' said Lee Chow, tight and close to Streeter, turning now, swapping hands, his back to the bar. 'No t'ouble. You likee dlink, Mr. Steeter?'

The other two, Whalen and Simpson, had nodded some secret agreement, starting to walk away, toward the door.

'Oi, Jonah! Sheet! Back with you,' Ember commanded. 'Want a word! Alright?'

Sheet Simpson kept going, but Jonah Whalen stopped, swivelled, and took the two steps back to

116

Streeter's side. *Bugger,* Ember thought, *that Simpson's going to return with friends, and while we're evenly matched now, I don't think we'd be up to it if Simpson brought back another pair of fancy dancers.*

'I've no quarrel with you, Mr. Ember.' Streeter looked uncomfortable, eyes trying to take in too much, searching them both and trying to look farther afield.

'No? Well, that means you've no quarrel with the Professor, then.'

'The Professor? Moriarty? You mean he's back?'

'You know bloody well he's back. What's more, he wants to see you. Wants it bad ... have a little chat with you.'

'He does? Why me?'

'Why not?'

'Well, we thought him gone. Gone for good, the Professor. Had to find work where we could.'

'Really?' Ember raised his eyes to the ceiling. 'You thought he'd gone and left you, eh, Sid? Left you all on your own? Dear, oh dear me. That why you went running to Idle Jack?'

'Idle Jack? I don' 'ave nothing to do wi' Idle Jack. The very idea!'

'You was wiv 'im last night, Sid. Don't deny it. We know you was wiv 'im, like you're wiv 'im most of the time. We know. The Professor knows.'

'P'ofessor want talk wi' you, S'teety. You wi' Irol Jack a'most twen'fou' hour ev-ly day. You stick him like shadow.' Lee Chow relaxed the pressure on the man's wrist and stroked it, slowly, as if stroking the hand of a woman. 'Si'ney, wha' we tewl P'ofessor if you no come wi' us? Eh?'

'Come wiv you? Me? Think I was brought up

117

by candlelight? Born on a Wednesday looking both ways to Sunday?'

'You know me, Sidney.' Ember took a pace closer, nestling in on the man, body touching body; and Lee Chow put out an arm to restrain Whalen, who made a move as if to leave again. 'Best come and see the Professor with us.' Ember turned slightly and said, harsh now, 'And you, Whalen. Both of you.'

'You're joking, Mr. Ember. Me, come into the same room as the Professor? Not on your trouble, mate.'

'You'll have to see him, sooner or later.'

Next door, in the Public Bar, they had changed the tune:

'Tinkle, tinkle! Let your glasses chink!
Bright and sparkling ruby we will drink,
Tinkle, tinkle, up my lads and bawl!
Hip hip hurrah! And jolly good luck to us all!'

Raucous as ever. Ember thought the Professor wouldn't like it here. He remembered, after Pip Paget's wedding, the big party the Professor threw for him in the warehouse – Moriarty's secret hideout. That got lively, a lot of singing and a good knees-up; but the Professor bowed out early, didn't like all the noise and rowdiness.

'Look.' Streeter was giving a lopsided smile. 'Look, Mr. Ember. I have an idea.'

Ho, yes, Ember thought, *an idea? A notion? A wheeze? Anything that come out of Sidney's ideas-box would have only one aim: to come to Sidney's aid. Probably not worth a jigger, but there's no harm in*

118

hearing out the bullet-headed rough.

Ember was no fool. His aim was to get Streeter to Moriarty by the quickest and quietest way possible, or if not, then to send him to Hades. The other toughy, Simpson, had made it out quickly, and Ember knew he'd be back. There were other people in the bar who kept glancing over, knew there was something dodgy going on. So—

'What's your idea then, Sid?' he said, smiling back, looking like he was ready to do anything to help the man. 'Speak out. Tell me and I'll see if we can oblige.'

'I take him to P'ofessor,' Lee Chow lisped, the Chinaman having already pledged his oath when they were all last with Moriarty. (*'I seek Sidney ou'. I a'ange Sidney.'*)

The chilling offer. Lee Chow making himself responsible for bringing the traitorous Streeter back, a penitent, to Professor Moriarty; or, of course, doing the other thing.

Streeter grinned at Ember, a worm stirring in each of his light brown eyes, revealing duplicity.

'Speak out,' Ember repeated.

'I was thinking.' Streeter's face crumpled up as though it was taking all his resources to concentrate and summon thought on the matter. 'Thinking,' he repeated, then, again, 'thinking, maybe I could first talk with Mr. Spear. I was in Mr. Spear's brigade, after all. He knows me, knows my worth. Before we take this too far and burden the Professor with it...'

'With what?' They were now in the first stages of haggling, Ember thought. They were engaging

119

in a Jew's friendly.

'Wiv whatever lies they're telling about me. This deliberate falsehood as I bin hanging around with that napper, Idle Jack Idell.'

'You'd like to see Bert Spear before anyone else?'

'I think that would be the way forward.'

'Yes.' Ember gave Lee Chow a long look. 'Chow, this is a good idea, I think.'

'Goo' ideah.' Lee Chow sounded like an infant learning to speak. 'Velly goo' ideah.' As he said it, the Chinee slid his arm round the back of Streeter's waist and came back with what Ember later described as 'a damned great metal pen-nib,' which cleared the bar in two seconds flat. Lee Chow turned the long curved blade in his hand, gave an evil grin, and said, 'To clean fingernails, ay? Velly tidy, cleaning finge'nails.'

In the Public they were now singing 'Pretty Little Sarah':

'Oh! Pretty little Sarah, with lovely golden hair,
Her beauty jealous maidens may be scorning.
She ought to be an angel, but if rich I were,
I'd marry her so early in the morning.'

Josh Osterley had his cab outside, the growler that would take all four of them, sitting facing each other, Lee Chow hanging on to Whalen, who did not look happy, and Ember with his arm linked to Sidney Streeter, who, from the moment they set off in the direction of the West End, gave the impression of a man worrying about some grave problem in his life: He was moving about like a bored child, pursing his lips and sighing noisily.

They negotiated the heavy traffic around Piccadilly and were headed along Coventry Street toward Leicester Square, when he finally started to speak.

'I got to tell you.'

'What?' Ember asked.

'A piece of intelligence. Something the Professor should know. He won't like it, but I know what's happened, and I think it should be passed on. It's Sal. Sal Hodges.'

'What is Sal Hodges?'

'The Professor's been away too long. It's about his bit of cuff.'

'Sal was Mother Judge to all the Professor's girls.'

'She was more than that, Mr. Ember. We all knew it. She was the Professor's seamstress, his needlewoman, and the mother of his child.'

'That's as may be, but what's your special intelligence?'

'Now don't be angry, Mr. Ember. Don't be angry.' Streeter was pressed back against the leather padding behind him, almost trying to find some way out of the carriage.

'What would I be angry about?' Ember puzzled at this rough bully who was attempting to calm him. It must be something terrible, he thought.

It was.

'She's dead, Mr. Ember. Sal Hodges is dead. Strangled. I'm not supposed to know but I've heard. Sal's murdered, with her body stowed away in a house near Brick Lane, what used to be part of the Flowerydean.'

121

'You...' Ember did not know what to say to him. 'Down the Flowerydean?'

The Flowerydean had at one time been the most notorious street in London – Flower and Dean Street in Spitalfields, on the edge of Whitechapel. Two victims of Jack the Ripper in 1888, both prostitutes, had come from the Flowerydean, Polly Nichols and 'Long Liz' Stride. But the Flowerydean was no more; it had been removed, taken down, flattened, its inhabitants moved on, the cheap lodging houses destroyed and all but a few houses restyled and rebuilt.

'Go Awber' Speah.' Lee Chow swallowed, anxious.

If this was true – if Sal Hodges was indeed murdered and dead – what then?

'Jesus,' Ember said aloud.

Back at The Mermaid in Hackney Wick, they were still singing and drinking in the Public Bar:

'Champagne Charlie is my name,
Champagne Charlie is my game,
Good for any game at night my boys,
Good for any game at night my boys,
Who'll come and join me in a spree?
Who'll come and join me in a spree?
Champagne Charlie is my name...'
Taddle-ta-rar-rar-rar ... la-la...

7

Death of a Courtesan

LONDON: JANUARY 17, 1900

Captain Ratford's place, where Moriarty had arranged for three of his Praetorian Guard to lodge, was generally known as Captain Ratford's Rooms, just off Lisle Street hard by Leicester Square. Ratford himself was a small, fiery man with a little spiky moustache and a crimson face, his nose bulbous and blue-mottled, which silently signalled drink. If the truth be told, the Captain had not been near anything more military than walking alongside Horse Guards Parade, nor more naval than occasionally travelling across the Channel in the packet from Dover to Calais. If faced with this, he would bluster and say that 'Captain' was an honorary rank. That was as far as you got. No more. Captain Ratford was not given to explanations.

He had six rooms, some large and made up in pairs on the upper two stories of the big old house left to him by his grateful wife, who had departed this vale of tears on a hot summer Thursday two years previously, her death sudden and never fully explained but categorized as an accident by the coroner, an old friend of Ratford's who, it was said, owed the Captain money. Ratford also had a

123

pair of water closets and two rooms fitted out with baths and wash hand basins, though by the look of him you would wonder if he ever used these facilities himself.

Albert Spear had been given the largest set of rooms, a spacious parlour adjoined by a smaller room containing only a brass bedstead with a side table. The decoration was not the finest, but the Captain catered to men who cared little for fripperies: There was wallpaper tinted with a small pattern of dog roses, and a pair of paintings copied from the work of Arthur Boyd Houghton, who specialized in groups of contemporary people, reflecting the constraints on ordinary folk, their uncertain lives and the strangeness of individuals within big-city life in the 1850s and '60s. One group on Spear's wall showed anxious children with men and women who appeared careworn, possibly begging, living on the edges of respectability, in a way threatening, some of them macabre. Certainly some were sinister, especially when you looked at individuals in the crowd: big, hard-faced grotesques, men you would never like to be left alone with, or women you'd never trust with your child, potential monsters, the kind of people who spring from nightmares. These were all persons instantly recognizable to Spear, though who knew if he would look at the pictures in a way that might bring about an understanding of what they were trying to say – something about the manner in which life was seen as cheap in London, and the impermanence of present-day existence in this, the first decade of a brand-new century.

The sitting room, or parlour, smelled of

camphor, lamp oil, and the carbolic soap that Ratford's women servants used for washing the stiff and irritating bed linen. Its two windows looked out onto the grey and dirty gable wall of the house next door, and down into a dingy courtyard where on a fair Monday the women would hang out the linen to dry.

In the parlour on that late afternoon sat three men, with Harry Judge outside on the impenetrable dark landing above the equally pitch-dark stairs. Spear sat upright and serious as he discussed their current employment problems with Terremant, who looked far too big for his chair, *like a drum on a pea*, Albert Spear thought with a smile he did not show. Sitting in the third chair, sprawling really, with legs outstretched, was young Glittering George Gittins, a big, friendly lad you would not wish to upset, with wide shoulders, smiling open face, bulging muscles, huge hands, and confidence obvious in his look, his eyes steady, his voice countrified, mixed up with a farmer's burr and the speech of a man not often heard in the great metropolis of London town.

'As oi sees it,' he is saying as we join the trio off Lisle Street, 'oi think the Professor aught 'a be told, but we casn't tell 'im till we've assured ourselves of the truth.' This was a long speech for George Gittins, and he was speaking about the main topic of their talk – the number of men, and women, once true to Professor Moriarty but now lapsed, having been snaffled by Idle Jack and sworn to his work.

'I've already told him,' Spear assured them.

'What? With numbers an' all?' Terremant

asked, taken aback by this news.

'Near as damnit. Far as we can tell.'

'And 'ow did he take that, then?' asked young Gittins, open-mouthed, running a hand through the thick mane of hair that grew halfway down his back.

'What you'd call philosophically. He said we should look to the future, and start fighting back.'

'I'll warrant he did.' Terremant gave a deep phlegmy chuckle.

'And that's exactly what we're going to do, beginning tonight.' Spear thumped his chair arm. 'We'll head out into the pubs and taverns, the sinks and the stews. We'll seek out our former comrades and associates. Think what the Professor said the other day...'

They shuffled in their chairs, Terremant and George Gittins, neither man happy with Moriarty using words picked straight from Holy Writ – after all, they had heard, vividly, from Lee Chow of the dreadful sacrilegious acts of which Professor Moriarty was capable. For Moriarty had told them, 'Do as the Bible commands. Go ye into the highways and byways and compel them to come in. Luke, chapter fourteen: verse twenty-three.'

They were just starting to decide who should go to which public houses when the interruption came. Spear was patiently naming 'flash' pubs like The Three Tons, The Waggon and Horses, The Gun, The Leaping Horse and Bar, The Four Feathers, The Bird in the Hand, and dozens more frequented by men and women of Moriarty's family, where they planned to go, with other loyal men, 'looking for trouble,' as Spear accurately put

126

it, trawling for former members of the Moriarty family who had recently deserted to become collaborators with Idle Jack's people. 'Then we shall put the arm on them: compel them to come back, return to our master's service, with all that it entails,' he added.

'Looking for trouble's about right,' Terremant had just agreed, when there was a commotion outside on the landing, and Harry Judge opened the door, sticking his head into the room. 'Mr. Ember and Lee Chow are coming up the stairs!' he gasped. 'Couple of jokers with them.'

Hard on Judge's heels Ember appeared, clutching hold of a struggling Streeter wiggling and waggling, trying to get himself loose, while Lee Chow pushed Jonah Whalen into the room, Whalen red-faced and angry, held in Lee's harsh arm-locked grasp.

'So,' Spear greeted them. 'You found friend Streeter, and he has a little apostle with him.'

'Says he should talk to you because he was your man. Said he should be brought to you first, before we arraign him before the Professor.' Ember looked hard at Bert Spear and shook his head as though trying to warn him of some arcane matter. 'Though, if he's to be believed, he has hard and brutal tidings.'

'What so?' Spear gave Streeter a venomous look.

Ember took a deep breath, his face somehow squashed partly in rage, partly in emotion. 'He says Sal Hodges is dead,' he blurted. 'Only just told us. Dead and stowed away down Brick Lane.'

'What?' Spear almost shrieked, his voice rising,

127

rasping, near screaming. 'Is this true, Streeter? You're not trying to make booberkins of us? Sal Hodges, dead? How? When? Dear God, if you don't tell us you'll wish you were never born.'

'Last night, Mr. Spear,' Streeter said, now quite terrified at being before his old captain, 'but I only heard in the small hours, this morning, from Jacobs, who used to be one of yours.'

'Which Jacobs? There were two. Brothers. William and Bertram.'

The Jacobs brothers had been prime men in the old days, lurkers and strong-arms of exceptional skill.

'The Jacobs boys who the Professor sprang from the Steele?' Spear asked, looking up from under his heavy lids. Indeed, Moriarty had got the brothers out of Coldbath Fields prison, known to everyone as 'the Steele,' short for Bastille – an amazing coup, for Coldbath Fields jail was known to be exceptionally tight and secure.

Streeter nodded. 'William Jacobs. He was with Idle Jack at his house. I happened to be there, downstairs with Rouster–'

'*Happened* to be there?' Spear roared. 'What do you speak about, you little foozler? *Happened* to be there? You're *always* there. You're his shadow, Sidney, his bodyguard, and we know it. Which house?' he added quickly.

'The one in Bedford Square used to belong to his father, Sir Roderick.'

'So you were there, right? And where was Sal?'

'Sal was visiting him on what she said was a matter of some urgency.'

'And what matter would that be?'

128

'I don't know for sure, Mr. Spear.'

Terremant stepped forward. 'Let me sweat him, Bert. I'll have it out of him.'

'I don' know the ins and outs of it, honest,' Streeter whined, glancing about him as if looking for a way of escape. 'Honest, I know nothing, but it was about one of the girls ... and don't arsk which one ... I don't bloody know...'

'I'll warrant Idle Jack knows,' muttered Terremant.

Spear took an angry deep breath, shuddering with tamped-down violence. 'You tell me the truth, Streeter, or by Christ I'll be topped for you...' He lifted one closed fist and reached for the bullet-headed thug with the other hand. 'I'll wring it out of you...'

'I know she was there. Late on last night... Knew she'd come to see Sir Jack about something. He was with her in his room with William Jacobs, Bill. I *did* hear raised voices. They was shouting at each other, well, you know how Sal could be when she had the devil in her... I just got on with me dinner.'

'And...?' Spear asked, cold and uncompromising.

'And eventually Jacobs come down. Wanted someone to help him with a job. I had to stay there with Sir Jack, so he took Rouster–'

'Rouster? Rouster Bates?'

'Rouster Bates. Used to work with Mr. Ember.'

Ember spat. 'That little tangle-monger! By God, I'll get Lee Chow to do his worst on him! Get him to do his cheek job. On you an' all, Sidney.' At which the unhappy Streeter began to

129

wail like a child getting the whipping of its life.

'So what was it that Jacobs wanted doing?' Spear asked with chilling calmness.

'Disposal of a body,' Streeter sobbed, gasping for more air with which to wail.

'Shut that fucking row!' Terremant ordered in a voice so loud, commanding, and frightening that Streeter went silent in the space of one breath.

'Whose body?' Spear asked with crisp coolness.

'That's just it.' Streeter was struggling to get control of himself. 'I didn't know till much later when Rouster come back. Early hours it was. He come in dead tardy, and I asks him straight away, "What was the job?" And he tells me, "Disposing of the Hodges woman's corpse." Well, I felt sick as a cat and asked him what had happened, and he tells me she was strangled. It's got to be Sal Hodges. Don't know another.'

'Who did the strangling, Sid? And think careful. Was it Idle Jack?'

'I think not, Mr. Spear. But I don't know for sure. How could I? I can't point the finger at no one. In honesty I could say I suspected it to be Jack Idell, but I could never prove it; and once I said that, how could I go back close to him, for you're right. I own it. He relies on me now.'

'You're not going back, Sidney.'

'What you mean, Mr. Spear?' he asked, truly frightened now the cat was out.

'Well, how could you go back, Sid? Your true place was always with the Professor, wasn't it?'

'Of course. *You* see that, don't you, Mr. Spear.' He was whining again, trying to curry favour, this bully boy with the shaved bullet-head reduced to

130

a pleading padder caught in the act.

'You were always a good man, Sidney,' Spear soothed. 'Always. I've got a job for you, and I know the Professor has something in mind for you as well.'

'Even though I worked for Sir Jack, Mr. Spear?'

''Course, Sid. The Professor likes people with spirit. But there's one particular thing you can do for us first.'

'Say the word, Mr. Spear.'

'The Professor will probably want a word with Idle Jack, so when would he find him out and about on his own?'

'Never on his own, sir. But Friday nights he goes to the Alhambra: first house as a rule. Goes in for half seven and has his hansom waiting for him the minute he comes out around half nine.'

'Tomorrow's Thursday, so it'll be the day after. That'll be Friday, the Alhambra, Leicester Square. Maybe Moriarty'll have a word with him there. The Professor likes the halls, loves palaces of variety. Enjoys a bit of a sing-song, a conjuring turn, and a comic.'

'Ah. Hold on, Mr. Spear. Yes, Friday night. He *will* be there, but there's only one performance Friday. They're having a benefit night for the *Daily Mail* war fund. Only one show. Nine o'clock, but he'll be there because all the big names are coming along later. Even Marie Lloyd's going to be down from Peckham. And he won't miss Marie.'

The previous October, for the second time during the nineteenth century, war had broken out between Britain and the Afrikaner Republics of Transvaal and the Orange Free State: the

South African Boer War. The war touched the feelings of the British public like none before, and people gave much at benefits run by individuals or newspapers, to send help to the beleaguered Tommies, treats of chocolate, Bovril, or fags. For some strange reason the Tommies seemed close to the man-in-the-street, who suddenly couldn't get enough of the jingoistic songs and spectacles designed to urge 'Tommy Atkins' on.

Spear nodded. 'Good man. The nine o'clock, then. Friday. The Alhambra, Leicester Square.'

'And he'll have his cab ordered for a quarter past midnight. With Marie and such you never know what time they'll finish, but Jack'll have his cab ordered for fifteen minutes past midnight, no matter. Like a clock, Jack is.'

'Carriage clock,' Ember grunted.

Spear nodded, then added quickly, 'And where did they stow Sal Hodges's body?'

Streeter did not answer promptly; for a second it was as though he suddenly saw through the soft soap with which Spear had been clouding the water. Then he gave a little nod and said, 'Brick Lane. The common lodging house up the top. I think they call it The Beehive. Dropsy Carmichael runs it, with his missus, Dotty.'

'Dropsy and Dotty Carmichael, yes, I recall them. A convenient pair I remember. When is the body to be discovered?'

'Tonight, as I understand it, Mr. Spear.'

'A good old dodge,' Terremant wheezed.

'Ah,' from George Gittins, who looked straight at Streeter and gave him an enormous wink. 'Yes,

132

you pops the stiff into a kiphouse bed with the connivance of the keeper. Then at some point, maybe twenty-four hours later, when everyone else has woken and gone, you find the stiff's died in the night and nobody knows its name. So nine times out of ten the stiff goes to a pauper's grave and the lodging-house keeper is five pounds richer, and maybe a couple of other officials turn a blind eye.'

'And we wouldn't want Sal done out of a proper Christian burial, would we, George?' Spear was sick at heart by the news of Sal's death but he tried to be bright, nodding toward Gittins. 'So, George, you'd better go along with Ember here and our Chinese friend. Sidney'd better go as well, add a bit of realism; tell Dropsy Carmichael that it's Idle Jack's instructions.'

'Of course, Mr. Spear. I'll go willingly.' Glittering George Gittins gave a broad golden smile.

'Right, Mr. Spear.' Streeter seemed less convinced.

'And take care of that other matter for me.' Spear glanced in the direction of Streeter: just a slight movement of the eyes and the barest nod of the head.

'Of course. Of course I'll deal with everything, Albert.'

'If we've a boy handy, Jim,' Spear turned to Terremant, 'best send him round and arrange for old Cadaver to meet them there with his van in about an hour.'

Terremant said he'd see to it. Cadaver was their nickname for Michael Cadvenor, an undertaker much used by Moriarty when the need arose.

'Better leave him a bit more time,' Ember cautioned. 'We were caught in a blockage in Piccadilly this afternoon. Really bad. I don't know what they'll do about the traffic eventually; there's more cabs, carriages, and vans around these days. You can't move on some streets for the crush. It's bloody madness; soon, folk'll not be able to get anywhere in London.'

'Yes, they'll have to do something, and sooner, not later.' Spear rubbed his hands briskly. 'Right,' he barked, 'I'm off to break the news to the Professor.'

'Wouldn't like to be in your shoes,' Gittins said, swallowing. 'He's going to raise a riot, the Professor.'

'He'll be like a hare in a hen house,' Terremant growled.

'He'll go doolally,' Ember muttered. 'Doolally tap.'

Ember and Lee Chow closed in on each side of Streeter to walk him out of the room, followed by George Gittins.

'Who else going to be in this big night at Alhambra, then, Sidley?' Lee Chow asked.

'All the big names, they say.' Streeter swallowed hard. 'Vesta Tilley, Little Titch, Dan Leno, George Robey.'

'Plime Minister of Mirth.' Lee Chow grinned. 'Vely funny man.'

When they had all left, Terremant turned to the concerned-looking Whalen. 'Well, young Jonah Whalen, so what're we going to do with you, you pasty-faced leatherhead?'

In life Sal Hodges had been tall and slender, with sparkling bronzed hair that, when loosed, would waterfall down her back to almost just behind her knees – 'like spun gold. Old gold,' Moriarty would tell her, which was odd, as the Professor was not often given to clichés. She had been a bubbly woman, quick with the joke, or the double entendre. Flicking at her long tresses, Sal would say that some men told her she sat on her greatest asset, and she would raise an eyebrow and pout so you were not certain if she was talking of her hair at all. Then she would give you this huge wink, just like Marie Lloyd when she was performing her cod French song, 'Twiggy Voo,' bring down the house, that wink when she sang:

Twiggy voo, my boys? Twiggy voo?
Well of course it stands to reason that you do;
All the force and meaning in it you can 'tumble'
    in a minute,
Twiggy voo, my boys? Twiggy voo?

Ember, standing beside the raggedy bed, sucked at his teeth and shook his head. 'She doesn't look well at all,' he said to Lee Chow, standing next to him.

''Course she doesn't look well,' big George Gittins sneered. 'You wouldn't look well if you'd had the life strangulated out of you.'

'Her hair all gone gley.' Lee Chow put out a hand and almost touched the now dirty white hair spread over the greasy pillow, fanned behind her head. 'Not gold now. Gold gone.'

'Poor lady,' Sidney Streeter mumbled. 'Poor

lady.' Streeter did not like being in the presence of a dead body, particularly in this unpleasant room that, on a full night, would have to accommodate some thirty people, where at one time it could have done for a couple of servants. Just.

When the Flowerydean had been in full flood it harboured record numbers of thieves and prostitutes, and the main reason for this was the propagation of cheap lodging houses. They had flourished like the biblical green bay tree in this part of London – even after 1851, when an act of Parliament had tried to reduce the number – but now this was the last in the area where the Flowerydean rookery had once stood.

Dropsy Carmichael was just behind the little group as they awaited the arrival of the undertaker. Michael – Old Cadaver – Cadvenor was yet to get to them, no doubt delayed by yet another blockage on one of the crowded highways.

'You sure this is right? Jonnick?' asked Dropsy, speaking from the corner of his mouth, a wraith-thin individual, unshaven and looking quite unkempt and filthy from the food droppings on his coat to his somewhat matted hair. Dropsy was not a good advertisement for his lodging house.

'What you mean, is it right?' George Gittins mouthed at the lodging-house keeper. 'What's not to be right? You've got a dead person in one of your bug-ridden beds, that's not right for a start...'

'Well, the people who came last night, Bill Jacobs and Rousty Bates, said she wasn't to be discovered till tonight, when we made up the rooms. That was on the instructions of Jack Idell. Now here you come, not half past four in the afternoon, and tell me the orders is changed. She's to be found now, and I already got a line of people waiting out there for beds tonight.'

'You'll have an extra one to give them then, won't you, Dropsy? An extra threepence in your pocket.'

'She really don't look herself.' Ember was still chauntering on about Sal's body, and at that moment Lee Chow brought his hand down on the deceased's forehead with a loud slap that made George Gittins wince. 'You got rice and bugs ever'where,' Chow turned and addressed Dropsy. 'You eve' do anything 'bout the bugs, Dlopsy? They o'ganizing own army here.' Lee Chow dramatically scratched under his arm. 'The rice got legements o' their own. The Bug and Rice B'igade.'

'You saying my house is not clean?' Dropsy asked belligerently.

'Hampstead donkeys everywhere,' Ember said. A Hampstead donkey was a body louse.

'Yes, we are saying that, and you'd better look to it, Mr. Carmichael, because our gaffer knows people who'd close you down quick as a fuck on a train, and don't open your mouth to me' – Carmichael had already done so – 'because I'm likely to close it for a few months, if not forever. Where's that bloody undertaker? The stench in here's enough to cut my phlegm.' Glittering George had a foam of spittle round his lips.

'Fart-e-bellies,' Lee Chow said plainly.

'Ar, and there'd be plenty of them here, an' all.' Gittins had reached the point where he wanted to hit somebody – preferably Dropsy Carmichael

137

– but there was a call from someone on the stairs. The undertaker had arrived.

'I hear that someone has departed from this house,' old Cadvenor said in the trembly, parsonical voice he used regularly for the bereaved.

'Up here, Michael,' called George Gittins, so loudly that Streeter flinched.

'She really doesn't look herself,' Ember said for the umpteenth time.

'I'll need the name and other details,' Cadvenor said, entering the room, a portly, fastidious-looking kind of man, the sort that would fuss over his appearance and be adamant that everything be done 'by the book,' as they say.

'You won't need those details, Mr. Cadvenor.' George Gittins turned so that what light there was caught his face. 'You'll be doing this on behalf of the Professor.'

'Oh!' The undertaker seemed to be pulled up short. 'Oh, yes. Of course. You're Mr. Gittins, are you not? Yes, I had heard the Professor was back in London.'

'Then you'll expedite this matter with haste, and receive payment in the usual way.'

'Certainly, Mr. Gittins. I'll get my lads up and we'll remove the corpse forthwith.'

'Good. Quick as you can, then.'

George looked at the body. The head was screwed to one side at an unnatural angle and the flesh had the flabby grey-white look of uncooked pastry, the lips lacking blood, the nostrils flared, and the eyes filmed over with all spark gone. Not being a squeamish man, George leaned over and closed the eyes with the thumb and forefinger of

138

his right hand, for which Cadvenor thanked him as his two assistants came into the room carrying a litter between them. Gittins gave a peremptory order and they all began to descend the stairs, leaving the undertaker to his work.

At the door to the street, Gittins turned to Dropsy Carmichael. 'I shouldn't go noising this abroad, Dropsy. Not if you've got any sense.'

'I'm not a fool, Mr. Gittins.'

'I wouldn't have known,' and George was away from the house as though he couldn't move quick enough, telling the others to get into the growler fast as foxes; pausing to tell Josiah Osterley to 'take us back by the river, I need some air after that place.' 'By God,' he said to Ember, 'what a place to take poor Sal Hodges!'

'What a place indeed,' Ember agreed. 'But she did not look herself, did she, George?'

'Anyone in a rush?' Gittins asked. 'Any of you got appointments tonight? No? Good, we shall meander back,' and he put a foot on the box and whispered in Josh Osterley's ear; and so they wandered off with, it seemed, no particular destination in mind until, some two hours later, when the streets were lit by the electric lighting and the odd window was illuminated by candles, the growler finally took them west of the London Docks, down Nightingale Lane into Wapping, turning east again, then off to the right down a pitch-black cul-de-sac lane to the riverside itself, where George Gittins climbed down, saying, 'I must strain me taters,' and proceeded to relieve himself into the river.

'Sidney?' he called, patting Valentine's muzzle

139

as he returned to the growler. 'Sid, get down here, up on the box with you, next to Josh Osterley. He'll need two pairs of eyes to get back up this lane.' Indeed the lane was dark; there was not a glimmer of light for two hundred yards or so back up to the road.

So Streeter climbed up and settled himself on Osterley's left as Glittering George Gittins went back to the coach, passing beside the driver, opening the door, then swinging himself up, one foot in the coach, left hand on the roof as his right hand went down inside his jacket and pulled out the Smith & Wesson hammerless revolver. Lifting himself up he blew Streeter's brains out with a single shot from behind, startling the horses and shouting, 'Josh Osterley, get rid of him!'

As he turned the coach around, so Osterley nudged Streeter's body into the river and Gittins swung inside the coach.

It was almost half past seven and, back in the real world, Albert Spear was about to call on Professor Moriarty with the news of Sal Hodges's murder.

8

At Home with the Professor

LONDON: JANUARY 17, 1900

Now that Terremant was spending much of the time away from the house, Moriarty called in Daniel Carbonardo to watch him there, both on the premises and when he went abroad into the streets. He also had Wally Taplin, the freckle-faced boy with the smooth, neat, copper-coloured hair, living in as his errand boy. During Wednesday morning he had sent the boy over to the nearby stables where his cab driver, Ben Harkness, lived in rooms above the big shed where the Professor's hansom was stored, next to the stable he rented for Archie.

In the late morning they drove out, Daniel sitting in the hansom with the Professor, vigilant, armed, and ready to move should anyone attempt to harm his gaffer.

They drove to the General Post Office in St. Martin's le Grand, where Moriarty sent a telegraph to a Karl Franz von Hertzendorf at an address in the fashionable Stephansdom quarter of Vienna. The message read:

COME AT YOUR EARLIEST CONVENIENCE STOP INFORM ME OF DATE AND TIME OF

BOAT AND TRAIN STOP YOU WILL BE MET
AND ALL WILL BE READY FOR YOU STOP BEST
REGARDS JAMES

The message cost the standard rate of 3d a word
for foreign telegrams, the entire cable being
charged at seven shillings and nine pence. They
then returned to the house without incident, the
entire outing taking roughly one hour. Moriarty
found himself so impressed by Daniel Carbonardo's behaviour – the way he held himself, his
alertness and general demeanour – that he
seriously considered him for a place in his aptly
named Praetorian Guard.

Once home, the Professor repaired to his room
and poured himself a generous glass of a dry
sherry, of which he was fond, while young Wally,
good boy that he was, went and fetched him a
rabbit pie from Mrs. Belcher at The Duke of York
public house on the corner. The pie came hot,
and the boy carried it upstairs with a cloth over
the two plates – one turned on top of the other –
so that it would still be warm and fresh for the
Professor, who, by the time the boy arrived, had
laid a place for himself at table and sat there
ready to eat, a pristine white napkin tucked into
his collar and a bottle of Hospices de Beaune
decanted and breathing beside his right hand.

Ada Belcher's rabbit pie was alright, not great
but certainly edible, though the pastry lacked
something, possibly the way a good rabbit pie's
pastry should absorb the juices of the gravy and,
so enriched, melt in the mouth. The actual rabbit
was done to his liking with the tender meat

142

peppered with cloves, and an onion spiked in the same way; carrots and diced potato were also provided, and there was plenty of gravy, delicious and full of flavour, to which he needed to add only a trifle of salt and a little English mustard for the meat. The mustard he made for himself, once a week, with Mr. Coleman's powder, sometimes, in the summer, after the French manner, mixing it with a white wine vinegar.

As a cook, Ada Belcher was almost good, though not quite great. Ada, he considered, narrowly missed the mark of perfection. The people he really wanted were those from the old days, particularly Fanny Jones; but Fanny had married Pip Paget so was Fanny Paget now, and would be to the end of Paget's days.

James Moriarty's fork, carrying rabbit flesh and pastry, replete with the succulent gravy, to his mouth, paused halfway up as he thought the unthinkable, drops of gravy falling back to the plate.

But was it unthinkable? Paget had denied him, and got away with it free and gratis. Though if the secrets of all hearts were laid bare, as they would be on the Day of Judgement, Paget doubtless expected to pay for his sin at some time, and it would not be difficult to make him cough and pay the final price. Oh, the idea of tasting Fanny's pastry again sent an almost sexual shiver through James Moriarty's body!

He sat back, relishing the flavour and thinking how much better it would be had Fanny Jones prepared and cooked the pie. At this moment he would gladly give a king's ransom for one of Fanny's meat or game pies, and possibly her

143

speciality, baked apple, to follow, the centre of the apple stuffed full of demerara sugar, studded with sultanas, and laced with a pinch of ginger. In his head Moriarty was singing:

And here we sit, like birds in the wilderness,
Birds in the wilderness, birds in the wilderness,
And here we sit like birds in the wilderness,
Down in Demerara.

A remnant of his childhood.

He drank three glasses of the burgundy with his meal, and in the postprandial glow, the Professor leaned back in his favourite chair and thought again of the final days and hours when he took over his elder brother's life.

First, he recalled how he had worked hard in taking on his brother's outward appearance; once he had perfected this skilful method of disguising himself as the professor of mathematics, young Moriarty set the final moves into play. From the years they had spent growing up together, the youngest brother knew the darkest secrets of the true professor's soul. Certainly he was aware of the professor's besetting weakness: For all his command of mathematics, James Moriarty was hopeless with money, forever living beyond his means. It was quickly clear to the young Moriarty that the professor had formed an attachment to a pair of his wealthiest students, and in this he may have met his nemesis.

The young men – Arthur Bowers and the Honourable Norman de Frayse – were in their late teens, both already bearing the marks of early degeneracy: the languid good looks, limp hands, weak mouths, bloodshot eyes following days of overindulgence, and a style of conversation that affected a quick, if cheap, wit.

Young Moriarty had both the young men marked. Bowers's father was squire of a small village in Gloucestershire, while de Frayse's father, the baronet Sir Richard de Frayse, was not beyond playing at the high-and-fast London life himself. The boys seemed already set in their ways, spending the bulk of their time with the professor of mathematics, sometimes staying out until the following morning and having little aptitude for the kind of studies that should have consumed their professor.

Through carefully cultivated friends, young Moriarty, judging when the time was ripe, spread the word that both Bowers and de Frayse were being corrupted by the older academic, and the whispers quickly reached the ears of their families – young Moriarty saw to that.

It was Sir Richard who reacted first, obviously concerned lest his beloved son be lured into the web of destructive pleasure and libidinous ways that were so obviously dragging himself toward eternal damnation. Sir Richard descended on the university and, after spending an uncomfortable hour or so with his son, arrived, wrathful and spleen-choked, at the Vice-Chancellor's lodgings.

The situation could not have been bettered, for the older man had acted true to form, even stretching himself further into trouble than his younger brother had estimated.

In all, the professor had funded his nights of

eating, drinking, gambling, and, presumably, debauchery by borrowing heavily from the two young men. When all was made known, the mathematician owed some three thousand pounds to de Frayse and a further fifteen hundred to Bowers. The Vice-Chancellor's anger was horrible to see. Moriarty's name was blackened in the groves of academe and he was asked to leave the university forthwith.

Naturally, rumours abounded: The professor had been discovered *in flagrante delicto* with a college servant; he had stolen money; he had abused and struck the Vice-Chancellor; he had used his mathematical skill to cheat at cards; he was a dope fiend; he was a Satanist; he was involved with a gang of criminals. The only truth that was undecorated was that Professor Moriarty had resigned.

The younger Moriarty chose his moment with care, arriving innocent and unexpected at the professor's rooms late one afternoon, feigning surprise at the boxes and trunks open and the packing in progress.

His elder brother was a broken and beaten man, the stoop more pronounced, his eyes sunk even deeper into his head, his gait slow and stumbling, and his hands unsteady. Slowly, and not without emotion, Professor James Moriarty unfolded the sad story to his youngest brother.

'I feel you might have understanding at my plight, Jim,' he said, once the terrible truth was out. 'I doubt if Jamie ever will.'

'No, but Jamie's in India, so there is no great or immediate trouble there.'

146

'But what will be said, Jim? Though nothing will be publicly revealed, for the sake of the university, there are already stories. The world will know that I leave here under some great cloud. It is my ruin and the destruction of all my work. My mind is in such a whirl, I do not know where to turn.'

The young Moriarty faced the window lest any sign of pleasure could be read on his countenance.

'Where had you planned to go?' he asked quietly.

'To London. After that...' The gaunt man raised his hands in a gesture of despair. 'I had even considered coming to you down at your railway station.'

The younger man smiled. 'I have long given up my job with the railways.'

'Then what...?'

'I do many things, James. I think my visit here this afternoon has been providential. I can help you. First let me take you to London; there will be work for you to do there, to be sure. Courage, brother; have faith in me, for I have the power to unlock doors for you.'

So, later that evening, the professor's luggage was loaded into a cab and the brothers set out together for the railway station and London.

Within a month there was talk that the famous professor's star had fallen. It was said that he now ran a small establishment tutoring would-be army officers, mathematics now playing a greater part in the art of modern warfare.

For some six months following his resignation, people knew that the former professor of mathematics seemed to go faithfully about this

147

somewhat dull and demanding work. He conducted his business from a small house in Pole Street, near its junction with Weymouth Street, on the south side of Regent's Park – a pleasant enough place to live, handy for skating in the winter, friendly cricket in the summer, and the interest of the zoological and botanical societies all year round. Then, with no warning, the professor closed his small establishment and moved, to live in some style in a large house off the Strand.

These were the known facts about the professor's movements directly following the disaster that overtook him when he was driven from the high echelons of academic life. The truth was a very different matter, as it marked the most important, ruthless moves in the career of the Professor Moriarty we now know as the uncrowned king of Victorian and Edwardian crime.

After he had lived in Pole Street for some six months, on one chilly autumn evening, the professor, having dined early on boiled mutton with barley and carrots, was preparing for bed when a sudden loud and agitated knocking took him to his front door. He opened it, revealing his youngest brother, Jim, dressed in a long, black old-fashioned surtout and with a wide-brimmed felt hat square on his head, the brim tilted over his eyes. In the background, the professor saw a hansom drawn up at the curb, the horse nodding placidly, and no cabbie in sight.

'My dear fellow, come in...' the professor began.

'There's no time to waste, brother. Jamie's back in England with his regiment, and there's trouble. Family trouble. We have to meet him immediately.'

'But where...? How...?'

'Get your topcoat. I've borrowed the hansom from an acquaintance. There's no time to lose...'

The urgency in young Moriarty's voice spurred on the professor, who trembled with nervousness as he climbed into the cab. His brother set the horse off at a steady trot, going by unaccustomed side streets toward the river, which they crossed at Blackfriars Bridge.

Continuing along side alleys and byways, the hansom proceeded down through Lambeth, eventually turning from the streets to a piece of waste ground, bordered by a long buttress, falling away into the muddy, swirling water of the Thames, much swollen at this time of the year. The cab was drawn up some ten paces from the buttress edge, close enough to hear the river, and the distant noise of laughter and singing from some tavern on the far river bank, together with the occasional barking of a dog.

Professor Moriarty peered about him in the black murk as his brother helped him down from the cab, his topcoat flapping open where, in his haste, he had not buttoned it.

'Is Jamie here?' His tone was anxious.

'Not yet, James, not yet.'

The professor turned toward him, suddenly concerned by the soft and sinister timbre of his brother's voice. In the darkness, something long and silver quivered in the younger man's hand.

'Jim? What...?' he cried out, the word turning from its vocal shape and form into a long guttural rasp of pain as young brother James sealed the past and the future, the knife blade pistoning smoothly between the professor's ribs, three times.

The tall, thin body arched backward, a clawing hand grasping at Moriarty's surtout, the face contorted with pain. For a second the eyes stared uncomprehendingly up at young James; then, as though suddenly perceiving the truth, there was a flicker of calm acquiescence before they glazed over, passing into eternal blindness.

Young Moriarty shook the clutching hand free, stepped back, and peered down at the body of the brother whose identity he was so cunningly about to assume. It was as though all the kudos of the dead man's brilliance had passed up the blade of the knife into his own body. In the professor's death, the new legend of the Professor was born.

Moriarty had stowed chains and padlocks nearby against this moment, so first he emptied the cadaver's pockets, placing the few sovereigns, the gold pocket watch and chain, and the handkerchief into a small bag made of yellow American cloth. He wound and secured the heavy chains around the corpse, then gently tipped his departed brother off the buttress and into the water below.

For a few silent moments Moriarty stood looking out across the dark river, savouring his moment. Then, with a quick upward movement of his arm, he flung the knife out in the direction of the far shore, straining his ears for the plash as it hit the water. Then, as though without a second thought, he turned on his heel, climbed into the

150

hansom, and drove away, back to the house off the Strand.

On the following afternoon, Albert Spear, accompanied by two men, went to the small house in Pole Street and removed all traces of its former occupant.

Young Moriarty had murdered his brother, disposed of his body, and ever since had posed as him in the world. He felt no remorse, rarely thought of his older sibling, and certainly never spoke of him. This was the first time in years that the manner of his brother's death had even come into his head. He was able to immediately banish the memory once more, so that it was as if the older Moriarty had never been.

He sighed deeply, got up, and crossed the room to pour himself a small glass of brandy, for Ada Belcher's rabbit pie had caused him to think that his stomach lay upon his chest. Settled again in his chair, glancing up at Georgiana, Duchess of Devonshire, his mind slipped onto one of the more pressing matters of the moment: the loyalty of individual members of his so-called Praetorian Guard. Now, without delay, he allowed his thoughts to roam over the four men closest to him.

The traitor had to be one of them. After an absence of almost three years, he had known it from the moment he stepped back onto English soil from the packet at Dover and boarded the train for London's Victoria Railway Station. The four men had been the only people in the world who knew when he was to return – even Sal Hodges, who had come back ten days earlier than he, did not know.

151

Yet the moment he arrived at the bottom of the gangway he knew that he was watched by shadowy figures, lurkers almost as good as his own.

Men and women, some half recognized, flitted around him, many like spectres, floating along the platform or passing among the passengers in the boat train's corridor. *Surely*, Moriarty thought, *I am not paranoid*, this new term for those who almost fear fear itself; those who live in dread of being discovered in even the mildest of actions. God knew, he, James Moriarty, had huge sins to hide, considering his final actions against his brother alone; surely he was not imagining these silent watchers because his conscience hung heavy, and filthy, with guilt?

But he *was* being watched and he knew it. One of his four lieutenants must have passed the news of his return to others. *Quod erat demonstrandum.* But which one?

Could it be Lee Chow? Unlikely, he considered, though the Chinese was not easy to read; like all his race, the smiling sallow little man was inscrutable. He showed a streak of ruthlessness that was always geared to the Professor's needs and requirements. Moriarty doubted that Lee Chow had the necessary motivational guile to betray him.

Likewise the foxy, ferrety Ember. Ember did not appear to have any desire for betterment; he did not dream, like some, of a future starred with great success. Ember, the Professor reckoned, was mainly satisfied with his lot, and asked only to remain in Moriarty's service with modest rewards. In plain words, Ember knew his place.

Which left Terremant and Albert Spear. On reaching Dover, Terremant had also noticed the watchers lurking nearby, and he quickly detected those on the train. He had also spotted the shadows close by since they had settled in the house on the fringes of Westminster. Anyone inclined to be deceitful or scheming would have chosen not to perceive the men and women who seemed to be permanently charged with keeping their eyes on the Professor and his household. Any new signs of a watcher, or some strange face coming within their purlieu, and Terremant would report it – he was quick to tell Moriarty of any changes. To the Professor, these did not appear to be the actions of a guilty man.

There are three of them and Spear, he had told Daniel Carbonardo.

So what of Spear?

Albert Spear was the first man ever to work under the Professor. Together with Pip Paget, Spear had been his most trusted man for years, and he knew, literally, where most of the bodies were buried or, in some cases, exactly where they had gone into the water.

Moriarty considered Spear to be the most intelligent of his immediate lieutenants. There-fore, following this private reasoning, he was possibly the most likely of his close associates to betray him, though he found it increasingly difficult to face up to the fact. If it were even-tually demonstrated to be true he would, naturally, be white with anger, yet he also knew it could be years before he would find the ability in himself to take care of the matter – look how it

153

had been, indeed how it was, with Pip Paget.

As was often the case when he thought of the probable duplicity of Albert Spear, James Moriarty turned away from the subject in the hope that it might go away.

He ran his right thumbnail down his cheek, from below the eye to the jawline, pressing hard so that the nail made a distinct impression on the skin, taking his mind away from the question of Spear.

He drained the remaining brandy – 'looked at the maker's name,' as the saying had it – then rose to his feet and walked to his desk, unlocking the longest drawer and removing a small, leather-bound book: the book that contained notes concerning the amounts of money he had harvested during the past three years. Sadly, he could see at a glance that the takings of his family in London had dropped by thirty, maybe even forty percent over the time he had been away. True, he had earned large sums in the Americas; there had been banks in New York and Boston that they had robbed blind using forged bonds and stocks drawn on nonexistent banks in London, like the Royal English Bank and the British Bank of Manchester. Spear had handled himself wonderfully during that time posing as a bank representative, and they had laughed much at how they had passed themselves off as wealthy businessmen in some of New York's and Boston's best hotels, living off the fat of the land.

Those had been good years, keeping their distance from the detective force at New Scotland Yard yet turning many a trick to guarantee a fine income. Alas, what they made on those roundabouts did not quite make up for the losses on the swings of the daily criminal earnings of what he thought of as his family in London.

James Moriarty's lawyer, the solicitor Perry Gwyther, looked after the money and kept the books and there was plenty of cash to keep, even taking into account the dramatically falling returns during the years Moriarty had been away from London.

The Professor took a healthy percentage from every robbery, every blagging, every smash-and-grab or knock-off, every break-in, whizzing, and dip that took place in the London area; he also took a slice from the money raked in by the whores and fancy girls, plus a good sum from any man or woman in his area who was on any street dodge, from the three card to thimblerigging, find the lady, or hoopla for that matter. It was why men and women from the larger criminal fraternity swore personal allegiance to him, using a carefully proscribed form of words:

Those who enjoy my protection have certain allegiance to me.
I pay you. You have an allegiance to me.
You promised, so you have an allegiance to me.
You belong to my family, so you have allegiance to me and to the family.

Some had broken the oath and absconded to work with Idle Jack Idell, and those who broke the oath would pay. They would certainly pay

155

more than those who gave their normal tribute.

Every day of the week, two smartly dressed hard young men, one carrying a Gladstone bag, would pass along various London streets, stopping at stalls and shops, pausing to speak to people on one dodge or another, in eating places and public houses, thieves' kitchens and bordellos, and with the good manners insisted on by the Professor they would say, smiles on their faces, 'We've come for the Professor's contribution.' In this way hundreds, nay thousands, of pounds would come eventually to Perry Gwyther to be salted away in special accounts kept by him for James Moriarty. The Professor.

The lawyer would often rib the Professor and tell him that really he could manage very well without all the money that came in from the various nefarious activities of his family. Indeed, the Professor had a good income already from his honest work. He owned a trading company called The Academic Vending and Service Company Limited, which dealt with the income he received as managing director of six purpose-built music halls and several relatively novel dining rooms and eating places throughout London. The three main well-run good dining rooms, which ran to serving four- and five-course meals for luncheon and dinner, were named The Press off Fleet Street, The Royal Borough in Chelsea, and The Stocks in the City. These places were rivals to the restaurants of the great hotels and to rooms like The Café Royal.

Apart from these excellent places, he had a series of chophouses and pie shops that provided simple

156

but plain English fare, and altogether, the profit from these establishments brought Moriarty some five or six hundred pounds a week – a sizeable sum, much of which he ploughed back into the business of his criminal family.

So Professor Moriarty did not go short of anything, and he was known to be generous and charitable to those who worked for him. Albert Spear in fact was often heard to observe that the Professor was too generous for his own good, as the saying went.

And now, sitting here in his temporary accommodation on the edge of Westminster, he owned that he probably was just that: far too generous. Look how he had let Pip Paget get away free with his betrayal.

Soon after the wedding of Pip Paget and Fanny Jones, the Professor had ordered him to kill. What was worse, the victim was a woman known to him: Kate Wright, who had been their housekeeper in the great warehouse headquarters in Limehouse. He knew that had been the straw, the one that caused the breaking of Paget's back, the final breaching of Paget's trust, for he had done what was asked of him, yet after it was done he left with Fanny Jones, never to return. In his strange, paradoxical way, the Professor had known the cause of his desertion and had left the matter alone, willing to find within himself an excuse for the big, good-looking lad with the fair hair bleached by the sun. He, Moriarty, was to blame for Paget's reaction, and while he knew nothing of love, he had in some strange manner loved Pip Paget as a substitute son. Yet now his

157

mind altered. With luck and guile he would soon have a secret headquarters again and the one person he wanted as his housekeeper was Paget's wife, the country girl Fanny Jones; and whatever the morals, Moriarty usually got his way. Even now he felt his mouth water, and in this salivation, he imagined he could taste Fanny Jones's boiled leg of pork with pease pudding.

He rose again, stretched, and walked to the door, opening it and going out onto the landing, hearing, as he did so, the secret knock far below, down the stairs and along the passages to the back door. The secret knock that was not so much a secret, it being the music-hall comedian's get-off dance – dum-diddy-dum-dum dum-dum, shave-and-a-haircut, me-next.

Then he heard the voices: Spear, with watchful Harry Judge in attendance.

'I fear it's hard and brutal tidings, Professor.' Spear parroted the words Ember had used when reporting to him. The Professor stood in front of the fire, Spear looking directly into his eyes, with Harry Judge on guard outside the door.

'Go ahead, then. I dare say I can take it.'

'It's Sal. Sal Hodges.'

'What of Sal?' Moriarty did not even sound alarmed.

'It seems she's been murdered. Dead. Strangled in Idle Jack's house. The house that was his father's in Bedford Square.'

'And when did this take place?' Still unruffled.

'Yesterday evening. The body's at old Cadvenor's parlour.'

158

'The undertaker?'

'The undertaker,' Spear spoke low in affirmation.

'And you've seen the body?' the Professor hissed.

Spear shook his head, still wondering at Moriarty's unaffected manner.

'So you haven't seen the corpse?'

'Not yet, sir. No.'

'But you've talked to those who have?'

'I've talked with George Gittins. He says she don't look herself.'

'I don't suppose she does; not if she's been strangled.' Moriarty nodded. 'Right, then perhaps we'll go together and take a look at her when you've given me the hard and brutal news.'

'We know where Idle Jack will be, more or less on his own. Out in the open. On Friday evening.'

'More or less alone?'

'He'll have a bodyguard with him. Maybe two.'

'Sidney Streeter?'

'I don't think you'll be worried by him anymore.'

'I wasn't worried by him in the first place.'

'Well, I think he is gone to Rotisbone. Been removed from the parish.'

'I wish him bon voyage. But who will take his place?'

'I have no idea, though I wager that young Rouster, Rouster Bates, will be one of them.'

'What, that hoddy-doddy little man?' It summed up the tubby little tough.

'He used to work for us. Yes. Probably him, and possibly another. But Jack'll be outside and walking to and from his cab. Outside the Alhambra,

159

Leicester Square. Going in for the benefit performance, which begins at nine o'clock. Heaven knows what time it'll end. Midnight, maybe long after. But I'm reliably told he will order his cab for fifteen minutes after midnight.'

'Good. Let me concern myself with the time.' Moriarty squeezed out a thin smile, showing his teeth. Then, from the back of his throat came an unholy cackle. 'Albert, that is the best news. Don't you think it's time for Idle Jack to become Jack-in-the-Box?' The cackle was totally without mirth and was delivered in a snakelike hiss.

Albert Spear, steeped in sin as he was, felt a long furrow of fear pass through him, meddling with his brain and seeping dread into his bones and internal organs. His old grandmother would have said someone had just walked over his grave, but from Spear's viewpoint it was as though someone had got down into his grave and was trying to pull him in after him.

'Is Daniel in?' Moriarty asked.

'He is, yes. With the boy.'

'Send them both up on your way out. And Terremant, is he back yet?'

'He's still out with Ember and Lee Chow. They're sifting every piece of dust to find our people and drag them back.'

'And you'll join them, no doubt.'

'No doubt, sir.'

'And you'll get on with finding a suitable warehouse.'

'Sir, there's much to be done.'

Moriarty nodded. 'Get on with you and do it then, Bert. Send the others up.'

Spear had reached the door before Moriarty stopped him again.

'And Spear...?'

'Sir?'

Moriarty let him stand there for ten ... fifteen seconds, unable to make up his own mind. 'Spear old friend...?' Still without his mind made up. Another ten seconds. Then he thought, there's a French saying, *pour encourager les autres*. To encourage the others. 'Do you happen to know where that blackguard Paget has got to?'

'No idea, sir.' Spear's voice cracking a little.

'Find him. Let me know where he is. Right?'

Spear wondered, *If I find him should I first warn him? First, before I tell the Professor.* 'I'll find him, guv'nor,' he said, knowing he would if he put his mind to it. 'Sir, I think you should know that it's said William Jacobs was present when Sal Hodges met her end.'

Moriarty nodded, an almost dismissive gesture. 'Spear,' he began. Then, 'Idle Jack is a man who delights in forbidden pleasures – not just the perversion of man lusting for man. Idle Jack is worse; much worse. And when a man has the desires of Idle Jack, and the murderous sly cunning that goes with them, then he is somehow warped, and not worthy to be called a man at all.' He raised a hand, almost a farewell wave. 'And in the morning be here. Half past nine. Be here so we can go and look at Sal's body, eh?' He gave a throaty little laugh that puzzled Albert Spear as he left the room and hurried down to the basement, Judge at his side, wanting to know everything as usual.

161

Back in his quarters, the Professor smiled to himself. He was thinking of Sal, whom he had seen last night, and again first thing in the morning, before she went off to catch the train to Rugby, where she was to visit their son.

Lying on his desk was her telegram sent from Rugby General Post Office at four this afternoon:

ARRIVED SAFELY ARTHUR LOOKS WELL AND SENDS LOVE WITH MINE STOP I SHALL RETURN AS ARRANGED STOP MY LOVE SAL

9

Resurrection

LONDON: JANUARY 18, 1900

Terremant taught young Wally Taplin to make firelighters by rolling whole pages of *The Times* newspaper into long tight sticks, then twisting them into a kind of granny knot. 'They'll help start the fire a treat,' Terremant told him. 'Three or four of 'em topped by some dry kindling and you'll have it going in no time. Just add coal.'

One of Wally's jobs was to get the Professor's fire going of a morning. 'Only works with the old Thunderer,' Terremant counselled the boy. 'I've tried other newspapers, but the Thunderer's the one. It don't work with the *Telegraph* or the *Express*, and the *Graphic*...? Well, the *Graphic's* no

162

bloody good at all ... just smoulders, then goes out.'

The Thunderer was *The Times*.

Down in the basement, they had slept in. This was partly due to Terremant not getting home until three in the morning and young Wally sitting up talking to Daniel Carbonardo – listening to grisly tales – as if waiting for Terremant, who had been out around the stews and sinks talking former Moriarty men and women back into the family.

'Some of 'em required a little encouragement,' he said in the morning when they were crawling around sleepily, just waking up. 'I encouraged them, never worry.' He slapped his gloved palm with the heavy stick he carried. The stick had a great knobbled head, like the tip of a mutinously erect pego. Hard as a brick and heavy as lead. Until he came across the stick in a Berlin shop, close to the Hotel Bristol on the Kurfursten-damm, where Moriarty was staying in the spring of 1898, Terremant always carried a neddy – a short, truncheon-like weapon also shaped similarly to the male member.

Now, he slapped his open palm again. 'Oh, I encouraged them alright. They understood what I was saying. They comprehended my meaning.'

Young Taplin shuddered, then sat bolt upright, hearing a thunderous knocking at the front door.

'I'll learn *him* an' all.' Terremant was off, quick as a butler on Palm Sunday, as the saying had it.

It was a telegram boy, all neat in his blue uniform, heavy coat collar turned up against the cold, with the leather pouch unbuckled on his

163

belt and a telegram for James Moriarty.

'I have to wait. See if there's a reply,' the boy said, trying out a bit of cheek on Terremant, who nodded at him, then summoned a drowsy Daniel Carbonardo from below stairs to take the telegram to the Professor.

Carbonardo had barely turned the handle on the Professor's bedroom door when Moriarty sat up, eyes open, awake and alert, a hand reaching for the Borchardt automatic pistol that was never far distant from his grasp, awake or asleep.

'What is it?' he asked, flat and seemingly disinterested. 'What was all that knocking? "Knock, knock, knock. Who's there? A farmer that hanged himself on th'expectation of plenty," was it?'

'I thought it was ill luck to quote from that play, sir.' Carbonardo was uncharacteristically arch.

'Daniel, yes. Ah, the Scotch play. So, I have a literate assassin. One who knows his Shakespeare.' Then, raising his eyebrows in query. 'The knocking?'

'A telegram for you, sir.' He offered the buff envelope. 'The boy awaits an answer.'

The Professor ripped open the flimsy envelope and quickly read the contents:

ARRIVING ON THE PACKET IN DOVER FROM CALAIS DUE AT NOON ON MONDAY 22ND JANUARY STOP THENCE TO LONDON BY THE BOAT TRAIN STOP WIRE MY INSTRUCTIONS STOP GOOD WISHES VON HERTZENDORF ENDS

'No answer,' the Professor smiled, as though to

164

himself, then asked Carbonardo if he would draw a bath and see if Terremant had prepared breakfast.

Outside it was heavy cold, with a north wind that had brought thick snow and a hard frost in the hours before dawn, its rime a carapace on plants and trees, the windows thick with freezing hard geometric patterns both outside and in.

Eventually, bathed and shaved, James Moriarty went through to his main room, dressed in his dark blue silk dressing gown with the military frogging on the sleeves and across the fastenings. Running a hand over his freshly shaved jowls, he thought of Mysson and the need to have his razor freshly ground and stropped.

Christopher Mysson – Sharp Kit – was their knife-grinder; he prepared all knives and razors and was paid two pounds a week to do it. A little man with an untidy mop of hair and some malformation of his back from stooping since childhood for hours on end over his footpedalled grindstone, he was a diligent worker. Daniel Carbonardo, for instance, swore by him. 'Never had knives so sharp,' he would say. 'Sharp as a hornet in heat.'

Wally Taplin waited to serve him the breakfast Terremant had cooked.

Years previously, Terremant had been taught the basics of cooking, from how to boil an egg to the method of grilling a beefsteak and preparing vegetables. His teacher was Kate Wright, who had been the Professor's head cook and housekeeper before she, with her husband, was discovered in duplicity, and so paid the price, at

165

the hands of Philip Paget as it happened – the reason Pip Paget had left Moriarty's employ in a somewhat deceitful manner.

Now, Jim Terremant was a reasonable, if rough and ready, cook. This morning he had prepared a small rump steak and some grilled kidneys, with potatoes after the French manner: parboiled, then fried, in deep beef dripping, until they were a golden brown. He had learned a little about French cuisine from a sous-chef at the Crillon while Moriarty was staying in Paris.

Young Taplin poured the tea, a strong Indian brew, the kind that Moriarty liked best. He could not do with what he termed 'thin and insipid tasteless Chinese Limehouse mistwater.' He would say loudly that he preferred something strong, 'brewed from a good Indian particular, with sugar and a teardrop of tiger's milk.'

So, Wally poured the Darjeeling and kept the toast coming while the Professor ate his way through the steak and grilled kidneys, and put a sprinkle of lemon juice over the potatoes.

When he tasted the tang of lemon on the crisp potatoes, the old rhyme went through his mind:

Two sticks and Apple,
Ring ye Bells at Whitechappel,
Old Father Bald Pate,
Ring ye Bells of Aldgate,
Maids in White Aprons,
Ring ye Bells at St. Catherines,
Oranges and Lemons
Ring ye Bells of St. Clemens.

'Breakfast,' he would often say, 'should be the best meal of the day: the most enjoyable.'

On completing the meal he wiped off his mouth with a crisp, freshly laundered napkin – Ada Belcher again – and went over to his desk to write a letter to Joey Coax, the society photographer:

Dear Mr Coax,
I have been much taken with your excellent photographs which have appeared in Queen *and* The London Illustrated News. *In particular I found your portrait of the young Lady Beamish to be one of the best portraits ever done in this medium. However, I would much like to talk to you about other photographs that have come to my notice. These are your artistic poses of young women of great beauty, providing physical comfort to well-endowed young men. Regarding these, I think I have a plan from which we can both benefit. If you would like to discuss this matter further we could meet, I would suggest at one p.m. tomorrow, 19th January, at my dining rooms called* The Press, *where I can give you luncheon. I look forward to our meeting.*
Cordially
James Moriarty

When he had first seen the 'artistic' photographs, Moriarty had scoffed. 'Nothing but lazy lasses having their way with skinny little men blessed with enormous haricots,' he said. But later he came to realize that Coax had the knack of positioning the subjects and lighting them so that the pictures were indeed erotic in substance.

167

Now, he addressed the envelope to Mr. Coax's studio in New Oxford Street, sealed it, and instructed Wally Taplin to deliver the letter by hand. 'You must place it directly in Mr. Coax's hand,' he told the boy. 'He is a tallish man, dark hair going bald at the back. A tonsure like a monk.' He placed his own right hand over the crown of his head, a gesture for the benefit of young Taplin. 'He dresses in a dandified way,' he continued. 'And, Wally, don't let yourself be caught alone with him inside his studio. Conduct all business with him outside his door, even in the street. You follow me?'

'I'm ahead of you, Professor. Mr. Terremant's told me about dandified gents...'

'I'm sure he has, Walter.'

'Has a name for them.'

'That wouldn't surprise me...'

'Begins with a *P*...'

'Yes, my lad.'

'And I'm to kick 'em in the baubles if they try anything on.'

'Good boy.' Moriarty smiled benevolently and ruffled the lad's hair. 'On with you, then,' he said, as Terremant came in to say that Spear had arrived and Harkness had the cab out front.

Changing into his dark jacket over his waistcoat, then getting into his topcoat – the one with the heavy fur collar – Moriarty pulled on his gloves, flexing his fingers to stretch the leather and lacing the gloved fingers of each hand, improving their tight fit. Finally he put on his hat, giving it a tiny pat on the right side to set it at a jaunty angle, and took the ebony silver-topped cane from Terremant. Thus dressed, he joined Spear outside, noticing with pleasure that the steps had been swept and cleared of snow.

'Good boys,' he muttered to himself, nodding and looking pleased.

'Cadvenor's funeral parlour,' he told Harkness as he climbed into the cab with Spear close behind him.

Michael Cadvenor ran his business from a gloomy house in St. Luke's Road that was in the area where the Kensington gravel pits were once grouped around the Uxbridge Road. In the fourteenth century it was known as Knottyngull. In reality it was Campden Hill or North Kensington, lately Notting Hill, and once the turnpike was opened it became Notting Hill Gate.

Quickly alerted to Moriarty's arrival at his premises, Cadvenor came out of his front door, dry-washing his hands in his usual unctuous manner, bowing from the waist as if to royalty. 'You do me an honour, Professor, coming to my home.'

'I have come to your business, not your home, Michael. I wish to see the corpse you brought back last night from Brick Lane.'

More bows and the stretching out of an arm, gesturing with flattened palm toward his mortuary, a brick structure built onto the west end of the house – not the most wonderful place to visit. Inside there was the faintest scent of decay, which, Moriarty considered, would be unbearable had it not been freezing cold. Inside, unshaded electric bulbs sent a glare of harsh light down on the six-wheeled stretchers that sat neatly arranged in the clinically bare room. The shape of a human form

169

showed under a somewhat grimy white sheet thrown over the stretcher nearest the door.

'I only have the one visitor at the moment, so.' Cadvenor's Irish brogue was just detectable. 'Just the one, Professor, and I was wondering if you–'

Moriarty cut him off sharply. 'Let me see.'

He had already handed his hat and cane to Spear as he strode to the terribly still figure under the sheet and told Cadvenor to uncover the head. 'Let me see her.'

The Professor had to use his legendary iron control as the head and shoulders were uncovered, for at first sight this was Sal Hodges. It was only as he bent closer to the face that Moriarty realized there were things about the face of the corpse that did not apply. Yes, at first sight she was the twin of Sal Hodges, and he was surprised to feel a long shaft of pain travel through his body, close to his heart. Then, looking closer, he saw that this woman had grey hair and that the hair was in fact covered with what initially looked like some kind of chemical residue. Brick dust, he thought to himself; then he corrected it. Henna. This person had used henna to colour her hair, and James Moriarty knew, sure as there were four aces, that Sal Hodges had never used any kind of colouring for her hair. Many a time he had run his fingers through the long fall and lifted the hair in his hand, heavy and sleek as it was, coppery gold and full of body. Sal had no need of colouring.

Yet he still admitted that the face had Sal's features, sunken now, in death, the lips blue and horrible bruising about the throat where the strangulation had taken place. Despite the decay, he could not deny that the features were those of Sal.

Taking a handful of the sheet, just below the neck, Moriarty tugged mightily and stripped the body so that it now lay unclothed and awful in death before their eyes.

'Spread her legs!' he ordered, nodding at Michael Cadvenor, who, mistaking his meaning hesitated.

'But, sir...' he stammered.

'Spread her legs, damn you, Michael. Do as you're told and remember who pays your stipend.'

Hesitantly, Cadvenor reached over and gently pulled the woman's legs apart, a hand on each knee. Then, Moriarty leaned forward, took the right thigh in his gloved hand, and turned it so that he had a full view of the skin on the inside of the thigh – pasty, bluish, marbled dead flesh.

'Now turn her over, Michael. Over with her.'

Michael Cadvenor gave the body a well-learned flip over, one movement, so that now it lay face down, the flabby, dimpled buttocks quivering like fleshy jelly on a plate.

The body had a scar, a long whitish laceration running from just behind the left shoulder almost to the shoulder blade. Livid white it was, a scar of some deep wound from long ago.

The Professor nodded, then straightened, and took his hat and cane from Spear. 'Keep this body another two days. No longer.' He looked hard at the undertaker. 'Just in case I need others to see it. After that, unless I give you back word, get rid of it. Drop it in a pauper's grave.'

So saying, he turned on his heel and marched

171

from the mortuary, the clicking of his heels on the bare concrete falling on totally deaf ears.

Giving Harkness an order to stop at the first available post office, he sprang into the cab, Spear behind him not daring to speak for there was an atmosphere that, he told Terremant later, 'you couldn't cut with a knife, let alone your fingers, it was so thick. The Professor seemed to glower from all parts of his body. You could touch the glowering of him. Made me truly frightened.'

At the first post office, Moriarty swept in, people parting to allow him to enter – such was his commanding presence – like the sea parting from the bows of a ship. He took a telegram form and addressed it to Mrs. James at the hotel in which Sal was staying close to Rugby School. The text of his message read:

YOUR PRESENCE URGENTLY REQUIRED IN LONDON STOP TAKE THE FIRST CONVENI-ENT EXPRESS AND COME STRAIGHT TO MY HOME WITH HASTE STOP GOOD WISHES JAMES

'Home,' he ordered peremptorily on returning to the cab, and on reaching the house he paused before the door, turning to Spear.

'Albert, you're to bring me that slimy toad Jacobs. William Jacobs. He was supposed to be there when that woman died.' Then, quickly: 'I don't know who she is. Almost the spit and image of Sal, but it's not her. We looked, didn't we?'

'We did, Professor, but I must own, I first thought it to be Sal Hodges. I just couldn't tell.'

Moriarty gave a one-note, barking laugh. 'No, but I could. Sal's got my mark on her. That woman had not. It's not Sal. Damned if she isn't like her though. William Jacobs. Bring him. Even if you have to lift him off the street. Bring him to me. I want the truth.'

'I'll find him, Professor. I'll take Lee Chow with me. He'd frighten the devil in Hell, Lee Chow would. I've told him that, mind. To his face.'

'I don't want a hair of Bill Jacobs touched, Albert. But I want you to lift him and bring him here.'

Sal Hodges returned to the house at half past eight. She said she would have been sooner but for the snow on the railway line out in the country. 'They had men out digging the rails clear,' she told Moriarty.

'Lucky they didn't have to dig you clear, Sal,' he said with what amounted to a dark smile, but she detected something shadowy and sinister behind his words.

'Dear God, James. What d'you mean?' It was his look as well as the words that disturbed her, deeper than anything had ever distressed her in all her life. She knew James Moriarty and his moods, but this was something she had never seen before, a lingering, worrying concern behind every movement and the way he spoke, every word and the manner in which he pronounced them.

'Later.' He looked at her, his eyes seeming soft as she had never seen them before. She wondered, *What's happening to him? Smitten, distracted, or what?* But, then, Sal admitted that she was

173

cursed with unsolved queries. Sal's conscience was riddled with doubts. She had her own secrets, her own deceptions, her own lies, and they all lay heavy on her grimy soul.

It was even more disturbing because of what had passed here, in this room, barely thirty-six hours previously. On their last meeting, on the night before she had left to see their son, Arthur, at Rugby School, James Moriarty had been particularly combative.

'Did you know I sent young Danny Carbonardo after you, Sal?' he asked.

'Why would you do that? To kill me? Why...?'

'To get at the truth. You have always been close to my main men, to my Praetorians.'

'I'd never deny that.'

'Then I reasoned that if one of them had gone bad on me you would have known which one.'

'You're probably right there. But, surely that's not the case, is it?'

'It could be. Someone's been gabbling where they shouldn't. I suspected as much in New York, and in Berlin, and again in Vienna. So I set a small snare. Only the four of them – Spear, Ember, Terremant, and Lee Chow – only that quartet knew the day of my return to London. Even you weren't told, Sal.'

'True enough. I had no idea. It was a wonderful surprise to get your note saying you were here.'

'Yet when I landed at Dover there was a reception committee: They were there when the boat came in, they were there on the train, and they awaited me at Victoria Station. Even took post outside this very house.'

174

'So it has to be one of them,' she agreed, looking troubled. 'Those four. I would not have ever guessed it, James. Trust me. I've been loyal to you, I swear it. Always. I've heard nothing, seen nothing.'

'I believe you. But you've been warned, so watch them, Sal. Hang by your eyebrows; keep your eyes skinned and ears akimbo. If you detect something out of collar–'

'You'll be the first to know of it, James. You must believe me. I remain true.'

Then the boys came in with the food Mrs. Belcher had cooked specially: pork chops, bacon, potatoes in their jackets with a butter cream and onion dressing that she had made, hoping Mr. P. would like it – very tasty, with a smidgeon of horseradish to tickle the taste buds. She knew him only as Mr. P., didn't know his real name or anything; and if she suspected, Ada Belcher had the sense to keep quiet.

The boys piled their plates high, and Wally poured the wine. Champagne, Mr. Terremant uncorked for them, and had already taught Wally to pour without the bubbles overflowing the glass.

When the lads had gone, James Moriarty looked across the table, into her eyes, and with soft firmness, asked, 'Who would look very like you, Sal, but without the tattoo on your thigh, and with a nasty scar behind her left shoulder? Used henna on her hair. Who would that be, Sal? Because she's dead.'

'Dead?'

'As a herring.'

'How?'

'Strangled.' A count of maybe two, during which Moriarty drew his right thumbnail down his cheek, from just below the eye to the jawline. 'Who, Sal?' Demanding.

She gave a shivering sigh, then nodded. 'That would be my half sister. Sarah Maddingley. By my father out of a different mother. Amazing, though. Two peas in a pod. Ringers, they said.'

'The spit and image, but for her being older and gone more to seed and dyeing her hair badly.'

'She was actually younger, James, and she had taken to passing herself off as me, yes.'

'She was successful. Whoever killed her thought he was killing you.'

'And who was that? Who strangled her?'

'Like as not it was Idle Jack. We'll know later, but ninety-nine percent Idle Jack in his house at Bedford Square. Bert Spear's looking for the witness now, and we're taking care of Jack on Friday. Tomorrow. I didn't even know you had a half sister.'

'It was nothing to be proud of. If I'd had anything at all of value, she'd have bled me white for it. It's irony that someone's killed her thinking it was me. Mind you, I always worried that she would talk herself into dangerous conditions. She had a fearsome quick temper on her; she would go off like a bomb. Look at her sideways and she would crack off in your face.'

Sal had grown up in a Berkshire village, Hendred – there were two Hendreds – not a long way distant to the country house Moriarty owned close by Steventon. 'My father used to ride over,

176

see this woman in West Hendred: used to go diving in the dark with her, name of Beatrice Maddingley. I suppose he took one dive too many. I remember her – big woman, a shade blowsy, had hair the colour of dishwater, my mother used to say. Dishwater Beatty, my mum called her. I can hear her now.' Her voice rose, imitating a loud Berkshire burr: 'You been wi' Dishwater Beatty ag'in, Charlie? Well don't come near me. I don't want to catch anything she's got, where your maggot's been burrowing.' Sal smiled, fondly recalling her mother.

'What did she become, Sally? Your half sister in Hendred.'

Sal gave a gurgling laugh. 'By the time she was thirteen she was the village stargazer. Lay on her back in the fields, or under the hedges, stargazing. They all knew her. Stargazing Sarah. Even in the winter she would be out there giving the local lads a ride. And she was a lustful girl, what Bert Spear 'ud call a gobble-cock. Enjoyed the work. There was even a time when she suggested that perhaps we could work together.'

'And she came to London, Sal? Recently was it?'

'She's been coming to London a long time now, James. But she's become a nuisance lately. Dropping in on me for a little swig of the O be joyful; a handful of silver; wanting me to tip the quids; or maybe just a kind word. Sarah didn't get many kind words, James.'

'The lot of the common whore, Sal.'

'That's true. I gave her the occasional kind word, but I never gave her trust. I couldn't trust her. I knew she'd steal from me, lie to me, do me down.' She paused there, as if coming to a decision. 'Lately she's worried me.'

'How so?'

'We looked so alike. I simply had the feeling that she was on some dodge of her own.' She frowned deeply. 'Some dodge that would affect me, because we looked so alike. I thought she was passing herself off as me, James, and it looks as though she was.' She went silent, troubled thinking about her half sister and a whole maze of deceptions. 'Maybe all she wanted was a knocker on her front door. Respectability. A penn'orth of paradise. We *were* alike, James, and I think that was a great temptation.'

'I have a theory.' For a moment, the Professor looked as though he was about to dispense great wisdom. 'I've had it for some years now. I believe that every person here on earth has what they call a double, like you and your half sister, though not always for the same reason – not always because of a bloodline. What in the horse-racing world they call a ringer, a horse that can be substituted; and there is a German word – a doppelganger. That has a touch of the spook about it – shivery, makes you wonder. There are stories – come face to face with your doppelganger and you die. Well, that's maybe how it works sometimes.' Once more he ran his thumbnail down his cheek. The Professor knew about doubles, ringers, doppelgangers. He had spent the past eighteen months looking for one, in Berlin and other cities nearby, and he had finally run down the one he was searching for in Vienna.

'The scar on Sarah's back. Left shoulder. How

178

did she get that?' he asked, changing tack, swerving from the general back to the particular.

'Poor little cow. Stargazing under a hedge. Felt the pain but didn't want to stop. Found out later she'd been lying on a broken bottle. Great laceration she had, very deep, cut to ribbons, and she used to laugh about it. Horse doctor sewed it up for her.'

They finished the meal almost in silence, and the boys came in to remove the dishes. When they had gone, Sal suddenly, with no warning, started to weep – not for her half sister, she said, but for herself. Moriarty told her that was usual in cases of grief. 'We weep for ourselves,' he told her, not that he had ever been known to weep.

Softly he stood and moved across to her, put an arm around her shoulders, helped her to her feet, spoke quietly to her, murmured an endearment, and guided her to the bedroom, where he pleasured her, with what passed for softness and feeling in a man like Moriarty. The act incidentally provided huge pleasure for the Professor, which was an expected bonus.

They were entwined one with another, under the sheets and blankets on the Professor's bed, and so fell asleep. Indeed, James Moriarty slept like a baby, untroubled by the knowledge that, for the larger part of his waking hours, he walked in the paths of extreme darkness.

10

The Lifting of Billy Jacobs, and What Happened to Sarah

LONDON: JANUARY 19, 1900

So the word went out: first from Moriarty to Albert Spear.

Bring me that slimy toad Jacobs. William Jacobs.

From Spear to Terremant; then to Lee Chow and Ember, and so filtering along the invisible rivers of sound that ran through the great arterial roads of London. Passed from mouth to ear. Whispered. Muttered. Called softly. Always moving, sluicing through the streets, passed on from dips and whizzers to magsmen, rampsmen, cashcarriers, punishers, and demanders, trickling down the tributaries of lanes, the brooks that spread out from the roads; emptying into courts and alleys; caught, noted, and passed on; waterfalling down steps, then building into waves of intelligence, rivulets of instructions. Bring in William Jacobs: Billy Jacobs. Wanted by the Professor. Bring him in. It rippled even into police stations, into the ears of men who, for a fee, informed the Professor's people, passed them secret intelligence, spies within the police giving Moriarty what he needed to hear.

So the call dripped into Moriarty-owned whorehouses, carried along by the boys now working for the Professor, his shadows; into public houses and meeting places, into whirlpools of men lurking still on the streets; the whisper taken on the tide until most men and women out and about on this cold winter night heard the call and were skinning their eyes, tilting their heads, earwigging for the first word of Billy Jacobs, onetime Moriarty's man, brother of Bertram Jacobs.

So the word hit gold and one of the shadows passed it on to Albert Spear that Billy Jacobs had been seen, earlier that night, drinking heavily in the Blue Posts tavern down Berwick Street, by the market, deep in Soho on the fringes of London's West End. Billy Jacobs, a small man, young, in his late twenties, gone grey, though, from being in prison six years before. Smiling Billy Jacobs, who tried to please everyone.

Spear, with Lee Chow and Terremant, were in Josiah Osterley's growler, turning into the great sweep of Regent Street when they spotted him swaggering in the direction of Piccadilly Circus, not a care in the world, swaying slightly. Happy. In good humour, helped by a liberal libation of spirits.

'Hallo, then. What we got here?' he called loudly. 'If it ain't Billy Jacobs, my old mate! Come along then, Bill. Come for a ride with us, then.'

But Billy, even slightly tipsy, knew better. He saw big Bert Spear, and behind him caught sight of the evil Chinee, Lee Chow, and knew him not just from reputation, for in his time he had worked with Chow and had seen what he could do to a person.

'Hold hard there, Billy!' Spear shouted as Jacobs took to his heels.

But he didn't get far. Lee Chow slipped from the coach in less than an intake of breath and was after him, hellity-split, had him down on the paving stones in one quick movement, sending Jacobs sprawling with a crash and a howl, then feeling the tip of a knife blade close to his neck, terrified, as he had once seen the Chinaman do his speciality act, the cheek trick: how the knife was there one minute and the next two lumps of bleeding flesh were being flung across the street and the poor bugger that was the victim stood, shocked and sucking air, could not understand why his tongue couldn't find the inside of his cheeks, why his throat was full of blood and what the blinding pain was across his face.

'No!' Jacobs cried out. 'No, you horrible little yellow bugger. Leave me be!'

'Then you get up, Billy, and come for a ride with us.'

It was almost a relief to see Bert Spear standing there looking down on him with his cracked, scarred face and shark's smile.

'Yea, you come lide wi' us,' the little Chinese grinned, very happy with the idea that he could terrify someone by just showing him his filleting knife, the one he had stolen years ago from a fishwife down Shanghai docks, with its simple wooden handle and the little cropped blade kept razor sharp by old Mysson with his hunched back and grinding stone.

Inside the coach, they put Billy Jacobs between Spear and Terremant.

'You've led us a right polka, Billy.' Terremant wrapped a huge hand around William Jacobs's arm.

'Oh. I have, Mr. Terremant? How come?'

'Birry Jacob,' Lee Chow breathed quietly. 'Farte'bellies.'

'Wouldn't surprise me.' Terremant leaned back. 'We looked everywhere, Bill.'

'Led us all round the town.' Spear leered at him. 'Looking for you, Billy. Lot of people looking for you.'

'Looking for me, Mr. Spear?' Coming the old innocent. 'Why would you be looking for me?'

'Now, Bill. The Professor wants a word with you and don't you give me that newborn-babe look, because we know, and the Professor knows. Last night you were there when a lady was done to death in Bedford Square. You sent Sidney Streeter and Rouster Bates out on a job, palmed off a corpse on old Dropsy Carmichael at The Beehive lodging house up Brick Lane. Slipped him some tin for his trouble. Memory coming back now, is it, Billy?'

'I'm not sayin' nothing.' Billy Jacobs looked all around the coach, avoiding what he could see of their eyes in the glimmering light from the street-lamps.

'Please yourself.' Spear leaned back. 'The Professor's got an old pal o' yours waiting. Danny Carbonardo. Danny the Tweezers. Remember him, Billy?'

'What you mean, the Professor? Everyone knows the Professor's gone away. Left years ago. Idle Jack's King Coal now. Ask anybody.'

183

'Oh, we have, Billy; and I suspect you know the truth: that Moriarty is back. Unexpectedly, I'll grant you, but he *is* back. Twice the size and four times as natural. So you'd better make yourself ready. Poor old Dropsy's had a good hiding for his part, so if I was you I'd start pleading for mercy as soon as you see the Old Man.'

Indeed, Spear himself had ordered the four men to do the work. Dropsy Carmichael came out of his grubby lodging house at half past four that afternoon to buy a pair of kippers for his tea. Instead of kippers he found himself facing these four grim coves, big as bull-beef, demanders by trade and ready to give him a fanning, which they did, advising him to keep out of the Professor's way in future and never to speak with any from Idle Jack's family again. Within fifteen minutes, Carmichael had three broken ribs, a broken arm, a cracked cheekbone, a badly swollen eye, and was minus five teeth.

'Where did you get all this from? This *Comic Cuts* about a corpse and Dropsy Carmichael – haven't seen old Dropsy in I don't know how long.' No doubt about it, Billy Jacobs was tenacious; he didn't give up easily.

'Alas.' Spear pitched his voice high and parsonical. 'Alas, it came first hand from your old friend Sidney Streeter, who has since, sadly, departed this life on account of it. But you, Bill, and young Rouster Bates, you are still here and have to answer for your sins.'

They took him straight up to find Moriarty waiting for them, Daniel Carbonardo in attendance and looking dead leery. Sal Hodges was in

184

the little bedroom, the Professor having coun-selled her to stay hidden until he called for her.

'Professor, sir.' Sudden, surprised. Surprised and delighted, both. 'Oh, it is good to see you, Professor. We all thought we'd never set eyes on you again.' Billy Jacobs took the view that he might best bluff it out, using the disappearing Professor defence. And why not, for he, together with his brother, had been close confidants of the Professor and his family, even adjuncts to the Praetorian Guard. *Close as God's curse to a whore's arse*, Bert Spear thought, crudely, as he looked upon the scene before him. Only a few years ago these men would have sat down as friends, con-federates in crime, with William Jacobs on easy terms with Professor James Moriarty and Terremant lolling back in sociable camaraderie with both of the Jacobs boys, for he, under Mori-arty's direction, had played a large part in getting the Jacobs brothers out of the 'Steele,' Coldbath Fields prison.

Now young Jacobs sat, with Terremant's un-friendly hand on his shoulder, weighing him down, and Moriarty boring into him with those dark mesmerist eyes.

'William, this is a sad pass.' The Professor spoke in a quiet, almost whispering voice. In-deed, because it was pitched so low and soft, the Professor's voice was more frightening, more fearsome.

'Have I not proved my friendship to you and your family, Billy?' He sounded weary, as if this was something too much. 'Did your mother, the good, God-fearing Hetty Jacobs, not come to me

185

first when you were so wrongly accused and sent for an impious season of imprisonment? She trusted me, Billy, not the cash-hungry leeches who pose as lawyers. She trusted in me and I acted on her behalf. I had you unlocked and out of the Steele in no time. I had it hidden and was like a father to you both: gave you work; paid you well; saw that you were clothed, watered, and fed. Is this a way to repay me, Billy?'

'No, sir,' Billy Jacobs said, subdued and ashen-faced.

'No, sir, indeed, Bill; and what should I do with you?'

'I plead for mercy, Professor. We were told that you had gone, left us all in the lurch...'

'And you believed that? You truly believed that I would do such a thing... Me?' He thumped his chest with a balled fist. 'Me, the one who has stood for you over so many years? You believed this tissue, this insubstantial story? You believed it, with no scrap of evidence to substantiate it, to prove it, Billy?' A pause for breath, then, 'I am ashamed of you!' The sentence was delivered as though it had been cast down on the floor at Billy's ungrateful feet.

'Idle Jack can be most persuasive, Professor. He had both me and my brother convinced that you'd had to flee, never to return.'

'And nobody converted you otherwise?'

'There were so many, Professor; so many had the same story; we became totally sure that you had gone.'

'Well, it's true that I had to flee, but only for a few seasons. You should know I'd never leave my

186

family for good. Not me.' He made a big shrugging movement, as if trying to physically rid himself of blame. 'Now I am back. What say you to that?'

'You must know, Professor, that now I know you are back all I'll want is to serve you as before. I'm sure my brother Bert will do likewise. I beg to be invited back into the family.'

Moriarty's hand went to his cheek, drawing the right thumbnail from just below the eye to the jawline as he grunted. 'What do you think, Bert Spear?' he asked, his eyes so intense in fervour that Spear was forced to look away. 'Should we take him back, or cast him further into the darkness he has chosen?'

'I think that depends, Professor.'

'Depends?'

'On what surety he can give.'

'Aye, that's a fair way,' he agreed, turning once more to Jacobs. 'Billy, our intelligence has it that you were present when Sal Hodges died in Bedford Square, in Idle Jack Idell's house. Would you like to tell me about that?'

'What can I tell you, sir?'

'Don't be a fool, Billy. Who did it? Who did the killing? You?'

'Not me, sir. No. Strike me dumb if I did. I was flabbergasted! Distressed, for she was a proper lady, Sal.' His eyes roamed from side to side, looking around the room as if for a way of escape. 'Made me sick as a cat what happened.'

'If not you, then, Bill, who?'

'Why, who else? Idle Jack himself of course.'

'You were there?'

187

'I was. Saw it all – well, most of it all – and there was nothing I could do. If I'd been able, I'd have saved her, but when Sir Jack's temper is frayed there's no reasoning with him.'

'Why was she there in the first place, Billy?'

'There was a message come in the afternoon that Sally Hodges wanted to see Sir Jack. On a matter of great importance, it said. So word was passed back that he would see her at six.'

'And she arrived? You saw her come to the house?'

'I did, Professor, yes...'

'And...?'

'I let her in and showed her upstairs. Jack has his office up in what used to be the withdrawing room, up there, second storey. Big room, all done up like a tart's parlour. He has little real taste, Idle Jack. Not like you, Professor...'

'Enough of the flannel, Billy. There's no need for it.'

'Sorry, guv'nor.'

Spear could see that Jacobs was frightened – what in the Bible they called sore afraid. Indeed, he thought to himself that Billy Jacobs was sorely sore afraid. Sore afraid enough to piss himself.

'You took her upstairs?'

'I did, and was concerned for her.'

'Why so?'

'She had become so reduced, sir. Lost all her sparkle; become dowdy even. It was like she had slid from favour and didn't look over clean, if you follow me.'

Moriarty nodded. 'But Jack greeted her, welcomed her in?'

188

'He did, yes. Said it was good to see her and even asked after you.'

Moriarty grunted. 'After me?'

'He said, "It's good to see you, Sal Hodges, and how's the Professor? I hear he's been listening to the music in Vienna."'

'Really? He actually said that about me and Vienna?'

'Those were his words, Professor.'

'And what had she to say to that?'

'She said you were well and back in London.'

'And how did he take that news?'

'He said he already knew you were back, sir, and he was hoping to talk to you.'

'And they were comfortable together?'

'Perfectly. He bade Sal be seated, asked if she would care for a glass of something, but she said no. Said she'd rather talk.'

'Mm-hmm. So what did they talk about?'

'This is where it becomes difficult, sir, because Sir Jack asked me to leave the room.'

'So you heard none of the conversation?'

'I didn't say that. I said I was asked to leave the room.' A tiny part of the old Billy Jacobs's sparkle was back.

'Go on then.'

'As I was leaving, I heard her say that she had something that would be of great interest. It was about some girl she had working in her house.'

'In Sal's house, in the Haymarket?'

'That was the meaning, and I saw Sir Jack stiffen. He's been finding ways of getting into your houses, Professor. Begging your pardon, he's taken over some of them. Little gold mines, he says they are, and he's been trying to find a way into the Haymarket house. I know that to my certain knowledge.'

'So you stayed, listening, outside the door?' Moriarty raised a hand to cover the lower part of his face, to hide his smile at Billy knowing to his certain knowledge.

'I did my best. Those doors are fearsome solid, Professor. I could hear little.'

'Just what did you hear?'

'She said she had this secret, but it would cost pretty.'

'You heard that clearly. That Sal wanted money?'

'I don't think just money. I think she wanted money and favours. Position, I would guess. She was after a good place in Jack's family.'

The Professor nodded. 'And they fell out over this?'

'She wouldn't tell him what it was, her secret. And he wouldn't set a fee or the promise of whatever she wished. They were at loggerheads, screaming at each other within fifteen minutes.'

Spear saw Billy Jacobs's fear again: His hands were shaking so much he had to cover one with the other and hold them down, hard, on the table.

'And what were they screaming?'

'She called him a louse, a brandy-nosed counter-jumper – you know, Sir Jack has two grocer's shops, one in Hackney and another in Pimlico; he's very touchy about that, being in trade. He was calling her a Drury Lane vestal and they were going at it hammer and tongs. I become concerned.'

'At the shouting?'

'Sir, Idle Jack's temper is ... how can I put it...?'

'Volatile?'

'That would be one way' – unsure of what volatile meant – 'Then I heard blows. I think she struck his face. That worried me greatly. Then there was this ghastly noise. A choking... I didn't think, just put my shoulder to the door, barged in...'

Billy Jacobs, eyes downcast, shook his tousled head violently, and, Spear noted, clenched his fists so that the knuckles were drained of blood.

'And, Billy?' Moriarty asked, still quiet, pitched low, in almost a throaty whisper.

'And I was too late, Professor. Jack was enraged, face scarlet and the veins on his neck standing out, contorted. He had her at arm's length, holding her by the throat, her on her knees, Sal. When he looked towards me I thought he'd do me an' all. His look was terrible. Then he just took his hands off her throat and she fell like a child's tupp'ny rag doll. Crumpled on the floor.'

'And you still didn't know what the quarrel was about?'

'It was about neither one giving way to the other. She wanted to sell her secret about a girl in her house; and he wouldn't make any promises of payment, or whatever else she wanted.'

'And he told you to get rid of the body?'

'He turned to look at me and let her fall – she flopped down like a sack of feathers chucked on the floor. He looked suffused with anger, if that's the right word; it was coming out of his face, out of the skin. And he said to me, 'Clear up the mess, Billy. Now. Do it now. Clear it out. The rubbish.'

'So you got Rouster Bates and Sidney Streeter to go out and lay her in a lodging? The lodging dodge?'

'That was about it.'

'You obeyed him?'

'You don't argue with Sir Jack, Professor. Jack's mighty persuasive.'

It seemed that death had come to Sal's half sister in a crawling, even trivial way, unexpected and unsought. Sal had said that Sarah was hot-tempered, and he knew of Jack Idell's reputation. 'Jack will go mad at people at the drop of a coin,' someone had once told him.

'You don't argue with me, either, Billy.' He looked hard and severely at Jacobs.

'Just give me the chance, Professor. You'll not regret it. Just one more chance.'

Moriarty looked up at Spear and gave him a nod, as if to say 'we'll talk later'; then he put back his head and called, 'Sal! Sally Hodges,' so Sal drifted into the room, coming from the bedroom, her hair down and hanging over her shoulders, this lovely red-gold canopy, as though she carried a burning flame down her back, wearing the white working dress she had hung up on her return from Rugby, her face ruddy and full of life.

'Hallo, Billy,' she said, her eyes lighting up – sparkling.

'Jesus!' Billy Jacobs hissed. 'Oh, Jesus Christ.' There was a general intake of breath.

'It was her half sister you saw topped by Idle

192

Jack.' And Moriarty laughed, a full-bellied laugh, then looked at Terremant and told him to take young Jacobs downstairs. 'Give him a pistol shot,' he said, which meant give him a drink. 'Make him comfortable for the night. Keep him close.' He told Lee Chow to go as well, but bade Albert Spear to stay behind.

'We will give him one chance, Albert. Feed him, make him happy, then tomorrow send him off to find his brother.' He nodded. 'I'll need to talk with him again. But in the meantime, tell him to get his brother and return to the fold. Talk to him. Talk about what else he knows. How Jack gets information concerning me and our family.' This was, of course, a double-edged command, for Spear, like the others, was also suspect as a spy in their midst. So Moriarty added, 'Keep tabs on him, mind. We don't want him among us spying for Idle Jack.'

When Spear had gone, the Professor returned to his bedroom where Sal waited for him and they had much sport, both out of bed and in – a joyous and rewarding night, and they drank the best part of a bottle of brandy between them, which kept them warm. During a rest from their lovemaking, Sal read the Tarot for him and couldn't understand why the Hanged Man came up in each of her three readings.

When at last they slept, Sal dreamed of strong men working, digging the ground with spades, while birds sang contentedly. But Moriarty dreamed he was out on a heath in a huge and dreadful storm, like the one experienced by King Lear in Shakespeare's play; and he was enshrined

193

in teeming rain, to the sound of cracking thunder, and rent by forked lightning gouging at the black sky. And he shouted Shakespeare's words – 'Blow, winds, and crack your cheeks! rage! blow! You cataracts and hurricanoes, spout, Till you have drenched our steeples, drowned the cocks!'

He danced in the storm, and with him were six young girls, dressed only in cotton shifts, soaked, dancing with him, wrestling him into the short sopping grass.

And when he woke, Moriarty found his manhood huge and strong, like a bold neddy cudgel, so that he had to wake Sal to ease the pain of it.

At breakfast, Moriarty explained to Sal that he would have to be out all day, though he didn't tell her he was to lunch with Joey Coax the photographer. Moriarty was always careful and rarely discussed his family business in front of others; the two boys were there, in the room, serving the chops and eggs, pouring the strong tea, and passing around bread and toast, making sure Moriarty had the Gentleman's Relish to hand – very partial to the Gentleman's Relish was Moriarty, particularly with chops.

Only after they went out did Moriarty tell Sal that he would be back here at the house by six in the evening when he had a meeting with Carbonardo, Ben Harkness, and others, 'to discuss Idle Jack's future,' as he put it. 'But say nothing,' he cautioned her, not wanting his closest lieutenants to know his immediate plans.

Sal said she would probably go down to the Haymarket house, and he told her to have a care,

194

to take someone with her, maybe that Harry Judge, Spear's man.

He sipped another cup of tea. Then–

'Sal, my dear, your half sister, Sarah. Do you want a proper burial for her? Perhaps have her taken back to Hendred to be buried in the churchyard there? If you'd like that, I can arrange it, and for you to be at the funeral.'

Sal asked if she could think about it, and he nodded, knowing at moments like this, relatives needed time to adjust to the grief of parting.

'While we are talking of Sarah,' he went on casually, like an aside, 'Billy Jacobs had this story – you may have heard him – that Sarah had come posing as you and told Jack Idell there was some secret to do with a girl in the Haymarket house. Your house, Sal. What d'you make of that? What would be worth passing on to the rapscallion Idle Jack from your house? A girl? Something not quite right, possibly? Any ideas?'

Of course she had no idea. 'Sarah was good at making up stories. She had a romantic turn of mind. Sly with it, mind you. I wouldn't put it past her making up some tale about a lost well-born, moneyed girl in the house, worth thousands, trying to sell it to Jack. She listened a lot, must have heard the stories going round about you leaving, having to flee the country from that Sherlock Holmes and Inspector Crow.

'Knowing Sarah, she always had an eye for the main chance. If she believed Jack was really the coming man, going to take over your family, James, maybe she was trying to side with him. Get a good position in his family.' She gave a

195

little two-note laugh, her voice like a little phrase played on a cello. 'It would be like her to want what was mine. If she saw it was an opportunity to get the Haymarket place for herself, she'd tell any tale.' Sal laughed again. 'I shouldn't say it, but I'm pleased she's out of it. Always a trouble, Sarah.'

Moriarty gave a quiet nod of understanding, but he scribbled a note in his mind to make a few enquiries concerning the house in the Haymarket. Look about and see if there was anything unsatisfactory. Sal was efficient, but she was a woman, so, like all women, she was prone to making mistakes.

The Professor did not normally go out and about on family business as either his real self or his alter ego Professor Moriarty – he of the tall stooping walk, the sunken mesmeristic eyes, and the reptilian movement of the head. As well as his great power to organize, James Moriarty was an actor – a man of a thousand faces, and two thousand voices. Today he decided to meet Joey Coax as the character he christened 'the banker.' This was a disguise he had used many times and knew well, a part he could take on with ease, a role he disliked but one that he could fit inside, like a second skin. He even had a name for him: Tovey Smollet, financial genius and parsimonious pedant.

So, around eleven o'clock that morning he began to prepare, first clearing his mind of all other problems and taking on the personality of Smollet. Then came the makeup, starting with the excellent wig, made by the same wigmaker who had supplied his amazing Moriarty wig.

Smollet's hair was dark and thinning, combed straight back, slick and smooth, with a touch of grey at the temples and behind the ears. The role also demanded him to straighten his nose, lengthening it a fraction and making it a straight Roman beak, using the nose putty he found so useful; also, he had long ago purchased a special pair of spectacles that distorted the eyes so that they appeared to others to be much smaller and closer together. The resulting image was of a man without humour, whose mind was centred on money; a one-dimensional man, pernickety and unattractive, just the sort of person to bore Joey Coax stupid, he imagined.

Just as Moriarty was preparing to leave, Spear came up to see him with the news that Billy Jacobs had been out and about and had brought his brother, Bertram, back with him. 'Says he has plenty to tell you, Professor.' Spear looked as though he doubted the fact.

'Bertram Jacobs?' Moriarty asked.

'No, sir. Billy.'

'Wants to talk to me?'

'Says it is urgent.'

'Well, he'll have to wait until after my meeting this afternoon. Is he behaving himself?'

'Good as gold. Helped with everything. Was polite and obedient – better than the two boys, 'cos they're young rips, the pair on 'em. Anyway, Billy toddled off and came back with Bertram, who's looking a picture, healthier than brother Bill.'

'I'll see him later, then, Albert,' and so the Pro-

197

fessor went off in the hansom with Harkness at the whip, too busy to hang around. Something that was later to give him pause.

11

The Hanged Man

LONDON: JANUARY 19, 1900

Of all the public dining rooms, restaurants, and chophouses he owned, Moriarty liked The Press above the rest. It was sumptuous, yet somehow managed to capture the air of a private club. Possibly this was because its clientele was made up mainly from people who worked in the business of writing and publishing newspapers.

Located on the second floor of a building tucked away in an as-yet unadopted, narrow road running off Fleet Street, parallel to Chancery Lane, The Press Dining Room was ideal for journalists and editors working nearby, who could eat there in some style and much better than they could at home in Wimbledon, Woolwich, or Putney. Certainly, some of these good people used The Press like a club and they would often bring names to have luncheon or dine there – the kind of names that were well known, and who made the news: Politicians, men of business, actors, writers, captains of industry, and men of the cloth would all be taken to this large, elegant

198

room on the second floor of a building owned outright by Moriarty, upon which he got a good return for letting all but that floor, mainly to newspapers and their publishers, or those working for firms adjunct to the papers.

The Professor in fact cultivated people connected with the newspaper business and secretly had some journalists, and at least one editor, on a retaining fee, for they were often the first people to get hold of important information. They, naturally, had no idea they were working for the Professor. Just as he had his lieutenants of what he called his Praetorian Guard, he also had lieutenants on a completely different level: men with offices and desks, men in charge; leaders; men with responsibility. It was for them that his spies in the newspaper industry worked, and from them Moriarty gained much knowledge of financial, legal, and political value. 'It is better,' he would often say, 'to have the gentlemen of The Press with you rather than against you.'

The Press was pleasant, even lavish, in the way it was decorated and organized. When full, it could dine a little over one hundred and fifty people at the forty-odd tables scattered across its wide floor, the tables smart, covered in immaculate starched white linen, with gleaming silverware and glasses and spotless napery, the whole against a background of mahogany panelling set on a deep carpet the colour of fresh thin blood and with rich dark blue velvet curtains sashed aside its four high windows, floor to ceiling, arched at the top, all glinting from the light that splintered, night and day, from three plump crystal chandeliers.

The manager of The Press was a smooth, silky, immaculate little Frenchman by the name of Guy Grenaux, known to friends as G.G., a man whose whole life appeared to be absorbed in the restaurant and its daily course. G.G. was consulted on even the smallest detail: He knew the menu and chef's limitations backwards, was familiar with all his kitchen staff and waiters, and knew their families, their hopes, fears, and most intimate problems. Some six years down the road, after he died, suddenly of a seizure on a Friday morning as he inspected the freshly bought fish with Chef Emile Dantray, it was revealed that G.G.'s interest in even the trivia of his employees was to a purpose: He had skilfully skimmed some twenty to twenty-five percent off the top of both takings and individual tips, not to mention his side deals with the butchers, fishmongers, and grocers from which the food was bought. Some of this money was shared with the man who turned out to be his lover, the fastidious, perfect head waiter, Armand – the relationship quite unsuspected by all, including the Professor. But that is another story.

Moriarty arrived before Joey Coax, as he had planned; the head waiter, Armand, had already been warned of the Professor's impending pseudonymous appearance by a note brought over by Billy Walker, he of the unruly hair and cheeky grin. Already there were people at the tables, and he was met by the appetizing smell of food, the pleasant murmur of conversation, and the occasional clink of silverware on plates.

It was only when Coax appeared, being shepherded to the table by Armand, that Moriarty was alerted to the possibility of having made a mistake.

He had no trouble with the fact, already known to him, concerning Joey Coax's sexual persuasion: He was a homosexual. What people did in their private lives did not matter to the Professor. 'As long as they don't expect me to do it with them,' he would laugh. 'And as someone else has already said, as long as they don't do it in the streets and frighten the horses, they won't bother me.' He would always be quick and amusing on the subject, and he would certainly never criticize men for being what in those days they referred to as 'queer,' an offence thought to be so serious against both God and man that it was punished by lengthy terms of imprisonment. Indeed, in the early years of the nineteenth century, buggery itself was punishable by death.

What he had not been prepared for was the overt mincing queenery of the man, and he blamed himself; he knew he should have taken a closer look at this person before setting things in motion. The trouble was that Joey Coax was the most able man for the job the Professor had in mind – in fact, he was the *only* professional who could be relied on; and here he was, this swinging cockatoo, in a public place, and everyone aware of him.

The fact that he did not criticize men like Coax did not mean that the Professor approved. Certainly there were whole areas of some people's sexual mores that Moriarty loathed;

indeed, he may well have allowed Idle Jack's businesses to exist close to his own, on a live-and-let-live basis, if it had not been for one area of Jack Idell's work.

Coax was not likeable in looks, but portly, a shade ungainly, and pudgy-faced; he dressed in clothes that were flamboyant, a plum-coloured suit of his own devising, with a lavender-coloured full scarf knotted below an exaggerated wing collar, the scarf flapping about, with four tails making its wearer look like some cartoon of an artist from a humorous paper. The man's hands floated about him, dipping and fluttering like two uncontrolled birds, his beringed fingers turning this way and that; his shoulders moved back and forth independent of his trunk, while his voice, loud and lisping, could have been heard in the street below – 'Over here, dear man? Really, where next, then? Where next? Oh this is too much. Where?' – and was drawing all eyes in the room toward him.

Moriarty's rule was that under no circumstances should you call attention to yourself. That had been part of his long success and the aim of disguise: the way in which he moved, invisible among ordinary human beings out and about in the world. His greatest coups had all contained within them this one magnificent moment, the final act in which he revealed himself as the Professor: James Moriarty. Complete invisibility was demanded of those who went with him in public. In a sentence, Joey Coax offended and embarrassed him. He also drew attention to him – a cardinal sin.

Now Coax was fast approaching the table, with his little squeaks; the grimace at other people already lunching; the occasional pretence of knowing individuals, mainly women; and the nodding bowing of the head, 'Hallo, dear, and how are you?... Ah, Sir Duncan... How are you, Cecil?'

Moriarty made some instant decisions, thinking on his feet as it were, preparing small changes to his plans. Moving this, replacing that, to get ready to face this walking gee-gaw.

'*You* are James Moriarty?' The tubby, almost bloated face of Joey Coax, with its inflated nostrils, rubbery lips, and eyes enhanced (Moriarty could hardly believe it) with a few touches of bluish makeup, looked down at the – thank God – disguised face of Tovey Smollet. '*You* are James Moriarty?' as though this just could not be possible. Heads turning, ears twitching.

'Alas, no,' Moriarty answered crisply. Then, with eyes showing intense distaste, 'Mr. Coax, I presume?'

'Yeeeaaas,' drawn out, an embroidered acknowledgement that sounded uncertain as to his own name.

'Then sit down, sir. Be quiet and let me explain.' Charming and at the same time cold. Pleasant, yet with a hard block of steel not under the surface but clear and visible. If Joey Coax knew what was good for him, he would take his seat quietly and listen with every fibre of his being.

For a second or two he seemed to behave himself, as Armand held the chair for him and as Moriarty indicated to the waiter that he would have to return with the menu later. Then Coax

203

opened his mouth, but Moriarty lifted a finger and hissed, 'No! Listen! James Moriarty has been delayed. He bids you start your lunch without him. I am his representative and we can deal with the business side of this meeting now, before Moriarty arrives. Understand?'

Again he had to hush Coax, who had taken a further gulp of air prior to holding forth.

'My Principal has asked me to make you an offer. It is that you spend one day working for and with James Moriarty. The purpose will be to take a series of photographs similar to the artistic pictures already referred to in his letter. Understand?'

Once more he had to hush the man, who was ready to burst out chattering again. 'In a matter of days you will be told when and where these photographs are to be taken. Moriarty will supply the models, and the studio. You will supply your photographic equipment, and you will be paid handsomely.' He slid a small piece of card across the table. 'That will be your fee, plus, of course, any monies you may lose through a clash of my Principal's set date with any work you have to put aside.' Damnit, he thought to himself, if he only had more time to get another photographer as good as Coax! But von Hertzendorf would arrive on Monday, and he could not have the man hanging around in London waiting to do the pictures. The session of photography would have to take place on Wednesday or Thursday – most probably Thursday, to enable von Hertzendorf to get some rest before the event.

Coax was looking at the sum of money written on the card. It was more than his entire earnings for the past calendar year – and Moriarty knew it. 'Agreed?' Moriarty asked, and Coax gave a soundless but firm nod, eyes wide with amazement.

Moriarty often said, 'There is one thing people of all classes, creeds, and stations find hard to resist. Money.'

'Good,' he told Coax, with a thin, humourless smile. 'It will be on one day next week. Hold yourself in readiness and do not breathe a word of this to anyone. You must understand that.'

Coax looked alarmed. 'Are you threatening me?' he asked.

'In a word, yes.' The affirmative came as if from a long way off, borne on a bitter blizzard. 'If this gets out, my Principal will kill you. No doubt of that. Now enjoy your luncheon. The rare roast beef is excellent here, but don't forget to tip the carver.' Then, as he turned: 'Oh, yes. It is not certain that my Principal will put in an appearance. Go with God!'

Moriarty stood, bowed, and left the dining room as unobtrusively as possible: 'Give that popinjay whatever he wants to eat,' he told Armand. 'And then never, ever serve him in this room again.'

Armand bowed deeply as the Professor went to the cloakroom to retrieve his coat, hat, gloves, and cane. Within ten minutes he was safely in the cab again with Ben Harkness guiding them away from the area, Archimedes between the shafts, trotting well.

'Ben, I'm hungry,' the Professor said, leaning back, and Harkness turned the hansom up Chancery Lane toward Holborn, where there was an Eel Pie Shop that did the delicacy his master enjoyed most.

On the way there, Moriarty thought of Joey Coax and his preening ways. He would have to take care when he oversaw the photography next week. He would have to handle Coax with a chair and a whip, like a lion tamer.

The Eel Pie Shop tucked away in High Holborn had a window with eels laid out on deep beds of parsley, with pies, or replicas of such, in tins tastefully displayed around the eels: The slimy, secretive, and sinuous creatures were at last on view, enticing and tempting those with taste for a gastronomic delight, for when skinned and prepared this is the sweetest of fish, and in addition to making pies, this shop did it in the way Moriarty liked it best, not in a pie, or jellied, doused in pepper and vinegar, but, as it stated, chalked on the big menu board, *Eels Prepared in the Norfolk Manner*.

The shop was busy this lunchtime, though not as busy as it would be at night. The owner, in his long white apron, was behind the counter, helped by his two winsome daughters, the pies appearing as though from nowhere – as though an unseen assistant, concealed under the counter, was popping pies up from an endless supply. The owner was running his knife along the inside of the tin and tipping the pie onto greaseproof paper, handing it to the customer while his wife, at the receipt of custom, took the money, the pies coming thick and fast. It was always like watching conjurors doing that favourite trick, the multiplying bottles, where bottle after bottle appears from a metal tube, and from the last one the prestidigitator pours any drink called for.

Ben Harkness asked for two portions of Norfolk eel, the skinned creature cut into segments of two or three inches, smothered in batter, and deep-fried.

The Professor would never eat the dish in public, for you ate it like playing a mouth organ, which he could do with great delight in the back of the hansom.

And he did just that as they trotted quietly back to the house on the fringes of Westminster.

The moment he stepped out of the cab in front of the house, Moriarty knew that some disaster had taken place. Like his gift for mesmerism, he could not explain this heightened instinct, but he felt his heart race suddenly and his stomach clench, as though he were rapidly descending in some contraption as yet never experienced.

It was still bitter cold and, as though to loosen the sense of doom he was feeling, the Professor began muttering some familiar Shakespeare under his breath as he toiled up to his front door.

'When milk comes frozen in a pail,
When blood is nipped and ways be foul,
Then nightly sings the staring owl,
Tu-whit, tu-who – a merry note.'

And he remembered the old superstition that if you hear an owl hoot in the city, then it is the harbinger of death.

In the hall, just inside the door, Billy Jacobs's

brother, Bertram, stood close to the stairs with Spear next to him, one arm on his shoulder, and young Wally Taplin leaned against the wall beside the green baize door that led to the kitchen and servants' quarters. Each of them was ashen-faced, breathing heavily, while Bertram Jacobs appeared to be beside himself and in shock, his eyes watering, mouth twisted in grief, lips trembling and hands shaking, weaving around, uncontrolled.

'What has happened?' Moriarty demanded, shrugging himself out of his coat and handing it, together with his hat and the other items, to Wally.

'Professor! Oh, thank God! Thank God you've returned!' Bertram, breathless, threw himself onto his knees, took Moriarty's hand, and kissed the signet ring on his right middle finger – as you would venerate a bishop. In itself this was not unusual; members of the Professor's family often performed this act of homage quite naturally. It was a sign of affection as well as a kind of serfdom within criminal families.

'What has happened?' he repeated, and Spear replied, stone-faced, 'It's young Billy. He's dead. Hanged in the attic.'

'Hanged himself?'

'I have no way of knowing, Professor. We've only just found him.'

Moriarty thought to himself that the lad had wanted to speak with him before he went off to The Press for luncheon, and he could not find the time to do so. This was his second mistake of the day: First was not taking enough care over Joey Coax, and now this. He should have *made* time for Billy, and now it was too late.

'Where was everyone when this took place?' he asked, and gradually the story came out.

All four members of the Praetorian Guard had been in and out of the house over the past few hours. The boys had been washing up dishes and pans downstairs in the old kitchen. Ember and Lee Chow were in and out seeking old family members to, as Spear put it, 'talk them back into the family.' Terremant had done the same, and Billy had been running around helping to tidy the place up with his brother. 'We was doing women's work, Professor. We really must have women to deal with the cleaning soon.' Spear sounded put out.

'I sent Billy up to clear out the waste in your basket upstairs. Fold the newspapers. Stuff like that, Professor,' Spear told him, still surly. 'He seemed to be taking an awful long time so I went up with Bert Jacobs here. We couldn't find him at first. Then I went to the top of the house, to the attics, and there he was, just hanging there. Dead.'

The attics ran the length of the house, left and right, east and west, off a wide landing right at the top of the stairs. Each had two dormer windows, but no ceiling; instead, the inside of the roofs was visible, and there were great-beam A-frames high up, where normally the ceilings would begin.

A ladder, leaned against the cross-beam of the A-frame farthest to the east, and a rope had been knotted around the cross beam. From the rope hung the muted, fractured body of Billy Jacobs, his head crushed to one side at a sharp angle, the neck obviously broken, ripped aside. No man could have told how it had happened. All that was certain was that he was dead. And Moriarty recalled the Tarot that Sal had read for him, and the Hanged Man.

God's teeth, Moriarty thought, *this is the worst yet, and it looks black for Bert Spear.* 'You didn't leave the house like the others?' he had asked Spear on their way up, and the big man shook his head, puzzled and sullen. The lad had wanted to talk privately, and he had little doubt as to what Billy wished to talk about – after all, Moriarty thought, he had ordered Spear to question him. This would concern Idle Jack and the spy he had inserted among the Praetorians.

Says he has plenty to tell you... Says it is urgent.

There are three of them and Spear.

Bert Jacobs was weeping openly now, not even attempting to hide his sorrow, moaning, 'My brother. My little brother. Oh my suffering brother!'

Moriarty turned on the lad, sharply. 'Strong men of our mettle don't weep, Bert. Control yourself.' Then, to Spear, 'Where's Sal?'

'She went out a good hour ago. Down the house in the Haymarket. Down to see her gay ladies. Said she'd be back by four.' Spear, Moriarty noted, did not look him in the eye.

With Spear's help, the Professor cut Billy Jacobs down from his gallows and Moriarty reflected that the man could easily have measured out a length of rope, constructed a noose, then jumped from the beam to break his neck. On the other hand, just as easily, one man could have rendered Jacobs

210

unconscious, lugged him up the ladder, and let him go with an already prepared noose, tight around his neck, the knot hard just behind the left jawbone. That was Jack Ketch's trick, the one that threw the head back, breaking the spinal column at about the third vertebra, killing instantly. Until only just over thirty years ago you could see it yourself on execution days, outside Newgate Prison or Horsemonger Gaol. Now, though, there was no knot to go behind the left jawbone. Instead they had a purpose-made rope with a pear-shaped eye woven into one end, the work of William Marwood, the 'humane' executioner who made many changes in the apparatus of death and was followed by the first of the Pierrepoint family, Henry. The brutal, often bungling Ketch, of course, became the generic name for executioners, Jack Ketch having served during much of the seventeenth century.

They laid out Billy on the hard planked floor of the attic, Moriarty thinking what a sad little fellow he looked, now he had departed this stiffening body. He thought of the man's mother, Hetty, who had originally pleaded with him to save her sons, who had been arrested while visiting an old family friend who just happened to be a fence. Bertram, who was helping, seemed to be trying to catch the Professor's eye, as if wanting to speak with him.

Down below, in the servants' quarters, they heard the rear door close and voices, Terremant's rising above the others.

'Albert. Go down to them and wait for me. I wish to speak with Billy's brother here.'

'Would it not be better for me to stay, sir?' Spear asked.

No indeed, Moriarty thought. *No. This time I wish to speak with a Jacobs boy on my own.* Aloud he told Spear, No. He would take Bertram to his rooms, give him a drink. 'You wait downstairs with your colleagues, Albert. I'll be down directly.'

Bert Spear left reluctantly, his footsteps echoing on the bare boards down the stairs, the sound sinister in the near-empty house. So much so that Moriarty decided there and then to summon George Huckett as quickly as possible so that the house could be decorated and made habitable throughout. Tomorrow, he thought, would be good, for by then, if all the plans went well, it would be the right time to begin a new phase in his family's fortunes.

Once in his set of rooms, Moriarty told Bertram Jacobs to sit down, then poured him a liberal dose of brandy. 'There, have a warm-up, Bertram. You want to talk with me, I think.'

Young Bertram was shivering like a man on the edge of a fit, but it was the horror of what had happened to his brother, combined with the bitter cold outside.

'Come along with you, Bert. We've known each other long enough to speak our minds,' Moriarty said, not unkindly, reaching out to the man.

Jacobs's cheeks were still wet with tears, and he gulped once or twice before he was able to control himself. 'I wanted to say how sorry I was. How sorry both of us were, Professor, for believing all that rubbish Idle Jack told us about you not coming back. Billy was outcast by it;

212

couldn't hardly forgive hisself. Told me that when he come over to fetch me. I'd be obliged if you would take us – me – back under your protection, where I should've stayed.'

'I'll be glad to have you back, Bertram, as long as you stay true to the family.' He leaned forward and patted the man on his shoulder. 'Now, having said that, what else do you want to tell me?'

'Well...'

'Come on.' Moriarty's voice took on a sharp edge. 'What was your brother so keen to tell me?'

'You are going to be angry, Professor.'

'Just tell me, man,' he said quietly.

'There is a spy in your family. Close to you, Professor.'

'Oh, I know that. Have known for some time. What I need to know now is who the spy is. What's his name? One of my closest people, I think. Who?'

Bertram Jacobs shook his head fiercely. 'I don't know, Professor. Billy didn't know either...'

'Then, damnit, what *do* you know?' The anger was bubbling like lava in his throat.

'We know ... well, Billy knew, and told me, how Sir Jack made contact with him. How he meets with him, or his representative.'

'Well, tell me; it's dead important. I mean *dead* important. Tell me.'

'Idle Jack has a house. Bought it specially. Keeps it empty most of the time, except he has a woman stays there, Hannah Goodenough. Looks after the place. When his spy wants to meet, or is sending someone with special word, he puts an advertisement in *The Standard*, uses a cipher,

"Who Killed Cock Robin." He puts the advert in saying he would like to see Cock Robin in the usual place; that means the house...'

'Where is this house?'

'Near Paddington. Near the Railway Station. It's a small house in Delamare Terrace, hard by the canal.'

'And all he does is put this advertisement in *The Standard?* Either Idle Jack or his man puts it in?'

'That's it, sir. Says, "Would like to meet Cock Robin usual place at six P.M. on Monday," or whenever it is.'

Moriarty smiled a grim smile. *Then we have him*, he thought. Telling Bertram Jacobs to stay where he was, he left the room and went down to the servants' quarters where his Praetorian Guard were gathered in the kitchen – except for Albert Spear, who seemed to be lurking in the passage that led from the stairs behind the green baize door toward the back door.

'I want you to send young Walker to Cadvenor. I'll prepare a letter.' He planned for Michael Cadvenor to look after Bertram for the time being. 'Tell him to come over after dark, and with his plain van, not the one that shouts his work at the public. I want Billy prepared decently. Have we got a priest who won't ask questions?'

Spear seemed preoccupied, but he answered smartly. 'Yes, Professor. Reverend Harbuckle round St. Saviours. He'll not chatter.'

Terremant appeared in the kitchen doorway. 'What do we want with a God botherer?'

'You haven't told him?' The Professor stared

214

at Spear.

'No sir. No, I haven't.'

'What's wrong with you, Albert?'

'I was fond of young Billy, to tell the truth, Professor. Really quite fond of him.'

'Tell the others, then,' Moriarty cracked directly at Spear. 'Tell them, then get on with your work. Watch yourselves.'

He went slowly up the stairs, thinking with each step that he might have to put Danny Carbonardo to work on Albert Spear before the night was out, after he had done the biggest job. He could not recall a time when he felt so out of joint and dejected.

The house that was known as Sal Hodges's House had plenty of protection all around: a lurker regular on each corner, four punishers downstairs and another two up, plus the two tough dikey women – Minnie and Rosie – who looked after the girls and watched out for rough customers. At one time, Sal's house had been in St. James's, but building and new planning had eased her out and she had moved the few yards to the Haymarket.

Sal had taken the Professor's advice and brought big Harry Judge along with her for protection. When they got there she told him that he could take any girl in the place and have her on the house, but he smiled shyly and, to her surprise, said no. 'I have a young woman I expect to marry, Miss Sal. And I don't go romping elsewhere. 'Tis not in my nature.' She found this refreshing, as it was most unusual among mem-

215

bers of Moriarty's family.

Everyone was glad to see Sally back, because there had been some awful stories floating around.

'Sal's back,' one of the punishers at the door called up, and the cry went all around the house, even from the girls entertaining in their rooms. 'Five in and paid for,' Minnie told her.

'I shall be in my office, Minnie. Tell Polly I'd like a word with her.'

'I'll have her come up straight off,' the plump and happy Minnie replied.

Polly was not one of the whores, but a young girl, no more than twelve or thirteen, whom Sal employed to do the mending and similar jobs concerned with the girls. She was slim and lithe, a little over five foot six, pretty in a striking way with dark curls that came bustling down her neck, romping onto her shoulders.

She tapped at Sally's door some three minutes after Minnie told her to go on up, and she came into the room with a smile that almost enveloped Sal Hodges.

'Mama!' She flung her arms around Sal's neck. 'Mama, thank heaven, there have been terrible rumours that you had been injured. Even killed.'

'Don't ever call me Mama when people are near, my darling girl.' Sal held her close and kissed the top of her head. 'Dreadful things are happening. We must take even greater care, you and I.'

12

Benefit Night at the Alhambra

LONDON: JANUARY 19, 1900

They had found an old table in one of the rooms off the kitchen passage that ran right to the back door, and some quite good chairs in what was probably at one time the servants' hall. They set them up in the kitchen and Moriarty spread thick cartridge paper across the table, pinned it down at each corner, then drew, in ink, a neat plan of Leicester Square, showing the Alhambra on the east side and all the exits and entrances to the Square; Coventry and Cranbourne streets coming in from west and east; and the area of grass known as Leicester Square Gardens in the centre, with its marble statue of Shakespeare, the corners decorated by dolphins and the inscribed tablet that read *There is no darkness but ignorance.* He had also picked out the four statues, one at each corner of the fields, depicting Reynolds, Hunter, Hogarth, and Newton, the great men who had all, at one time or another, lived in the area.

Though he knew that members of his Praetorian Guard would, with their common sense, divine what was going on, Moriarty did not want to give them any details, so he banished them from the house. They had plenty to get on with,

217

continuing to reorganize his family, bringing the lost lambs back into the fold, slaughtering some on the way. Spear still searched for a new warehouse that they could turn into a secret headquarters. 'I want you to come back with the news that things are under way in that department, the warehouse,' he told the big ramper, who nodded and smiled his shark's smile. Then, as Spear reached the door, the Professor called him back. 'And there's the question of Paget,' he said, in a dark, near threatening voice. 'Don't forget Pip Paget, Bert. Paget and his lady love who was Fanny Jones.' He drew his right thumb down his cheek, almost scoring the skin, from under the eye to his jawline.

Spear stopped dead in his tracks, then turned, giving Moriarty a curt nod. 'I haven't forgotten,' he told him before going off into the darkening, cold evening, a frosty mist in the air, to join the other members of the Guard. In truth, Albert Spear already knew exactly where Pip and Fanny Paget could be found. Or, to be more accurate, he was fairly certain where they could be discovered: almost under Moriarty's very eyes if he used his considerable brain. Paget was working not a hand's turn from where Moriarty had his country house, close by Steventon not far from Oxford, near the Hendreds and pretty villages with names such as Kingston Bagpuise and Hanney. Pip Paget was happy as Larry, acting as gamekeeper to Sir John Grant and his lady wife – Lady Pam, as she was known locally – who owned a huge estate bordering on the lands attached to Moriarty's house, Steventon Hall.

The Professor sat at the table now, nigh on six o'clock, with Ben Harkness next to him and places for the boys, Wally Taplin and Billy Walker, who would both have star roles to play in tonight's deadly business. The one person missing was Daniel Carbonardo, who had, as Wally Taplin put it, 'nipped over to Hoxton, over to his house to get the necessary.' This meant that he had gone to Hawthornes, letting himself in around the back and creeping through the rooms with a small lantern, aware there was a high probability that Idle Jack would have a lurker watching the place. He still couldn't really understand why Jack Idell had let him go alive, unless, as Moriarty had suggested, Idle Jack himself wanted to employ the many-talented Carbonardo.

Daniel found his way into the front parlour, where, using his keys, he opened the desk and activated the secret panel that gave him access to the deep hidden compartment where he had placed the Italian pistol he so liked. He knew that the Professor in all probability would offer him the Borchardt automatic or some other handgun, but he would be happier with his Italian iron, with which he had practised in many situations, on both moving targets and still, in all weathers and conditions. The weapon had a long barrel and high foresight, which made for greater accuracy: Danny reckoned he could score well with eight out of nine shots, and he had indulged in some training from an army man, a sergeant who had been a sharpshooter, trained in all weapons. Carbonardo had a high opinion of his own skill, and considered that he could outshoot most people with both rifle and handgun. He had outshot the sharpshooter with little difficulty, the sergeant greatly impressed.

He checked the ammunition and slid the pistol into the specially reinforced pocket built into his trousers, just behind the right hip, dropping extra rounds of ammunition into his jacket pocket. He then left the house the way he had come, walking back to the church of St. John the Baptist, where he had told his cabbie to wait for him. Now he ordered the man to take him to Westminster, an address around the corner from the Professor's house, his eyes skinned, watchful at all times lest he was being followed. From there he paid off the hansom and walked the few yards back to Moriarty's house.

In the kitchen, Moriarty waited quietly; he had plenty to occupy his mind, apart from tonight's work, for he had written to George Huckett, the builder and decorator from Hackney, telling him he wished his firm to make a start on refurbishing and decorating the interior of his house as soon as it was convenient. Huckett would not keep him waiting long, as he knew that work for the Professor came before any other business, and it didn't do to be in any way slapdash or tardy where Moriarty was concerned.

Now he looked around the big old kitchen with its red glazed tiles and the large brick-red and white flagstones that made up the floor. Already, in his mind he had Fanny Jones working here with a couple of kitchen maids, a scullery maid, and a second cook. They would need the big old sink replaced and he was giving much thought to the cooking arrangements. He favoured putting in the Improved Leamington Kitchener, the one with the ventilated wrought-iron roaster that had moveable shelves, a draw-out stand, a double dripping pan, and a meat stand, the roaster easily converted into an oven by closing the valves. It also had an iron boiler with brass tap and steam pipe, with round and square gridirons for chops and steaks, an ash pan, an open fire for roasting, and a set of ornamental covings with an attached plate-warmer. It was fifty years since the Leamington had won the first-class prize and medal (at the Great Exhibition in 1851), but with its improvements there was no other Kitchener to touch it. Expensive, yes, at around £24 from Messrs. Richard and John Slack, 336 Strand, but Moriarty was not inclined to spare the expense. He already had novel plans for the big walk-in pantry and the large scullery, as well as work that would double some of the other rooms here in the basement, eventually allowing ten or twelve of his people to sleep down here at any one time. Then there would be the decorating up in the main house, some new fireplaces, wallpaper, carpets, curtains, and the like, about which he would consult Sal Hodges, who had a good eye and taste in these matters.

After half an hour or so, Daniel Carbonardo returned and took his place at the table while the Professor went over the plan once again, tracing his finger along the map he had drawn, pointing out potential problems: for instance, the traffic in that area could still be heavy, causing blockages even relatively late at night.

Then he asked Ben Harkness if he was happy about the part he would play.

'I shall take you down to the theatre, Professor. Then I'll put the cab and Archie in for the night. My arrangements are that a couple of our lads, Ned and Simon Day, will go to Bright's yard off the Strand where the night watchman'll look the other way, for a consideration, and they will take out a cab and a nice horse I already know, name of Apple. He'll be as good as gold. Very obedient is Apple.'

Most of the hansom cabbies hired their vehicles by the day from the large cab-owners who had considerable numbers of cabs and horses, the hire fee being somewhere between nine and twelve shillings a day.

Ben Harkness was a jewel among cabmen, for, as a profession they had a terrible reputation, which came from the temptations that lay with the job. There were over four thousand cabs plying for trade in London, and many of them worked from ranks close to what were termed 'watering places,' namely the public houses. A large number of the men drank, some of them drinking round the clock, with rarely a home or a bed to go to. It was not uncommon to find cabmen sleeping in the taprooms of inns, taverns, and public houses, or quietly in the back of their cabs. Thus they could be intemperate and quarrelsome, often untrustworthy and unreliable. Ben Harkness was different, an old macer, a gentlemanly swindler, good at many of the dodges used on the streets. Glib of tongue and not possessed of much conscience, he could tip the flash with the best of them. But early on, Harkness had looked to his future and learned to handle a hansom and horses with skilful ease, and had been with the Professor almost from the start of Moriarty's rise to command his own family. 'I'll pick up Daniel around eleven,' Harkness nodded at the assassin who gave him a spot for the pickup.

'Charing Cross Railway Station,' Carbonardo told him. 'Stay apart from the rank and tell people you're booked for a fare.'

Harkness nodded his agreement. 'About eleven, then. We'll do a couple of circuits around the Square, then park ourselves somewhere at the top, where Cranbourne Street filters into the Square, so that when the time comes we can go straight down past the Alhambra.'

The Professor asked Daniel Carbonardo what he thought of the plan.

'What d'you mean, sir?'

'Are you happy? Can you do it, Daniel?'

'If I'm put within fifty paces of the target, I can remove it, sir. I can hit a postage stamp at fifty paces. Still or moving.'

'At fifty paces?' Moriarty gave him a glaring stare.

'I have a natural aptitude, Professor.'

'A natural aptitude? Good.'

Moriarty nodded again, turning to William Walker. 'Now, Billy, you've arranged your part?'

'I'm all Sir Garnet, Professor. I've set things so's I take another boy's pitch selling papers directly outside the Alhambra from about half eleven onwards.'

'And you can recognize Idle Jack?'

223

'Seen him twice. Once pointed out to me going into The Café Royal, then again the other night outside the place where they took Mr. Carbonardo. Know him anywhere.'

'Good boy. And you, Wally?'

'I'll be opposite the Alhambra, by where they have to park their cabs. Soon as Billy gives the signal, I'll put me arm up and signal Mr. Harkness.'

'Then all hell will break out,' Danny said with a dark chuckle.

'And we will say good-bye to the ambitious Idle Jack.' Moriarty smiled his thin, grim smile.

'Please God.' Danny crossed himself, and Moriarty took out the shining gold half-hunter attached to a chain in his waistcoat pocket. He flicked it open and read off the time. It was now four minutes past seven, meaning they had a little under two hours before the curtain went up at the Alhambra. He closed the watch, feeling nothing as he glimpsed the engraving on the lid, which read, *To My Dear and Beloved Son, Professor James Moriarty, with Pride From His Mother Lucy Moriarty*. The watch was, of course, the one Moriarty had removed from his brother's corpse on the evil night when he had killed him close to the Thames all those years ago. Moriarty smiled at the men and boys ranged around the table and, feeling not the slightest remorse, wished them all good luck, then left the kitchen, returning to his quarters to disguise himself as yet another of his characters.

Tonight he would be going to the Daily Mail War Benefit Night at the Alhambra as an elderly country cousin: a man he liked to call Rupert Digby-Smyth from one of the Cotswold villages, one of the Chippings, he thought, a man for whom a trip to London was a huge change in his routine, an exciting business.

In his sixties, Rupert was already set in his ways, nervous yet still with an eye to the good things of life. He was slim, with a full head of greying hair; a somewhat bulbous nose, blue of hue; tired eyes; and the beginnings of a stoop to his shoulders. He dressed well, though in a slightly old-fashioned way: dark trousers and a black swallowtail evening coat that showed signs of mildew, a dull silk cravat that had originally been costly, and a shirt front that could have been stiffer, while on his feet were boots outdated many years, the soles a patchwork of mended leather. His cloak looked fine from a distance, with its silver lion's-head clasps, but on close inspection was frayed and dirty.

When Moriarty came down the steps to the cab, Harkness marvelled at his master's skill. Not in a thousand years would anyone take this old mutton as the evil, fit, and cunning Professor. This fellow looked as if he would require help to get across the road, and even more help to get across a woman – and there would be plenty of willing girls promenading at the Alhambra tonight; there always were.

The two boys, William and Walter, stood by the coach, ordered there so that they could identify the Professor later, when he came out of the theatre. Like Ben Harkness, they could hardly believe their eyes.

'I'll do my best to pick you up, Professor,' Harkness said as they set off for the theatre. 'But it'll be a shade warm around Leicester Square by the time you're ready to leave.'

'Don't worry about me, Ben. I'll find my way back. Those two good boys have orders to shadow me. They learn quickly. It'll do 'em good.

There was a huge and excited seethe around the front of the Alhambra, people crowding in for this special night. A good thing, Moriarty thought, that he had sent young Taplin over to pick up tickets to his box that afternoon. He sat well back; even though disguised, he would never take for granted that no clever shins might see through his disguise. 'Err always on the side of caution,' he would tell his people. Even though, in the deep confines of his mind, he knew his disguises to be impenetrable, Moriarty seldom left anything to chance – his lack of readiness concerning the sexually intermediate photographer, Joey Coax, being the kind of exception that proved the rule.

He usually knew far more than he let on to those around him. For instance, before Sir Jack Idell arrived, all done up in his finery, the Professor was aware, through a man he had in the Alhambra's front-of-house staff, that Idle Jack had five seats booked in his favourite part of the theatre, the fauteuils, close to the promenade where the night ladies would usually parade unless the management had been got at by the many public decency organizations who held the old music halls were an abomination in the sight of the Lord: places of drunkenness, debauchery, and coarseness. The Alhambra was a theatre, not a hall, remember; people did not sit at tables drinking during a performance as in the old, true music halls, which were often rough, dangerous, and rowdy places, far from the incorrect collective memory of gilded and glittering theatres of fun. The real old music halls gave access to alcohol throughout performances, which were often enjoyed because of the drink, not in spite of it.

Here, tonight, the Alhambra was sucking in its large audience, particularly the seats in the stalls, and dress-circle stalls were filling up with the better-class clientele and the wealthy young bucks who frequented the palaces of variety: men and women in full evening dress, white tie and tails, some in dress uniform, a cut above the rough, coarse audiences of the ordinary halls. But there was that same hum of expectancy that Moriarty had always found exciting in places of entertainment. He smiled to himself, remembering the last time he had been in this theatre, when he had been concentrating on the act presented by the illusionist Dr. Night, whom he had manipulated and used in his dreadful attempt upon the life of the Prince of Wales back in 1894.

He was quickly pulled out of his reverie by the arrival of Idle Jack and his party, Jack Idell clumping to his seat, flat-footed and slack-jawed. Tonight there were two bodyguards with him, Moriarty noted: a big, argumentative bruiser he knew as Bobby Boax and the short, pudgy Rouster Bates, whom he had expected. As Bates appeared, next to Boax, a childhood rhyme coursed through his memory:

Long legs and short thighs,
Little head and no eyes.

That pretty much summed up little Rouster, whose eyes all but disappeared into his pudgy face.

Somewhat to Moriarty's surprise, Idle Jack was tonight escorting a lady, and he recognized her instantly: the Honourable Nellie Fletcher, youngest daughter of Viscount Pitlochry, said to be worth millions and none too concerned about the kind of company he kept, a great one for the gaming tables and the fast life. Now that would be a match, Moriarty considered. What an ideal thing that Danny was to take care of Jack that night, for the girl looked to be an innocent, and he had heard of Idle Jack's sexual proclivities, which he would not wish on any young maid. Certainly one of Idle Jack's many unprepossessing traits was his known penchant for rape. Jack was not the kind of man you could leave with your daughter, he had been told. 'Nor your young son, either,' a particular friend had remarked. 'Likes his greens violent,' Sal had heard.

Indeed, Jack Idell had few scruples about his urges and desires; other people's susceptibilities were never held much to the fore by him. Just as he was light-fingered regarding other folks' wealth, so he was light-handed in another sense. 'A liar, a cheat, a thief, a womanizer, and a sacrilegious bugger to boot,' had been the way one cheated banker had summed him up. Moriarty had recently told Albert Spear, 'I am a veritable

Goldilocks compared to that liver-faced trossano.'

Yet it was the fifth member of Idle Jack's party who interested the Professor most, for he had never actually seen Broad Darryl Wood in the flesh, the large, balding broad-shouldered, and undoubtedly highly intelligent ramper said to be Jack Idell's right-hand man. Another person of low morals and ruthless cunning, it was said of him that he had more pockets in his clothes than a normal man, for he needed them to hide the spoils he picked up while walking through any gathering. Ember said he had India-rubber pockets so he could filch from the soup kitchens; and the saying was that Darryl Wood could thieve the keys from St. Peter, while Idle Jack would never even wait for the keys – he would force the locks of the Pearly Gates to get in, and would bring a forged life history with him.

As he watched the arrival of Idle Jack's party, Moriarty was aware of the orchestra tuning up, and it was obvious that for tonight, the pit had been enlarged: Many new players, particularly among the brass, had augmented the usual pit band. He also caught a glimpse of two extra drummers, one settled behind a full set of timpani. There was obviously going to be a joyful noise put up tonight.

He took in a deep lungful of air and smelled the heavy redolence of tobacco, mixed with the scent of the many bottled bouquets the ladies liked to use – 'their perfumes of Arabia,' as he had heard them called. The Professor had a good nose, and so he also detected the remnants of human sweat that joined with the other aromas hanging and jostling with one another.

Moriarty cast an eye over the entire house, putting names to faces, watching the audience settle and seeing the thin blue haze of tobacco smoke hanging a few feet above their heads, swirling and thickening in the rays from the spotlights operated from behind the dress circle.

Now, as the excited buzz and ripple of the audience reached its peak, the conductor finally took his place, tapped on his music stand, and raised his baton. The house lights dimmed and slowly the chatter died out, leaving in its wake the expectant hush of an audience brought to readiness. Then, the brass bellowed out *Tan-ta-ra-ra-ta-ta-tum-ta-ra-ra–*

The curtain rose on a hundred men and women dressed in military red coats, blue trousers, and busbies, seemingly marching in time toward the footlights as they sang the simplistic jingoism of an opening song written especially for tonight's benefit, sending thoughts toward the war in South Africa, the brass blaring loud above the strings and the drums keeping up a persistent military beat–

Ta-ra-ta-ta-rat-ta-ta-rum-ti-tum-ti-ta!

'The Queen's soldiers are marching,
To keep our Empire free,
The Queen's soldiers are fighting,
Fighting for you and me.

Bar-ra-bapa-ta-bapa-ta-tum-riti-tum-titi-tum!

'The Queen's soldiers are marching,
Fighting,

230

Marching for glory,
And fighting and riding and shooting
And clashing,
And fighting the Empire's foes.'

Pa-pa-pa-pa-pa-pa-pa-ra-taaaaaaaar!

'I feared for the roof,' Moriarty said later, and the audience loved it as the singers and dancers seemed to form fours and march in time to the banal song. They clapped and cheered, Idle Jack's party yelling with the rest, Jack leaning over toward Boax, exchanging a joke, heads back, mouths open in laughter.

Let him have his fun, the Professor thought. *He has little time left.*

The chorus ended, the stage cleared, and the tempo changed for Eugene Stratton, The Dandy-Coloured Coon, black-faced with white lips and eyes and a magnificent style in his soft-shoe shuffle as he quietly danced on–

'She's my lady love,
She is my dove, my baby love,
She's no girl for sitting down to dream,
She's the only queen Laguna knows,
I know she likes me, I know she likes me,
Because she says so,
She is my lily of Laguna,
She is my lily and my rose.'

And on with his expert dancing – certainly better than his singing – the drummers giving the soft-shoe a counterpoint on the skulls.

There followed a plethora of popular acts: Kaufman's Trick Cyclists, billed as 'Twelve Cycling Beauties,' circling the stage performing impossible bicycle tricks, very eye-catching in their pink two-piece costumes, form-fitting to show off their figures and excite the gentlemen, the lower half hugging the thighs but ending just above the knees; the amazing juggling Cinquevalli, 'The Human Billiard Table'; and to close the first half, the much-loved Fred Karno and His Speechless Comedians with their manic slapstick sketches.

The Professor had arranged to have a glass of brandy brought to his box in the interval and he sipped it with relish, watching half hidden by the decorating drapes as Idle Jack moved about in the audience, greeting acquaintances, always with the roguish Boax a foot or so behind him like a leech. As he became animated, it seemed to Moriarty that Idle Jack lost his slack-jawed Farmer Giles look, becoming almost suave as he moved around, introducing the Honourable Nellie Fletcher to friends. Moriarty had heard that much of Jack Idell's outward appearance, the walk and drooping jaw, was put on to throw people off his actual astuteness. He wondered now if this could be true.

The most difficult position on the variety bill was always the second-half opener, and tonight the job fell to an immaculately dressed – white tie and tails – good-looking, slight young man who walked on carrying only his opera hat and cane, introducing himself, 'Good evening. I am Martin Chapender. He crushed the hat and laid it on a small table, then proceeded to amaze the house

232

with effects that seemed to be true magic. He swallowed his stick and produced it from his pocket, conjured full-sized billiard balls from the air; freely selected cards from a shuffled deck rose eerily from the deck placed in a glass.

Chapender then flicked open his opera hat, looked slyly at the audience, and asked, 'Were you expecting a rabbit?' – immediately pulling a kicking bunny from the hat. He then wrapped the rabbit in newspaper and tore the newspaper into small pieces to show that the animal had gone.

Chapender next went into the audience and borrowed none but Idle Jack's handsome heavy gold watch and chain, which crumbled to nothing in his hands, startling Jack Idell. Then, drawing attention to a box that had been suspended from the flies throughout, Chapender asked for the box to be lowered and unlocked it to reveal the rabbit, with Jack Idell's watch around its neck.

Now the huge old music-hall names were beginning to arrive, fresh from a night's work somewhere else in London, and the first to be greeted with a roof-lifting cheer and applause was Mr. Dan Leno, 'The Chief of Comedians,' indisputably the greatest comedian of his day and 'Champion Clog Dancer of the World.' Tonight, the little, comic-faced, sad-eyed man introduced one of his beloved characters, Mr. Pipkins, recognizable by many a man in the audience:

'How we met, 'twas quite romantic, in the
    Maze of Hampton Court;
Love, I thought, would drive me frantic, in
    three weeks the ring I'd bought.

> A peck of rice, a bag of slippers, bought but one
> small week of bliss.
> Ma-in-law she came to see us; then my hair
> came out like this—

'That's her mother's doing. 'Pon my word, I don't know whether I'm married to the mother or daughter sometimes. Oh they do beat me, and of course you daren't hit a woman; well, I know I daren't. I can assure you I'm one mass of bruises; if my coat wasn't sewn on me I could show you some lovely bruises. I suppose it's because I enjoy bad health that I bruise so nice. I don't know what I wanted to get married for. Yet I might have done worse; I might have got run over or poisoned. My life's one long wretchedness; and it's

> All through a woman with a coal-black eye,
> All through a woman who was false and sly,
> For when she said she lov'd me,
> She told a wicked lie;
> And her mother's at the bottom of it all!

'It was very strange that I should first meet my wife in the Maze. I'd never been in the Maze before. (Well, I've never been out of one since.) I think every married man's a bit mazy, more or less. Well, to make a long story thick, I was walking up and down, and after walking for about two hours I found I hadn't moved; somehow or other I'd mislaid myself–'

And so on and on, with the story becoming more ludicrous as well as hilarious, until Dan Leno

234

finally quit the stage to make way for the one-and-only Miss Marie Lloyd, 'Queen of Comedy.'

She advanced to the limes and apologized for being late: 'I got blocked in Piccadilly,' she explained with a leer.

Then she had a problem opening her parasol. Finally the parasol opened and she sighed, 'Thank heavens, I haven't had it up for months.' Another of her winks before she went into one of her old favourites:

'The boy I love is up in the gallery,
The boy I love is looking now at me,
There he is– Can't you see
Waving his handkerchief
As merry as a robin
That sings in the tree.'

She did two more songs before the audience reluctantly let her go to be replaced by Miss Vesta Tilley, the great male impersonator in white tie and tails. With her top hat jaunty on her head and a swagger in her walk, she sang a sad song that touched on the danger of crossing the class barrier:

'From the sad sea waves back to business in the morning,
From the sad sea waves to his fifteen bob a week,
Into a cook shop he goes dashing,
Who should bring his plate of "hash" in,
But the girl he'd been mashing
By the sad sea waves.'

Vesta Tilley gave way to the night's top of the bill, Mr. George Robey.

Looking like an unfrocked parson, with his little black hat at a rakish angle and the black almost cassocklike garment reaching to below his knees, his little cane whirling in his hand, on he bustled to loud applause, which seemed to puzzle him. The audience was certainly a surprise to Mr. Robey, and once he had spotted them he advanced to the footlights, his nose a heavy red and his black eyebrows arched violently, his eyes shining like headlamps.

As ever, the sight of Mr. Robey produced titters and even guffaws of laughter, which brought him to a halt. 'Desist!' he called out. Then a commanding, 'Out! Out!' When this did not stop the laughter he declared, 'Let there be merriment by all means. Let there be merriment, but let it be tempered with dignity and the reserve which is compatible with the obvious refinement of our environment.' And he would be off in a storm of staccato gags about bullying wives and henpecked husbands, noisy landlords and interfering relatives. 'Kindly temper your hilarity with a modicum of reserve,' he would say, and the audience would giggle and hoot even louder at this pompous comic.

Tonight he ended with a song telling the sad tale of how he had sought a father's permission for him to marry his daughter:

'He told me my society was superfluous,
That my presence I might well eradicate.

236

From his baronial mansion he bade me exit
And said I might expeditiously migrate.
In other words, "Buzz off!"'

By the time he finished, the audience was help-
less, for he was able to play them like an instrument. Even Moriarty, not the most humorous of
men, wiped tears of laughter from his eyes.

The stage cleared once again and, as at the
start, filled with the chorus and dancers in their
military costumes. The orchestra struck up the
best-loved popular song of the day, the chorus
again seeming to march toward the audience –
two steps forward, a step to the side, and two
steps back – bellowing out:

'It's the Soldiers of the Queen, my lads,
Who've been, my lads,
Who've seen, my lads.
In the fight for England's glory, lads,
When we have to show them what we mean:
And when we say we've always won,
And when they ask us how it's done,
We'll proudly point to every one
Of England's Soldiers of the Queen,
It's the Queen!'

The audience joined in Leslie Stuart's well-known
chorus, and applauded louder than they had done
for the entire evening as all the artistes lined up to
take their final call, the orchestra quickly changing
to waltz time to get the audience out of the building, a cold blast of air signalling that the doors at
the front of the house had been opened.

Moriarty took his time; he did not want to be present when the deed was actually done, so he lingered, putting on his long cloak and gloves, grasping his silver-topped walking cane. He watched from the back of the box as Idle Jack clumped, flat-footed, up the aisle. *Moving heavily toward his death*, the Professor thought. *Jack Idell wouldn't be walking at all if he knew what waited for him.* Moriarty smiled grimly and began to leave the box slowly, not hurrying at all.

It was bitter outside, with the wind knifing across Leicester Square and a crowd starting to build up in front of the Alhambra's elaborate façade, some already crossing to the hansoms that were lined up on the far side of the road. Billy Walker shouted his paperboy cry, a pack *of Evening Standards* under his arms, his eyes moving, sweeping the interior of the Alhambra's foyer. Across the road, leaning on the rails bordering Leicester Square Gardens, Wally Taplin kept his eyes on William, occasionally glancing to his left, catching a glimpse of where Harkness had the stolen cab by the side of Cranbourne Street; Apple, the quiet little grey, snuffling, turning slightly, wanting to be off and Daniel Carbonardo sitting back, the Italian pistol held firmly in his right hand and his hat pulled down over the top half of his face.

Billy saw the big Boax, with Wood by his side, as they emerged from the auditorium. The woman Jack Idell was with was laughing up at him. *You'll laugh the other side of your face before long*, Billy thought, and waited until the group had pushed through the crush, almost out of the doors, before

238

he lifted his arm with the newspaper in it.

Accordingly, across the road, Wally's arm went up in a kind of salute, his fist closed, and up at the top of the square Ben Harkness thumped on the roof of the cab, and Daniel shifted, bringing up the pistol and looking forward as Apple started to trot quietly down the road.

This isn't going to be easy, Daniel thought; there were people and other cabs to his left, a whole crowd of folk out on the freezing pavement, but he could see Idle Jack's brilliantly white shirt-front as he pushed forward.

Daniel had Jack in his sights, his left forearm running along the left side of the cab, forward of the hood, which barely kept the flakes of snow off him in the wind. His right hand held the pistol comfortably, the barrel lying across his forearm as he squinted toward Idle Jack and adjusted his aim as the foresight came to bear on the shirt-front.

Harkness urged Apple forward, and Danny Carbonardo began to squeeze the trigger.

Matthew Shotton pulled on the leash and cursed his little dog, George, a sparky Yorkshire terrier whom he was taking for its nightly walkies lest it would foul one of his good carpets. This was not one of Matthew's usual jobs. As a rule, when he got home to their little house in Poland Street, George had already been walked by his wife, Ivy. Matthew worked in the ticket office at The Prince of Wales theatre, sometimes doubling as front-of-house manager, which earned him an extra couple of pounds a week. But tonight Ivy had a heavy cold coming on and she had told him he would have to do this late-night chore. Matthew didn't care for taking George out to do his business, but thought that needs must when the devil drives – and Lord knew, Ivy could be a real devil at times, particularly when one of her head colds was upon her.

George performed near one of Shakespeare's dolphins, looking up at Matt as though this was the cleverest trick in the world. He then barked twice, and Matt Shotton gave the leash a sharp pull. He was aware of the crowd spilling out from the Alhambra and of the traffic and people. Then George barked loudly again and slipped his leash, pulling it from Matt's hand and heading off, barking and jumping, through the railings and out onto the road, as though the great three-headed dog Cerberus had been let loose and was at his heels.

The problem with George was that he thought he was human, a spunky, tough little lad with no fear. After all, hadn't he tried to break down the parlour wall to smash through when next door's bitch, Dippin, was on heat? When he sensed things were right, he would hurl himself at the wall: This little ball of black and ginger hair would take a running jump at the wall in his heartfelt attempt to smash his way through. George reckoned he could go anywhere and do anything. One of his favourite pastimes was worrying horses.

All little George was aware of was the hansom and its horse trotting down the centre of the street. George did not particularly like horses, so he barked louder than ever and ran out, yapping, snapping, and leaping up toward the larger animal.

Ben Harkness was taken by surprise. Apple, usually the most docile of creatures, reared to the left; then, finding himself heading toward a crowd on the pavement, he reared up again, pulling to the right just as Danny Carbonardo squeezed the trigger.

Danny was thrown back in the cab but could not stop the pistol from firing: once, twice, three times; and Ben Harkness saw first a woman stagger back, wheeling around as a bullet thumped into her shoulder, and then, to his horror, young William Walker stagger, mouth open in a soundless scream as blood blossomed on the boy's shirtfront and splashed over his newspapers as he dropped them. There were screams and an agitated movement in the crowd. Harkness gave Apple a flick of the whip and pulled hard on the reins, dragging the cab to the right and urging the horse on as their speed increased and they made their way toward the only possible exit.

Left out of Leicester Square, bearing left. The Old City Hall coming up on their right, then hard left into Charing Cross Road, going straight on until they reached Cranbourne Street again, turning right, away from Leicester Square, and so into Long Acre, where they planned to ditch the cab and escape on foot.

Danny Carbonardo cursed roundly throughout. 'I've let him down!' he shouted. 'I've let the Professor down.' And Harkness quietly said, 'It happens to us all sooner or later. It was that fucking little canine.' The fucking little canine had followed, barking, until they almost got to Charing Cross Road.

'I should have shot the little bleeder,' Carbonardo said with a lot of feeling.

'Oh, Danny; you're not a child or a pet killer. Wouldn't have done to have shot him.'

Finally, Moriarty pushed through the doors out into the wicked cold of Leicester Square, with tiny particles being carried on the wind. There was an ambulance pulled up close to the theatre, two big horses between the shafts, blowing steam into the freezing air. There were police bustling around and some nurses. But no sign of Idle Jack. *My God*, Moriarty thought. *What the hell's happened? Don't say that Carbonardo's missed him. How could that be?*

Then, with horror, he saw they were lifting the body of young William Walker into the ambulance, blood dripping from the stretcher. The Professor swallowed hard, almost weeping. *My poor good boy*, he thought. *Daniel Carbonardo, where's your natural aptitude now?*

'What's happened?' he asked a police constable nearby.

'You move along, sir. There's been a terrible shooting: lady over there wounded, and the paperboy killed outright. Didn't know what hit him, poor boy. There one minute, gone the next.'

'Good, brave lad. Dear God,' Moriarty breathed, turning to see a young woman weeping and a nurse bandaging her shoulder, which dribbled blood.

The woman was only some seventeen or

242

eighteen summers old, seated on a step, upset and beyond comfort by the man with her, who murmured, 'Come, Jessie. It'll be fine.'

'How would you know?' The woman spoke sharply; and as Moriarty turned, he was sure that he glimpsed Albert Spear in the crowd, with the boy Sam who had worked at the Glenmoragh Private Hotel, but when he looked again they had gone, melted away.

So the Professor, filled with anger and rage, stumped off toward Piccadilly, where he would get a cab. His cloak filled with air, billowing and floating like a great sail behind him, and he spotted young Taplin across the road, trying to keep pace with him.

They had failed to kill Idle Jack, God rot him. He put his head down against the wind, which carried particles of snow and ice painfully into his face.

Moriarty reached back into his long black Irish past and pulled out from many generations ago an old curse, from his travelling ancestors, the diddicoi, and he murmured it onto Idle Jack's head:

'Ekkeri, akai-ri, you kair-ari,
Fillisin, follasy, Idle Jack, ja'ri:
Kivi, kavi, Irishman,
Stini, stani, buck.'

As he made his way up toward the 'Dilly,' the wind blew stronger and the snow hit his face like needles, as though nature itself was reacting to his muttered spell.

13

The Monkery

LONDON & OXFORDSHIRE:
JANUARY 20, 1900

From the moment he stepped through the back door into the passage running past the kitchen, Albert Spear was aware of the sense of disaster pervading the house.

The down he could feel seemed to have reached saturation point, as if it even affected the dust motes floating in the thin sunlight shafting through the windows from the cold early-morning air. It was not actually freezing today, a mild thaw having set in during the night.

Spear already knew what was up, or was near certain that he knew. The morning papers had given him the tip with headlines like SHOTS FIRED WOMAN WOUNDED BOY KILLED. And MURDER OUTSIDE ALHAMBRA. Or MAN IN HANSOM SHOOTS NEWSBOY.

That was enough to pique interest, made you want to read on, and while he did not recognize the woman's name – Jessie Rippon – the boy's was almost too familiar.

William Walker (14), newsboy of no fixed abode.

Wally Taplin's eyes were ringed raw red from

244

weeping, and Danny Carbonardo could not even crack a smile sitting there in the kitchen with an enamel mug of tea, hands trembling when he raised the mug to his lips; Ben Harkness was pacing around, looking miserable.

Carbonardo acknowledged him with a curt nod and a 'Bert.' Ben Harkness just looked right through him.

'They been on the carpet,' Jim Terremant told him, muttering low as they stood together at the door to the little room Terremant had appropriated for himself. 'Well and truly on the carpet after the balls they made of things last night. Even the gaffer's upset about Billy Walker. Tears. Blowing his nose.' He shook his head hard. Then, with a catch in his voice, 'Everything,' and shook his head again.

Spear asked if this was the Professor's plan. 'Settling with Idle Jack? Topping him?'

'Reckon so,' Terremant said, and warned him not to mention dogs for a bit. ''Specially yappy little terriers.'

'Well, maybe I'll cheer up the old man.' Spear gave his fearsome shark's smile, showing the inside of his mouth, gums and all, and his sharp broken teeth. Bert Spear had big teeth, some of them pointed as if they had been ground by Kit Mysson's machine, the one he used on the knives. 'I got good news for him.' Spear gave another of his smiles.

'What's that, then?' Terremant sounded dead interested.

'You'll hear soon enough.' Bert Spear had long learned to keep quiet, not to blab about the

Professor's business before it was all clear with the gaffer.

Terremant shrugged and said he should watch himself because George Huckett's men were all over the place, 'Saturday morning an' all. Measuring and sanding, even using blowlamps. Said they'd be in here, in the kitchen, on Monday. Professor's having the whole house done up.'

They were there all right, men in overalls working away in the hall and on the staircase, stripping off the old wallpaper with blowlamps and scrapers, sanding down the paintwork, a singeing smell in the air. Some of them threw furtive peeps at Albert Spear, sideways looks, turning away quickly, put off by the lightning-flash scar and broken nose, the way he held himself: a dangerous man. Spear wondered if the Professor's plans had changed, now he was setting this fine house to order.

Things went off well, though, after what you might call a hesitant start, for the Professor looked grim as a shroud, showing no pleasure at Spear's unheralded arrival.

'Yes?' he said flatly, looking up from the desk where he was writing. 'What is it, Bert?'

Even when he told Moriarty he had found a warehouse, the Professor's initial reaction was tepid: just a questioning, 'Well?'

Only after Spear had enthused and told him the details did the Professor show a little pleasure. It was the largest of three warehouses standing parallel to the river – the closest, protected by a wall, with its own gate, the warehouse being sold off by an import firm that usually brought in tea

246

but had recently lost one of their biggest suppliers, so was currently going through a difficult time.

'Absolutely ideal, Professor, sir. A mite larger than the one we had in Limehouse.' This one was in Poplar, about two and a half miles from where they had been on the night Daniel Carbonardo had been snatched: The Sheet Anchor public house.

'You want to see it, sir?' Spear asked, but the Professor shook his head. 'If you say it's ideal, then it's ideal. First thing Monday get Perry Gwyther to do the business. Buy it. I want to move on. Buy it, and talk to Gwyther about an architect.'

Spear nodded. 'Thought I'd go and find Pip Paget today.' Casual, as if he had just thought of it – like the idea had popped into his mind that very minute.

Moriarty looked up, startled. 'You know where he is?'

'Got a hint.'

'Don't let him see you,' he ordered quickly.

'As if I would, guv'nor.'

And this time the Professor gave him a straight smile. 'Find him,' he said. 'Find him, then come and tell me. I'll want to see you all bright and early tomorrow morning anyway. Something important is coming off. I'll send young Wally round to those I don't see before then, but I'll need you all here first thing. Eight o'clock Sunday morning.'

Spear simply nodded and left to find Harry Judge, stamping his feet and blowing on his hands outside the back door, drawing on a cigarette.

'We're going for a trip out; going on the monkery, Harry,' Spear told him.

'Where, boss?' The monkery was tramps' talk for the countryside, or becoming a tramp in the countryside.

'Out Oxford way. Going to look up an old chum.'

'How we getting out there, then?'

'Go on the rattler. Take less than two hours. Hour and a half, maybe.'

Judge stamped again. 'Bloody fast, them rattlers. I don't like 'em all that much.'

Spear laughed and said something about the queen not liking her first ride in a steam train, but that was half a century ago.

'If we was meant to ride rattlers, God 'ud 'ave given us wheels instead of feet.'

Albert laughed again and said they would have to ride a gig at the other end.

'I just hope the roads are clear of snow. You can never tell out on the monkery. They don't do things like we do here in the city. They're not as quick as in the city. Not as efficient.'

Spear said it would be fine. 'If the roads aren't clear we'll just have a nice dinner in some tavern; quaff some ale and come home again.'

'That sounds more like it,' Judge said, grinning the grin of a man who likes a little adventure but wasn't happy about travelling to find it.

Idle Jack was incandescent with rage. 'I'm going to tear his heart out,' he declared loudly, striding across the withdrawing room in his Bedford Square house, the room Billy Jacobs had likened to a tart's parlour. 'I'll show him he's not wanted here, damn his eyes. I'll reach into his chest and

248

tear his black heart out, throw it down. Feed it to the dogs.' He stamped his foot in time to his threat. 'In the street! I can't believe it! Tried to shoot me! Me? In a London street, with innocent people standing near. Tried to shoot me from a hansom cab!' The room did not look like a tart's parlour. It was just that the Idells had always preferred bright colours.

'Jack, calm down. You'll have a turn, do yourself a mischief.' Broad Darryl Wood was sprawled in a nursing chair over by the fire, coal and crackling logs throwing flames up the chimney. 'We don't yet know it was him. Not for certain.'

'Course it was him. I've showed him what's what and he's angry. I wouldn't mind wagering it was Carbonardo himself doing the shooting. The police'll be outraged. And that's no good to any of us. All we need is the rozzers out in force. Moriarty's too arrogant by half; he's attracting the coppers like a magnet, and we can all do without that.'

In private, Jack dropped the pretence of looking like his father, flat-footed and slack-jawed. In effect he was slim, tall, and rather fine-looking: a bit of a dandy, who walked and moved elegantly, with light, neat, peppery hair, and cold grey eyes that could freeze you cold as a corpse.

While Idle Jack Idell was proud of coming from a military family, the darker side of his lineage was seldom far away. Jack's grandfather, Roger Idell, and his great-grandfather Kimble had been slavers; that was where the money came from, where the house in Hertfordshire, and the estate, and the entire village of Idellworth some five miles from Hitchin came from. It had been serious wealth in the day of his father, Roister Idell, huge riches when his grandfather ran what was left of the slaving – half-a-dozen ships and a private army, with outposts in Africa, now gone to rack and ruin along the Slave Coast, between Cotonou and Lagos.

Idle Jack had slavery in his veins, and the stories he heard from his grandfather were enough to keep the dream alive in his head. Jack had that ruthlessness in his character, that merciless streak that allowed him to take people, drag them down, and inflict pain without a second thought. He treated all men and women as if they were inferiors. Darryl Wood, a man of wit as well as brawn, once said that Jack Idell would expect the queen herself to do his laundry if he was invited to stay in Buckingham Palace. It was the old family bloodline into slavery that gave him a start in his cunning life of crime. He was prepared to see other people work for him until they dropped, and for little wages if necessary.

Some of the seafaring men who were young lads in his grandfather's day now owned their own vessels and were more than willing to work, illegally, at the slavery for Jack Idell. There were four men in particular who were little less than pirates even in this modern age, the start of the twentieth century. In the late 1890s, and even now in 1900, Ebeneezer Jephcote, William Evans, Corny Trebethik, and Michael Trewinard sailed regularly on what were well-organized slave-acquisitioning voyages. They sailed from Portsmouth, Plymouth, Bristol, and Liverpool, heading to his

250

family's old stamping ground, around Lagos. But they would also call in at Naples on the Italian coast, and Dubrovnik on the Serbian shoreline.

The slave trade, like so many other things, was now illegal, society having become infected with what Idle Jack called 'the prude germ.' Yet Jack Idell's captains still managed to return with human cargo to smuggle into the country. More females than males now. Always girls and boys of eight or nine years, even younger. The blacks from the old gathering grounds of Africa, but whites also from the poor regions of Serbia and rural Italy: Told they were heading for a good new kind of life, they quickly became pliable, for most had suffered the trauma of being orphaned – mainly by Jack's press-gangs. 'Make them motherless and fatherless,' Jack would instruct his captains. 'Let them see what happens when they cross us: easy lesson for them to learn. Then don't kill them by kindness, but show them how they can win treats by doing what they're told.'

Idle Jack had no scruples regarding how he used these children. There had been a lively and lucrative trade in children some fifty or so years before, so, he reasoned the demand would be the same now. He recalled his grandfather's stories of the Haymarket in the '40s and '50s: How girls of twelve – the age of consent – or less would take men by the hand and bid them to follow, in the most beguiling manner. So, he reasoned, it would still be the same now. There would be men today with those self-same appetites who would gladly pay in order to spend time with very young girls of twelve, eleven, or even only ten summers, just

251

as there would be men who would pay good money to buy, or spend time with, a catamite. All the children Jack put to work in London could, in many ways, be classed as exotic. The dark-skinned children certainly were, and his men had a good eye when choosing the white Italians and others.

Only the previous week, Ebeneezer Jephcote had suggested sailing his barque, *Midnight Kiss*, into Cadiz, because 'I have a contact there with a source of pliant gypsy girls, young and ready to fuck a horse for money. Beautiful, loose-limbed, and with obvious passion in every movement. Oh, Sir Jack, you should see them dance; then you would know what the word *sinuous* means.'

And Jack had told him, 'Do it and bring me two samples.'

Certainly, Idle Jack had branched out into the selling of protection to commercial businesses on high streets; running casinos and night drinking dens and bucket shops, and demanding a per-centage of money made illegally in his satrapies and all the other dodges and money-makers on the edge of illegality that Moriarty ran, or took his cut from, in London and other large cities. But his main source of cash was from the sale and prosti-tution of children, something that made James Moriarty's blood boil. It was an area of prosti-tution that the Professor would have no part of, and it was the overriding reason why he was determined to win back the rights to his criminal empire. Above all things, this was the one crime Moriarty wished to expunge, the one he would not go near even with the proverbial bargepole.

Thinking that Jack Idell possibly had the same proclivities as those he tempted with small and young children, Moriarty would often say, as he had said to Spear recently, 'The man who would delight in lusting after a young child is somehow warped, and not worthy to be called a man.' And in a manner he was right, for Idle Jack was not above stealing children from their parents if it suited him.

Look hard at Idle Jack; look into those cold grey eyes and you might possibly glimpse the real man – heartless and cruel. The misshapen character glowers from his face, revealed by his physical flaws: the twist of his smile, the teeth that show uneven, and the mouth slightly askew. Idle Jack was a robber of innocence, a pillager of families, a thief of time and decency.

Albert Spear, with Harry Judge in tow, hired a gig from a man he knew near Oxford railway station, and they drove out on the road to Steventon, Harry handling the reins of the little piebald pony called Smudge. It was cold, but they had not suffered the same heavy falls of snow as London; still, Harry grumbled a lot during the railway journey, and now he grumbled again because he was hungry. Spear had to be sharp with him in the end, and he went quiet, a shade sulky but still handling the gig sensibly and with dexterity, which went in his favour. Some five miles from Steventon they stopped in the hamlet of Twin Willows, where there was a coaching inn: The White Hart.

Twin Willows stood on the edge of Sir John Grant's estate, with its farm, several acres of wheat and good grazing land; the big house, Willow Manor; a wonderful stretch of river with fine fishing; and his shoot, which was much talked about in fashionable circles in London itself. It was also here that Sir John had the kennels and runs for his hounds, the savage pack that ran with the Grant-Willow Hunt. Sir John and Lady Pam were out with the Grant-Willow every other Saturday during the season, and Sir John was, naturally, Master of Foxhounds. It was a hunt looked up to by members of the Royal Berks, the Quorn, the Beaufort, the Old Berkely, and other great hunts. Foxes were no trouble to the many hens kept by local farmers – not with the Grant-Willow hallooing and tantivying across the local fields.

The White Hart was a fine old Tudor Inn that had seen better days. Until the advent of the railways it had two stagecoaches going through from London to Oxford every day – one in each direction – with all the extra gain they brought with them: ladies, tired from the journey, who would book in to stay a few nights until rested, and the many travellers who required feeding, or simply needed to use alcohol to dull the boredom and pain of journeying.

The main taproom was large, scented with wood smoke from the big open fire, clean, and with respectful locals: two old granddads, wearing the ancient country dress of smocks, who pulled their forelocks to Spear, and three or four men who obviously worked the land nearby. All of them showed deference to Spear and Judge, who, to their eyes, looked, they supposed, like gentlefolk, for they were both dressed in jackets

254

and trousers of good cloth. The Professor insisted on his men being neatly dressed and polite of manner. Spear of course wore a short top hat.

Confidently, Spear asked the landlord of The White Hart if they could get some dinner, and the landlord, one Jonathan Booker, said there was not such a call as there had been when the coaches still ran, but he liked to keep some victuals to hand for travellers. In the end he gave them a tasty and nourishing vegetable soup followed by generous slices of a veal-and-ham pie that was bulked out with hard-boiled eggs, mushrooms, and oysters mixed in with the meat. Spear recognized it immediately as the kind of veal-and-ham pie that Fanny Paget – Fanny Jones as was – used to make when she cooked and cleaned in the old warehouse headquarters in Limehouse. So, right away, he mentioned to Booker that he had come to look up an old friend who he had heard was now Sir John's gamekeeper.

'Oh, that'll be Paul,' Booker nodded. 'Lives just up the road. Tell the truth, the pie you're eating was made by his wife, Fanny.'

'Little Fanny! Well I'll be damned!' Spear gave him a special shark's smile and reached up to clap him on the shoulder, then asked where he could find old Paul, mentally noting that Pip had changed his Christian name at least. 'Big lad,' he said by way of description. 'Broad-shouldered, light-coloured hair, thick as a good maid's thatch but straight and floppy, bronze of face an' all. Liked to be outdoors; a smiler, with bold blue eyes and a way with him that demanded respect.'

'That's Paul to a T,' Jonathan Booker declared.

'Like looking straight at him, how you describe him.'

'So, how do we find him?'

'Nothing easier. Straight on up the road half a mile, t'wards Steventon, and there is a road signposted to Willow Manor, on the left. 'Tis a track really, right along the four-acre meadow they use for grazing the cattle. Quarter of a mile and you come to two clumps of cottages. The first two – big ones, more houses than cottages really, with two dormer windows jutting out of the roofs. First one is the Huntsman's cottage, Mr. Grosewalk. Lazarus Grosewalk. But the second, new painted last summer, that's Paul's cottage. You should find him there this time o' day. Goes home for his victuals, and a bit more I've no doubt, for he has the most tasty wife in Fanny.' And they all fell to laughing, merry as grigs.

'Eat up, then, Harry.' Spear touched Judge's forearm. 'We'll go along and surprise Paul. It'll be lovely to see him again.'

'And Fanny,' Harry Judge said, and Spear recalled how Harry had fancied Fanny Jones like a fandangle. Never would have done anything about it, though, for Harry had his own one-and-only girl and nothing would ever change that.

Spear failed to see the pot boy, who had been washing the mugs and jugs, slip away from his work and leave the inn by a side door.

It took less than ten minutes to drive up to the track with the fingerpost that pointed to the left, neatly painted, black on white, saying WILLOW MANOR. Spear gave Judge his instructions to stay pulled in to the track, but with Smudge

256

facing the road. 'Mark any sod that comes my way,' he ordered. 'I'll whistle for you if I need you. My good two-fingered whistle.'

'Your shrieking one. Right. You whistle and I'll come trotting down for you.'

'Good man.' Crossing into the field, Spear made his way up the side of the track, hidden by the thick and high hedgerow with its evergreen bushes and trees at intervals.

Albert Spear was wise to the ways of London streets, but knew little of country matters. There was no ditch running along the hedgerow – his eyes told him that, just as they also told him he was well shielded from the cottages when he came to them. Behind him, looking out of place in the middle of the meadow, was a clump of trees: some firs, and a pair of oaks, clear of leaves in winter, the branches curled against the sky. There was, he noted, a gap in the hedge, flanked by two elms almost directly opposite the cottage that he marked down as Pip Paget's bolt hole – and a nice little place it was, built in red brick with a slate roof, and big enough to warrant white barge boards at the gable ends. The remaining wood-work – door and window frames – was a neat, clean white as well.

New painted last summer.

There seemed to be no sign of life from the cottage, but behind him in the field there were cattle, restless, anxiously lowing, expectant even. Then the cottage door opened and out came Fanny, unchanged, with her long, dark hair just as lustrous as Spear remembered. She was shaking out what could have been a tablecloth, cracking it

257

in front of her, holding the ends far apart, her eyes raking the hedge and peering to the far distance. Spear crouched down; she was, he thought, a sight for sore eyes. Pretty as any picture. Oh, Fanny was captivating. Always had been. Even though he had his own beloved wife, Bridget, Albert Spear thought nobody could fail to be captivated by Fanny with her slim waist, that jet hair and her big brown eyes: captivating and fascinating. He was so fascinated with her now that he could not take his eyes off her every move, and felt the need to circle her waist with his hands.

Until he heard the unpleasant deep and menacing growl.

Then the click of a shotgun being cocked, the thumb pulling the hammers back, one after the other.

He spun around, his right hand going for the pistol he kept – like Carbonardo – in a special pocket behind his right hip.

'Don't, Bert. Don't make me blow holes in your guts.'

Philip Paget stood four feet away from him, a grey-black lurcher with its teeth bared growling close to his booted and gaitered leg and a two-barrelled shotgun, steady and pointing, aimed at his stomach.

'Bugger me. Pip Paget.' Spear opened both eyes and tried to look innocent.

Which made Paget laugh aloud. 'Bert Spear, you old fraud. You've seen Fanny come out, so don't be surprised when I'm here.'

Spear nodded slowly. 'How d'yer manage to creep up on me like that, Pip?'

'Because all these years I've been living like Billy Bones.'

'Who's Billy Bones when he's at home then?'

'A pirate, Bert. A pirate in Mr. Robert Louis Stevenson's wonderful book, *Treasure Island*. He comes to this inn on the cliffs and pays people to watch out for him. To watch out for anyone asking about him. In particular to look for a one-legged seafaring man. Well, I pay people, Bert. Good people, and I pay them to watch out for me.' He gave a strangled little laugh. 'I told 'em to watch out for a big bully-boy over six foot tall, and a little foxy man, a Chinaman, and a big man with a broken nose and a scar shaped like a lightning flash down his cheek.'

'Me,' Spear grunted.

'Yes, you, Bert Spear. And the pot boy from The White Hart came running over here not a half hour ago and said his gaffer was telling you where to find me. Do you not recall that in the old days, when you were a lad, pot boys were known as squealers?'

'So how did you get behind me, Pip?'

'I been with them cows, Bert; then a'course Fanny come out and that got your attention. Now, Snapper!' He spoke to the dog, which growled and looked alert. 'Stay, Snapper! Watch!' He moved a pace closer to Spear. 'Snapper here will have your throat out if you move against me. Who else you got with you, Bert?' He came very close now, removed the pistol from Spear's right hip, and gently felt in all the right places for other weapons, Snapper the dog circling close. His forelegs and body were grey, but his right eye was

259

circled with black. Bert Spear thought of Bill Sykes's dog, Bullseye, in *Oliver Twist*.

'I got Harry Judge up the end of the lane. But, Pip, I come here first to warn you. I swear to God I did, not just to seek you out, or do you harm. The Professor's looking for you. Told me to find you. I thought I could come down and warn you that where I've been he'll soon be watching.'

Paget said they should walk gently over to the cottage. 'Fanny's got a shotgun in there as well, Bert, and she's not afraid to use it.'

'I'm not going to cause you any trouble, Pip, I swear. On my mother's eyes I swear.'

'We'll see. How can you summon Harry?'

'Me piercing whistle, Pip. Two blasts with me fingers stuck in me mouth.'

'Not yet. Just walk, quiet; slow; don't do anything stupid, Bert Spear, because Fanny has a twelve-bore trained on you as well.'

Spear looked toward the cottage and saw that Fanny, standing just inside the door, had a second shotgun at her hip, up and pointing toward him.

'Whistle when we get to the gate,' Paget told him.

So, at the gate, mindful of the shotguns, Spear slipped his two forefingers into his mouth, above his front teeth, resting on his tongue. He turned his head and blew two long, piercing double whistles that actually hurt his ears, so Lord knew what they did to the dog. Snapper looked bewildered and pained but settled again, staying with him as they got to the door.

'Snapper!' Paget commanded. 'Stay! Watch!'

And the dog gave another low growl, moving quietly in as Spear stepped over the threshold. Paget was to one side, out of sight, and Fanny remained just a blur somewhere in front of him but in a dark patch, just inside her kitchen door, pretty much in line with the front door and leading off the parlour. Later he saw that the kitchen door was a latched half door, like one in a stable – nice though, painted a deep cream, as was all the interior woodwork. 'Hello, Mr. Spear,' she said in her lovely deep and soothing voice. 'It's been a few years.'

'I need to talk to you both...' he began, feeling inadequate.

'Let's deal with your chum Harry first,' Paget said. 'I want to make sure he's not lurking around with a barker ready to puncture me.'

The gig pulled up in the middle of the track, right in front of the cottage gate, and Spear called to Harry Judge, 'Come on down, Harry. Come and say hallo to Pip Paget.'

Paget left his shotgun behind the door, calling back to Fanny not to let Judge see the weapons before gently pushing Spear toward the garden, the dog close to them both, looking up, interested, as Harry came through the gate, meeting Pip Paget as though he had no care in the world. Which was an accurate description. Harry was a literal person. He knew Paget had left the Professor's service suddenly and without permission, but that was as far as it went. Nobody had directly charged him to take any action against Pip, or Fanny for that matter.

'Hallo, Pip,' he called, coming up the path,

261

boots crunching on the neat gravel. 'That's a fearsome-looking dog you've got there.'

Paget said it was good to see Harry again and responded to Judge's remark concerning Snapper by agreeing, 'Yes. Yes, old Snapper'll have your socks off before you know it, if you give him cause.'

They talked for a few minutes, though Harry, of course, had only small talk, mentioning how cold it was and how they'd had grievous hard frosts, and crippling heavy snow up the Smoke, and how lucky Pip and Fanny were to have moved to such a nice spot as this.

'Gets righteous cold out here, as well,' Pip told him. 'Cold as a witch's tit some nights.'

Fanny came out after a while and Harry blushed, probably to the roots of his hair only you could not see, so bundled up was he against the weather. At last Spear told him to go and wait in the gig as he had to talk with Pip and Fanny, and the dog watched as Judge left, dividing his time between Spear and Judge, alert and intelligently aware of everything, his body flat, low on the ground.

Pip had always been good, Spear considered: covered himself all ways; knew how to post people on the watch and how to protect himself and others. Now he seemed to have got even better, living out here in this pleasant place. 'Wouldn't do for me, though,' he said. 'Too quiet out here in the sticks, not enough going on.' Away from the city streets and houses, Spear felt unmercifully vulnerable.

'I'm not here to harm you,' he said now that

they faced each other inside the nice room that was the Pagets' parlour: two comfortable chairs pulled up to the fire; a fair-sized circular table and stand chairs; a pair of oil lamps standing on the table; even ornaments on the mantel, which was draped in a cherry-red cloth with a fringe hanging down. There were three little statues – naked women, they looked like – and a glass ball the size of a man's fist, and two little pottery vases.

A looking glass in a gilt frame hung over the mantel, and on one wall were two framed reproductions of paintings: long-haired sheep grazing on a rocky hillside, and some horned cattle crossing a brook. Curtains, a deep red heavy material, hung from brass poles fitted above each window.

'Not here to harm you,' he repeated.

'If you're not here to harm us, Bert Spear, why are you here at all?' Fanny asked in a cool, somewhat calculating, way, her eyes fixed on his face, steady, not shifting. Getting to the heart of it, Spear thought. Fanny did not faff around; she preferred to get straight to the nub of matters.

'We been away for several years,' he began, then launched into the manner in which Moriarty had started to show interest in the whereabouts of the Pagets. 'He ordered me to find you, won't leave it alone. And I found you with little trouble.'

'Do you have to tell him that?' Pip Paget asked. 'That you've found us?'

'Now what's that mean, Pip? You forgotten what it's like to work for him? Forgotten his demands, the ways he has? I have no means of hiding you from him. If you take my advice you'll go. Put distance between you and him. I don't know what he plans, but it can't be good for you. He's a fair master, the Professor–'

'–and I ran out on him,' Pip Paget said, a gloomy edge to his voice.

'As he sees it, Pip, you are a traitor. You gave up one of his greatest secrets to an official enemy. You sold him to the rozzers, Pip.'

Paget gave a solemn nod. 'Aye, I did. Folly. The most foolish thing I ever did. Going without talking to him. But, Bert, I could not have killed for him again – not a defenceless old friend.' And he told them about Kate Wright, one of their own, whom he had been forced to murder, garrotting her with a silk scarf.

The story was so touching that tears started in Fanny's eyes. Fanny had worked close to Kate Wright. 'But Kate and her husband had betrayed the Professor,' she said. 'Really betrayed him.'

'So did we, my dear,' Pip said, matter-of-fact, unemotional.

'We're under threat again now,' Spear told him, and then explained about how Idle Jack had stolen so much, taken over so many areas of Moriarty's organization, his family. 'He's vowed to tip Idle Jack Idell into the sea, smash him utterly, and we've begun to make headway.'

'Then perhaps he won't come after us all that quickly,' Fanny said.

'I would not bank on it, my love,' Paget told her. 'Unless he's a changed, man, he'll come for the easy target first.' Then, turning to Albert Spear, he asked how long he could possibly expect to keep quiet.

'Couple of days at the most. I certainly have to

see him, tomorrow. No doubt about that. He's got something going on, Monday I think. I don't know what it is, but I can't avoid seeing him and he's bound to ask. Knows I am searching for you now. Today.'

They talked on for a good hour, chattering of days gone by, Pip and Fanny Paget telling Spear how they had laid low after getting out of London, then how Pip had reasoned it would be safer if he settled himself close to where Moriarty had property. 'We've made ourselves a good and happy life here,' Fanny said, her voice, to Spear, still soaring and deep, like a well-tuned string instrument. She made some tea, brought out a cake, and invited Harry Judge in to warm himself by the fire.

Finally, almost four in the afternoon, Bert Spear said they must go as it would be getting dark soon, they had to be getting back to the Smoke, and how nice it was to have seen them. As though they were relatives on an afternoon visit. 'I'll do my best to put off that business,' he told them, giving nothing away in front of Judge, out by the gate.

The light was going, and the skeletal trees looked more stark than ever against the squirrel-grey sky that hung over them as they urged little Smudge into a walk, heading back on the long ride to Oxford.

On the road again, Spear glanced back over the flat fields and could just glimpse the Pagets' cottage, where he saw lights starting to come on. He thought of their cozy parlour, and the oil lamps that Fanny would be lighting; how she would be drawing the dark red curtains over the windows, making it cozy for them once the night drew in.

Then, from away behind them, from the big meadow that contained the cattle, he thought he heard the whinny of a horse, and it concerned him because it sounded uncomfortably like the whinny of Archie, Moriarty's horse, though he knew it could not be. There was no time for the Professor to have driven from London. Just impossible, unless he owned some unknown form of travel that simply ate up the miles, that went at some incredible speed.

So they drove on toward Oxford, the air biting cold now and dusk giving way to misty darkness. They passed The White Hart on the edge of Twin Willows, picking up a nice trotting run. Spear would be glad when they were on the train, happier still when back in London.

If he had some magic ability, and was able to return for a moment to the meadow by the track leading to Pip Paget's cottage, Spear might just have made out a figure stepping from the stand of trees out in the middle. A dark figure in a black greatcoat with a fur-edged collar.

'I shall go round to the back, I think,' Moriarty said softly to Daniel Carbonardo, who remained with their horses deep among the trees.

'That 'ud be your best way, Professor. Round the back and in through their kitchen door. I'll keep an eye on the front.'

Moriarty started to pace silently through the meadow, heading for the track and the cottages that lay beyond. The evening mist was coming up, hanging heavy near the ground. Carbonardo thought the Professor looked as creepy as some avenging ghost advancing, floating gently above the grass, moving inexorably toward the cottage.

14

The Pagets and Their Future

OXFORDSHIRE & LONDON:
JANUARY 20, 1900

Moriarty had been with Spear, Judge, and the Pagets for most of the day, waiting and watching, and this was all thanks to Wally Taplin, who had overheard Albert Spear talking to Harry Judge that morning, early, outside the back door. The Professor expected Wally to report any interesting conversations, and often tipped him well if the exchange was important enough. 'You are my one good spy now, Walter,' he told the boy. 'You must live up to the high expectations I have of you. You must always walk in my ways.'

One of the things Wally liked about Professor Moriarty was that he often talked like the Sunday school teachers talked when he was in the home for boys, after his parents had gone. He did not particularly like the home, but he did like the certainty presented to him at Sunday school. In the end everything was going to be all right, forever and ever, amen. That was a good and helpful thought.

Moriarty knew well enough what comfort his boys, men, and women drew from the pious words spoken in church, from the Bible and the prayer book; he was well aware of the way the archbishops, bishops, and priests went about their work. Indeed, he had used this knowledge in allowing Lee Chow to see him dance with the devil by celebrating a Black Mass. You can control people with eternal promises, he thought, make them do exactly as you wanted. So why shouldn't he control in that manner also? Religion offered a giant prize in return for dull humiliation in life, and they could well be right. The Professor, in turn, promised a satisfactory life with enough money and safeguards if you remained true to him, to James Moriarty – if you did what he asked, used your skills in his service. Moriarty without end, amen. Fear and promise were two sides of the same coin. To mix metaphors, it was the carrot and the stick: exactly what religion did.

That morning Wally had wanted to pee and he slipped out the kitchen back door, as opposed to the house back door along the passage. He had decided to pee outside, in the bushes round the back, because he was averse to following Terremant into the downstairs lav in the mornings. This was wise, because following Terremant anywhere after he had been out on the booze, round the pubs looking for the Professor's backsliders, could be daunting.

So, Wally nipped outside, unbuttoned, and had his slash into the bushes. It was during this procedure that he heard Spear come out of the back door and engage in conversation with the Beak –

as they called Harry Judge, beak being the general slang for a judge, so they thought it a mite witty to call Harry the Beak.

'*We're going for a trip out; going on the monkery, Harry.*'

'*Where, boss?*'

'*Out Oxford way. Going to look up an old chum...*'

'*...If the roads aren't clear we'll just have a nice dinner in some tavern; quaff some ale and come home again.*'

'*That sounds more like it.*'

This was the conversation Wally reported back to Professor Moriarty, who was well pleased, tipped him half a tosheroon, and told him to send Mr. Carbonardo up. 'Good boy,' he said, giving Wally's hair a ruffle. 'Very good boy.'

Wally Taplin came back into the kitchen after giving the message to Danny Carbonardo, delighted with himself, clutching the silver half-crown. Not seeing Terremant, who was in one of the larger sculleries, and thinking himself alone, Wally lifted a leg and broke wind, loudly in the key of G, and sniggered, as boys do.

'You dirty little bugger.' Terremant came out of the scullery. 'When I was a boy...'

Bloody hell, Taplin thought, *here he goes again.* Terremant was forever harping on about when he was a boy, trying to draw parallels with his childhood, a tack that did not succeed because his experience of childhood was in a different age, at a different time, so you could not draw any conclusions by placing one against the other. The world had moved on.

'When I was a boy in Cumberland, learning to be a pugilist, if you did what you just done the

269

other lads would gather round and pinch you, pull your hair, punch you, kick your shins, stamp on your toes and chant–

'Rannel me! Rannel me!
Grey goose egg,
Let every man lift up a leg,
By the high, by the low,
By the buttocks of a crow,
Fish, cock or hen?

'Then, if the answer be "cock" they would shout, "Give him a good knock." If "fish," it was "Spit in his face." So you think on, lad. Could be better these days, but stop your arse from singing when I'm around.'

'Yes, Mr. Terremant. Sorry, Mr. Terremant.' Wally had learned to be polite with Jim Terremant because he had big hands and was not averse to catching you a thump round the earhole. Wally turned away, about to shed a tear because he would have liked to share this with Billy Walker, make him laugh, but he was never going to be able to do that ever again. This made him deeply sad.

'Well, he's going in the right direction,' Moriarty said to Danny Carbonardo when he came up-stairs. Then he explained that he had sent Bert Spear looking for Pip Paget. Of course it was not a question of looking for Paget, because Moriarty – with his army of knarks – knew exactly where Paget was. So, once more it was a question of test-ing Albert Spear's loyalty.

'We shall follow at a discreet distance,' the Pro-fessor said. 'Train to Oxford, then on horseback

270

to see what they're playing at.' Hoping against hope that Spear was being straight with him. He didn't know what he would do if Spear had turned traitor.

Already he knew exactly what he would do about Pip Paget.

Presently the Professor came down and summoned Daniel Carbonardo to go out with him, and while Daniel was getting into his ulster, the Professor told Wally that he would soon be having company again. 'I've told Mr. Spear to bring over the boy Sam who used to be at the Glenmoragh Hotel, the boot boy. He's coming to work with you here, and it will be your business to teach him manners and show him how to behave.'

After they had gone, Terremant said that he did not think Sam the boot boy would be much of an addition to the household. 'I reckon you'll have your work cut out learning that boy,' he told Wally. 'I reckon that Sam is a quarter-flash to three parts stupid.'

Moriarty and Danny Carbonardo did not call for Ben Harkness but hailed a hansom at the street corner close to The Duke of York, instructing the cabbie to take them to Paddington station, where they caught the first available train to Oxford.

They travelled first class. Moriarty always travelled first unless he was in a disguise that prevented it, and they found a compartment on their own, where Moriarty held out at length to Carbonardo about Pip Paget and his wife, Fanny.

'I want you to remember, Daniel,' he said finally, a couple of minutes before the train pulled into

Oxford station, 'whatever's said and done in the end, when he has served his purpose Pip Paget will be *your* business. He lives now on time loaned to him by me. He is alive only by my generosity of spirit. He is a dead man living. You understand?'

'Perfectly, guv'nor.' Carbonardo gave a little nod, just a simple, single inclination of the head that would not even be noticed if they were being clandestinely observed.

Once at Oxford, Moriarty headed to the livery stable he always used in that university city, near the railway station; he had used it years ago, on that fatal picnic near The Rose Revived public house when he had done away with the Draughtsman. Now he hired a pair of horses: a spry little roan for Carbonardo and a big black gelding for himself. While making the arrangements, he questioned the owner of the stables about others who had hired horses that day and so learned of the two men who had taken the gig a couple of hours earlier. From the descriptions, they were obviously Spear and his man Harry Judge.

'We'd best go by a circumlocutious route,' he told Carbonardo, and led them along side roads and across fields, finally coming out in Steventon itself, where they stopped for some fifteen minutes. Then across the fields once more, down to Willow Manor and so crossing Sir John Grant's estate, ending in the glade of trees that gave summer shade to Sir John's cattle in the four-acre meadow but was today bleakly chilling to the marrow, tree branches slick with ice.

The wait was long and numbingly cold, relieved

only by the bread, cheese, and brandy that Moriarty had bought for them at The Swan in Steventon. Finally, however, as the winter light died and the mist unfurled over the grass of the meadow, as Tom the cowman came down and herded the beasts off for milking – the milk, Moriarty thought, would certainly come frozen in a pail today – so they saw Pip and Fanny Paget leave the cottage with Albert Spear and Harry Judge, all talking together a mite too friendly for the professor's liking.

Don't let him see you, he had counselled.

Inside the cottage, in the parlour, Fanny and Pip Paget now settled down for a quiet evening, talking amicably in front of the fire. Fanny had some thick bacon rashers in the kitchen cold safe built into the wall at the back of the house and screened with tight metal mesh. She planned to do them in the oven for a nice supper later, with mashed potatoes, cabbage, and an onion sauce, because Pip adored her onion sauce and, since they had been here on the Willow Manor estate, she was able to do it properly using butter and fresh milk, which they were never without.

But tonight Fanny was, not unnaturally, deeply concerned. 'Does Mr. Spear worry you?' she asked now, as Pip leaned forward to give the fire a poke and pat Snapper as the dog made himself more comfortable, curling and settling himself on the mat to doze.

After a moment's pause for reflection, he said, 'The Professor worries me far more than Bert Spear.' He straightened up and reached over to clasp her hand. 'Life has been ... what's the word

273

I'm searching for, Dove?' It was his favourite word for her, Dove.

'Peaceful? Tranquil? Idyllic... ?'

'All three of them and more besides.'

'And now it is over, Pip. That's what you want to say, is it not?'

'I don't *want* to say it, my Dove, but it is what must be said.'

'We are just going to walk out on Sir John and Lady Pam?'

'What option have we? I think we must go, and the sooner the better. To France, maybe. I hear there's a community of English gentlefolk there in the south at a place called Mentone, got their own church, like an English village church and everything. We'd be bound to get places there with some family, and the weather is clement.'

Fanny nodded, not even attempting to hide the tears starting in her eyes.

'Look, Fan,' he said quickly. 'We talked about this some time ago. When we first came here. We knew it would not last.'

'Could not last,' she said. 'But now it has...'

Snapper, the dog, was suddenly alert, rising up and growling, pointing toward the kitchen door, his right paw raised in expectation. Anyone could walk in through the back door, be in the kitchen in a trice; folk around here had no reason to lock their doors.

Pip got to his feet, standing, silent, moving behind his chair. Fanny, who had been seeing to some mending, dropped it into her lap and looked around, noting that one of the shotguns was in its usual place in the corner. Then her hands flew to

274

her face as both sections of the kitchen door swung back and, as though by some theatrical illusion, James Moriarty stepped into the room, his presence almost electrifying, certainly commanding; he was carrying his silver-topped cane and wearing his half-tall top hat, the long, bulky black greatcoat with its handsome fur collar, and a white silk scarf around his neck, stylishly tucked inside the coat.

'Sit down, Pip. I have not come to kill you.' A little bow. 'And good evening to you, Fanny.' He began to remove his soft, hand-stitched leather gloves.

Snapper's growl became louder, the dog crouching, baring his teeth, ready to spring. Moriarty gave a low-pitched whistle, a hissing sound, one arm moving, a finger pointing. The dog gave a little yelp and trotted over to sit in the corner to which the finger had been pointing. The Professor's uncanny mesmeristic skill spread to the control of animals, legendary among those close to him. 'Are you going to invite me in, Pip? Fanny?' he asked, calm and not unfriendly.

Paget's eyes flitted toward the door.

'Do not even consider it,' the Professor cautioned, his face like stone, the eyes still and heartless. 'I have Daniel Carbonardo at the front. You recall Danny the Tweezers, Pip?'

Paget remembered Carbonardo as a confident who lived apart from Moriarty's family. He remembered him as a short man, splendidly fit, always glowing with good health; a man with sallow good looks, adored by women. What he remembered most were the screams.

275

'Come, let us sit together.' Moriarty took Paget's vacated chair and Fanny slowly got to her feet, indicating her chair to her husband, who sat in it, with Fanny sinking and finally squatting on the floor at his feet.

'So, here we are.' Moriarty smiled at them, like a father happy to embrace his family; he ran his right thumbnail down his cheek, from just under the eye to the jawline.

'Let us get right to the heart of matters. Albert Spear has been to see you today. What had he to say for himself?' He raised a hand as though to stop them speaking immediately. 'I should tell you that I bade good Spear not to let you see him. Not to show himself to you. Yet it is obvious he did.'

'He couldn't help himself, Professor. He is more used to city ways. I had him here, over a barrel as they say. Well, over two barrels – the shotgun, that is.' He tried a cheeky smile, and Moriarty nodded, showing that he understood.

'I have good friends here,' Paget continued, 'and was warned so that I got to him, rather than him getting to me.'

Moriarty gave a grim smile and a nod. 'I can understand that. You were always exceptionally good at your work, Pip. When you disappeared after your wedding it was like someone vanishing and leaving no trace. It took several months for me even to get a whiff of you, and then only because Sir John Grant is a good and valued friend. Now, both of you. Do you admit to your sin of disappearing from my employment? Do you admit to the manifold sins and wickedness which you have committed most grievously by thought, word, and deed?'

'It was my fault, sir. I take the full blame. Never was it Fanny here.'

'So.' He appeared to be weighing up the situation. 'You put me at risk, Pip Paget, and you have both provoked my wrath and indignation. Can you show any sorrow for what you have done? Can you repent?'

Fanny gave a little sob, and Pip looked at her, saw the tears, and felt a little indignation of his own. 'I repent. Sincerely,' Fanny said, her eyes downcast.

'And you, Pip Paget. Is there any reason for me not to set Daniel on to you?'

'I betrayed you, Professor. I knew what I was doing and I have dreaded this moment of meeting you again. Coming face to face with you. I know you have extreme ways of punishing those who are disloyal.'

'Can you show any repentance, sorrow for what you have done?'

A whole album of pictures ran through Paget's mind: the times he knew of when Moriarty had ordered the deaths of those who had crossed him. In the back of his head he heard words from the past, in the Professor's quiet voice: 'You have played the crooked cross with me, so be it.' Names floated through his head, people he had known who could still be alive today had it not been for them crossing Moriarty.

'Of course I'm sorry, sir. Anyone would be sorry to offend you as I have. God knows I've been looking over my shoulder ever since.'

'So you can promise me repentance?'

'Sorrow, sir. Yes.'

'And to go back, what did Albert Spear have to say to you?'

'He told me that you were looking for me, and that he had found me, and that was not hard. He would have to tell you where I was.'

'He give you any advice?'

Paget shook his head. There was no point dropping Spear into the sewers that wait for all men to drown in.

'So, when you looked over your shoulder for all those years, Pip, what did you eventually expect to see?'

Paget did not know if he could explain it; he wondered if he had the words to draw the nightmares that sometimes disturbed him, even when he was not asleep. 'I expected some terrible creature, sir. Some fanged hound coming at me out of the night, its teeth dripping and its eyes on fire wanting vengeance.'

'So, I am reduced to a hound? A dog? Some mythical beast?'

'No, sir. I was bound to you by oath. *Am* bound to you. I would expect you to look for a terrible revenge because I broke that oath.'

Moriarty nodded as if in agreement.

'Well.' He turned to Fanny, smiled at her, then looked at Paget. 'Whatever happens between us, Pip, I trust Fanny will return and work for me. I have so missed her cooking, and besides, in my London house I am having my kitchen rebuilt especially for her.'

Fanny's head was raised, slightly cocked to one side, arrogance guttering in her eyes. 'You did so many good things for me, sir. You stood by me and paid off that black-hearted butler who tried to take advantage of me and then had me thrown out of my place. You were good to me and Pip, helped us with our marriage...'

'I was like a father to you both, Fanny, and I wouldn't have you forget it.' Moriarty's voice was rising, cracking stern now.

'If you do something terrible to my love, Pip Paget, I'll never come near your house again, Professor,' she said with huge affirmation. 'You do away with Pip and you must do away with me also.'

A good, spunky girl, Moriarty thought. *The kind of girl I need by my side.* He hoped against all hopes that Sal Hodges would bear witness in the same way should Idle Jack wish her to come under his employ.

Aloud he gave a little nervous laugh. 'Pip, you would surely expect some kind of penance, some way to expiate the huge and mortal sin of your betrayal?'

'Of course, sir. I would do anything to make it right. I am heart-sore and sorry.'

'Then maybe there is one way.' James Moriarty looked him down. The eyes that had the power to drug a man bored into Paget's brain, making him want to telescope into himself and so disappear.

'One of my Praetorian Guard is, even now as we speak, betraying me. I know one way of catching out this man, but I would rather find him fair, run him down by stealth within my family.' He took a long and deep draught of air. 'Philip Paget, I want you to come back and take your place, your old place, in my Guard; and from there I will charge you to winkle out the traitor in our midst. If you do that, then I shall pronounce complete forgiveness and raise you to the highest position within the family. If you don't or can't do it, then I'll see you crushed, and your wife with you.'

Paget and Fanny exchanged a look, both knowing that once more they had little option. To survive, Pip had to take on the task. Quietly he said, 'I shall do it, to the best of my ability, Professor,' and, without even thinking about it, he took Moriarty's right hand, raised it to his lips, and kissed the signet ring on his finger: a sign that, once again, he was owning to the Professor as his master, his liege lord, the one he would obey and defend through thick and thin.

Following her husband's example, Fanny curtseyed and kissed the Professor's ring, knowing deep within herself that this would be their last chance, that Moriarty was being uncharacteristically merciful, and that if matters went wrong again, Professor James Moriarty would leave no stone unturned to see them both crushed, obliterated from both this life and the next. She had heard it from Pip, who often told her, 'He'll have us killed and after that he will extract the worst possible vengeance on us. He will have our bodies burned so that all hope of the Blessed Resurrection will be gone for us.'

Followers of the One True, Holy Catholic and Apostolic Church believed that to burn the physical body made it impossible – except for those martyrs miraculously saved – to be raised from the dead and made one with Our Lord Jesus Christ on the Day of Judgement. The expunging of the flesh and excommunication from Holy Church were the two most terrible punishments that could be meted out on a Christian man or woman. Moriarty was careful; most of his key followers had been Roman Catholics, or at least held the Catholic beliefs.

Pip Paget, one such, put on a contented look, his face suffused with goodwill. Inside, he felt nothing but dread, because he knew Moriarty, probably better than most men. The promises made by the Professor were so out of character with the man he knew that it was impossible for him to believe in the olive branch Moriarty had offered them.

The Professor believes I have the skill and cunning to entrap whoever is betraying him within his Praetorian Guard, he reasoned. *Once I have done his bidding he will dispose of me with as much emotion as he would show in swatting a fly away from his food. I am a means to an end: no more, no less. I have shown a certain weakness, a lack of complete trust, so Moriarty will never have faith in either me or my Dove, Fanny, ever again. The trick will be to outfence him and get us away from his circle of dominance before the axe falls.*

Moriarty clasped both of them in a tight embrace, then told them that there was much work to be done. 'You will have to be at this address,' he said, handing Pip Paget a discreet business card that omitted his name but showed the address. 'I would suggest you arrive at the back door before eight in the morning—'

281

'Tomorrow?' Fanny cried. 'That soon?' Then again, 'Tomorrow?'

'That is entirely your choice.' Moriarty did not even look at her.

'We have a meeting of the Guard at eight in the morning. I would like you there. Go to the back door, Terremant will let you in, and Fanny, you can start in the kitchen. I shall leave money. I am known locally as Mr. P. That is the only name by which I am known. I trust you will come, and I look forward to seeing you. Good night.'

He left behind him a kind of emptiness, as if his bulk, his quiddity, had removed air from the house. For one split second Pip Paget thought that he caught the man's essence, a trace of French cologne, the quick burn of cognac in his throat, and an eerie sense that he could feel the white silk scarf running through his fingers. His voice also seemed to linger. *'I trust you will come.'*

Idle Jack had been out with Broad Darryl Wood. Using a trusted cabbie, they had done the rounds of his best places – the knocking houses, drinking dens, bucket shops, and nightclubs where his word held sway. He was a little perturbed, because it was obvious that a slight trickle of men and women had begun to return to Moriarty's camp, though it had not yet become a haemorrhage.

Now, Jack thought hard and long about the situation. He had, some time ago, put out a plea to other leaders of criminal factions in Europe for a meeting in London proposing an alliance, just as Moriarty had done some years before. As yet none of them had responded.

One thing was plain to him. It was necessary to crush Moriarty and so loosen the hold the Professor had on a large section of the criminal underworld.

Broad Darryl Wood was not given his soubriquet in any reference to his physique. He was broad of neither chest nor shoulders. The fact was that Wood had been an excellent, even legendary broadsman, a card sharp, leader of the famous broad mob that had operated in some of the more louche gambling dens around Bond Street. Now he sat, dozing before the fire burning gaily in the withdrawing room of Jack Idell's house in Bedford Square.

Jack woke him, shaking him hard by the shoulder, bringing a hot toddy to warm him thoroughly before going to his bed.

'I have made a decision, Darryl,' he said, his eyes glinting in the firelight. 'A momentous decision.'

'About what, Sir Jack?' Wood was always careful to address his leader by his title. Idle Jack could be touchy when it came to what he thought of as his place in society.

'About James Moriarty. About the so-called Professor. I have come to a decision about Moriarty.'

'Well?'

And as Idle Jack Idell told him what he planned, Darryl Wood's face became as grave as the tomb. 'I will not do that,' he said at last.

'Not until the summer,' Idle Jack said with his sinister twisted smile. 'Give things a chance to settle down first.'

'I could never risk doing that, even for you, Sir Jack.' Wood looked troubled.

'I don't expect you to do it, my friend. I've already decided. I am going to get Micah Rowledge to do it.'

Micah Rowledge had the emotions of a stone. His first position, some years ago now, had been working for a notorious baby farmer. His particular job had been strangling unwanted newborn babies.

It was said that Micah had loved his work, could not get enough of it.

15

Georgie Porgie

LONDON: JANUARY 21, 1900

Spear was not on time for the meeting of Moriarty's so-called Praetorian Guard due to be held at eight o'clock on Sunday morning. He had to go to Pembroke Gardens, Kensington, to catch Perry Gwyther before the solicitor set out for church with his wife, Alice, and their daughter, Lena. Gwyther was still in his dressing gown, having breakfast – coffee, kedgeree, kidneys, and toast – in the dining room, and Spear felt out of place telling him that he was to buy the warehouse first thing Monday, and to inform the Professor as soon as it was done.

Gwyther was a kind of wall, a barricade, between Moriarty and officialdom in its many and varied forms. The Professor often felt that, if it came to it, Perry Gwyther could prove beyond all doubt that James Moriarty had never existed.

Spear shuffled his feet, looking down at his boots as they then talked, for some twenty minutes, about Gwyther's recommendation of an architect: a man by the name of Iain Hunter, a large, gentle fellow, but most skilful according to Gwyther.

'We want it just like it was last time – in Limehouse,' Spear said.

'Fellow who designed that hung up his boots some years back,' Gwyther told him between mouthfuls of kedgeree. 'Tell Hunter exactly what you want and he will do you a good job – oversee the builders and everything.'

Spear was, therefore, not at the Professor's house when Pip and Fanny Paget arrived just after seven, let in through the back door by Jim Terremant, who had been warned and had instructions to take them straight up to the Professor.

Terremant thought Fanny Paget looked washed out and tired, as though she had been up all night. Which in fact she had.

Moriarty was having breakfast with Sal Hodges, during which he outlined to her his requirements for later in the week.

'In all probability it will be Wednesday,' he told her. 'I will know later tomorrow, but, whatever day, my needs will be the same – six of your prettiest girls: young, big-eyed, and willing to have photographic likenesses taken of them *au naturel*, possibly with a male installed, if you follow me.

Eyes the size of cow's eyes would be good – eyes that look like a fellow could drown in them.'

Sal smiled sweetly. 'I think I shall have the right girls for you, my dear James. Who is the man?'

Moriarty shook his head. 'Not in your interest to know, but we shall be using a studio I have hired in St. Giles's. You will want to be there, of course?'

'I shall have to look after my girls' interests, my dear; of course I will.'

'And *my* interests, Sal, my love? What of them?' He looked her straight in the eyes and laid one hand over hers, resting on the table.

For a moment, Sal Hodges was mystified; she did not know how to reply. 'Your interests are mine, of course, James my dear,' she said eventually.

'Then I believe we should take a bold step.' His eyes never leaving hers.

'Yes?' she said, still mystified.

'You have borne me a child, Sal. We live more or less as man and wife. I think we should regularize the situation.'

'You think...?'

'Yes.' He smiled the most wonderful smile, lighting up not just his eyes, but his whole face, crinkling the corners of his eyes and revealing the laughter lines at the edges of his mouth. The kind of smile that men and women dream of when thinking about those most private, intimate, and romantic thoughts. 'I am suggesting that, when we have finally bought another warehouse, and it has been altered to my specifications, we should marry.'

Sal dropped her right hand to her breast, her

mouth shaping a letter *O*, as she took in a swift, almost involuntary breath.

But at that moment, Terremant tapped on the door, ushering Pip and Fanny into the room.

'So, Pip, you have taken the wiser course?' the Professor said. 'I greet you, and salute your common sense.' Then, turning to Fanny, he told her that she was to take immediate charge of the running of the house, particularly the cooking. 'I have left a purse with several sovereigns on the kitchen table,' he told her. 'Terremant will show you. And, Tom,' speaking to Terremant, whom he still refused to call by his proper name, Jim, 'when Spear arrives with the boy Sam, you are to tell him and Wally Taplin here that they must obey Mrs. Paget to the letter.' He turned to Taplin, who was serving the breakfast. 'You understand that, Walter. You are to do as Mrs. Paget tells you. You will meet Sam shortly and he will tell you what happens to boys who do not do my bidding, eh, Tom?'

'I've already told him, but I don't think the little bug ... boy believes me, Professor.'

'Disabuse him, then. And I shall want to see the boy, Sam, after we have held our meeting. Go now; you also, Fanny; and you, Wally. Go with Mr. Terremant.'

Terremant was somewhat bewildered, and had been from the moment he had found the Pagets on the doorstep. 'Very well, Professor,' he burbled, betraying the fact that he could not understand how this could be – Paget being welcomed back into Moriarty's household. It made no sense to him. After all, it was less than a week ago that Moriarty had spoken disparagingly of Pip Paget, a speech that had been whispered among the gang, more or less verbatim:

Pip Paget saved my life. Shot a murderous skunk dead and saved my life, yet he'd already betrayed me. Me, who was a father to him, who had been present at his wedding, stood for him, provided his marital feast, blessed his union with another member of my organiz-ation ... my family... It is meet and right for those who earn their stipend through me to know of my justice.

'As soon as friend Spear decides to put in an appearance we'll start our meeting.' Moriarty's words were laced with sarcasm, and he gave a dismissive gesture of the hand, leaving no doubt that he wanted to be alone with Paget.

'I will help you take the breakfast things down, Mr. Terremant,' Sal Hodges said, brightly start-ing to assist in clearing the crockery away in a manner that made Taplin, Terremant, and Fanny Paget move to help.

Terremant felt sinful stirrings of lust as he brushed past Fanny Paget, catching a tiny trace of the clean, clear scent she wore. It reminded him of the lemon aroma he had often caught when in the vicinity of well-bred ladies in Paris – different from the cologne worn by the Professor, and certainly more affecting than the cheap perfumes used by the girls he was often close to in the Professor's houses. Fanny Paget put about her a veritable scent of heat and Terremant appreciated it, as indeed did his loins; it was the most robust case of Irish toothache he had experienced for many a long day. Go on at this rate, he thought, and he would have to visit Delilah, the slim, little dark girl with the amazing thighs who worked in Sal Hodges's House. She would pull his tooth for him and no mistake.

Yet it set Terremant thinking as to how a game-keeper – because that, he understood, had been Pip Paget's work lately – could supply his wife with a delicious French perfume. He could do with some of that himself; those perfumes were worth gold as gifts to some of the perfect ladies who worked Moriarty's houses. He would have to put down a lure, perhaps.

Then, within the hour, Bert Spear arrived downstairs with the boy Sam, whom Terremant had last seen when they had lifted him from the Glenmoragh Private Hotel the day he and Spear had given the lad the hiding of his life. He was pleased to see that young Sam was quiet and respectful, and that he moved forward to shake hands with Wally Taplin when they were introduced one to the other.

This did not stop Terremant giving the pair a short homily on the way they would be expected to behave. 'And you'll do everything and anything Mrs. Paget instructs you,' he ended. 'And if you don't I've no doubt she'll inform me, or Mr. Paget, and the Professor will require me to dispense his particularly harsh punishment, same as they do it in them public schools. Understand me?'

'Yes, Mr. Terremant,' the boys chorused, like pupils conning a lesson by rote in one of the board schools.

'Old Terremant's bark is worse than his bite,' Wally told Sam when they were left alone a moment later, after Fanny Paget had slipped off down the shops on her own. 'Clip around the ear

289

occasionally, but nothing worse to speak of.'

'I would not like to risk it.' Sam sounded most serious, and explained the circumstances of his error, and its aftermath, that night when the boys were becoming good friends, now sharing one of the smaller rooms down in the kitchen area.

'You mean Mr. Spear flogged you?' Wally could hardly credit it.

'Mr. Spear and Mr. Terremant both. I still bear the weals,' and Sam lifted his nightshirt and showed Wally Taplin the stripes and bruises remaining on the cheeks of his backside.

'Bloody hell, like railway lines!' Taplin was well impressed with the brutality.

'Mr. Spear's told me since that it is the Professor's way,' Sam said, starting to be a little proud of having come through such an ordeal. 'I would never cross him again, Moriarty. That's learned me my lesson.'

But much had happened between Sam and the Professor since the morning, things he could not and would not share with Walter on pain of much worse than a flogging.

Yet the intelligence from Sam had set Wally Taplin to thinking, and he resolved to watch himself from now on.

Before the meeting began, Moriarty sent for Fanny once more, bidding her send the boys to The Duke of York to fetch jugs of porter. He also asked her to prepare a tray and put out one of his best bottles of brandy with a bottle of Champagne. If his men were to have porter, the Professor decided that he would have his share of Champagne cocktails, his choice being the

Vauban Frères Champagne of which the family had a huge supply, squirreled away over the years from consignments diverted from their original destinations by bribery and the more barefaced forms of violent robbery.

By nine o'clock the Guard were finally gathered upstairs, an hour late for the meeting: Spear, Terremant, Ember, and Lee Chow were all shaking hands with, and welcoming back, Pip Paget.

'Never thought to see you again, Pip,' Ember told him.

''Tis a sign of the Professor's mercy. He's a true gentleman,' Paget told them, looking mightily relieved and speaking loud enough to let Moriarty hear.

Daniel Carbonardo, who had also been summoned to the meeting, sat to one side, not at the round table, as if to signify that he would remain slightly apart from the Guard as such.

As he took his seat, Lee Chow grinned his evil grin. 'Now 'ee ar sit at lound table. Rike the knights of King Althu'. Rong ago,' he carefully enunciated.

'That is good, my Chinese friend.' Moriarty nodded to him. Then he quoted some Alfred, Lord Tennyson:

'Live pure, speak true, right wrong, follow the
   King–
Else, wherefore born?'

The five men looked at one another, not knowing the words came from Tennyson's Arthurian poem *Idylls of the King*, so not following its significance. Daniel Carbonardo smiled to himself. The Professor could be a terrible romantic at times, and often saw his way of life, and those around him, as good and quite the reverse of their reality in the wicked world. Carbonardo knew that Moriarty was adept at deceiving even himself of the true facts of evil. In his master's mind, the words he had just spoken probably transposed themselves into 'Live impure, speak lies, wrong rights, follow Professor Moriarty. That is what you are born to perform.'

The Professor brought the meeting to order, first welcoming Pip Paget back to what he described as 'his rightful place.' He then continued, 'Terremant, you recall the man I met a number of times when you were guarding me in Vienna?'

'Indeed, sir. Yes I do.'

'And you would recognize him again?'

'Of course, Professor. Recognize him like shot.'

'Good. Then take four of Ember's best lurkers with you and get down to Dover in the morning. That gentleman will be arriving on the packet from Calais, due to dock at Dover, midday. He will then be making his onward journey to London by the boat train. You are to stay with him, at a distance. Protect him and give him help should he need it.' He looked around his men before his eyes alighted on little Ember, and he continued:

'Ember, you will also take four good lurkers and be ready to take over this man from Terremant here, when he shepherds him into Victoria Station. I warn you both that you must take the utmost care: Do not make obvious signals, for you may be watched; and be careful should it be necessary to speak to one another. I would suggest that you use a cipher to describe the gentleman you are to watch. Nursery rhymes are the easiest to remember, so maybe we should call him "Little Boy Blue." You understand?'

They all nodded, and Lee Chow spoke aloud. 'Ah, Ritter Boy Brue,' he said. And again, 'Ritter Boy Brue.'

'He's the one what blew up his horn,' Ember said, somewhat lasciviously.

'Quite right, Ember. Quite right.' The Professor, unsmiling, glanced around the table again, then asked for individual reports.

Both Spear and Terremant, sounding most happy, said that the backsliders returning to the Professor's employ seemed to have built into a steady flow. 'Word is getting around,' Terremant told them. 'Now, I don't have to issue any threats at all. You are back, Professor, and they know it; there is general happiness about that. Last night, for instance, everyone down Cheapside knew you are here in London, and they was all keen to make sure you knew they had come back, true to you.'

The Professor looked pleased and gave out a farthing's worth of praise; then he asked how matters were in King Street, meaning at the house where Detective Inspector Angus McCready Crow lived with his wife, formerly the widow Mrs. Sylvia Cowels.

It was Spear who answered. 'The people I've put on there – Cresswell, Dixon, Roberts, and Wilson – all say the same thing, Professor. They reckon Mr. Crow is getting short of money. Almost coals, some say. Mrs. Crow is running him ragged; never

293

rests, always out at the shops. Buying much on tick, and the bills all wait to be paid. She is beggaring him.'

'And his contact with Holmes?'

'None. Nor while we were abroad either. Cresswell and Dixon kept a loose watch all the time we were away. There were no reports of contact with Holmes.'

'That's all to the good then.'

Lee Chow appeared to be puzzled, preoccupied. Suddenly he asked, 'Rittle Boy Brue? Where he rive when we bling him in London, chop-chop. We bling him hea'?'

'No,' Moriarty explained carefully. 'No. He is to come with you to Captain Ratford's place, where you are living. Keep him well hidden there; I do not want to see him abroad on the streets. Provide him with any luxury he requires. Understand, Bert?' His eyes gimleted into Spear's head, as though carrying some special message physically into his brain.

'I'll see to it, Chief,' Spear remarked. 'You need have no fears on that score, sir.'

Moriarty nodded in a sage manner, then asked if there were any other matters they wanted to air at this point and they began muttering one to another, exchanging ideas, as Moriarty ran a thumbnail down his cheek, from a little below the eye to his jawline. Then his head moved, reptilian-like, from side to side for almost a full minute as he waited.

A shade too loudly, Terremant spoke to Pip Paget. 'A fine French perfume your wife Fanny's wearing, Pip. How does a gamekeeper go around buying that kind of bottled juice?'

Paget did not seem in any way perturbed. 'I have a good friend who is first mate on a barque that often calls into a French port on its way back from longer journeys.'

Moriarty seemed suddenly most interested. 'What's the name of this ship and her captain, Pip?'

'She's the *Colleen of Cork*, out of Plymouth usually, Professor. Captain name of Michael Trewinard, Devonshire man. His first mate a man called Carpenter. Bernard Carpenter. I know about the captain because Mr. Carpenter's told me about him. Lived at one time in the village of Twin Willows, on Sir John Grant's estate – Bernard Carpenter, that is. It was Sir John who introduced me to him. A nice, good-hearted man who brings in things like perfume, silk, and the like and sells them off cheap – no excise duty, I suppose.'

Moriarty's hand went to his face once more, and he again ran his thumbnail down his cheek, as far as the jawline. '*Colleen of Cork*,' he said, as if musing. 'You know who that captain works his ship for, Pip?'

'Well, hisself I suppose.'

'No!' The head movement from side to side again, as though the great man had started to become anxious. 'No, Pip. Captain Trewinard, and his crew, and I suppose his first mate also, work for someone else. They work for Idle Jack, bringing in youngsters, children – girls mostly – to satisfy the lusts of Idle Jack's customers.'

A few moments later, Moriarty gave another

295

instruction after some careful questions: 'Bert Spear, who do you trust more, your man Judge, or George Gittins? Glittering George Gittins?'

'I trust both of them equally, Chief.'

'Let us use Gittins, then. I want him to pick a team of loyal men, as many as he thinks he will require. He is to put a permanent watch on Idle Jack's house in Bedford Square, front and rear. This is to be quiet, no flash moves, nothing that will stand out, but he is to watch, mark, and learn, make note, deduce what is going on.'

Spear said he understood and would see to it.

'Get him up here, Bert. Get him here today. I shall need to speak with him. Instruct him in certain matters.'

Then each of them in turn, except for Pip Paget, began to go through all the people who had expressed a wish to talk face to face with the Professor. Spear ticked names off with his fingers: 'Knight and Richards want to talk about a blagging they have in mind; Stimpson, Taylor, Murch, and Smith all wish to talk over various matters. Then Amy Stencil, Gertie Ward, and Emma Baisley kept me for nearly an hour last night. They have a proposition to put forward that is good, worth thinking about.' He explained that they had this clever idea: advertising for men visiting London on their own and wishing to have a lady for company – nicely spoken, well turned out, and intelligent young women. 'Good conversation and all that, just to go out around the town. No strings attached; go to the theatre, have dinner, what have you. Flat fee paid directly to the business. If the man wants more, then the girl is free to indicate her willingness – or not, as the case may be. You follow, Professor?'

'This sounds promising. Yes, of course I will see them, and I shall talk with Sal about the idea.'

Ember had a man called Roger Prince who reckoned he had been swindled by two other members of the family and wanted to see justice done; while Lee Chow was desirous of the Professor meeting a young Anglo-Chinese girl called Jeannie Chang, with whom he was seriously thinking of setting up house, wanting the Professor's blessing first. 'She good housekeeping, and make excerrent bang-bang in the night – a'ways wirring.'

The others tried to hide their smiles, and 'a'ways wirring' became a catch phrase after the manner of George Robey's famous 'Kindly temper your hilarity with a modicum of reserve.'

At just before midday, the meeting finally broke up, but only after Moriarty had given vent to a heavy head of ire. 'There are four ships,' he told them. 'I grant you had no way of knowing, Pip; the *Colleen of Cork* is but one. The others – so you will know next time – are *Midnight Kiss*, with her captain, Ebeneezer Jephcote. There is also William Evans and his craft, *Sea Dancer;* also Captain Corny Trebethik, a fine Cornishman this time – he has a barque named *Pride of the Morning*. All four of them work for Idle Jack Idell, and I would be obliged if you would all do me a great service. Put your heads together, and so decide how we can put an end to this vile trade in children. For mark me, that is what these ships are for; their cargos are

297

children, nothing but children, set aside for unnatural practises. Think about it. Then come and tell me what we should do.'

At fifteen minutes past noon, Sam knocked at the door and came in to face the Professor, exactly as he had been instructed to do by Terremant.

'Ah, my boy.' Moriarty gave the lad a welcoming smile, putting him at his ease. 'You are Samuel. Sam. Am I right?'

'Yes, sir. Samuel Brock.'

'Brock, eh? Brock as in badger. Samuel. Do you know who I am?'

'You are the Professor, sir. Professor Moriarty.'

Moriarty grunted. 'Not quite, Sam. I am Professor Moriarty' – he pronounced the name in his own unique way, rolling the second *R* and seeming to add a letter so that it came out as 'Mor-ia-rrri-ty.' It was the manner in which he always pronounced it, singular to him.

'Now, Sam Brock. Are you loyal to me? Will you do as I tell you? Will you keep your mouth shut? Can I depend on you?'

'Of course, sir. You can depend on me in all things. I will be loyal to you. Loyal and true unto death.'

'Did Mr. Terremant tell you to say these things?'

'Mr. Terremant and Mr. Spear both, sir. But I mean it. I shall remain loyal to you. Unto death I shall be your man.'

'You were loyal to Sir Jack Idell once, though, Sam. You reckoned Idle Jack as your master. Why did you do that?'

'I did that for money, Professor. Now I pledge

298

myself to you for deeper reasons.'

James Moriarty gave a dark smile of satisfaction that reached cavernously into his heart but not to his eyes. 'It may be, Sam, that you are to be tested.'

'Good, sir. May I serve you well.'

'Indeed. Listen to me and answer faithfully and true. Did Idle Jack trust you?'

'Completely, sir. Yes.'

'Would he trust you again?'

'I think so. If you want me to make him trust me, yes, I can do that. Idle Jack is...' He searched for the word. 'He is ... pliable, sir; he will believe what he wishes to believe.'

Moriarty nodded and his head moved from side to side once more, as though he had no true control over the movements. He thought to himself, *out of the mouths of babes and sucklings*. This boy, he reckoned, would go far, for he already had the makings of a man who could read the ways of others. Moriarty had long believed that Jack Idell could be manipulated by a deviously minded man. 'Good boy,' he said. 'Now, tell me about yourself. What and who was your father?'

'Robert Brock. Ostler at a coaching inn, well known in Canterbury.'

'And your mother?'

'Elizabeth Spurgeon. Chambermaid at the same inn. They was married on account of me, sir.'

'Ah, that is good. A family spliced together and tightened by children and vows is a family that will last and stand all the tests of time. Have you any schooling?'

'Yes, sir. I can read and write and do my sums.'

'Is Mr. Spear paying you properly?'

'He is, sir; and I am sending a portion of my wages home to my mother, just as Mr. Spear suggested.'

'Now, Samuel. None of what I am about to say should go outside this room. You are not to prattle about it to anyone else.' Then his voice barked, 'Anyone. You understand me, lad? Nobody, not even Mr. Spear or Mr. Terremant is to learn of this. And certainly not the boy Taplin. Not a soul but you and myself, young Samuel.

'Do this right for me and I can promise you a place in my family as high as Mr. Spear's. If you are disloyal then, even if I am dead I shall hunt you down and destroy the last traces of you. Make no mistake about it, Sam.'

'What am I to do, Professor?' Samuel sat back, looking contained and in good humour; yet inside, his brain seemed to be roiling with excitement. This was, to him, the start of a huge adventure.

'You are to return to Sir Jack Idell. You are to crawl back to him like a whipped cur. You are to tell him that we attempted to coerce you – you understand? – that we beat you and ill-treated you; that we scoffed at Idle Jack and his designs on my family. Mock us, Samuel, mock us; tell him we are the very dregs of society – he will like that. Tell him that the Professor is rebuilding his family. Tell him that we hold him in contempt. You follow me?'

'I follow you, yes, Professor.'

'Now,' Moriarty continued, 'this must work

both ways. Here, people are to believe that you have slipped out, got away. Make your own plans for that. Everyone here in the house has to believe that you have gone of your own volition. You understand that? Of your own free will.'

'Of course, sir. Nobody will know...'

'It must come as a surprise, and I shall show great anger when your absence is reported.' He held out a key to the boy. 'This is an extra key I have had cut, in secret. It will fit the back door and help you steal away.'

'And what am I to do, sir, when I get to Idle Jack? I would kill him if you so ordered it.'

'No. I want you to keep your eyes and ears open. Watch and listen, because I wish to be warned about all Jack intends to do; I want to know which people are closest to him, what they are plotting. I need to know everything well in advance.'

'I will find out everything and anything, Professor. But how shall I let you know what I find?'

'You say you can write. So, write this down.' He made the boy sit at the table, gave him pen, ink, and paper, and dictated Perry Gwyther's address, which Samuel Brock wrote down in a most fair hand, after which the Professor instructed him to commit the address to memory until he could repeat it again and again. After it was fixed in the boy's mind, Moriarty destroyed the paper.

'You must send me details of what you have heard; send them by post to that address, and you must put a small cross in the top left-hand corner of the envelope.' He had provided paper,

301

envelopes, and two pencils, for nobody could possibly guarantee that ink would be available. 'Keep the paper and pencils well hidden, and don't give them any action or word which they might think odd and therefore suspect you. And never fear, Sam; if I want to get a message to you, I shall find a way.'

His penultimate advice was to give young Sam a large yellow silk handkerchief, a good eighteen inches square. 'If you have any real worries, if you think you are suspected and you wish to run and get back here, you must contrive to hang this wipe in one of the windows overlooking the Square itself, then try to escape. I doubt we can be of any help to you, we can but try.'

Finally he told him that to be safe, they must use some kind of code. 'You know your nursery rhymes, Sam?'

'Most of them, sir. Yes.'

'They are the best for secrets. You will be Georgie Porgie. You remember him?'

'Kissed the girls and made them cry, sir.'

'You must sign all your intelligence to me in that name; and if anyone with my authority approaches you, he must use the words "pudding and pie." If he does not, then you cannot be certain of him. And Samuel, if you fail me and pull the crooked cross on me, even if I am dead and in my grave, I'll hunt you down and send you to eternal damnation. Even if I am dead, I shall do that. I will hound you, Samuel. I will hound you down the nights and down the days. I will hound you down the arches of the years. You hear me, boy?'

302

'I hear you, Professor.'

In the afternoon, Glittering George Gittins came to the house and was closeted with the Professor for over an hour. Moriarty started the conversation by telling him, 'Everything I tell you in this room must stay in your ears, George. None of it must go to your tongue.' When he left, George Gittins reverentially kissed the signet ring on the Professor's right hand.

And the next morning, Samuel Brock had mysteriously vanished, and Moriarty's fury knew no bounds. He was consumed by his anger, and those close to him felt they would be shattered and utterly destroyed by it.

When he had exhausted his terrifyingly violent temper, the Professor returned to his quarters and sat looking at the painting of Georgiana, Duchess of Devonshire, his mind full of joy and laughter, almost a sense of frivolity. Then, as he sat there in comfort, he played, in his mind, Beethoven's Piano Sonata no. 14 in C# Minor.

Soon he would have his piano again and would be able to play such pieces.

He thought of his mother, who had taught him to play, and, at peace, he thought of the last time he had seen moonlight on Lake Lucerne in Switzerland.

16

Little Boy Blue

LONDON: JANUARY 22, 1900

First thing on Monday morning, Albert Spear, with Harry Judge in attendance, met the architect, Iain Hunter, at the warehouse in Poplar, a huge building standing what amounted to a little over two stories high, almost two hundred yards in length, and at least forty, nearer fifty, yards wide, with large double doors at both gable ends, east and west. This great building was surrounded by a high brick wall topped with shards of sharp glass set in cement; entrance was limited through one set of high iron gates, fastened with huge locks and guarded by a solid block-built gatehouse.

In his mind's eye, Spear saw how this site in Poplar could be an even better headquarters than the old warehouse they'd had up the road in Limehouse, and he quickly set about rehearsing Hunter in exactly what would be required of him.

First, the interior of the whole building would need to be lined, sealed with strong, seasoned oak, leaving any broken or slack timbers on the outside still looking damaged. A brick and plaster wall would then be built some six inches in front of the wooden cladding, the space between the two filled

304

with sawdust and wood shavings to deaden sound. A similar, more complex arrangement would be put in place for the roof, so that the entire interior virtually became a new building, seated within the old, and near as damnit soundproof. Then the false walls would go in, behind which the secret passages and rooms could be constructed.

Nothing would ever be as it seemed.

A person straying into the warehouse would see only an empty, dilapidated, disused huge storehouse, the walls peeling and rotting. In fact, the final result would be a remarkable piece of trompe l'oeil. At the far end, the walls would hide secret passages and rooms that would be able to sleep between fifty and sixty men and women; they would include communal wash houses, kitchens, storerooms, and a mess hall where people both permanently living and working at the headquarters and those simply visiting could eat well.

At the other end – the west side – Professor Moriarty's quarters, comfortable and spacious, would run the width of the building, built above a room that would eventually be known as the waiting room, where those wanting an audience with the Professor could rest quietly, sip tea or something stronger, and even read the daily newspapers, while above them, in his rooms, the Professor would dispense his kind of justice, send out people to do his bidding, or plot the latest blagging, smash, grab, or careful theft to order.

The builder, George Huckett, was present with his most senior foreman, while Hunter had a pair of assistants measuring and making notations. At one point, Huckett revealed that he still had the original plans they had used in Limehouse. The measurements would be undoubtedly larger, but the architect could get a clear perception from these old plans; and, after a lengthy talk with George Huckett, Hunter reported that he expected to have the place finished and ready for occupancy around Christmas – eleven months hence. Huckett agreed, looked happy, and promised that his men would be 'brisk as body lice when they get down to it. Won't let the grass grow.'

Standing there in the bare shell of the warehouse, Spear thought he could smell the old odours of Limehouse headquarters: the lovely cooking smells, including the pleasant aromas of baking, sausages frying, and nourishing soups simmering on the big hobs in the kitchens, combined with the scent of fresh flowers the girls brought in every day. He could almost hear the old echoing sounds, the horses' hooves on the interior stone flooring, the music as Ember played his Jew's harp in the evening, or one of the other lads picked tunes out on a squeeze box.

The Professor was delighted when Spear brought the plans back to him. The house on the fringes of Westminster would take another two months to complete – ready in time for his son, Arthur, to come home from school for the Easter holidays.

That very morning Sal Hodges had gone off to choose fabrics and furnishings, carpets and additional accessories. 'I am leaving all those choices to her, because she has a good eye for colour and decoration,' Moriarty told Fanny Paget. 'But, Fanny, if she needs any assistance, I

306

would be delighted if you could give her some hints and general advice. After all, you have had a better opportunity to see how aristocrats and people from the upper classes, people like Sir John and Lady Pam, decorate their properties.' He gave Fanny a warm and tender smile. 'I was much taken by the way in which you managed that cottage on Sir John's estate; it looked so smart. It will be good to have you here, and in Poplar, running the domestic side of things. Quite like the old days.'

Fanny was not so certain she wanted a return to the old days, but clung to the fact that Pip had told her he had spoken with Sir John Grant, and the cottage would be waiting for them as soon as they were able to return from the business he had told Sir John that he had to attend to in London.

In fact, at the moment Sally had no need for extra help. She had taken her protégée, Polly, with her, the young woman who assisted so well in Sal Hodges's house in the Haymarket. Over the years she had seen to it that Polly was well educated; that she spoke excellent French, a little Italian, and some German. Also she wrote and read well, had studied Latin and Greek, was an exceptional needlewoman, and had that parti-cular talent to manage staff with discretion and a strong sense of discipline. Sal Hodges had great hopes that Polly would one day be in a position to take over the running of the house.

Even the working girls of the house liked Polly, for she could be an even-tempered, sweet-natured girl, blessed with common sense. She had also studied art and been exposed to the great classical cultures of Greece and Rome, so was undoubtedly a suitable person to advise Sally Hodges as she strove to choose the soft furnishings and accessories that would be a background anchor to which Moriarty's impeccable taste could be tethered, both in the house close by Westminster and at the new headquarters being prepared, close to the river in Poplar.

They sought out the right colours and patterns, going as far afield as William Whiteley's gigantic store in Westbourne Grove, Bayswater; then coming back into the West End to visit Arthur Liberty's shop and that of Messrs. Swann and Edgar in Regent Street.

People complained that the rise of these big department stores, with their range of goods all under one roof, had sounded the death knell for the personal service that had always been the hallmark of great London shops until the middle of the last century, but Sal and Polly found their shopping in no way hampered by the huge range of choice. On the contrary, in the space of some three and a half hours, which included a leisurely luncheon at the restaurant in Claridge's Hotel, off Brook Street and Grosvenor Square, Sal had chosen several shades of velvet that would be made into curtains for the main rooms of the house, with the promise of a carpet fitter and two experienced men to visit the following day for measuring and putting in hand the making of the curtains – a sumptuous deep red for the drawing room, a light blue for the dining room, and a lilac and a lime green for two of the bedrooms. Polly had also persuaded Sal to order extravagant carpets for the drawing room and the Professor's study, together with a conveniently unfussy patterned carpeting that would do well on the stairs.

'I shall have to get the Professor's final permission for these choices,' Sal told young Polly, who said how lucky Sally was to work so closely with James Moriarty. 'I would like to be given that chance myself,' Polly said, to which Sal Hodges replied that it was not always a pleasure, that sometimes it could be difficult. 'He can be frightening, you know, Polly. His reputation is not as savoury as that of more conventional men.' But Polly thought this could perhaps add some spice to life.

Sally Hodges had never told her the truth concerning her relationship with the Professor, but the child had heard the rumours among the girls in the house. Young ladies would, naturally, grow up quickly and become wise in the ways of the world when they lived cheek by jowl with the girls in a house of pleasure.

Meanwhile, at the noon hour, Terremant and his lurker assistants had taken their places close to the gangway following the steam packet's arrival at Dover from the French port of Calais. Quickly he spotted the man whom the Professor had met so many times when they were in Vienna, and whom he referred to as Karl Franz von Hertzendorf – the man they now knew as Little Boy Blue. Once more, as he looked at this stranger, Terremant had the strong feeling that he knew the man, not simply from observing his meetings with Moriarty in Austria, but from some wider knowledge outside the circle of people within Moriarty's family. He wondered if it was true, what some people said, that you lived from life to life; and that he had perhaps known him in an earlier existence, from a divergent world.

Surrounding Little Boy Blue, the lurkers kept tabs on him as he went through the revenue hall, showing his papers to a waiting officer, a porter carrying his two bags. With a pair of lurkers ahead and a pair behind him, the man climbed the sloping ramp that led up to the railway platform, Terremant staying well to the rear, keeping back, never getting close, simply seeing that Little Boy Blue got himself settled on the train with one of the lurkers in the same compartment.

So they travelled on to London, Victoria Station, where Ember's men took over the watching.

'This the bloke you reckon to have seen before?' Ember asked, without moving his lips, after the manner of an experienced old lag. Foxy little Ember had, if the truth be told, spent time in a pair of jails – at Her Majesty's pleasure, as it was said.

'That's the fellow,' Terremant grunted. 'He's familiar as Mrs. Palmer the five-fingered widow. But I do not know from where.'

'Can't you see why, Jim? It's plain as Salisbury.'

'What is?'

'Your man here. He is what the racing people would call a dead ringer for the late lamented Prince Albert, the Prince Consort.'

'Bloody hell, you're right!' exploded Terremant. 'Blow me, I never saw that in him before.' Sure enough, if you looked at him so he was the living image of the late Prince Albert – not the young prince who had come, years before, full of life and hope, not to mention the dread of seasickness in crossing the Channel – but Prince Albert in his last days, exhausted, his face thickened by worry about the young Prince of Wales and the mountains of work that had bowed him down, that work of the king that he never was. A man buckling under the weight of being the uncrowned king. Undoubtedly the man who had arrived this day could be taken as the dead prince.

'That is passing strange,' Terremant said as they made their way in a hansom, following a growler and a second hansom, heading through the teeming streets toward Captain Ratford's Rooms, where they made Little Boy Blue comfortable, gave him victuals and a good glass of Hock, and told him to rest after his journey.

Later in the afternoon, after the darkness of dusk arrived and the lights had come on in the streets and shop windows, Moriarty himself visited the Captain's rooms, with Daniel Carbonardo very close, protecting him and certainly coming between the Professor and other members of the old Praetorian Guard – something that particularly worried and concerned Terremant. Moriarty talked for a good three-quarters of an hour with Little Boy Blue and left looking pleased as a dog with two choppers, muttering something about Wednesday being the day.

When Moriarty got back to Westminster, he found Lee Chow waiting to see him, also Bertram Jacobs lingering around the kitchen area

311

while George Huckett's men worked their nuts off, diligent and giving their particular best because it was for the Professor.

Lee Chow left about an hour later, following a long talk with Moriarty. He headed for Paddington Railway Station to pick up one of his special boys, a tall Chinese, name of Ho Choy: a most serious man, taciturn, a man who spoke only when it was absolutely necessary.

At Paddington Station they boarded a train to Bristol, travelling third class and assuming positions of great humility, helping men and women with their luggage and generally showing that they knew their place.

Back in his house on the fringes of Westminster, Professor James Moriarty looked at the letters that had come in the afternoon post, around four o'clock. There was a packet sent on that very morning by Perry Gwyther – papers requiring his signature, and concerning the purchase of the warehouse. Also there was an envelope addressed in pencil, shakily written and bearing a small cross in the upper left-hand corner of the envelope.

This is Gorgie Porgie writing, the short letter began. *I have done as instructed and hav some gud things to say. Here they are getting in tuch with some one called Shleyfstine; also another called Grisomb and a third man who is named Sansionare. There is a forth man called Seegobey. Some of this I have seen rit down. Others I have eared. These fulks are all from foren parts and Idel Jak seems to think it is important for him to plot sum thing with them. I will keep workin and wachin.*

Moriarty knew immediately who these men were in Sam Brock's report. He had already had dealings with all of them: Jean Grisombre, the short, slim Parisian, leader of one of the largest gangs of thieves in the world, based in Paris and ruthless in their quest for the acquisition of rare and valuable jewels; the one Sam called Shleyfstine was the tall and correct Wilhelm Schleifstein, who looked more like a banker than a criminal yet held sway over the criminal classes of Berlin, particularly the trade in human flesh. Then there was the fat, suave Luigi Sanzionare, son of a baker who had risen to become one of the most sought-after criminals in Rome. Lastly, there was the man spoken of as the Shadow of Spain, Estoban Bernado Segorbe, a quiet, dignified, neat, and unassuming man with a controlling interest in crime and vice, based in Madrid.

Moriarty had been involved in close dealings with all these men in the past and had no doubt that Idle Jack was now attempting to forge a partnership with them. If this was so, there were things he could, and must, do now to circumvent any activity Idle Jack planned with the continental mobsters. But first, he considered, he had to take care of matters concerning Karl Franz von Hertzendorf: Little Boy Blue.

Fifteen minutes later he was ringing for Wally Taplin, whom he charged with taking a letter by hand to Joey Coax. 'And do not forget,' he reminded Wally, 'do not go into the man's studio.'

'Don't worry, Professor, sir. Mr. Terremant calls him a–'

'Yes, Walter, I know what Mr. Terremant calls him.'

At four o'clock in the morning, down by Bristol Docks there was a violent explosion as a ship burst into flames and burned and burned, sinking low in the water, then finally disappearing, leaving only an oily slick on the surface where it had been moored, and three of the twenty men aboard did not make it to shore again.

People who flocked down to help with the fire almost tripped over a body lying on the dockside, about a quarter of a mile away from where the ship had been moored. The body – that of a man – had been badly beaten about the head, and also had a strange injury to the face, where the soft flesh of the man's cheeks had been cut out and removed.

Later the body was identified as Ebeneezer Jephcote, captain of *Midnight Kiss*, the ship that had burned beside the docks.

On the morning of Wednesday, January 24th, Sal Hodges travelled with the six girls she had chosen to go to the studio in St. Giles's. They were quiet and sitting patiently waiting for things to start, and to be told what they were to do: Red Annie, Gypsy Smith, Connie Best, Sukie Williams, Dark Delilah Amphet, and Goldie Goode. Excellent choices, Moriarty thought, as he viewed them from the balcony. All were attractive, voluptuous, and had that special quality in their eyes, the one that appeared to invite men into their arms and, indeed, further.

The balcony was one of the reasons he had chosen this nice room, which was once a public ballroom for the good people of St. Giles's. From the balcony he could observe without being himself observed, for he had no desire to become personally involved with Joey Coax and his photography.

Coax presently appeared, with three assistants lugging in cameras, tripods, and other jigamarees connected with the business of taking likenesses, and, as soon as work began, Moriarty was pleasantly amazed at the excellent and professional way in which Coax approached the job in hand. He seemed to know exactly what he required of all concerned, and issued his instructions without any of what the Professor thought of as 'effeminate faffing on.'

Only once was there a problem. He had positioned Dark Delilah Amphet on a couch, hard by Little Boy Blue. 'Now,' the photographer instructed, 'look as if you're whipping the harpoon into her.' The Austrian did not understand the instruction and, in the end, Moriarty himself had to call out an impolite expression in German, which made von Hertzendorf give a somewhat injured sigh.

First thing the following morning, a boy left a thick buff envelope for the Professor.

The photographs were magnificent, Moriarty considered. Coax certainly knew what he was doing. He had positioned the lighting so exactly that the flesh of the women on display seemed to glow, breathe, and live in the likenesses.

The posing was also done with a certain taste-

315

fulness that stopped short of crudity, though few would doubt what they were viewing: the late Prince Albert, the Prince Consort, lickspittaling and poodle-faking with six different luscious, partly clad women, on chairs, draped on a chesterfield, and one – Dark Delilah Amphet – across a large bed.

Moriarty rubbed his hands gleefully, summoned Harkness and the hansom, and set off immediately, with Daniel Carbonardo as protection, to Gray's Inn Road, to see what kind of an impression the photographs would make on his advisor, Perry Gwyther.

17

Holy Week

LONDON: LATE JANUARY-APRIL 15, 1900

Peregrine Gwyther was well-heeled, rich, prosperous, tall, and immaculate of dress, confident, and gleamingly clean. He sported a bald head, one of those sleek heads of skin that glisten in any light, shining, bordered by neatly barbered snow-white hair: soft, lying smooth and silky at the back and sides. By the sight of Perry Gwyther's head you knew of his cleanliness.

Perry was normally a person who would greet people with a smile and open-armed gestures, welcoming in a way that was completely unthreatening. He was not smiling now, as he looked up at the Professor from behind his desk. 'And what are these?' he asked, passing his hand over the pile of photographs, his voice tilted to the brink of revulsion.

'What do you think they are?' Moriarty smiled, amused and jovial.

'I know what I am meant to think.' Gwyther's face was sombre, no trace of pleasure. 'Sir, what did you imagine you were doing?'

'I am set to put the Queen at a disadvantage.'

'Have you taken leave of your senses, Professor? How did you think you could use these unpleasant photographs?' he asked, his voice on a rising note.

'The idea was that she would do almost anything to stop them being distributed to the newspapers. She pined for long enough after his death – the Widow of Windsor – surely she would do anything to stop a scandal of this magnitude. I pay you to advise me, Perry. I know you can reach into the royal court. I hoped you would be in a position to–'

'The Queen, Professor, would not even look at these...' his voice barking, angry, cheeks flushed, and his hand again sweeping over the photographs, '...these...' a frustrated note from the back of his throat, 'from ... these ... these ... filthy fraudulent pictures.'

'Not even look?' Moriarty shuddered, taking a deep breath. Then again, 'Not even look?'

Gwyther shook his head slowly, three times, not meeting Moriarty's eye with his. 'One glance and she would be near fainting. The late Prince

Consort is sacrosanct. Even if she looked at these, she could never believe them. She would deny them utterly. She would see them as the stupid, irrelevant, dirty trick that they are.'

'But he is the spit and image of Albert...'

'Indeed, your model looks like Albert. Looks to a great degree like Albert, but nobody would possibly believe this, least of all Queen Victoria. It simply could not happen.'

'Why on earth not? Even in royalty there must be such a thing as jealousy. You yourself have said that she—'

'Much enjoyed the pleasures of the marriage bed? Yes, indeed, that is true, but that pleasure was tinged with a strange prudery, Professor, and a total trust in Prince Albert. What your photographs show just could not occur. The idea is ludicrous.' Gwyther could hardly credit Moriarty with plotting such idiocy. 'My information is first class. Yes, I can, as you put it, reach into the court. If you had come to me with this absurd plan I would have advised you to bury it in the deepest well, sink it in the darkest ocean. How can you have expected this to give you any hold over Her Majesty?'

'I met the man, the man in the photographs, by accident. In Vienna.' Moriarty laid a hand, palm down, on the corner of Gwyther's desk. 'Schleifstein, the criminal overlord in Berlin, put me on to him, and the moment I saw him I imagined we could use him... And now...' He appeared to struggle for the right words. 'And now... This is hopeless... You mean I have spent time and money – a lot of money – for nothing?'

'Nothing, Professor. Victoria is a sad old lady, in her eighty-first year, with declining health. She is like to die at any time. Her doctors say she has indicated that she would not fight hard against a mortal illness.'

'So she would in no way fight against these photographs being published?'

'I have told you. She would not even believe them. This is the woman who relied on Albert in all things. Who enjoyed, as you have said, the marital bed, yet could not even bring herself to explain human reproduction to her daughter – the Princess Alice – and left it to Albert; she is the woman who claimed to know of her son's shenanigans with the girl Nellie Clifden, but said she did not know "the disgusting details." Do you not see what I am getting at?'

Moriarty, usually the most stoic of men, almost wrang his hands. 'All that time!' he cried. 'All that time; all that money. For nothing?' In his mind an even worse thought prowled – that he had been foolish to think this plan could have worked at all; that he had allowed himself to believe there was any merit in this threadbare scheme.

'Professor, you would be advised to bring your energies to bear on Idle Jack. You have such talent, and have made such a difference to the class we are both proud to share. You have so much more to give. I beg you, concentrate on that villain so we can see him put to rights.'

Moriarty gave an animal-like cry, a small howl that made Gwyther jump in his skin. 'Na-ntaaacht!' The sound, part snarl, part cry of anguish, and part warning of attack, echoed through Perry Gwyther's rooms in the Gray's Inn Road so that two of his clerks in an adjoining office recoiled as though they had heard the call of some feral beast about to harass them, and were thrown into such terror that it drove them shivering into the street and, so, home at this early hour.

Moriarty left Gray's Inn Road some twenty minutes later, refreshed by a cup of Indian tea made for him by Abott, Gwyther's chief clerk, who was, as Perry himself remarked, a 'dab hand when it came to infusing tea.'

Moriarty was refreshed, but still raging inside: furious and, worse, questioning his own self-confidence, as he sat shoulder to shoulder with Daniel Carbonardo in the hansom, silent, locked within himself for fifteen, nearly twenty, minutes, swaying against Carbonardo as the cab rolled back to Westminster.

Finally he leaned close and spoke quietly. 'Tomorrow, Daniel. Tomorrow, take the Austrian home.'

'All the way to Vienna?'

Moriarty shook his head. 'No, Daniel. No. You take him *home*.'

Indeed, on the following day Carbonardo accompanied von Hertzendorf onto the packet sailing from Dover to Calais. Nobody saw him with the Austrian when they reached France. Twenty-four hours later Daniel returned alone to London, where Moriarty had been particularly busy. Von Hertzendorf was not heard of again.

During the night – around three in the morning – Moriarty had personally wakened Joey Coax with the news that there was special work, dangerous work, to be done, after which the photographer would be paid in full. He then drove him, Moriarty himself at the whip, at great speed, to a remote house on the Ratcliffe Highway, where he handed over the terrified Coax to a pair of his most adept punishers. The house, between Wapping and Stepney, was destroyed by fire a year or so later, and the site has since been rebuilt upon. Joey Coax is possibly still there, sleeping through the years, fast in the reddish soil of the area that gave the name to Redcliff, and so Ratcliffe. This tale bears out the truth that it was not in your best interest to become professionally involved in any scheme put to you by Professor James Moriarty, particularly if you had some signal skill that he required to use. Rarely did the Professor leave witnesses in the present to speak of what had happened in the past.

Also, in the early morning of that same day, the barque *Colleen of Cork* was returning to Plymouth, coming in to The Sound, making way for Devonport, after calling in for a day at the French port of Le Havre, where two members of the crew – both Chinese – appeared to have deserted ship. A box of firecrackers, accidentally ignited, set fire to a powder keg kept under lock and key. In turn, the keg set off other inflammable and unstable materiel. The explosion was heard from as far away as Polperro, and several bodies were washed up along the coast, notably that of her captain, Michael Trewinard, and her first mate, Bernard Carpenter, both of whom were identified, in St. Austell, by family members.

So the wheels continued to turn, slowly, and the work began to take shape in the warehouse hard by the river in Poplar; also in the great house on the fringes of Westminster, which pleased the Professor so much that he even spoke to George Huckett about the possibility of his little firm doing some further restoration at Steventon Hall, on the road to Oxford. With this in mind they visited Steventon one day in mid-March accompanied by Sal Hodges, who brought a basket containing a loaf of Fanny Paget's homemade bread and some cold sausage and pickle with mustard, and a flask of Fanny's excellent cock-a-leekie soup made from a fine capon, her simmered chicken stock, and several parcels of leeks so that the soup was finally thick and most tasty. Sal said that even though this was a Scotch soup, she could remember the days in her childhood when people, coming to assist in gathering in the harvest, would each bring their own bunch of leeks to add to such a soup to be consumed as the first course at their harvest home banquet.

So, freezing January slipped quietly into a February that lived up to its old name of February fill-dyke, then to a March during which the days began to get a mite longer and the temperature started to rise a fraction, and they passed quietly into April with its soft refreshing rains. It was on All Fools Day, April first, that a thundering great robbery occurred in Hampstead, that place of groves once infested by wolves, and where during the reign of Henry VIII, London's washerwomen soaked the clothes of the nobility. This particular event, the clearing out of an entire house of goods, jewels, precious stones, and furniture, was a robbery to order. The thieves were three men and a boy, all under Ember's control, the object of interest being a single piece of furniture: a magnificent hand-carved Swiss sleigh bed, fashioned from pine, with outward-curving head and foot boards, complete with ridged foot blocks that Moriarty later called his 'mounting blocks.'

Ember presented this large bed as a personal housewarming gift just as the carpets, curtains, and other furniture were being brought into the house. Eventually, the Westminster house was decorated and in perfect order, and it was almost time for Arthur to return home from Rugby for the Easter holidays.

The sleigh bed was wonderfully comfortable both for James Moriarty and his love, Sal Hodges, just as foxy little Ember knew it would be; and in the cozy darkness of the night, Moriarty would shrug off all traces of evil, and the dark phantoms that must have invaded his dreams; and he would whisper in Sal's ear, 'Oh, my dolly darling, my donah, my sweetmeat,' and running his hand between her stunning thighs, he would say, 'Oh, my dilberry bush, my sweet garden ripe for planting, my honeycomb. My love.'

Stirring deep in the night, Sal Hodges would come awake and find great apprehension facing her in the gloom, for she kept one dark, terrible secret that she wished to hold on to until the end of her time. In her distress, she wondered if that would be possible, and dared not consider the consequences should the secret be revealed to her lord and master, to Professor James Moriarty.

Through the previous months, Moriarty had received regular messages from Sam Brock, his spy in place with Idle Jack, and the intelligence he was able to obtain, particularly concerning the passage of ideas between Jack Idell and the continental crime lords, he considered invaluable. But as they approached that Easter of 1900, the messages became more alarming.

I heard them again last night, Professor, Georgie Porgie wrote with a sense of urgency on Thursday, April fifth. *They seem to be planning your downfall. I thing they are after you life. You are in great dangor.*

And on that very evening, the Thursday before Palm Sunday, there was a great reunion at the house in Westminster. Young Arthur Moriarty – known in the world as Arthur James – returned for the Easter holidays, greeted lovingly by his mother, Sal Hodges, and his father, James Moriarty.

There was pride in the Professor's heart as he faced his son, who had been met at Euston Station by Daniel Carbonardo and driven home by Harkness in the Professor's hansom. The young man stood in the tiled hall of the great house, embraced his mother, and gave his father a firm handshake.

Moriarty thought he would burst with pride, for the young man had grown in stature, filled out, and was blessed with a new confidence after just over a year at Rugby. He spoke clearly in a firm classic voice with no trace of Moriarty's former Irish accent, but with the clipped consonants and sharp, slightly elongated vowels of what was obviously the inflection of the upper classes; while the way in which he held himself was after the manner of a leader, a man born to be at the head of whatever profession he chose. The investment Moriarty had made in Rugby School was already paying off a hundredfold.

That night, after dinner, Sal left father and son alone over the port and, for the first time, Arthur spoke to his father about his place in the family, and what his father actually accomplished in life.

'Father of the chap I share a study with is something in the city and says you, Papa, are a bit of a dark horse.'

'Does he now?'

'That's what he told, Peter – Peter Alexander, my friend. Said you had holdings and a lot of property. I've never thought about the kind of business you are in, Papa. Or what I shall do when I leave school.'

'I am what the French call an entrepreneur, Arthur. Know the word?'

Arthur looked his father full in the face. 'Oh, indeed, sir, I do.' A smile and the merest shadow of a wink. 'It can hide a multitude of sins, Papa. Yes?'

Moriarty smiled back, thinking his son was wise beyond his years, and leaning forward told the boy that he would, in due time, inherit a fortune, not simply in terms of money, but in human realities. 'You will become heir to an army of workers, men, women, and children, people who are skilled in their various trades. You will be their rock and the one from whom they will derive their livelihoods. You will direct them, and be their master and their guide, both. You will be their reason for life.'

'And I shall be delighted to see to them, Papa.' Once more, the shade of a smile.

In that moment, the Professor's heart sang, for he knew that he had bred a whelp after his own heart. 'You should first study the Law, my son. That will make you ready to take on the great future I shall leave to you.'

So, a bond was forged between father and son. For the remainder of that week the two would sit and talk into the night, Arthur entertaining his father with both tales of life in the great public school and his own youthful ideas of how life should be lived, and how the great obstacles in life should be surmounted, and life's difficulties overcome.

Arthur was, of course, as yet unlettered in the world, and required years of experience to grow and become familiar with the many pitfalls of that adventure from birth to knowledgeable rebirth. Yet in those days the Professor could clearly see how the son he had longed for at the time before his birth would be a beloved credit to him and to all with whom he had dealings. In the fact of Arthur, James Moriarty first began to sense what love may really be for a father.

Lucy Moriarty had been a devout Roman Catholic and had brought her children up in the holy Roman Catholic and apostolic faith. Moriarty naturally had followed his mother and in his own makeshift blood family insisted on an adherence to that faith. When in London, they would worship at the Pro-Cathedral in Kensington High Street, going there quietly and with no fuss, as they did for the High Mass on Palm Sunday when, with the whole congregation, they remembered Jesus Christ's triumphal entry into Jerusalem on that first day of the most momentous week in history for Christians. As in former years, they came away bearing palm leaves and crosses made out of palm leaves. They were there again on Good Friday, where they joined in the liturgy that seeks to focus hearts and minds on the agony and death of Jesus by the stripping and washing of the altar and the individual veneration of the instrument of death, the holy cross; the bells usually rung at the Sanctus and during the consecration now replaced by the harsh sound of a mallet on the sanctuary steps, reminiscent of the nails hammered into Christ on the cross. Then the prostration of the clergy before the large crucifix, followed by the veneration, the entire congregation coming one at a time to kiss the feet of Christ on the Cross, an act not of idolatry but of mental and spiritual obeisance. On Holy Saturday, with the end of the Lenten fast in sight, they attended, early in the morning, the kindling of the New Fire, bringing it into the church, a sign of the Holy Spirit regenerating each member of the Church as though coming down in tongues of flame, and so to the lighting of the Pascal candle. Then, Easter itself, with a great High Sung Mass, praising God and the miracle of the Resurrection.

'How much of all that do you believe, Papa?'

Arthur asked when they assembled in the drawing room before the Easter lunch, their nostrils still lined with incense, which also seemed to cling to their clothes, at odds with the succulent new season's lamb Fanny Paget had cooked for them.

'How much do I believe?' Moriarty seemed to look into the far distance. 'A lot of it, I suppose. "Vengeance is mine sayeth the Lord." One cannot but believe in a God of vengeance...'

'And an afterlife?' Arthur prompted.

'Oh, there's an afterlife.' Moriarty nodded. 'I believe all that. There has to be Hell and Satan and retribution. Day of Wrath and Doom impending sort of thing. Fear all of it, son. Quake and fear all of it.'

Arthur could see that his father, James Moriarty, was moved following the surfeit of unrelenting prayer and ceremonial that told the story of Christ's promise to all men and women, from the glory, laud, and honour of His entrance into Jerusalem to the betrayal, death, and hope of the Resurrection.

In his head, Moriarty could hear the translated words of the Dies Irae, thudding in his brain like sombre, driving timpani beats:

Dies Irae, Dies illa,
Day of wrath and doom impending,
David's word with Sybil's blending,
Heaven and earth in ashes ending.

Oh, what fear man's bosom rendeth,
When from heaven the judge descendeth,
On whose sentence all dependeth.

James Moriarty was swept by a great fear and could not distinguish whether this was a fear of God or mankind.

18

Summer Term

LONDON: APRIL 17-30, 1900

Back on the evening of Palm Sunday, Moriarty had summoned Terremant to his room. In the old days, after Pip Paget had gone missing, and before his promotion, Terremant had been in charge of the punishers, that gang of hard and ruthless men used for inflicting violence, and even death, on enemies of the family.

'It's time we started to fight back, Tom,' the Professor began. 'How many of the loyal punishers can you muster?'

'Around three-quarters of them, sir.' He went on to explain that he had, in the previous week, brought back six of their toughest men, including the legendary Arno Wilson, onetime fairground and booth prize fighter, like Terremant himself, and Corkie Smith, a man almost as big as Terremant, who would go into fights wielding a small holy water sprinkler – a cudgel spiked with nails, set points to the fore – with which, it was said, he had already killed some four men in street fights.

329

He had also won back Rickie Cohen, the tall master of the knife, who cut people with his long, razor-sharp blade – almost an equal to Lee Chow in flicking a cutter across his enemies' faces.

'They'll be true to you now, Professor,' Terremant told him, and on being further questioned, he said that he would trust the reunited punishers with his own life.

'Then let's put them to the test.' Moriarty said the time was now ripe, and perhaps on the Monday or Tuesday of Holy Week, when the trade for the girls would be slack, they should take back the house that Idle Jack had filched from them up at the Marble Arch end of Oxford Street – the one Spear had gone to sniff out only a week or so ago, hidden deep among the warren of streets north of Oxford Street itself.

Terremant seemed pleased to get the chance of some real work, but later in the week he brought bad news. It had been as if Idle Jack's people had expected the assault. Instead of a sleepy and unprepared skeleton crew of minders and cash-carriers at the house, there had been a party of what the big punisher called fighting troops. 'It was as if they had been tipped off and were prepared, waiting for us,' he told the Professor on the Thursday evening. 'We was pushed back like a nest of ants being destroyed by boiling water. I've got three men who'll be on crutches for the next six months, and dear old Glittering George Gittins may not even pull through, he's so damaged.'

The tall, long-haired George Gittins had been shot in the head outside the house just as he was about to charge in with a group of six toughs as big as himself. (Eventually, he recovered.)

Moriarty had Bertram Jacobs keeping his eye on *The Standard* advertisements, but nothing had appeared summoning Cock Robin to a meeting at the house in Delamare Terrace. *Maybe they are using the Royal Mail, like me*, the Professor wondered. Or, perhaps one of the reunited punishers had not been reunited enough. 'Grill 'em,' he ordered Terremant. 'If necessary get Danny Carbonardo in, with his extra-sharp and hot pincers. He'll make them talk.' Even Terremant appeared to wince. He had seen Carbonardo at work before.

On the Tuesday morning after Easter, another packet of letters arrived from Perry Gwyther's office. *I urg you to beware, Professor*, Georgie Porgie wrote. *I know they are plotting dredful things against you. And there are strange people here, in the house. A little man with a cocked head: sort of skew-wiff. A bad un ever I saw one. He was with Idle Jack, alone and talking last night. Over an hour, and they talked about you. Jack said, 'this must finish him.' The little one is cheeky. Jack called him bum-shus, but I dono what bum-shus meens. I do no they plan sumthing teribul.*

The next morning, Wally Taplin came specially to tell the Professor that he thought someone had been watching the house. 'A hansom, parked right across the road, sir. In it was a smallish man, dark, and he seemed to be smiling. Watched intently for about an hour between eight and nine.'

Moriarty told him to report it to Daniel Carbonardo and tell him to keep an eye open for a similar kind of man.

With Arthur home, it looked as though Moriarty had little time for the usual family business, though he did see everyone who had a special reason to talk to him. He also spoke with Spear, and with Carbonardo for about a half hour each day, and, in fact, kept a keen eye on everything that was going on. Not even his newfound close relationship with his son could come between him and the smooth running of his family, now that he was back in London.

Indeed, he had taken Perry Gwyther's words to heart. Idle Jack Idell had had it too much his own way. The moment for Moriarty to reclaim his family was almost upon them, and his spirits were high. 'We shall show that twopenny ha'penny Lance Jack who thinks he is the great horn spoon!' he told Carbonardo one evening. 'Keep your pistol ready, and your wits about you, Dan. He'll come for me soon enough.'

Whenever Moriarty went out and about with Arthur, Carbonardo was not far away from him: A past master at hiding himself away in the crowds, sneaking behind nearby windows, or dodging into convenient doorways, Danny watched not the Professor but those near him, knowing that when Idle Jack unleashed his killer dogs they would come panting almost silently, not with a fanfare of barks and squeals. Death had a way of arriving unexpectedly when Jack Idell was behind the man who would pull the trigger.

The Professor showed no outward sign of his concern, taking Arthur out to The Press, The Royal Borough, and The Stocks, treating him to slap-up meals and giving the boy his small glasses of Champagne at every meal.

'Ever get bullied?' the Professor asked him one day as they ate oysters, followed by roast fillet of beef with vegetables and a Spanish sauce. 'Boys try to strong-arm you?'

'There is always bullying, Papa, but I can look after myself.' Arthur was bright, happy, and confident.

'Never let a bully see you are afraid of him, son.'

'No, Papa. What should I do?' He had in mind a boy called MacRoberts who was forever trying to pick on him and who liked to frighten and scoff at younger boys.

'First, you should always give the impression that you agree with everything they have to say.'

'I understand that. Agree with them.'

'Then, my son, if there is no other way, get even with them when they are least expecting it. Always take them by surprise, even at times when it is dangerous for you to show your true colours. When masters are about, for instance. It is also a good thing to perhaps win over one of the bully's particular cronies. Even if you have to bribe them with money it is a good way to turn the tables on those kind of people, and also to draw suspicion away from yourself. But choose your time carefully. The bully is usually a bit of a coward underneath his bluster, so use that fact to your advantage. And if that fails, well, send for Bert Spear; he'll fix them up for you.' He laughed at the joke, and Arthur laughed even louder. 'The thing to remember is you must treat friends and enemies alike. Never allow one to know whom you favour and whom you despise.' This was a constant in Moriarty's advice: that you should never reveal your real friends, or enemies, to anyone. Make it look as though you are the same to all men.

The 'little man with a cocked head: sort of skew-wiff' was, of course, Micah Rowledge, whose first job had been strangling unwanted babies; the man who had loved his work; the man who Idle Jack had said would be hired to settle matters with James Moriarty.

Micah Rowledge was an abomination, a horrible little man: small of stature, with his head permanently cocked to one side and a birth defect that had left him with an enduring physical handicap – a smile as insincere as a drunk's promise, the smirk forever curling his lips, saying that he always knew better than you, the amusement supercilious and leaping into his eyes, which regarded other people, in general, as being his inferior. His hair was long, to his shoulders, dark, and kinked with waves that put a rough sea to shame. All in all, Micah Rowledge was chock-full of a superiority, ripe with arrogance: insufferable.

He was now spending much time with Jack Idell, and claimed he had the perfect method to do away with Moriarty and so do Idle Jack's bidding.

'This has to be public,' Jack said to him, blinking his hooded eyes.

'Don't let that concern you,' Micah hissed, for he spoke low, in almost a whisper, dropping his voice at the end of each sentence, so making people listen even harder to catch his words. 'This will be as visible a killing as you would ever want. The world will know when I have done it, and it will certainly be the end for the so-called Professor Moriarty. Within days you will be monarch of all you survey, Sir Jack. You will have no enemies, for I shall do away with Professor Moriarty completely.'

His plan seemed to fulfil all Idle Jack's requirements: The murder would be carried out in public, the world would know who was behind it, but there would be no proof. Micah Rowledge had his escape route planned and he would disappear for several years. 'Nobody will even guess where I'll be,' he told Jack. 'And if they do guess, they will never be able to find me, or get to me.'

'No,' Idle Jack agreed. 'It will be as if you had never been.' He had learned much from watching the Professor's progress in the past. That was one of the reasons why Idle Jack Idell was such a threat to Moriarty: It was as though he had evil powers and kept an idol of the Professor in his den – an idol he could manipulate, alter, and destroy. There was a difference between Daniel Carbonardo and Micah Rowledge. Carbonardo killed professionally; Rowledge enjoyed killing for the sake of it.

On the afternoon of April twenty-ninth, the ship called *Pride of the Morning* sank without warning off the coast of Portugal. It was as though someone had unexpectedly opened her seacocks so that she suddenly foundered and sank taking her entire crew, with her captain,

Corny Trebethik, into Davey Jones's locker. A passing ship picked up one survivor: a Chinese employed to swab down the decks.

So, spring inexorably nudged the world toward summer, and all too soon the Easter holidays were over, and Arthur was forced to prepare himself to return to Rugby School on April thirtieth for the start of the Summer Term.

Harkness had the cab outside, and had loaded Arthur's box into a second cab driven by Josh Osterley while the young man said goodbye to his parents. 'Your father says if we leave in good time I can give you a treat, take you through Regent's Park,' he whispered to Arthur. Regent's Park was a little out of their way, but much loved by Arthur, who had been taken there, to the Botanical Gardens and the Zoological Gardens, as a toddler. A ride round the park, on the way to catch his train, would be a fine way to end the holiday.

'It has been my best time here, sir. The best I can ever recall, Papa.' And Arthur, on an impulse, embraced his father, who, as he turned, noted that Sal was near to weeping.

'The summer will soon be here and you'll return for the long holiday,' Moriarty told him. 'I thought we would take a short trip, perhaps to Deauville, where you can learn something of the impossible business of gaming. Learn you can rarely rake in the persimmon at the tables, eh?'

'I shall look forward to it, Papa.'

Moriarty smiled at him. 'And other things also, I'll be bound.' For he planned to see Arthur initiated into the way with women, and where

336

better to do that than at the French resort?

The young man, looking handsome and happy, kissed his mother, said good-bye, and turned, waving at the foot of the steps, before he got into the cab.

'There, Sal.' Moriarty put an arm around Sally Hodges, who now wept openly. 'He'll soon be back. We have made a good young fellow.'

But Sal turned away, the tears flowing freely and her heart heavy with the secret she dared not reveal to him, the secret locked away inside her. She stifled a sob, disentangled herself from him, and ran to her room.

And off he went to his study, for he had much to do.

As he turned he saw Carbonardo near the front door, and, on a whim, told him to follow Harkness in the other hansom. Carbonardo ran to it and jumped in, telling Osterley to stay close behind Harkness all the way to Euston Railway Station.

'I'll see Mister Arthur on the train, never fear, Professor,' he called, and Arthur waved from inside the cab as it pulled smartly away from the house.

It was a beautiful spring day, the sky cloudless, that deep blue that is a foretaste of summer: the kind of day they had called Queen's weather for the past sixty years or so. Harkness manoeuvred the cab gently so that they could take a pleasant ride to Euston Station, where Arthur would travel on the London and North Western Railway's regular morning express that stopped at Rugby. As he had promised, Harkness took a little turn in Regent's Park.

Most of the traffic was flowing toward the West End and the City of London at that time in the morning, and there were not many cabs as yet gently clopping through the Outer Ring of Regent's Park, so Harkness should have been alerted early to the cab coming toward them, the horse moving a little faster than normal, coming at a brisk trot.

Then, as the cab came closer, Harkness realized there was danger. He saw the small figure stand up inside the cab as Micah Rowledge pulled the twelve-gauge shotgun from the floor and pointed it directly at young Arthur. The gun had been shortened, the barrels sawn off, and he fired from the hip, pulling both triggers as the two cabs came abreast of one another, the horses both rearing and faltering at the sudden loud explosions.

Bam! Bam! as the cartridges were fired.

Arthur, seeing what was happening, had half risen, and the two blasts of lead shot caught him in the chest, ravaging his ribs, tearing into his lungs and heart so that he was thrown back in a great blossom of blood. He took two half, dreadful, fighting breaths, like the gasps of a dying fish, his head reaching up as though struggling for clear air. He died in seconds, still trying to draw air into his ruptured lungs.

Daniel Carbonardo saw what was happening and brought his pistol up, firing four shots, two at Rowledge and two at the cabbie, a small man called Lennie Adler, a man with a history of drink and infidelity to his long-suffering wife but a good cabbie who had worked for Idle Jack for almost two years, and had been chosen especially for this morning's job.

Both Rowledge and the driver were knocked down by Carbonardo's bullets, both hit square in the head and dead before they collapsed: Micah Rowledge trying to break the shotgun and reload, Adler attempting to whip up his horse, which took off at a near gallop and was finally stopped by a policeman close to the Botanical Gardens.

Harkness, looking down into the cab, saw Arthur's body and knew what he must do, so he whipped up the old horse, Archie, still nervy, disturbed by the shots, and set him off at a clip, heading as quickly as he could toward Notting Hill and Cadvenor's premises in St. Luke's Road.

Having taken care of the business of putting Arthur's body into Cadvenor's care, he cleaned out the cab as best he could and drove sedately back to Westminster, not drawing attention to himself.

When Moriarty heard the terrible news he behaved like a man possessed: giving out a great and long wail, grabbing at his waistcoat lapels and tearing down, popping all the buttons, like biblical women rending their garments. This was not the only act with religious significance. Reverting to the Bible study his mother had made him do for hours every Sunday, Professor Moriarty howled out words learned long ago, the grief of David on hearing of the death of his son, Absalom – 'O my son Absalom,' he cried. 'My son, my son, Absalom. Would God I had died for thee, O Absalom, my son, my son.'

His grief was so great, and so primeval, that Sal

would not go down, near him, fearing what he might do.

That's what Idle Jack meant, he thought in the lucid portion of his mind outside the horror of his son's death. *That's how Jack was to bring me down, by making me mad with grief, so that I would lose hold of my precious family.*

'It was as though they already knew we would be in the park,' Harkness told him when he finally went through the events of that morning. 'But nobody knew, Professor. Only I asked you if I might take him for a last ride through Regent's Park, and you told me I could do that. I told no one. So who?'

They looked at each other and both realized the truth at the same moment: It was the man on guard outside, the only one who could have known, listening at the door.

Dropping his voice, the Professor asked Harkness how the man could have got a message out.

'I saw the boy, Wally Taplin, run to the corner and give a letter to a cabbie who often loiters there.'

'Get Taplin up here.' Moriarty could barely control his speech; his throat sounded constricted and he looked most solemn when young Taplin faced him.

'Wally, you have done nothing wrong, I'm sure, but do you ever run errands for Big Jim Terremant?'

'Why, yes, sir. All the time. I take notes to Mr. Quimby, who he has bets with.'

'And where is this man Quimby?'

'Usually at the cab rank, Professor. The one by

340

The Duke of York public house, where Mrs. Belcher is.'

'You took one of these notes this morning, Wally?'

'Yes, sir. Mr. Quimby looked upset when he read it. Took off in his cab like there was the devil himself after him, sir.'

'And this was today? This morning?'

'Just before I helped with getting poor Mr. Arthur's box down, sir. Oh, sir. Poor Mr. Arthur!' and Willy Taplin started to weep like a seven-year-old having a fit.

'Good boy,' said Moriarty. 'Don't talk about this to anyone.'

When he left the room a few minutes later, with Harkness, Terremant was back, standing in his usual place on the landing, smiling his daft smile and looking pleased with himself.

Moriarty smiled back, went up to him, pressed close to the big man, and hissed, 'Cock Robin.'

At the same time he slipped his right hand under Terremant's jacket and took hold of the short, sturdy neddy cudgel the fellow kept in a leather loop on his belt. Stepping back, Moriarty swept the cudgel around in a great arc so that it caught Terremant an almighty swipe on the left side of his head. They were not to know it, but that one tremendous blow did the job: Terremant's neck was broken, which accounted for the strange angles of his head after the following blows. Moriarty swung the club the other way, smashing down on the right side.

Terremant grunted and dropped to his knees, looking up at Moriarty, shocked, as the Professor began to rain blows onto the man's head and face, beating him to a crushed pulp so that his face looked, at the end, like a mashed beetroot. Again and again he hit him, and the blood was spattered over the skirting, down the stairs, and across the heavy paper on the wall.

When he was done, the Professor let Terremant's body, with its battered stump of a head lurching to one side, go tumbling down the stairs just as Daniel Carbonardo reappeared.

He tossed the cudgel down onto the hall tiles and told Carbonardo to get rid of the body. 'Sink him like you sank that Austrian scum. Take him out and sink him deep,' he called, still shaking with anger. Then, like an afterthought, he told him to get Huckett's men up to redecorate the stairs.

19

The End Game

ENGLAND: APRIL 30- MAY 29, 1900

Grief swamped Moriarty. There were moments when he believed he would die of it: of a broken heart, inconsolable.

Sal Hodges did not see him for over three days, for he stayed in his work room, but, like other members of the household, she heard him weeping, and occasionally wailing, like a priest

342

from some bizarre old religion going through his private ritual, cleansing himself.

The letters were delivered by Pip Paget, straight from the postman at the front door. They spoke every day – Paget and the Professor – while Daniel Carbonardo borrowed a horse and cart from Huckett, threw Terremant's body in the back, and covered it with old sacking and off-cuts of wood before setting off for Devon, where he disposed of the mortal remains of James Thomas Terremant, suitably weighted, in a deep-water cove near Bolt Head.

Out in the world, the police were investigating the shooting of a cabbie and his passenger, a small man who had a twin-barrelled shotgun – probably a Purdy, the barrels sawn short and the maker's name and number filed off. The gun had been recently fired, but they had no idea about the target.

Cadvenor, the undertaker, had used his common sense and summoned up one of his tame doctors to sign Arthur's death certificate, listing the cause of death as a cardiac arrest, which, in a way, was the truth. He also altered Arthur's name to Albert Stebbings, a sixty-five-year-old labourer; and it was Albert Stebbings's funeral that Moriarty attended at Golders Green Cemetery on May fourth at two-thirty in the afternoon.

Sal did not stir from her room, but James Moriarty visited her on his return to say that their boy had been 'put away,' in a good and proper manner.

'They had "Love Divine All Loves Excelling," and "Soldiers of Christ Arise, and Put Your

Armour On." It was all very rousing,' he told her. Privately, he thought it was all the bellicose sweetness so beloved of middle-class women.

Sal was much distracted, anxious and concerned, hardly raising her eyes to look at him. This he attributed to their son's sudden and violent end. He then went back downstairs because he had much to do, particularly work regarding Idle Jack and the end game. The man could not go on living; that had been obvious for some time, and the Professor bitterly regretted Carbonardo's failure on the first occasion, outside the Alhambra Theatre. Now, following the callous murder of Arthur, things had to be speeded up, and the whole of the Professor's concentration became completely focused on the question of how Idle Jack could be lured to his death, and what form that death should take.

To some extent Idle Jack's future drove out the sorrow, so that Moriarty's days were taken up with the question of revenge – a totally personal matter.

Within a week, possibilities began to emerge.

That morning there had been yet another report from Georgie Porgie, Samuel Brock, his spy close within Sir Jack Idell's household:

Jack is doing som kind of bizniz with the foreners I tol you about. He wants to have a meeting with them but they will not give him a time or place. And I am getting worried because some of the people here are givin me odd looks, like they suspect me, or somethin. Last nite I cort Darryl Wood starin at me. He looked puzeled, like he knew wat I was up to. You think I orta come out? I am much afeared.

I would be much afeared, Moriarty thought. This was an immediate warning, and yes, he considered, yes, it was time he pulled out young Sam, brought him back here. But he also knew that George Gittins was not where he had put him to accomplish that job. Gittins, who was supposed to be on guard, watching Idle Jack's house; Gittins, shot in the head and laid up. The Professor, straight off, had second thoughts about George Gittins; after all, he had been close to Terremant, who had used him in the attempt to recapture their house off the Marble Arch end of Oxford Street. Possibly, Terremant, in his treachery, had sought to draw George Gittins away from the Bedford Square lurk. Now, Moriarty would have to get someone else to snatch young Brock from the possible jaws of death. Pip Paget could do it, but he wanted Pip for another part of this plan, so it would have to be either Ember or Spear.

It took Moriarty a night to make the decision and send for Albert Spear. *Take care,* he told himself, *do nothing hasty.* It was imperative that he make no mistakes. In situations like this you usually got only one chance. They had already had their one chance, outside the Alhambra. The second would be complicated. It also had to be foolproof.

Spear finally shuffled into Moriarty's room at eight in the morning on May sixth. He seemed uncomfortable and dejected, looking down at his boots and not meeting the Professor's eye.

'You alright, Bert?' Moriarty asked.

'You mean apart from feeling like a fresh-boiled owl, Professor?'

'You look uncommonly out of sorts, Bert.'

'I'm sad, sir, on account of Mr. Arthur.' Spear shook his head. 'I cannot tell you how sorry I am. He was a fine young man, We've lost a right don, sir, and that's a fact.'

'Thank you, Albert. I was proud of the young 'un. But we must go forward. There are things we have to do.'

'One thing in particular, Professor.'

Moriarty looked up at him, a quick squint, fast, his eyes lighting on the big bruiser for a fraction of a second, then down again.

'Yes,' he nodded. 'Yes, the one thing we both know. Requiescat to Idle Jack.'

'That's the one, Professor. Any ideas how we can get near?'

'I have the germ of an idea, Bert. A glimmer. A twinkle in the eye, as they say. I'll tell you when it has...' He gave a gruff, short laugh. 'Well, when the germ has germinated, so to speak.'

'In the meantime, Professor, what can I do?'

'You remember the boy, Sam? The one you chastised? Used to work at the Glenmoragh Hotel? Lippish.'

'How could I forget him? You gave him some work, I think, sir.'

'Yes.' The Professor then told him what to do. 'You must never take your eyes off the house, Spear. The boy is, I think, doomed unless you can pick him up from the street and bring him to me.' It was Moriarty's understanding that the boy was trusted enough to take any letters from

Idle Jack out to the nearby post box each evening. That would be the optimum time to lift him off the street and bring him back to the comparative safety of Moriarty's family.

Daniel Carbonardo returned from Devon, reporting that the disposal of Terremant's body had gone well, and on Thursday, May tenth, Spear went across to Bedford Square and joined the team Gittins had assembled there: a pair of tough, hard men, much steeped in the ways of the criminal world – Nick Palfrey and Joe Zwingli, men who had worked at one time or another under all four of the old Praetorian Guard.

'The lad does the post run every day?' Spear asked.

'Near as damnit.' Palfrey was a bright but intimidating fellow with a lumpy face, scarred and bruised by time lived within the Professor's family. 'Round about five o'clock, most days,' Joe Zwingli said in the husky, grating voice that made people think his throat was red raw with some infection.

Spear waited, and at a little after five the boy came out, walked around the corner into Bayley Street, and popped a small pile of letters into the pillar-box there. Then he retraced his steps back into Idle Jack's house.

Spear was glad to see that the boy appeared to have his wits about him and did not seem to be havey-cavey, or have a touch of the slows, but looked around, alert and bright.

'We'll do it tomorrow, same sort of time,' Spear said and left, disappearing as quietly as he had arrived.

347

Then, in the late afternoon of Friday the eleventh, he came back with Osterley and his growler. Palfrey and Zwingli were there again, having been relieved by another pair of Gittins's original team, Moggy Camm and a squat, silent rough by the name of 'Dutch' Nightingale. This last name was a bit of a joke, for a Dutch nightingale – and a Norfolk nightingale, come to that – was cheap talk for a frog, and Nightingale's physical likeness to a frog, or toad, was striking. Spear had often remarked in the past that he was never about when Nightingale got undressed, but he was prepared to wager that the little fellow had webbed feet.

Sam came out of Idle Jack's house at just before five minutes past five. Spear gave the signal and, accompanied by Joe Zwingli, the growler went across the square at a lick. Spear opened the door and leaned out to scoop up the boy, pulling him inside, whispering at him, 'Scream, Sam! Shout and scream like you are being taken against your will,' and Sam yelled and hollered his lungs out.

'They heard him,' Spear told the Professor when they got the lad back to the house. 'That evil feller, that Broad Darryl Wood, poked his head out of the door and made as if he would follow us, but then thought better of it. Good for him; I'd have had his deadlights out if he had given any bother.'

Sam was in a state, wailing and trembling like a leaf in a gale; he could not keep still. Then, when he was finally taken up to Moriarty, he couldn't stop thanking him, chattering on and kissing the signet ring on the Professor's right hand.

Moriarty sat the lad down, gave him a few sips of brandy to calm him, and then began to question him about what was actually going on in Idle Jack's camp, asking devious questions, slowly drawing out facts.

They talked round the clock for twenty-four hours with breaks roughly every three hours, when Fanny would bring them hot drinks and bread with cheese for young Sam, who had done well under Idle Jack's roof, keeping his eyes and ears open and his memory sharp as a Whitechapel needle.

'Nobody actually said as much,' he admitted, 'but you didn't need Mr. Charles Dickens's imagination to work out what was going on. They was planning to have this sit-down and talk with these foreign geezers.'

When he had, to use his own words, 'bled the lad dry,' Moriarty went down to the servants' part of the house, around the kitchen area. Fanny Paget worked away but seemed glum and miserable, and all of the old Praetorian Guard were now gathered together, talking, looking serious. Moriarty motioned Ember to come upstairs with him.

'I want four of my best shadows. I have an adventure for them, and they must be the most intelligent of my boys,' Moriarty told him, referring to the young lads he had working for him. 'My good boys,' he would say. 'My shadows.'

'Very good, Professor. Can I give them any hint of the work?'

Moriarty shook his head. Even though he had dealt with the traitor from the Guard, he was still

349

not ready to take chances. 'Just assemble them here. There will be about a week's work, and they will have to travel,' he instructed. Ember went away and began the relatively long process of deciding who were the most reliable boys to be chosen for this work, finally deciding on lads he knew well, all of them sixteen years of age or older: Dick Clifford, a boy who was always happy, singing away to himself, then Marvin Henry, 'Welsh' Bruce, and Benny Brian. These were lads who had always worked well together and he sought them out, told them where to report, and said they should look smart and be prepared for anything. The Professor's shadows.

Quietly, Moriarty made notes and checked dates, carefully working out his plans. Then he sent for Pip Paget and told him what he must do. 'You go and talk to Lazarus Grosewalk. After all, you lived next door to him for some time. Tell him that I will be his friend forever more, that if he does this one thing for me, he can call on me anytime and I shall give him whatever he asks. Even if it is something impossible.'

'He'll be anxious about his place in the future.' Pip himself was concerned for his own future, for things had been difficult with Fanny since young Arthur's murder.

The problem was that when Pip had taken on the gamekeeper's job with Sir John and Lady Pam, he had made a pact with Fanny. They had pledged not to have any children until things were more settled. Arthur's death had upset everyone, and in Fanny's case it had concentrated her mind on the fact that life was fragile, hung by a thread.

'You don't know what is round the corner,' she said to Pip. 'I do not think we should wait over-long before we start a family. Not now.'

Until then they had been using the rudimentary forms of contraception available to them: working things out from the phases of the moon, and Pip getting off at Hillgate, as the jargon had it. Now, all that was changing, and in bed Fanny had become a different person, clinging to him, making him complete the act and behaving like a doxy, as if she wanted to be at it all hours of the day and night. This Pip enjoyed, but found unsettling – well, who wouldn't?

Now Pip was away on the Professor's business. For at least a day, maybe two. And the Professor was in his room, keeping everyone away. Even Sal Hodges, who was most anxious to talk with him, was kept out.

Moriarty was composing a letter – four letters in reality, all to be taken abroad.

You are playing with fire. If you do not stop immediately it will consume you, and it will be as though you never existed. I refer, naturally, to your conversations with Sir Jack Idell, who can charm birds from the air and snakes from their lairs. This is not a threat made by me, but simple plain fact. This man, Idle Jack, is a usurper, a cheat, a thief, a liar, a murderer who would have you all hoodman blind. Playing the crooked cross is, to him, like a second nature. For some time now, he has attempted to gain control of my entire family here in London. You know me well enough, my friend. You know what is within my power and what I am not able to accomplish.

*Mark me well: this Idle Jack has all but been com-
pletely stripped of his power. Making a convenience
with him will only put matters off for a few weeks at
the most. I urge you to follow my instructions well in
order to avoid perishing with this common fellow.
There is no escape. If you are not with me, then you
are against me, and with Jack Idell. If you are with
Idell you will be swept away. Now, if you are with me
and wish to survive into a fruitful and rare future in
the broad and sunlit uplands of our common cause,
then this is what you must do. Send a message to Jack
Idell giving him the information he requires for a
meeting. You do not have to come and be part of that
meeting. I shall see to it all.*

He then gave them the precise time, date, and
place of the proposed meeting. Pip Paget had
returned from doing Moriarty's bidding. 'One
date is certain and best,' he reported. 'Tuesday,
twenty-ninth May.'

'Then that must be the day on which Idle Jack
will meet his nemesis.' Moriarty closed his mouth
and gave a thin, almost ghastly smile.

'At six o'clock in the morning, Pip?'

'Six o'clock precisely, Professor. Yes.'

'And the other matters are taken care of?'

'Near enough, sir, yes. Lazarus Grosewalk says
he has four rogues who will not fight one with
another, but who will turn the entire pack into a
set of death within seconds. They are, it appears,
born leaders. Males who will see to it that they
are obeyed.'

Moriarty nodded and returned to his letter:

352

If you are agreed, then send me a telegram stating in the simplest of terms that you are about to forward the instructions to Jack Idell.

The letters were then signed, the envelopes addressed and sealed; then they were passed over to the boys who would take them, by hand, onto the Continent and give them directly to the men who were the hinges of this plan: Schleifstein of Berlin; Grisombre of Paris; Sanzionare of Rome; and Segorbe of Madrid.

Moriarty spent much time instructing the four lads from what he called his shadows – Dick Clifford, Marvin Henry, 'Welsh' Bruce, and Benny Brian. He was most anxious that these lads did their job properly and with confidence. He was not concerned with the fact that they each had to travel a considerable distance – to Paris, Rome, Berlin, and Madrid; the fact that was most in his mind was the manner in which they made contact with the four men who between them controlled vast armies of criminals. These were men who did not enjoy being sought out or hunted for in their particular capital cities. All of them took great pains to remain hidden. If a friend from outside wanted to meet and speak with any one of these men, he would have to go through what amounted to a ritual. For instance, Grisombre, in Paris, had to be asked for in a small, unassuming café on the Boule Miche on the Left Bank, the Rive Gauche, of Paris. And you could not ask for Jean Grisombre by that name; you asked for a Monsieur Corbeaux, and you also had to be possessed of a recognizable name. With Grisombre it had to be a Paul Godeux from Lille, who had a wife called Annette and two children, Pierre and Claudine. There were further questions, of course – name of a grandmother, or sister, or even a dog.

All four of the crime bosses of Europe had similar labyrinthine secret passwords and traps to pass through before you even got to within an ace of seeing the man for whom you searched.

Moriarty went through this whole rigmarole with his chosen shadows, testing them, going backward and forward through each stage of the maze, until he was assured that all four boys could do the job to which each was assigned. At last the boys left at various times of day on Friday, May eighteenth.

Almost a week later, Moriarty received a telegram from Wilhelm Schleifstein under his assumed name, Gunther. The telegram read:

WE HAVE ADVISED OUR MUTUAL FRIEND THAT HE SHOULD MEET US AT THE APPROPRIATE PLACE ON THE TIME AND DATE SUGGESTED STOP HE HAS RESPONDED FAVOURABLY STOP SUGGEST YOU VISIT US SOMEWHERE ON THE CONTINENT WHEN ALL IS DONE STOP GOOD LUCK STOP GUNTHER ENDS

Moriarty knew as he stood in the darkness at the back of Paget's cottage at half past five in the morning of Tuesday, May twenty-ninth, that luck

354

did not enter into it. If you leave nothing to chance, you do not require luck. He had left nothing to chance.

Moriarty and the men of his Praetorian Guard, plus Daniel Carbonardo acting as his personal bodyguard, had arrived late on Monday night. They carried food and drink with them, which they ate following a careful reconnaissance of every possible hiding place within an eight-mile radius of the cottages on Sir John Grant's estate, the reconnaissance carried out by almost the entire army of lurkers and punishers, brought down from London for that express purpose.

'If there is any kind of emergency in London while we are here,' Moriarty said to the estimable Daniel Carbonardo, 'then we are most likely scuppered.'

'Half of the lads will be back in London by now, Professor,' Carbonardo told him. 'And we should be done here before seven, so everyone will be back before nine this morning. I don't think we need worry.'

In the darkness, Moriarty nodded.

The old huntsman to the Grant-Willow Hunt, Lazarus Grosewalk, had been awaiting their arrival – a small man, leathery of face and hands, with a deft and commanding manner that suited his position in life.

He immediately took Moriarty off to see the hounds, kept in their long wire run and big enclosed kennel area. They were noisy, giving tongue immediately Grosewalk appeared. 'They're a bit nervous,' the huntsman said. 'They know something is afoot; they're restless, and they can smell the other dogs.'

The four rogues, as he had referred to them, were a quartet of ugly-looking hounds, alpha males that had gone bad, each in a separate cage almost a mile away, but they, too, were nervous and showing signs of aggression, jumping up against the cage walls and snarling the moment the old huntsman approached with the Professor, who pulled a thick leather wallet from inside his clothing.

'No, sir. No. Not yet.' Grosewalk pushed at the empty air as if pushing the money away. 'I want nothing 'til it's all done. Taking it now would be bad luck. There's many a slip.'

'Well, it's all here, Lazarus. The money for restocking the pack, and the fee we agreed upon.'

'I've no doubt on it, sir. But I'll take it afterwards when you're gone and satisfied.'

'They'll do the job, though?' Moriarty asked. 'They'll kill him?'

'When we have the scent on him, yes. That's what I feel worst about. That's a country rule, sir, and I broke it. You don't shoot a fox like I did a few hours ago.'

Moriarty nodded again, and eventually they returned to the cottage, where Grosewalk showed them the blanket and everything else that was made ready. Then the remaining time ticked quickly past, in that silent brooding time as the world woke up.

They all stood in the darkened cottage as the first trembling rays of the new day's light filtered through the curtains. Then, on the dot of six

356

o'clock, they heard the sound of Idle Jack's horse, its hooves rattling out like a pair of great shells hitting each other in a steady rhythm.

'Right lads,' Moriarty said softly as the huntsman went out to greet Idle Jack, chatting respectfully and telling the boy he had with him to take the gentleman's horse away, look after it. 'Give him a drink,' he said, which was the signal for the four Praetorians to close in on Idle Jack and bind his arms, pulling him into the cottage, where Moriarty let himself be seen.

'Damn you!' was all Idle Jack said, and later even Moriarty commented that the man had shown considerable courage.

'Ah, but he didn't know what was coming at that point,' Spear said. And that was true enough, for they dragged Jack Idell around to the back of the cottage where Grosewalk had left the thick blanket – the blanket that he had wrapped the dead fox in, rubbing the animal's scent and blood into the rough wool until it was entirely impregnated with the creature's smell.

'This is disgusting,' Jack Idell said. 'What's to be gained...' He started to speak again, to say something further, then realized what was happening, for the pack of hounds were loudly giving tongue and the huntsman had released them, sounding his horn for them to give chase and releasing the four rogue dogs into the pack. They all got the scent immediately, the hounds holding off and yapping, uncertain until the four rogues came hurtling through the dawn light toward the back of the cottage.

Moriarty led his men back inside the cottage,

and as they went, they pushed Idle Jack onto the ground.

Jack let out one great high, terrified scream as the pack came onto him, the rogues breaking through, chasing him as he rolled, then staggered to his feet, running, trying to cross the lane. But they had him down, and Pip Paget for one knew that he would never get the sound out of his head, would never be able to come back and live in this place for Idle Jack's screams seemed to cut and cleave the air, screams of terror mixed with screams for help, for someone to aid him, as the hounds found his throat and shook and bit down with no conscience, so that all was still and silent but for the baying of the hounds after less than two minutes.

'Too quick,' said Moriarty as old Grosewalk whipped the hounds off and tried to deal with the rogue dogs. 'I wanted him to suffer,' even though he could clearly hear the jaws of the chomping hounds.

'A clean kill,' Grosewalk said after the hounds were back in kennels and he had, with difficulty, subdued the rogue dogs, who now had the taste and were slavering for more, their fangs still bloody and wet with blood and slime.

'It's going to be a lovely day,' Spear said as he stood in front of Paget's cottage. Daniel Carbonardo was just whipping up the horses, pulling the cart away toward the road. In the cart lay the bitten, crushed, and gouged remains of Idle Jack Idell, covered with old sacking.

The sky was blood red as the postdawn light sifted across the fields and hedgerows, and the

358

hounds kept up their terrible, ceaseless clamour.

'A clean kill, and that's for sure,' Grosewalk repeated, then sounded 'gone away' on his brass hunting horn.

20

Sal Hodges's Secret

LONDON: JUNE-SEPTEMBER 1900

Sometimes in the night Sal Hodges would ask herself why she had done it; but it was useless even asking, because she knew damn well why. She had done it because he was set on it, and he just did not give up as she inched her way toward the birth those years ago.

Now, she realized she was faced with choices: Either she came clean to him, risking a terrible wrath, or she tucked her secret away and lived with it for the rest of her life.

Sal Hodges returned to the Professor's bed five days after he came back from Steventon to London, following what must, she reasoned, have been an important and fruitful night. She knew a body had been found, no more.

The fact was that Daniel Carbonardo, on Moriarty's instructions, took the cart, under the cloak of night, and tipped the body at the foot of Nelson's column, where it lay like a pile of old rags until the morning. Idle Jack was, by this time, unrecognizable: a terrible sight, for the hounds and the rogue dogs had destroyed most of his face, and torn at other parts of his body.

The first senior police officer at the scene made the bare weighty statement, 'We're going to need help with this,' and sent for Angus McCready Crow, now a Superintendent in the Detective Division, who in turn paid a visit to Mr. Sherlock Holmes in Baker Street – but that is another story which will be told.

The clearing up of the fringes of Idle Jack's organization took place over the next handful of days. The barque *Sea Dancer* unexpectedly exploded in Portsmouth, tied up to a quay with only her captain, William Evans, aboard.

And there was the case of Broad Darryl Wood, the man who had been Idle Jack's second-in-command and was set to be heir to his family. It was sad, for he took to drink, and one night, during late July of this same year, 1900, he came staggering out of a pub in Oxford Street and bumped straight into Lee Chow, who said, 'Ah. So Mis'er 'ood. Nice to see...' and promptly did the cheek trick with his little razor-sharp filleting knife: flick-flick, and Wood's cheeks were no more. Lying at his feet. They sewed him up as best they could, and it has to be said that he was not a man you could keep down. There was more of him in the future, though his nickname altered from 'Broad' to 'Cheeky.' 'Cheeky' Darryl Wood, later a force to be reckoned with in Moriarty's family. There's a turn-up for the book, as they say.

But what of Sal Hodges and the dreadful weight of her secret? The night she returned to

Moriarty's chamber the bed springs sang their sweet harmonies, and when they were done, Sal was still weeping, distraught with the loss of Arthur. Or so one would have thought.

'Come, my princess, my dolly darling,' Moriarty soothed. 'Don't take on so. Arthur has gone and we must continue our journey in peace.' He lit a lamp and looked upon Sal and saw that she was shivering with emotion, her eyes scarlet and dreadfully blotchy, while her cheeks were raw with the salt tears, making the skin sore and rough. 'Come, dearest Sal. Arthur was a good boy and I miss him. But...'

And she said it before she could stop herself.

'But he was not your son!'

She looked at him hard, expecting this to maybe be the last moment of her life; expecting to see his face changed into a violent thunder-cloud.

Instead, Moriarty smiled at her and nodded, slowly and with infinite understanding.

She knew all about him, knew that he had killed, or ordered murder on a whim almost, knew that he had done horrific things; but she could not believe what she saw now.

'One gets a sense of what's what,' he said, quietly, in control of himself. 'I knew there was something, not quite...' The hands spread in a gesture more eloquent than words.

'You...?' she began, and he said softly, 'Tell me what happened.'

'You were so insistent. All the time you spoke of your *son*. You told me I was so good, being the conduit through which your son was coming into

361

the world. You spoke all the time of our unborn baby as *our son*. And I could not gainsay you. "*Our* son ... our *boy*... *My* son." Not a day went by without you talking of him. I began to dread the birth because I thought it might not be a male child. Then, with one thing and another, I became so fearful. I knew I could not fail you, so I went to your friend, the nurse. Gwendolyn Smith. Gwen Smith. I begged her and she saw to it the boy was smuggled in. He was there when I bore you a daughter.'

She looked at him hard, her eyes searching his face as though looking for some fissure, some fault, a crack in his physical makeup, but could find none. He looked down at her with affection, that smile playing over his lips and clawing up to his eyes.

'You are not angry?' she asked.

'The Lord takes away, and the Lord gives. Where is she? My daughter?'

'You have seen her, James, though you have never met her. She's the girl who assists me at the Haymarket house. Polly.'

'Polly,' he said, and nodded. Then he said they should sleep and he would meet Polly tomorrow.

Of course, Sal thought. *Of course. I should have known he would take it in his stride.* Moriarty was always flexible, tempering things to the changing winds. Always trimming his sails.

So, on the following morning Sal brought Polly to the house and introduced her to James Moriarty. 'This is Professor Moriarty, Polly. This is your father.' He took her in his arms and looked into her eyes and saw himself there, deep and devious, cunning as a cat, lovely as the first rose of summer, deadly as a lethal weapon.

It was during that summer that father got to know daughter, and daughter plumbed the depths of her father. She accepted him for what he was, admired his ingenuity and genius of organization, and he taught her all things: took her around his lairs, introduced her to those who worked in the world for her. In that one summer, Polly learned all the dodges from fawney dropping to the three card; she learned how to crack a crib, how to blow a safe, how to shoot, and how to handle a knife with dexterity, how to smash and how to grab.

As the summer progressed, Polly saw the way the warehouse in Poplar was taking shape, and even made some suggestions of her own.

In early autumn, one still, balmy evening when father and daughter had arranged to dine together at The Press off Fleet Street, they found that part of the road had been blocked, which meant they would have to walk some sixty yards or so over cobbles. Harkness helped Polly down from the cab and said he would make his way round and be outside when they had eaten.

She took Moriarty's arm, and the pair started to walk toward the famous restaurant where Sal would meet them, for she had been having a fitting for the dress she would wear for the wedding on Christmas Day in the warehouse, which would be ready by then.

As they paced along the road, some music reached their ears from an open window: the sound of a piano and a well-known voice. It came from a rehearsal room hidden away in this quiet side street, and the voice was that of the great male impersonator Vesta Tilley. That evening she was trying out a new song, which in a few months would have the errand boys whistling and people's feet tapping.

As Polly matched her stride to that of her father, and as they both took up the rhythm of the song, Vesta Tilley's voice floated out into the street, singing:

'I'm following in Father's footsteps, I'm
   following dear old dad.
He's just in front with a big fine gal, so I
   thought I'd have one as well.
I don't know where he's going, but when he
   gets there I'll be glad!
I'm following in Father's footsteps, yes, I'm
   following the dear old dad.'

The piano took up the refrain, and James Moriarty and Polly, arm in arm, almost danced together over the cobbles.

Glossary

In any book set among the criminal classes at the turn of the century you would expect to come across the criminal slang of the day. I have tried throughout to make the meaning of the slang obvious and clear. I include this small glossary of more arcane terms reluctantly. When I first published a work set in the nineteenth century and included such a glossary, some young reviewer wrote, 'Gardner has also been dipping into a slang dictionary.' What price erudition and scholasticism?

broadsmen: Swindlers, card sharps, etc.

demander: A beggar; or more likely one demanding money with menaces; i.e., someone on the protection.

dips/dippers: Pickpockets.

dodger: Anyone working one of the criminal dodges of the day.

dollymop: An amateur, but enthusiastic, prostitute. Brothel keepers would often allow dollymops to operate within the house.

fawney dropping: A ruse in which the villain pretends to find a jewel or ring (which is worthless) and sell it to a passer-by as a valuable article.

gonif: A thief or rogue.
lurkers: Beggars/watchers with criminal intent.
magsman: Swindler. Usually one who posed as a gent.
patterers: Fast-talking con men.
punishers: Obviously, those who meted out punishment.
whizzer: Another name for a pickpocket. Also someone outstanding, extraordinary.

The publishers hope that this book has given you enjoyable reading. Large Print Books are especially designed to be as easy to see and hold as possible. If you wish a complete list of our books please ask at your local library or write directly to:

Magna Large Print Books
Magna House, Long Preston,
Skipton, North Yorkshire.
BD23 4ND

This Large Print Book for the partially sighted, who cannot read normal print, is published under the auspices of

THE ULVERSCROFT FOUNDATION